LOVE AT THE ROCK SHOW

PAGANS & POP STARS
BOOK 2

KATTA KIS

JOIN MY NEWSLETTER

Keep up with me and my work by signing up for my newsletter! Once a month with freebies, exclusive behind-the-scenes fun, and no spam. :]

For my fellow spoonies and anxiety kitties.
For my partner, who makes sure I know I am loved, every day.

1

RK Does it Again
Like every other musician, ex-Beatboyz pop star RK recorded a pandemic
album to get through quarentimes. His sophomore album, Home With
You *is half an ode to new love, half a diary of a stir-crazy artist, and*
100% relatable. It runs the gamut from throwback 80's pop beats with
epic Bollywood influences to tender ballads about his mysterious new lady
love. His lyrics are poignant without being sappy, his featured artists are
phenomenal (Benji Omega! Doc Conjure!), and the production by fellow
former Beatboy Rick Jones ties it all together with a glorious bow.
—Music Daily

*F*ucking industry parties.

Lights flashed in his face. People yelled his name, his old stage name, *over here, look over here.* Step, pose, repeat. Ugh.

Patrick "Rick" Jones escaped the red carpet and sighed with relief as the stairway doors closed him off from the manufactured press frenzy. Climbing the three floors up to the actual party gave him time to breathe and work off some of his anxious energy. He paused at the landing, adjusting the fancy-casual outfit that cost way too much but fit the nebulous theme of the album release party.

You got this. You won't die if you see her. You won't die if you don't.

The door opened into an alcove right off the event room. A security guard gave him a look but Patrick flashed his VIP badge and a professionally non-threatening smile, breezing by.

Installing himself against the wall, he surveyed the room. The crowd spilled through the bar area to the open wall to the balcony of the boutique hotel ballroom—sorry *event space*. It was the kind of room that could be the site of anything from a wedding to a business merger, if you were trying to be edgy and hip. It was bright teal with flattering lighting and there wasn't a straight line in the whole place aside from—

Was that a Tarot reader table over in one of the selfie alcoves? Why? Were they a prop? Surely, his business partners hadn't stooped *that* low.

Whatever, he didn't have time for details right now.

He kept his gaze moving, but even with all the people, he could tell *she* wasn't here yet. Thank fuck. Just the thought of being in the same room as her turned him into an exposed nerve. Everything was too loud, too dim, too close, too warm. His stomach was in knots.

Parties drained his social battery within minutes but he was inevitably expected to be there for hours. Party Patrick was honed to be a tool, trained to sell a product with his face on it, to make someone else money. He smiled at a passing acquaintance and said something pleasantly banal—who knows what. He could work a whole party on autopilot, hating everything from behind his smile. One of the benefits of spending ten years in a boy band machine. But not now, not this party.

He kept his gaze roving, trying not to look at the publicity shots all over the place of his former bandmate, current business partner, and ex-friend. He could barely stand to work with Rohan, let alone stare at a fuckton of pictures of him. It didn't matter now, after tonight's launch of Rohan's new album, Patrick's contract was fulfilled and he was quitting. The thought was a lifeline as the bass thrummed under his feet, the susurration of small talk lapping around him like social-climbing waves.

The baby hairs on the back of his neck stood up. He'd recognize that voice anywhere.

She's here.

He turned slowly, trying to be casual. There she was, his ex-best friend, the one that got away, on the arm of the man formerly known as Patrick's friend.

Cazzi wore a cloth mask and make-up but he still recognized her from across the room. Even from here, he could appreciate her eyeliner, dark green witchy dress, and matching mask. He hadn't seen her this dressed up in years, maybe ever. She looked good. She looked up at Rohan and her eyes smiled.

Patrick's stomach tried to stage a full-on revolt. He jingled the coins he always carried in his pocket for offerings—Nana had schooled him years ago to never leave home without them because you never knew who or what you might run into—but couldn't hear the sound they made enough to focus on it. He fiddled with his own mask. The party was in a rooftop bar with fancy garage-style doors open to the night so theoretically he didn't need it. Neither did Cazzi, but he knew she wore it for more than COVID protocols.

She looked happy. Uncomfortable, sure but happy overall. A thousand times better than the last time he'd seen her, over a year ago.

You mean better than completely emotionally wrecked? That's a low bar.

It wasn't that. It was so much worse. She fucking glowed. She looked at Rohan like she loved him. Like she loved him and it didn't tear her apart.

He couldn't bring himself to look away. It wasn't all happiness. He could see the nerves under her poise. The too-straight line of her back, the smile in her eyes calcifying, the way she kept her distance to Rohan exactly the same no matter how he moved. Did Rohan even notice? Did he realize how much she was putting herself out there for him, just being here?

That could've been you she was hovering next to. But you fucked it up.

His therapist told him to be gentle with himself but goddammit how could he when he'd fucked up so miserably? When he was currently fucking up?

This was love, wasn't it? He hadn't been sure. It'd been tearing him up to not know if he'd actually loved her or that the idea of loving her made it easier to justify his actions last year. He hoped his feelings would have faded by now and he'd come out of this party relieved, maybe even happy for her. But fuck, this wasn't easy so it had to be love, right?

Say something. Tell her. Don't leave it unfinished, you never know how much time either of you have left.

The memories of holding the phone to his ear, as his grandpa couldn't speak, as he died alone in quarantine bubbled up. Patrick hadn't said anything then, hadn't known how to go through the motions of expected affection when he couldn't forgive the man who tore his family apart with his self-ishness.

The nurse said Patrick was the last call Grandpa Pat had taken.

His heart pounded so hard it made him even queasier. He was lightheaded, he was sick.

He ducked into the stairwell and down two flights of stairs.

Sitting on the landing, he put his head between his knees and tried to breathe through the shaking, through the pulse in his throat, the nausea. He patted his pockets for something, anything that could help but he hadn't thought to pack so much as a ginger candy. Dammit all, he was a mess. Why had he thought he could do this?

Fuck, I hope she didn't see me.

Judit Kemenes stood up from her table, straightened her Thoth Tarot deck, and tucked it away into its velvet bag. Everything ached, the pain getting sharper and her mind getting cloudier. Her wrists and fingers were banded with dull pain, her shoulders were wracked, and her hips were sore from sitting for hours. Dammit, she was too young for this shit.

She forced herself to focus. Her shift was over. There hadn't been an instant connection with anyone who might skyrocket her career but life wasn't a movie or a romance novel, as much as she often wished it was. Her business card stack was half gone, but her table hadn't been exactly popular. She'd gotten more confused glances than clients even though LA people loved psychics, but she was the first to admit a card reader didn't quite fit with the theme of Rohan's album release party. (Honestly, she wasn't sure what the theme was. People seemed to either be super dressed up or in expensive loungewear and the event brief had been... unhelpful.) Which made her ten times more grateful to Cazzi and Rohan for getting her the gig. Clearly, this party hadn't needed her as much as she'd needed the money.

It's fine, she told herself, *This way you were able to keep an eye on Cazzi.*

Not that her best friend needed a babysitter per se, but Judit knew half the reason she'd been invited was Cazzi wanted extra emotional support if Patrick got weird.

Patrick. Judit narrowed her eyes at the thought of him. Cazzi's so-called best friend and once the love of her life. The guy who'd very efficiently wrecked Judit's friend more than once with his ghosting and fuckwittery.

He was strangely absent.

Frowning, she straightened. Pain shot from her hip, down her leg. She suppressed a wince. Great, now her pelvic muscles wanted in on the pain party.

I hate you, she told them before immediately apologizing. Her therapist, back when she'd been able to afford one, told her hating her body would only make things worse.

She looked around for a chair that wasn't the metal folding shit she'd been sitting on for the last two hours. The bar featured those tall tiny tables you were supposed to hover around. There was a balcony with a view that attracted a lot of selfies (when people weren't trying to take a selfie at her table), a dance floor that mostly contained groups of people networking, and not one single chair.

Seriously? Were LA people too bougie to sit or was this a special torture reserved for parties only?

She spun in a slow circle, not caring if she looked weird. Weird was on brand. Cazzi shot her a puzzled look. Next to her, her boyfriend Rohan "RK" Kapoor raised his plastic cup at her and looked like he was debating coming over to ask if she was okay. He was a nice guy. He practically lived with Cazzi so Judit saw him whenever she dropped by. So far he'd been an absolute sweetheart and treated Cazzi like she was the best thing that ever happened to him.

She shot them both a thumbs up. She didn't need anything but a chair, or wait—

A door caught her eye. Stairs.

She texted Cazzi that she was going to sit somewhere and headed into the stairwell. The door shut, cutting the sounds of music and networking. She exhaled in relief and headed downwards to get away from the couple one flight up that was getting excitingly well-acquainted.

It was so much quieter down here and the pressure of being around so many people lifted as she descended to the landing. She popped a 20:1 CBD gummy in her mouth, enjoying the burst of sweet strawberry flavor. There were three left in the pack.

She sat down with a sigh, relishing the peace and removing her mask. Except—

Oh no, was that someone... crying?

She listened. The sobbing breaths were below her, ragged and fast. Panic not pleasure.

Fuck.

Grabbing the handrail, she dragged herself upright. Every bit of pain flared brighter. What she wouldn't give for some instant-release pill that made her feel like she was actually in her late twenties instead of prematurely ninety.

"Hello?" she called, approaching slowly. She checked the pockets of her dress. Phone, wallet, keys, deck, gummies... hmmm...

The sobbing didn't stop. She followed the sound until she found the source, doubled over, head between their legs, breathing fast. They were hard to discern in the yellow half-light but she thought they were skinny, dark-skinned, and definitely having a moment.

"Hi," she said again. "Are you okay?" Stupid question, but honestly what else did you say?

Their breath hitched. They raised their head, wide dark eyes catching hers. There were no tears but sweat beaded their hairline. "I feel like I'm gonna die." Their voice was a low rasp through their mask and it sent a chill down her spine.

"Okay." Judit sank down in front of them, about six feet away, crouching even though her hips protested. Vaccination was a requirement for entry but being close to people was still strange. "Do you want me to call 911?"

"No!" A hand reached out and grabbed her wrist, breaking

the social distance between them. Not hard, but the strength was there. "No, it's not real."

Uh-oh. She fought the urge to jerk away.

"What's not real, hun?" She kept her voice kindergarten teacher gentle.

A forced, tortured breath. The fingers on her wrist shifted restlessly. "It's all anxiety."

Oh. *Oh.*

"Anxiety spiral?"

Their eyes narrowed. "Attack."

"Been there." Not this bad but still. "Want me to sit with you for a bit?"

They stared at her like they hadn't even considered this was an option.

"Is that a yes?"

They dipped their head slightly. She nodded and gently removed her wrist from their grip.

They made a noise of protest but she just arranged her skirt as she sat. Then she offered her hand back.

They shook their head, closing their eyes. Their breath picked up again.

"Would taking off your mask help?"

They shrugged, making no move to remove it.

"Did you take anything?"

They shook their head.

Judit put her mask back on in case that made them feel more comfortable. "Does CBD help you? I have some twenty-to-one gummies."

Their eyes snapped open. "Yes... please."

She passed them a gummy. Two left. They turned away to lift their mask but she could still see them chew and swallow like their life depended on it. Probably felt like it did.

She sat in silence, tracking the way they breathed and

keeping her breathing deliberately slow. Eva, her semi-sister (long story), had once explained the concept of mirror neurons and people unconsciously mimicking each other with yawning and shit. She figured pretending to be super calm couldn't hurt.

"Wanna talk about it? Will that help?" She asked when their breathing slowed.

"You won't tell?"

Another chill went down her spine, a precognition. She would regret this.

"Psychic's honor." She held up two fingers like a boy scout... or someone out of the *Hunger Games*, she could never remember which.

They worried their hands together. "I feel like I'm having a heart attack and an aneurysm and about to pass out or puke or... the CBD is helping but..." They looked up, their gaze clearer as they met her eyes.

"Whatever you feel comfortable with. We don't have to talk about it." She really hoped they didn't puke. This was her nicest dress. It'd survive the dirt on the floor but puke? Probably not. (Plus, puking in a mask had to suck.)

"You swear you're not going to tell anyone?"

Aw man, either they were famous or a serial killer. Fantastic.

"Who am I going to tell? I have no idea who you are."

Their shoulders relaxed.

"What happens in the stairwell, stays in the stairwell." She smiled, then remembered she was masked. "Why don't you tell me what's going on? Helps me when I'm spiraling."

They smoothed their locs back and sighed. "The love of my life is here." They flinched at the words as if they couldn't stand to hear them.

"Oh?"

"With her boyfriend."

"Ohhh."

The stir of precognition tingled in her spine. *Surely not...*

"He's gonna ask her to marry him, any day now. They practically live together. He's, he was, my friend."

"Some friend," Judit said. *Fuck, fuck, fuck.* If she was right...

"She loved me. *Me.* But... but I fucked up and he swooped in... and stole her."

Like she was a fucking trophy. Judit made a sympathetic noise through gritted teeth. There was no way she could have the "women are not property" discussion without it devolving into an argument with him right now. (This is what she got for being nice, dammit.)

"I thought the pain would fade, that I was maybe deluding myself about how I felt. Then I saw her and she looked at him and... and... she's happy. She's in love." His voice was a gut punch and she suspected he was trying to get her to sympathize even as he visibly shook. Maybe he didn't realize he was doing it. He hugged his knees and looked up at Judit with big brown eyes. "It hurts so much."

He was very pretty, even obscured by the mask. But then, all guys in boy bands are to some degree. He didn't look like the boy who'd graced the Beatboyz poster on her wall a decade ago. He'd grown up hot but sad. A devastating combination. But now she knew what to look for, she could tell exactly who he was. Thank goodness they'd never met (Cazzi used to be super secretive about him before their whole relationship blew up) or this would be awkward as fuck.

She could see why Cazzi fell so hard. But Judit knew a trap when she saw one. She put on her sympathetic face even as her mind raced. Was she really going to sit here and let this asshole try to sway her to his side of things? (She couldn't just get up and leave, could she? Would it help anything if she gave him a piece of her mind? Because she had *thoughts*.) "That's rough. I can't even imagine."

That was mostly true. She'd had her share of unrequited love (what pansexual romantic got through puberty without a few heartbreaks?) but she'd never had a long-running thing for someone she'd known forever. After watching Cazzi wreck herself against Patrick, Judit was A-okay with that.

Patrick drew a shaky breath, pressing the heels of his palms into his eyes. He'd stopped hyperventilating sometime in the last five minutes and now looked like he was going straight from anxiety into a depressive slump. His body barely shook but his shoulders and neck drooped. He seemed utterly miserable.

It made her soft heart sad. Dammit.

"I-I lost someone to COVID," he continued. "Someone I never got a chance to clear the air with and I thought—I hoped—" He shrugged.

That sounded exactly like the kind of drama Cazzi was worried about. But maybe it would help them both if they actually talked?

Patrick drew another shaky breath and shook his head. "I can't let her see me like this. A man handles his shit."

Okay, no one needed that toxically masculine nonsense.

"We're in a pandemic," she pointed out. "Literally, no one is handling their shit."

His eyes crinkled in a sad smile. "I've been going to therapy for months. I should be better by now."

Boo-fucking-hoo, you can afford therapy.

When she didn't laugh, he cocked his head. "I'm not usually like this."

She shrugged, the adrenaline of dealing with a crisis fading and leaving her wrung out. The CBD was kicking in, softening her resolve and giving her munchies. Damn, she'd taken it on an empty stomach, hadn't she? That one milligram of THC was getting her lightweight ass. "Do you think there's any food left at the party?"

He looked up as if he could see from here. She smothered a giggle. *No giggling at the enemy.*

He glanced at the time on his phone. "I doubt it. The food budget was limited... um, I'm guessing."

Wow, his acting was worse than it was in that Beatboyz movie she saw back in high school. Surely, he'd gotten better since then... oh wait. "Is your gummy kicking in?"

He nodded. "Kinda."

She had a bad idea. But it was kind of brilliant? Like, what if she got him out of here and also got snacks? She hadn't eaten dinner at all and forgetting to eat was not an option when she'd gotten migraines from that before. No drama at the party plus having a cute-if-emotionally-constipated guy buy her food sounded like a great idea. Also safe. (Probably.)

"Hey," she said. "Do you want to get out of here? I saw an ice cream place around the corner. It's probably closed but I could use the walk."

He looked unsure.

"Come on," she wheedled. "Staying here isn't healthy. You said you didn't want her to see you like this."

It was a low blow, manipulative even. Cazzi told Judit how he'd shut her out of his emotions, to the point that he'd once dated someone for months without telling her, his supposed best friend. That had been a sore spot.

She grabbed the handrail, ordering her reluctant joints to work as she stood. He stood too, offering his hand to steady her. She took it, telling herself it was okay to accept help from the enemy when it served her purpose. Besides, she'd given him (mild) drugs so she was kind of responsible for him now.

God, he was tall. Her neck bent back looking at him but not enough to give her a crick. An acceptable amount of tall.

No, wait, not acceptable.

A loud moan echoed down from the couple above. Judit slapped a hand over her masked mouth to suppress a laugh.

"Is that—?"

She nodded frantically as some sort of ecstatic yipping filled the air.

"Yeah, okay, I could use a walk," he said, his fingers lingering to brush hers. His eyes crinkled with mirth.

A frisson shivered up her arm.

"Let me get my stuff," she said. "Stay here."

She hurried up the stairs, cursing the flaw in her stoned logic. Would he stay? Or would he follow her and cause a whole thing?

Judit cleared her table, tossing everything in the tote she brought with her. Sign, tablecloth, business cards, Tarot cards —they all fit easily.

"Where are you going?" Cazzi asked, appearing out of nowhere.

"Fuck!" Judit's hand flew to her chest. "You scared the shit out of me."

"Sorry, but I thought you were coming home with us." Cazzi's eyebrows furrowed.

"So, yeah, about that," Judit said, thinking fast. "I met someone and we're hungry and I think they're out of food here."

Cazzi glanced around. "I just saw a waiter—"

Judit shook her head. "Nope. No food here. Look, um, they're cute and—"

"Oh! Ohhh." Cazzi's eyes widened. "Okay, hey, look at you, getting out. They seem safe? Do you need an escape call?"

"Yes, they're safe," Judit said. "No, but I'll text you where we go and if we change locations."

"Good." Cazzi's eyes smiled. She reached into her dress pocket. "Do you need condoms?"

"Nooo." Judit's face went hot at the thought. If Cazzi knew

she'd just offered Judit condoms to sleep with her old crush... yikes. "I'm not ready for that."

"You know where to get some when you are." Cazzi patted Judit's arm. "Have fun!"

"Thanks!" Judit hugged her and dashed away before she could get further interrogated. She slowed on the stairs, panting. Dammit, her lungs were not used to this. Pausing, she glanced down.

Patrick stood on the landing waiting for her. His gaze fastened on hers, holding her in place. "You're back."

"You're surprised?" Damn, even in this light, she could make out the way his elaborately decorated blazer was tailored to fit his slender form. Under it, he wore a tight, short shirt and skinny jeans tucked into ankle boots.

He shrugged, glancing away. A slender loc fell in front of his face and she fought the urge to tuck it back behind his ear.

Danger! You're high and he's hot.

Dammit, now she had "Danger Zone" stuck in her head.

"Don't be," she said, forcing herself to move again. "You're buying me ice cream. I'm stuck to you until the cone is done."

He chuckled. "Oh, I'm paying?"

"Yep." She brushed by him, leading the way.

This was harmless. It was community service. She could be nice to him for a night. Maybe it would help him move on? Probably not, but she deserved the sweets anyway.

Next time she saw him though, she'd verbally eviscerate him. Even if he did seem sorry.

The Kenny Loggins song in her head was not convinced.

After sneaking out the back, Patrick stood awkwardly in the brightly lit store, staring fixedly at the menu. The ice cream place turned out to be a hole-in-the-wall combination ice cream/boba shop around the corner from the hotel. She— probably she, he hadn't asked but she was dressed very femme —stood next to him, bobbing her head to a song that had been a hit when he was in high school—thankfully not one of his. Wow, were the speakers in here bad though, everything sounded fuzzy and the low end was non-existent.

Focus.

How had he gotten from freaking out in a stairwell to buying a stranger ice cream? The CBD she'd given him blunted the edges of the question. Maybe he was having a spontaneous moment.

"You know what you want?" he asked.

Her brow furrowed. "I'm torn between ice cream and boba."

"Get both?"

She looked at him. "You sure?"

He shrugged. "I'm paying. It's fine."

"I was mostly joking about that."

He smiled under his mask. "Consider it payment for the listening and the CBD."

She squared her shoulders and nodded. "Deal." She stepped up to the counter and ordered three different flavors of ice cream with sprinkles and a taro milk tea. Huh. Maybe she'd had some of her own CBD gummies. She certainly seemed to have munchies.

He ordered a taro milk tea too with thirty percent sugar, boba, and no ice.

They sat at a table, waiting for their order. Should he ask her name? He took her in out of the corner of his eyes, trying not to stare awkwardly. She was pretty. Her eyes were accentuated by purple liner, her figure was softer than the LA standard, her dark hair was cut into blunt bangs and long enough to hit her bare shoulders. Her dress was a halter-necked affair with swirling purples and blue skimming her curves. There was a keyhole neckline cut into it. He refused to let himself look closely.

He knew it was okay to notice someone's beauty when you were in love with another person but he still felt like an asshole.

"Order up!" yelled the person working the counter.

They were the only customers so Patrick and the woman stood, grabbing their order. When they sat again, Patrick realized his mistake.

He'd have to take off his mask to drink his tea.

The woman ran her fingers over her black cloth mask and looked at him.

What if she recognized him?

"It's darker outside?" she offered. "If we don't want to actually see each other."

"Is it ridiculous that I want to take you up on that?"

She shook her head. "Let's go."

They ended up sitting on a bench in a nearby park, away from the lights. He held her drink as she took her mask off. It was kind of ridiculous, he could mostly see what she looked like. But he appreciated that she humored him.

She glanced at him and then away. She was even prettier without the mask, her face heart-shaped and lips soft-looking, painted a color he couldn't parse in the dark.

He took a deep breath and took his off.

"Well, we did that," she said, taking a sip of her drink. No surprise, no sudden recognition.

He sipped his drink, savoring the creamy taro and chewing on the boba. "I haven't had boba in a long time. I forgot how good it was."

She hummed in agreement.

They sat in silence for a while as they worked their way through their respective desserts.

"So, I guess talking about work is off the table since we're staying anonymous," she said, once her ice cream was done. "Wanna lie creatively to each other?"

He raised an eyebrow.

"I mean, we're probably never going to see each other again. Might as well make up some crazy-but-impressive-sounding life stories."

"You sound like one of those overly quirky girls in rom-coms." Cazzi hated that trope.

The stranger gasped in faked shock. "Are you calling me a manic pixie dream girl?"

He shrugged a shoulder. "If the sparkly shoe fits."

"Hey, you don't know, I could run a cupcake shop/be a dog trainer/professional hang glider. You seem like you could brood admirably. I'm sure you'd love for me to liven up your life whether you want it or not while having absolutely no agency of my own."

He wanted to frown but kept the expression off his face. There was an edge to her words but he couldn't parse why. "Is that the creative lie you're going with? Or was that your dissertation on media tropes?"

She paused. "Neither, you're welcome to be the manic pixie dream girl, if you want."

"You mean we can't both be manic pixie dream girls?"

She shook her head seriously. "It's like *Highlander*. How can she show how not like other girls she is if there are multiple MPDGs?"

His lips twitched, the image in his head was too weird, too funny.

"What?" she asked.

Fuck it. "I just imagined Sean Connery out in the middle

of Scotland dressed like Zoey Deschanel and screaming 'There can only be one!'"

She choked out a laugh, coughing. He patted her back until she recovered. When she could talk again, she asked, "Does he pull it off?"

Patrick considered this, turning the image over in his mind. "The make-up doesn't work but I think he's pulling off the dress."

"Fair. He's a little craggy for winged eyeliner."

Patrick snickered, ducking his head.

They stayed on that bench for hours, talking around everything important, saying sillier and sillier things until the occasional sharpness in her words disappeared and they were both limp from laughing. It was the most fun Patrick had had in months.

He almost asked her name when she yawned and ordered a ride home. He almost, not quite accidentally, looked at her screen but he looked away at the last second.

Maybe it was better this way, to have this one night away from their worries. The perfect illusion of what could've been more.

He walked her to her waiting car. She turned to him before climbing in. "I feel like I should say something memorable here."

"Anything coming to mind?"

Her hand reached for his chest then stopped, closing in a fist. Through his thin shirt, he could almost feel the heat of her. He was suddenly aware of how close she stood. "Be your own manic pixie dream girl," she said with deep seriousness and rapped a knuckle against his breastbone.

They paused and both broke down laughing.

"Thank you for tonight," he said, laying a hand over her fist on his chest. He wanted to lean down, pull her mask back off, and kiss her.

"Shockingly, I had fun." She did actually sound shocked.

"Shockingly, I did too."

"You getting in or what?" yelled the driver.

They broke apart and with an awkward wave, she was gone.

But Patrick was still smiling when his driver came to pick him up.

2

Whatever Happened to Ricky Rick?
Okay, I don't know about you but shy guys are my kryptonite. When I was
a teenager, if a boy could barely speak to me, I was hooked. That probably
says something but, whatever, this isn't about me. It's about the ultimate
shy guy, the one, the only Ricky Rick of Beatboyz. I mean, when he bought
his love interest a rare book in Boyz in Dublin! *and only communicated*
to her in notes (and songs, of course)? I died. That was it for teenaged me.
Stan 5ever. But after the catastrophic break-up of Beatboyz, Ricky's been
barely on socials. And since I got bored during lockdown, I did some
digging. Starting a by-artists-for-artists record label with RK and Benji
Omega? Producing arthouse soundtracks and his sister's album? Supporting
his ex-bandmate Leo's drag shows? Honestly, it's so wholesome I could cry.
Here are some recent pictures and videos I found (on other people's
accounts, come on Ricky!) so you can revel in how too pure for this world
he is.
—Boyz in the Band blog

J udit put her phone down and finished her muffin. Rohan
baked so damn well, you wouldn't even know these were
supposed to be healthy. She eyed a second muffin.

Anything was better than looking back at her phone. If she read that email from her high school reunion committee one more time she'd lose it.

"You are cordially invited to the ten-year reunion of the class of..."

Though, to be fair, it was better than the email above from her landlord informing her and her roommate he was raising their rent next month. Well, marginally better.

She glanced at her breakfast companions. Cazzi was reading and Rohan was on the phone with someone but the pinkies of their free hands were hooked together on the table. Judit looked away, mildly (deeply) jealous. She soaked in the sunny details of the apartment instead. It was a rental, cozy but definitely not cheap with a large kitchen, a nook, and a granite-topped island. The whole place was done up in cheerful colors, which meant Cazzi hadn't done the decorating. She wasn't paying for it either, given she mostly lived upstate in Clementine and Rohan was probably swimming in Beatboyz money, not to mention his recent success. He mostly spent his time in Cazzi's house but had a rental here because that was what celebrities did, Judit guessed.

Thinking about celebrities made her think about Patrick. She'd had fun last night, despite her best intentions. Should she feel guilty? Was she betraying her friend? Oh god, what if Cazzi found out?

"Oh fuck." Rohan hung up, dropping his phone on the table of the breakfast nook. It clattered away, heading for the lovely clay tile floor.

Judit lunged forward and caught it before it went over the edge. "All good?" she asked, handing it to him.

He thanked her but shook his head.

"What's up?" Cazzi asked from next to her boyfriend, blinking as she looked up from a book on menopause. Judit thought she was jumping the gun a bit, given Cazzi was years away from the change but she was pretty sure her demi-sister

Eva was reading it too, so maybe it was just a sex educator thing.

"Our merch team caught COVID and Doc Conjure's bassist broke his wrist." Rohan raked his hair back with a groan. "I told Benji it was too soon to do a damn touring fest."

"Eventful night," Judit murmured.

Cazzi snorted and closed her book, folding her hands over the pink cover. "Do you want to pull out of Endfest, Ro?" She asked like they'd had similar conversations before and she was cutting to the chase.

Rohan frowned. "No. Am I worried? Sure. The damn thing could shut down any minute, but the label needs the money and if I don't go, that lowers the draw of the fest which would hurt the small acts and…"

Cazzi put her hand on his. "Don't put that all on yourself."

"I have to." He sighed. "I'm the cash cow of our label right now. My success is keeping us from completely folding."

Judit patted his shoulder. "Anything we can do to help?"

"Cure COVID?" Rohan shook his head. "Kidding. You don't happen to know anyone who wants to work our merch booth for two months while we drag ourselves around the country sponsored by Green Brew Energy Drink and Lady-Water Hard Seltzer though, do you?"

Judit blinked. "That sounds fun." Her body would fall apart, sure, but it'd be an *adventure*. A *paying* adventure. She glanced at her phone and all the dreadful emails hidden within.

How much could selling T-shirts at a fest possibly pay? Not enough, she was sure.

She locked the screen. She was a freelance psychic with chronic pain, coming up on her ten-year reunion and what had she achieved? She wasn't even the weirdest person in her class. She'd been outdone by the guy who'd started a vanlife cult. He had a whole convoy of followers! Meanwhile, Judit... had no degree and barely made rent. Still.

Except no one had extraordinary expectations of her. Failing and barely surviving was exactly what they thought would happen to a sick little girl.

Her therapist would tell her to take a step back and not beat herself up about it but she couldn't afford her therapist right now. She was stuck in the awful middle ground of being too broke for decently priced insurance and not broke enough for Medi-Cal. So she didn't have any. She had about three months before she was fucked on taxes because of it too.

"How much are you paying?" she asked.

Rohan rattled off the pay and benefits like he'd set the rates himself. Maybe he had. The label he founded with Benji Omega and Patrick was a barebones artist co-op from what Judit heard. The number made her eyebrows hit her bangs.

"Healthcare is covered too," he said. "It's not great, we can't afford much but Ma would kill me if we didn't offer it. No dental or vision or anything but—"

"I'll work your merch table," she said.

Rohan brightened. "Really?" He frowned. "I think we'd need at least two people."

"My roommate is always looking for gigs," Judit said. "I'll text her."

"You're both fully vaccinated?" Rohan asked.

"Absolutely."

Cazzi frowned so hard it was almost a sound. Judit ignored her as she shot off a text to Helen.

Did Judit have chronic, inexplicable pain without a diagnosis? Sure, but she'd handled it her entire life. Was Helen missing her right leg below the knee? Absolutely, but she had a killer prosthetic and she hated her day job. Plus, it paid more than either of their gigs did.

Helen texted her back almost immediately: *Hell yes! I'll sell overpriced T-shirts any day for that much money.*

"You could read cards if you wanted to," Rohan said, growing excited. "I'll talk to Benji. They'll send you the contract."

Judit resisted a fangirl moment at the mention of Benji. She was sitting next to a celebrity, for fuck's sake. Though she knew from Cazzi, he couldn't pick up his socks to save his life. Celebrities were just people. Even so, Benji Nakamura was *the* goth/emo heartthrob when she was in high school. They'd only gotten hotter when they came out as non-binary a few years back. She caught a glimpse of them at Rohan's party last night and wow, did they look good in person.

Cazzi put her hand on Judit's arm. "I have reservations."

"I know," Judit said. "I'll be careful."

Rohan exchanged a glance with Cazzi before looking at Judit. "Are there any accommodations you need?"

"Two comfortable chairs. Let me double-check with Helen though."

"We can do that!" Rohan smiled like an excited kid. Judit resisted the urge to pat his head. "Let me know the rest, I'll make sure you're both covered."

Cazzi's shoulders relaxed.

"We'll hash out the details with Benji." He frowned, fingers flying over the screen. "Now, I just have to deal with Doc Conjure's bassist."

Cazzi rubbed his arm. "Don't you have a pile of backup possibilities?"

"Not one that knows their set. Tour's next week. Maybe if we got someone who could read music for the first few shows."

"Their shows get rowdy, a music stand might get knocked over," Cazzi said thoughtfully. "You're telling me the Control Freak General doesn't already have a plan?"

Rohan snorted. "Benji is already in overdrive, yes."

"So why are you stressing?" Cazzi asked.

"Because we've both gotta pull double our weight since Rick..." He trailed off and grimaced. "Sorry."

Cazzi sighed. "For the millionth time, I can hear about Patrick without losing it, even if it's not nice. I'm a big girl."

"I know, I know," Rohan said, squeezing her hand. "I just wish he'd pull his weight. That's his sister's band but is he going to help? I doubt it."

Judit remembered Patrick in the stairwell, barely able to function, and wondered briefly if he'd told his business partners how bad his anxiety was. Then she put it out of her head. It wasn't her business and if she said anything, she'd have to admit where she went last night. She wasn't sure how they'd react.

Rohan's phone rang. He picked it up, listened, and then said, "Okay, yeah. No, that makes sense. Thanks, Benji." He didn't look exactly pleased as he hung up. "Well, it might be fixed."

"That's a good thing, right?" Judit asked.

He shrugged. "Sabrina is going to try to get Rick to sub in for the tour."

"He won't say no to her." Cazzi put on a false smile. "He'll hate it but he did do most of the instrument parts on the album."

Rohan watched her carefully. "Yep."

It was a good thing he was so focused on Cazzi. It meant he didn't notice the blood drain from Judit's face or how she'd accidentally crushed the muffin she'd picked up in her fist.

Unfortunately, Cazzi *did* notice. She didn't say anything but her frown when she handed Judit a napkin said they'd have a conversation about it later.

Yeah, no way *that* was happening.

PATRICK SAT on the floor in front of the house ancestor altar, gathering himself. The altar took up an alcove at the back of the house by a window facing the backyard, the garden he and Nana planted, and Nana's ADU apartment where she lived and kept her workroom. She'd wanted the family altar to be in the main house where he and his sister lived so it was always accessible to them. It was comforting to have it in his home even if it was more a part of Nana's practice than his. But today, he laid out fresh offerings, straightened, and wiped down the already pristine surfaces. Nana usually handled it as part of her daily hoodoo rituals but this morning, he'd taken over the task to clear his head.

Quitting was a good thing, he reminded himself. It wasn't a failure to leave a toxic environment, especially now his contract was fulfilled. He wasn't leaving them high and dry. He'd given Sabrina the best album he could've given her and her band.

It was just a fucking phone call. An email even. Hell, an email would be better, then he'd have everything in writing, the Hollywood gold standard.

He looked at the framed photos Nana painstakingly gathered and preserved over the years of everyone she could find of their family tree. Her late, estranged husband, Grandpa Pat was notably missing. The pictures seemed to glow in the morning light, staring back at Patrick like he had their full attention.

He lit a white taper candle in a glass holder and held it. Nana had more complex rituals but after Patrick left home to join Beatboyz, he'd lost touch with those ways. Today, he preferred to keep it simple, so he didn't feel like he was messing anything up.

He closed his eyes. *Give me the strength please to do the right thing and follow my heart.*

He sat there for a while, soaking up the peace. There were no words, no sudden bolts of knowledge, just acceptance. When sitting on the wooden floor aggravated his knees, he silently thanked his ancestors and respectfully extinguished his candle—this was LA and he wasn't fucking around with fire. He replaced the candle in its spot, making sure he'd fully put it out.

He stood, taking out his phone to get this over with.

"Pat?"

He turned and almost walked into his sister.

"Hey, can we talk?" she asked, undeterred by being nearly mowed over.

"Hm?" He opened a blank email.

"Look at me, would you? It's important."

He sighed and lowered his arm, looking at her. His little sister looked like she hadn't been to bed yet which told him he really wouldn't enjoy this conversation. "Well?"

She grimaced, glancing away. "I know you're about to quit but I need a favor."

He froze. "What kind of favor?" She wasn't going to ask him to stay, was she?

"It's an emergency." She scoffed her foot on the floor. Once, twice, three times.

"Better be." She knew how much it killed him to work on both of Rohan's albums. Even though Rohan produced the songs about Cazzi without him, it was like she was there, ringing in the background of every track. But Sabrina didn't know why he'd stayed with the label. How Benji held making Doc Conjure's first album over his head so he couldn't quit. Until now.

"So, you remember that after party you ghosted me on? The one thrown by Lil Sparkz?"

"No." He hated parties. She knew that.

"Of course, you don't," she said, half under her breath. "Well, the band went without you. Kevon and I had a good time but Cyrus…"

Patrick couldn't help but roll his eyes at the mention of that shithead. It was like Cyrus had heard about the brainless bassist stereotype and made it his entire personality. Unfortunately, he was talented enough for the band to overlook that, mostly. Oh, and he was the drummer's cousin.

"…had too good a time."

"So? Is he passed out somewhere where Nana might see?" He did not have time to babysit a grown man who damn well knew better.

"No, he tried to jump off Lil Sparkz's mansion's roof into the pool. He's fine!" She said hurriedly, "He, um, just broke his wrist on his way down."

Patrick stared at her, trying to process this. "On his way down?"

"He took out a window too."

Patrick sucked in a breath. "Ow, fuck. Where is he? Do we have to take him to the hospital?"

"No, that's where I just came from." For the first time, he noted the dark smudges peeking out from under her fading foundation. "He can't play, for like *months*."

"Shit." Patrick squeezed his eyes shut. Endfest started touring in a week and it was Doc Conjure's chance to build a following in advance of the album he just cut for them. He mentally flicked through the Rolodex of musicians he knew. "Let me think, I can find you someone."

"That's not what I'm asking for."

He waved her words away. "It's fine. I just gotta make some calls."

"They won't know the music."

"I won't send you an amateur. You'll just have to jam your

ass off and give them the sheet music. The first few shows will be rough but—"

"Maow!"

He glanced down. "Hi, Scoot." His tortoiseshell cat stared up at him with her huge golden eyes. Her adorably tiny head and large round teddy bear body never failed to make his day brighter. He smiled at her. She rubbed against his leg.

"You could do it."

"What?" He stared up at Sabrina, half bent over as he scritched Scoot's head.

"You pick up music like that—" She snapped her fingers. "And you co-wrote most of the instrumentals." She gave him her best pleading eyes. "Please, Pat? It's just a few months. Everyone will be super busy and Rohan has a separate bus. You'll never see him."

He scooped up Scoot, cuddling her softness and listening to her purr. It helped keep the anxiety at bay, a bit. His thoughts hissed and buzzed, screaming at him. He was so close, he was almost free. "It's not that simple."

"What's not that simple?" Nana asked, poking her gray head out of the kitchen. She narrowed her eyes. "You better not be getting cat hair on your offerings, child."

Patrick stepped back from the altar. "It's nothing, Nana."

"Is it those label people again? I'm telling you, one good trick and they won't be bothering you."

"I'm not laying a trick on anyone."

"Of course not. You don't know how."

Patrick braced himself. Though he'd gotten plenty of his herbalism knowledge from his Nana, she was forever sore he hadn't fully followed her in the hoodoo tradition. Plants were well and good she said, but ritual and tradition were where the real power was.

Before Nana could prod him to try learning, Sabrina

blurted out, "I need Patrick to fill in for my bassist on the festival tour."

"I told you, I can't," Patrick said. "Someone needs to be here for Nana and Scoot."

"Nonsense," Nana said. "I can take care of myself and the cat."

"The whole label's going," Patrick said, feeling like he was a kid and tattling on his sister. "I can find you someone else." He turned to Sabrina. "Please, don't push me on this."

"I'm sorry... I just thought..." She shrugged, hunching in on herself. "You're such a good player and no one knows and maybe we could hang out or something."

"Sabrina, you live in my house. We quarantined together. We hang out all the time."

"Do we? You're either in the studio—"

"Recording *your* album—"

She rolled her eyes. "On *business*. Or you're hiding in your room with your cat. When was the last time you left the house?"

"I hang out in the backyard all the time." Scoot struggled in his arms, tired of being held. He put her down and she wandered off. So much for emotional support.

"Doesn't count."

"I went to Rohan's album release party—"

She cocked her head. "Did you? I didn't see you."

"I did and I didn't come home until late."

"Yeah, what about before that?"

"Before that, we were in lockdown!" And sorting out the mess of Grandpa Pat's death but he couldn't bring that up in front of Nana.

"We haven't been in lockdown for weeks!"

"Nana's immunocompromised!"

"Oh, so now I'm the asshole for going on tour?"

He reared back. "What?"

"Children!" Nana thundered.

Patrick and Sabrina's mouths shut immediately. Nana rarely raised her voice.

Their grandmother looked at Patrick. "I'm worried about you."

"Me?"

"Yes, baby. You've been moping around the house for the last year and a half. It's enough to make anyone depressed just looking at you."

"I'll be better when I *quit the label*." He glared at Sabrina.

"So quit and be part of my band," she said.

"You mean quit and then make Benji and Rohan my bosses? So much better."

She flushed.

Nana closed her eyes. "The spirits are talking to me."

The siblings fell silent again, glaring at each other.

Nana opened her eyes. "The spirits are giving me a good feeling about this."

"What?"

"Go with her. It'll be good for you."

"What about being trapped for months with two people who fucked me over will be good for me?"

"Language," Nana admonished. "Those people used to be your friends. Maybe this will work things out between you."

"What if I just let you lay a trick on them instead?"

She shook her head. "I'll divine to see if there is another way but this feeling is strong. You need love, baby. You need to go out and *live*. You need this."

Patrick didn't know what the hell love had to do with it but he knew he couldn't say no to his Nana, especially when her spirits tended to be right.

They damn well better be right now.

"Fine," he said. "But we're setting up contactless delivery

for your meds and groceries, and please, for my sanity, call my driver when you need to go somewhere."

"The bus stop is barely three blocks away," Nana protested.

"Nana!" Sabrina and Patrick said in unison.

"Please don't get COVID from riding the bus," Sabrina said.

"Fine, it's wasteful, but all right."

"You're making sure Mike gets paid while we're gone," Patrick said. That wasn't technically true. Patrick paid for Mike's on-call hours whether he got called or not. His driver had kids he was trying to put through college, after all.

"Oh well, I suppose I can find some use for him." She wandered back into the kitchen.

Patrick forced a smile he didn't feel, relieved but wrung out. Was he really going to do this? He hadn't performed in years, let alone without a track and with an instrument. Hell, at least he wouldn't have to do choreo. Or slather foundation over his skin until he looked airbrushed.

Sabrina gave him a hesitant smile and mouthed, "Thank you."

He nodded. He still was in his feelings about her putting him in this position, but hell, it was probably better than her touring with that dipshit Cyrus. Patrick would be boring compared to him.

Remembering the other bassist's injuries, he followed Nana into the kitchen to mix up a batch of tea to help ease his recovery. Cyrus might be an asshole, but Patrick didn't like to leave anyone in pain if he could help it. Physical pain, at least, he could help.

3

"Open my lips and speak for me
These are your words in my mouth
Sounds I can't pronounce
They pretend not to notice
Your hands moving my jaw

I'm no blank-hearted darling
With lines to fill
With words and your voice
As I lay still

My heart is full!
It needs no one
Not me, not you!
I'm not your blank-hearted darling!
My words can kill

Pose me, dress me
Curl my hair, paint me pretty
Color me giddy

Wind me up, turn the key
Make me say it…"
— "Blank-Hearted Darling" by Angela Alice off of *PhenoBarbie Doll*

Midtown Sacramento on a Sunday morning always felt distinctly hungover to Judit. The streets were quiet and mostly deserted. Though it was the coolest part of what promised to be a hot summer day, the only people out who weren't unhomed were a few chipper early folks ready for brunch and one or two night owls coming home in last night's clothes. Judit loved it, soaking up the post-revelry energy like she was one of those Saturday night hellions instead of just someone who'd walked to Grocery Outlet to avoid her family.

Okay, maybe not *avoid*. That felt more drastic than "accidentally" leaving her phone at home.

"Your sister just texted me." Her roommate Helen squinted at her phone. "She's threatening to come over and bring your parents."

Judit groaned, pushing her cheap knock-off Ray-Bans back up her nose. "What if we never went home?"

Helen patted her back. "My dad's been on me about this too. Over a decade of 'overcome and surpass your weakness' and suddenly he's not sure my leg can handle a cross-country tour." She rolled her eyes. "He dropped by yesterday with a whole new repair kit."

"That's kinda sweet, in a smothering way," Judit said. "My family just keeps trying to talk me out of it. It's moving out all over again."

"Which time?" Helen asked. "Moving in with me, Eva, or your exes?"

"Every time," Judit grumbled. "Mom demanded I come home when she heard about the break-up. Papi and Eva had to talk her down." Papi was Eva's dad, but given he shared a son with Judit's mom (his ex-wife) and was more of a dad than Judit's deadbeat bio-dad, she'd been calling him Papi ever since she was a kid.

They turned the corner and their quadplex came into view, shaded by some of the many trees lining the city streets. Two very familiar cars were parked out front. Judit groaned.

Helen bumped her shoulder against hers in commiseration. "Do you think they brought food, at least?"

Judit snorted. Helen was a great friend but her loyalties were questionable when her stomach entered the equation.

"Of course they did," she said. Judit was a passable cook, as was her mother, Eva's food was barely edible, but Papi poured love into his food and it was amazing—even if it was delivered with a heavy side of guilt.

"No time for avoidance then." Helen grabbed her arm and towed her towards their gate. "I wanna see if he brought molé —oh! Or those tamales he made last time."

"You couldn't stop gushing about them," Judit said, feeling steamrolled. "Of course, he brought them."

Helen hummed happily and wiggled her shoulders, unlocking the gate.

"You're still gonna back me up though, right?" Judit asked.

Helen paused to look at her. "Always. You may not be as good of a cook as your dad but you're still my ride or die."

The twisting in Judit's stomach eased and her breath came easier. She smiled, unlocking the gate. With her friend at her back, she could withstand any inquisition.

IT WASN'T SO MUCH of an inquisition as a lecture. No, a rant, a diatribe, a fucking browbeating.

"So, I don't think you should go." Mom leaned back against the cushions of the third-hand couch Judit and Helen had wrestled home from a local Craigslist free ad. It took them a sweaty, backbreaking hour to drag it two blocks but it had been worth it.

Eva sat next to Mom, her mouth a thin line. She knew better than to interrupt Judit's mother when she went into a rant but Judit didn't expect her help. Eva had made her position very clear over text.

Papi scraped his fork over the sauce left on his plate and sighed.

"I'm going." Judit took a sip of water. She glanced over at Helen. They both sat on the floor, backs against the wall. It was either that or folding chairs from the dining room table and Judit's hips were protesting already.

Her friend gave her a thumbs up from over her plate of tamales, her mouth full.

"Helen's going with me. We'll take care of each other. Cazzi's boyfriend will be there and he's super nice. If we need anything, he'll help us for sure."

Helen nodded enthusiastically, still chewing.

"You like the boyfriend? He's okay?" Mom looked at Eva, her voice sharp and her Hungarian accent hard-edged.

"Rohan is sweet," Eva said. "But he'll be busy, right? Running the label and doing tour stuff."

Cazzi dating RK wasn't a secret but it wasn't exactly out in the open either. Both Judit and Eva downplayed his fame to their family. No need to get everyone excited and asking questions. To them, Rohan was a working musician who had a side job helping out his label and making indie music they didn't listen to.

"Yeah, but I'll be there," Helen said. "We've been taking care of each other just fine for like a year now."

Mom frowned. Papi cleared his throat. "This job, does it have benefits?"

"Yeah," Judit said, "Medical."

Papi smiled. He knew she'd been uninsured since her last gig fell through. "Good. You need a real job for a while."

She contained her wince at the backhanded approval.

"She has a real job," Eva said.

Judit smiled at her.

"Maybe when you come back you can go back to school and get a degree like we talked about, mija," Papi continued, ignoring Eva.

"Or she could get a job with her cousin László right now," Mom said.

"László can't afford to give her health insurance, Mira," Papi said like he'd said this many times before.

Flashbacks to every conversation about her career goals she'd ever had with her family, flickered in the back of Judit's mind. Papi was an engineer who could never understand her psychic abilities no matter how many times she'd proved them because he couldn't measure them. Her bio-dad believed. He'd been the one to take her to his favorite psychic after six-year-old Judit predicted her mother's promotion using her brother's Pokémon cards. But he was never around and Mom couldn't see past the sick girl Judit had been.

"I'm right here," Judit said.

Mom sighed. "Bubala, you know I'm just worried about you. You're going to be so far away. Touring is hard work, I looked it up! And you're..."

"I *can* function, you know. I'm not an invalid." (Well, not completely.)

Mom looked at Papi and Eva, her expression despairing.

"Let her go," Papi said like Judit hadn't already signed a contract and Helen wasn't frantically looking for a subletter. Like it was their damn decision, not hers. "She's young. She'll bounce back."

Mom sighed and looked at Judit. "You'll be okay?"

Judit nodded.

"You'll call if you aren't, right?" her demi-sister pressed. "You'll send us regular updates?"

"All the pictures of dusty parking lots you can stand," Judit promised. If Eva agreed, maybe her leaving wouldn't be a living hell.

Eva nodded. "Don't worry, Mira. It'll be okay."

Mom heaved a heavy breath, closing her eyes and pinching the bridge of her nose. After a moment, she nodded. "Okay, bubala." She got up and kissed the top of Judit's head. Judit breathed in her mother's perfume and smiled. The gesture made her feel like a child, a deeply bittersweet feeling.

"Thanks, Mom," Judit said, carefully keeping her jaw loose so she didn't grit her teeth.

"But when you come back you and I are sitting down to make a five-year plan," Mom said. "You can't keep drifting through life like this."

Judit swallowed her objections. If she brought any of them up now, they'd be stuck here for the rest of the afternoon. "You got it."

4

"*I thought it'd be easy*
To never see you again
You go your way
I'd go mine
But fate didn't get the plan

Everything, everywhere
You're never far away
Everything, everywhere
I can't ever get away
Can't avoid you
Even though I try

How can I be without you?
You're around every corner
They say forget her
But there's no way I can
When you're everywhere I am"
— "Everywhere" by Beatboyz off of *Not Sweet, Not Simple*

The next week, Judit stepped onto the tour bus in the San Fernando Valley, sure it would all dissolve and she'd wake up any minute. That the burn in her nose from the COVID test was just an illusion. She'd been waiting to wake up since the paperwork had been finalized and Helen found them someone to sublease. When the subleaser came through, they'd had an impromptu dance party until they'd both had to sit down.

"I can't believe we're actually doing this," Helen breathed from behind her.

"Yeah." Judit's shoulders were already protesting carrying her duffel bag and backpack but she didn't care. If she dwelled too long on how hard this might be she'd run away screaming.

Instead, she handed her duffel off to the butch lady driver who tossed it into the hold. Judit glanced around, wondering if they were the first ones there. They weren't that early. But no one else seemed to be around, just rows of buses and dry heat, the air rippling over the blacktop of the bus depot. Damn, it was as hot as Sacramento down in SoCal.

She climbed the stairs, sighing as the A/C hit her. Oh my god, there was a lounge? On a bus? Was that normal? It was small but had a couch and a small TV on one wall. If it was empty she could probably do most of her daily stretches here.

She wandered past and took in the bunk beds. They were... practical. Each bunk was stacked two high and outfitted with curtains. Most already had stuff in them so she tossed her backpack on an empty top bunk and hauled herself to sit next to it with a happy sigh.

She knew she should probably go for a lower bunk since she'd be tired and hurting most nights, but Helen's prosthetic might have trouble on those slippery metal ladders.

Helen took the bed below hers. "Who else do you think we're

gonna bunk with?" She leaned over across the aisle to another bed and poked at the bag sitting on the blah brown covers. "Also, I'm scared to ask why they picked brown for the sheets."

"Gross," Judit said. "Didn't you read the tour handbook? We're with 'people of comparable skill sets.'"

"Number one: no, of course I did not. I binged festival documentaries instead. Number two: what the hell does that mean? Dickheads with T-shirt cannons?"

"Unfortunately, I left my T-shirt cannon at home," came a dry voice behind them.

Helen and Judit turned to see Benji Nakamura standing in the aisle.

Benji. Fucking. Nakamura.

They wore black linen, not a wrinkle in sight, with make-up so flawless they looked gorgeous, porelessly inhuman. Their black hair curled loosely over one black-and-silver-lined eye, emphasizing their sardonic expression.

"Hi," Judit said and congratulated herself for forming words.

"You're the merch girls?" Benji took their hand off the handle of their rolling bag and offered a fist bump. "Benji."

"Uh-huh." Judit bumped her knuckles against theirs on autopilot. She could feel Helen frozen like a statue behind her. "I'm um, Judit." Great, now it sounded like she was lying or didn't know her name. "This is Helen."

Helen nodded.

"Good." Benji fist-bumped Helen. "This is the Now or Never Records bus. It's us, Doc Conjure, and Steph Infection. Rohan and his dancers have their own bus. We're sharing roadies with the rest of the fest so don't expect a lot of help." They checked their smartwatch. "Now, if you'll excuse me, we have a label meeting in ten minutes and I need to claim my bunk."

Judit scrambled out of the way. Helen just tipped over into her bunk wide-eyed as Benji hefted their bags and squeezed by.

"Steph Infection is gonna be on our bus!" Helen hissed, "Omifuckingggawd! Pinch me, I'm dying." She glanced at Benji and Judit knew it was taking all her self-control not to fangirl about them too.

Steph was Helen's favorite drag queen, possibly because he'd been her favorite Beatboyz member. Unfortunately, he wasn't the only Beatboy on this damn bus because if Doc Conjure was on this bus... shit. Maybe if she hid on top of her bunk and only left the bus when it was dark... yeah, right. She wasn't even fooling herself.

The bus shook as someone climbed the stairs and a lovely Black woman appeared at the front. She was curvy, with natural curls constrained in a puffy ponytail, piercings up her ears, black denim shorts, and a faded pink Beatboyz T-shirt. She waved awkwardly at everyone and Judit waved back, earning herself a nod and smile.

"That's Sabrina," Benji said, nodding to the newcomer. "Frontwoman of Doc Conjure. Sabrina," they pointed, "Judit and Helen. Merch girls."

Before Sabrina could respond, there was talking and laughing behind her, people coming up, and then—

Oh hell. There. He. Was.

Patrick never expected to tour again. After ten years of nearly non-stop shows, not to mention the practicing, publicity, and filming the label stuffed in the band's supposed downtime, he was very over it. He'd been to nearly every continent, played all the big venues, all the talk shows, and in the beginning, half the damn malls in America.

"Stop brooding," Sabrina muttered from next to him in the back seat. "This could be fun."

For her, it was. Doc Conjure had never been on a big tour before, this was their chance to win over crowds who would otherwise never bother clicking on their music.

Patrick just wanted to stay home and pet his cat. Nana promised she'd send plenty of pictures but he already missed his dorky little tortoiseshell. He'd been looking forward to a summer without Rohan and Benji.

Also, now there was no way he'd run into that girl from the party again, his anti-MPDG. The odds of him running into anyone in LA were astronomical but they were a million times worse on the road.

What would he even do if he ran into her? Ask her out? What would he even say? *Hi, I'm hung up on my ex-best friend but you're cute too*—Yikes.

"We're here." Sabrina opened the door and stretched.

Patrick followed her out, retrieving his luggage from the trunk and saying goodbye to Mike. He'd already had his basses set up in the bus. No way Patrick was renting whatever shit the festival offered.

They'd parked next to the two hulking anonymous black coach buses the NoN people were traveling in. Patrick looked the buses over and grimaced. The last time he'd toured he'd had his own damn bus, now he was going to share that space with seven other people, most of them strangers.

"Remember when the buses used to come to us?" asked a voice behind him.

"Leo!" Patrick grinned for what felt like the first time in ages, turning to greet his ex-bandmate.

Leo grinned back at him from his ridiculous height, the June sun gleaming off his short blonde hair and blindingly white but very muscular arms. He wore half a shirt that said "Future Trophy Wife" written in rhinestones and most of a pair of red shorts. He opened his arms for a hug and Patrick stepped into them.

Not to his surprise, but slightly to his annoyance, Leo picked him up and swung him around before depositing him gently on the ground.

"Yeah, yeah," Patrick said. "You're very strong and manly."

"And don't you forget it, Twiggy," Leo said.

Patrick rolled his eyes. "Are you also crammed into the Now or Never bus?"

"Yep," Leo said, "but I got the bedroom."

"Fuck off! How?"

Leo gestured at his height. "Also, I'm currently more famous than your sister's band." He shrugged. "Face it, Rick, you're practically a peasant again."

Patrick groaned. "Normally I wouldn't mind but—"

"Come on, Pat!" Sabrina called. "Let's check out the bus."

She waved at Leo, who bounded over and scooped her up too. His sister shrieked in glee just as she had when Leo spun her around as a child.

"Stop manhandling my sister," Patrick said, trying to keep a straight face. "You'll make her puke. Again."

Sabrina shot him a glare that could've flayed him to the bone. "That happened once," she said through her teeth as Leo put her down with a laugh. "I was nine."

Patrick dead-eyed her back until she gave up and raced up the bus stairs.

"Are you two going to be fighting the whole trip?" Leo asked. "I need to know how much popcorn to bring."

Patrick snorted, handing his suitcase to the bus driver with a smile and a thank you. "You're such an only child."

"You say that like it's a bad thing." Leo tossed his head like he was wearing one of his long green wigs. He smiled at the driver too. "Thank you, honey."

The driver, a butch woman, looked him up and down and then at the pile of luggage next to Leo. She sighed.

Patrick snickered.

"Yes, I know," Leo said to both of them. "I'm high maintenance, but high maintenance reformed, I swear!"

Patrick shook his head, trudging up the stairs.

"Don't shake your head at me!" Leo called after him. "Just for that, I'm starting Tourgasm back up again!"

Patrick groaned.

"What's Tourgasm?" Sabrina asked from the top of the stairs.

"Leo pretending to be the Perez Hilton of our tour," he grumbled.

"Hey! I'll have you know that newsletter was gold-standard journalism," Leo said.

Sabrina laughed. He looked up at her but his gaze snagged on the people in front of her. Benji and two strangers he assumed were the merch girls: an Asian woman who was giving him the glassy-eyed look of a fan and—

Oh. Shit.

He was staring. He knew he was staring but she was staring right back through her dark bangs. Her big eyes widened and her lightly tanned skin flushed pink over her high cheekbones, which honestly was really distracting because would she look this flushed if—

"This is Helen," Benji was telling Sabrina, gesturing at the Asian woman. "And this is Cazzi's friend, Judit."

So the anti-MPDG had a name. Judit. He liked it, he—

His brain caught up with the rest of the sentence. Judit, Cazzi's friend. Cazzi's friend, Judit. Judit, her old roommate from the first time when he'd ghosted Cazzi. Judit, the psychic, *who knew exactly who he was.*

Suddenly, he processed the way she stared at him like she was waiting for a bomb to go off. She'd known exactly who he was that night. Was she being nice, letting him think his identity was safe? Or had she been trying to keep him away from Cazzi?

Static and feedback screamed in his head. He focused on his breathing, nodding at both women before turning around and pushing past Leo to leave the bus. He had to leave the bus. He'd kick Leo in his bad knee if he had to, but his friend just let him by, too busy responding to Helen's babbling fangirling to notice his face.

"Patrick?" Sabrina said, turning to watch him.

He shook his head and accelerated.

Then he was outside, breathing, the sun hot on his face. God, god, god, why did it always come back to Cazzi? Why was the universe torturing him with the one thing he could not have, the one thing he'd fucked up beyond all repair? He paced, weaving his way through the various buses, avoiding the one that Rohan's dancers were swarming around.

He barely saw any of it, all he could do was count his breaths until his thoughts retreated to a manageable buzz. The world came into focus and he realized he was on the other side of the bus rental place's parking lot, staring out the chain link fence at the quarry across the potholed street. The air was heavy with the oppressive heat that could only come from standing outside in the summer for more than five minutes in the San Fernando Valley, every inch of the sea of asphalt around him shimmering and hot. His shirt stuck to his back and his mouth was dry.

Turning away from the street, he aimed himself back towards the bus that was going to be the closest thing to home this summer. He had a good sense of direction, honed over years of sneaking out of hotel rooms with Rohan to explore or avoid Leo and Martin's latest fight—

"I'm going to miss you so much." Rohan's voice from around the bus next to him stopped Patrick in his tracks. He was talking to Cazzi, he had to be.

"I'm going to miss your cooking," she said, right on cue, her voice teasing and light. A mask of humor.

Rohan chuckled. "Just my cooking?"

She gasped softly. "Maybe."

"Are you sure?" His voice was so low, Patrick had to press himself closer to the front of the bus to hear it.

"Well, I wasn't expecting the Spanish Inquisition," Cazzi replied breathlessly after a moment.

"You wouldn't. Our chief weapon is surprise—surprise and seduction, our chief two—" His words were cut off. Patrick knew with horrible certainty it had been with a kiss.

"I love you, you absolute nerd," she said. No mask, no uncertainty.

"I love you too, Caz."

The sharp pain in Patrick's chest must be what being stabbed felt like or maybe he was having a heart attack. Those would be sane explanations. But no, he knew it was just hearing his nickname for Cazzi on Rohan's lips, like an evil echo of the boyfriend he had never been. One stupid fucking word, his word.

"Marry me?" Rohan said.

Apparently, there were worse words. Patrick had been bracing himself for these but they still stole his breath. Cazzi wasn't the marrying kind, he didn't think, the last time they'd discussed it she'd been in grad school and it turned into a discussion of the institution as a whole. She hadn't been a fan. So Patrick felt pretty sure she'd say—

"Someday," she murmured, her voice warm, raspy, *intimate.* "I want to, someday."

"No pressure," Rohan said. "I promise."

Patrick pushed off the bus and stumbled away. He knew

marriage wasn't the endgame to everyone's love lives but he wasn't like Grandpa Pat, he wasn't, even if he had kissed Cazzi while dating another woman. He shunted the guilt away before he went down another spiral. And Cazzi wouldn't marry just anyone, especially not a famous anyone.

She must really, really love Rohan.

Patrick stopped. Cazzi was really, really in love with Rohan. Rohan was head over heels for her. They'd been together for over a year now. They were talking about marriage. This wasn't going away any time soon. Why had Patrick thought he was special? Why had he thought she was secretly waiting for him?

Because she *had* waited for him until he'd fucked it up. Until he'd fucked it up and Rohan swept in.

The old anger rekindled, cold flooding his veins, and Patrick stalked back towards his bus. His phone pinged with a text. Multiple texts.

Sabrina. Sabrina was worried about him. Sabrina was the person he was here for. Not Cazzi, not Rohan, not Benji, and especially not Judit.

He stopped, the sun beating down on his head, his neck, all his exposed skin. He was so sick of this emotional roller coaster. He couldn't ride it non-stop for months while packed in close proximity with Rohan. Not if he wanted to help Sabrina and Doc Conjure build a fanbase.

"Let it go, Pat," he said, feeling somewhat silly talking to himself. "Let her go."

Maybe he'd been in love with her, but it certainly wasn't mutual anymore. Maybe by the end of the tour, his hopeless heart would get the damn message.

You need love, baby, Nana's words whispered in his head.

Yeah, right. That was about the last thing he needed.

5

The Fest to End All Fests
EndFest is here and it's literally everything you could ever want after
sheltering in place forever. With acts ranging from chart-topping pop (RK,
Martin Mejía) to indie rock (Doc Conjure) to the Bitch Queen herself, not
to mention drag queens, circus acts, and the occasional comedian. If this
doesn't get you out of the house, nothing will.
—HardYes Magazine

When he got back to the bus, Benji stood by the entrance. They hooked their arm in his and steered him away.

They grimaced. "I have news."

This couldn't be good but at least it would be a distraction. Patrick damn well needed one.

"Nicky called. There have been some developments," Benji continued.

Nick Sullivan was the promoter running the whole fest. Benji called him Nicky behind his back because he looked about twelve and had the temper of a child. But he'd run

49

several successful tours and festivals in the last ten years so the investors and the brands supporting the fest liked him.

Patrick let Benji lead him to the space between their two buses. It was easier than fighting. They might look like a goth stick figure but he knew firsthand they could be shockingly strong.

"So," Benji said. "Judit, who is she? Trouble?"

Patrick shrugged. "I thought you had news."

"Don't give me that," Benji said. "I saw the way you two were eyeing each other and I need to know if I should separate you. I got enough on my plate without more ex drama."

"She's not an ex," Patrick said quickly. Then his brain kicked him. "What do you mean *more* ex drama?"

"Line up additions," Benji said darkly. "Fucking pain in my ass." They stopped and looked Patrick in the eyes. "I may need your help. Can you give it?"

Patrick blinked. He'd been doing the bare minimum on NoN admin stuff more days than he'd like to admit but this was the first time anyone addressed it. Guilt, he suspected. "What exactly are you worried about?"

Benji took a breath and blew it out, lowering their voice. "It's Angelica and Martin."

"What?"

"They're the additions. Rohan's going to announce it any minute." They headed towards the center of the bus yard.

"*Fuck!*" Patrick hissed, following them. "Please tell me someone warned Leo."

Benji grimaced. "I haven't even told Rohan he's announcing it yet. The call literally just came in."

Patrick swore again, picking up speed towards the edge of the small gathering of crew and talent. The crowd milled around, circling Rohan like planets around the sun. Patrick immediately scanned for Leo as Benji broke off to talk to Rohan. The dancers in their workout clothes fidgeted, watching Rohan like he was more god than employer. Sabrina and her drummer, Kevon, vibrated with barely concealed excitement. Cazzi appeared to have already left, thankfully.

Judit stood in her long dress, hands in her pockets, watching with a smile behind her sunglasses.

He kept his gaze moving, unwilling to dwell on her. Judit's friend bounced next to her, in shorts with a prosthetic leg and a giant grin. She grabbed Judit and pulled her in for a selfie, the two of them cycling through a rapid succession of poses.

Where the fuck was Leo hiding?

As if Patrick summoned him, his ex-bandmate sidled up. "Is he going to give us the old run down? No drugs, no hookups, no bad press?" He winked.

Patrick did not want to know how much contraband Leo smuggled onto their bus. If he didn't know, it wouldn't stress him out. Same went for hookups and bad press. Out of the corner of his eye, he could see Benji talking to Rohan, and Rohan's face going stiller and more pleasant as his training took over.

"Hey Leo," Patrick said, "Bad news. So, um—"

Rohan clapped his hands, calling everyone's attention. "Just a few things to go over before we head to the festival's first stop."

"Tell me later," Leo said. "I want to watch Rohan pretend he's in charge."

"He's our headliner," Patrick pointed out as Rohan reminded everyone not to be an asshole and let him or Benji know if anyone was an asshole to them.

"I thought we were mad at him," Leo said, puzzled.

"Yeah, but—"

"Okay, now for some interesting news," Rohan said, his smile holding a brittle edge. "Angela Alice and Martin Mejia will be joining us on select dates as their tours intersect with ours." He looked directly at Patrick, his eyes begging him to keep Leo in line.

Patrick was already on it, grabbing Leo's arm, catching his hand as it snarled into a fist. "Not now," he hissed.

Leo's muscles tensed, his whole body taut. Patrick braced himself. Leo's temper, especially when he felt trapped, was destructive. He didn't hurt people but... well, those weren't calluses on his knuckles. Patrick had spent far too many nights dripping yarrow tincture on Leo's hands to stop the blood. Leo took a shuddering breath and his fist loosened, his arm muscles following. Patrick let go but stuck to his side, watching out of the corner of his eyes.

Rohan finished his announcements and appeared next to him as the crowd dispersed, smiling out at the other NoN folks, covering Leo's reaction as much as anyone can cover someone five inches taller and twice as wide.

"Two evil exes," Benji remarked. "What are the odds?"

Given that no one knew about Martin and Leo outside of the Beatboyz team, Patrick wasn't sure. The label carefully smothered any possible evidence of the on-again off-again relationship his two ex-bandmates once had. Couldn't have their boy band image tarnished by two members being queer, let alone with each other. He gave Benji a sharp look. They shrugged and Patrick wondered what they knew.

But everyone knew about Rohan and Angela fucking Alice.

What had Nick been thinking? Did he think Rohan and Angela sorted their issues out? Was he counting on *Angela* to be professional? The woman who'd blasted her break-up with Rohan out through an album complete with a movie-length music video on YouTube then gotten into a Twitter feud with Benji over it? Or was he hoping for exactly that notoriety?

"Why the fuck didn't you tell me?" Leo growled at Rohan, taking a step towards him.

Benji moved to get between them but Patrick put a hand on their arm.

"Let him handle it."

Benji raised an eyebrow.

"Trust me."

"Pull your head out of your ass and I'll trust you again," Benji said. Apparently, the gloves were off now. But they stood back.

"When? I found out two minutes before you did," Rohan asked with the mildness he adopted while handling Leo back in the Beatboyz days. It wasn't like any of them could take Leo in a fight. The one time Leo got so drunk he'd passed out, it'd taken Rohan, Patrick, and two roadies to get him out of the bar. Martin hadn't bothered to lift a fucking finger.

"You still could've told me."

Rohan sighed. "Our schedule is tight as it is. If I told you in private I'd have to wait for you to finish trashing the bus."

Leo flinched. Patrick glared at Rohan. Trashing shit was what disqualified Leo from winning that drag competition show he'd been on.

"Fuck you," Leo snarled, voice rising.

"*Leo.*" Rohan lowered his voice in admonishment. He managed to hit the exact tone, James, the Beatboyz manager and Rohan's stepdad, used to when Leo tried him.

Leo dragged his hands over his face, straightening away from Rohan. "I hate this."

"We're just damn delighted," Benji said drily.

"Yeah," Rohan said, matching his tone. "I'm so excited to see my worst break-up ever."

Patrick grimaced sympathetically. He was massively pissed at Rohan but he wouldn't wish that break-up on anyone.

"It's different," Leo rasped, his voice barely a whisper.

Patrick put a hand on Leo's shoulder.

"I know," Rohan sighed.

They shared a moment of silence for the year Leo lost to his broken heart when Martin left the band and him in one fell swoop.

"We'll minimize your interactions as much as possible. I'll get their schedules and we'll strategize," Benji said. "I don't trust Nicky as far as I can throw him."

"Purely hypothetically, how far would that be?" Patrick asked, enjoying the image.

"Not as far as I could," Leo said like he was actually contemplating it.

"I'm surprised Martin and Angela agreed to be last-minute add-ons," Rohan mused. "This seems below their pay grades."

Benji shrugged. "It's a surer gig. A venue show is easier to cancel than a traveling fairground with this many moving parts. Everyone's being careful right now."

"There's nothing we can do, is there?" Patrick asked.

"We don't have the clout anymore," Benji said.

The four of them shared a grimace, all of them probably wishing for the fame they'd had less than a decade ago.

"I'll mitigate this as best I can," Benji said. "But we're going to have to work together because Angela is a vindictive b—" They thought better of finishing their sentence at Rohan's stern look. "Will Martin be as bad?"

"Probably worse," Rohan said. "Getting a rise out of Leo is easy and that asshole enjoys it far too much."

"Right here," Leo hissed.

Patrick sighed. "I know you've been working on it but you still have a temper."

Leo growled again, took a deep breath, and dropped his shoulders. "So Benji," Leo's eyes twinkled with mischief. "Are you going to be my handler now?"

Benji raised an eyebrow at the subject change but gave him a blatant once over. "Do you want me to be?"

Leo blushed, his entire head flaming bright red.

Patrick sighed, settling in for the inevitable flirting. He accidentally looked over at Rohan and caught the other man casting a commiserating glance in his direction. Patrick looked away. It must've been an old habit, from the days when they were forever navigating the swells and pitfalls of Martin and Leo's relationship. It had been a long time since they'd been on the same side like that.

He almost missed it. Too bad Rohan killed their friendship when he seduced Cazzi.

The buses around them started their engines.

"We'll talk more," Rohan said with an apologetic smile. "See you in the next dusty parking lot." He dashed off.

The three of them trudged back to their bus. The damn bus Patrick would spend the next two months sharing with Leo's Martin issues while Benji probably ran a shadow government right under Nicky's nose. Oh, and Judit.

Judit. The thought of her was a landmine he didn't have the energy to poke. Maybe he could leave it that way for the entire—

He cut the thought off. That wasn't happening. Avoiding shit was what had blown his life up before. Maybe this time he should just face this mess head-on.

But when he climbed onto the bus he saw how she turned away from him. How dare she turn away from him, when she'd been the one to deceive him in the first place? Was she mad at him? He hadn't done anything wrong!

Anger prickled through him and he grabbed the only empty bunk, hauling his bass in with him. He plugged his headphones into his bass and pulled out the tabs he'd written for himself, blocking out the world as he practiced for Doc Conjure's first show. The bass lines thrummed through him, pulling him out of his thoughts as the bus left the lot. He relaxed into the repetitive rhythms, closing his eyes as he grew confident enough to practice without the written notes. If he didn't think about it, maybe he could forget she was sitting right across the narrow aisle from him.

Maybe avoiding her was the right call after all.

AM I THE ASSHOLE HERE? Judit texted Helen, though she sat in the bunk above her friend.

Helen popped her head out. "Context please."

Judit looked around to see if anyone was paying attention but Leo was in his room, Sabrina was watching TikToks, Benji was on their computer, and Kevon, Doc Conjure's drummer was asleep. Judit tipped her chin at Patrick, bent over his bass, his long fingers moving deftly over the frets. Dammit, now she was noticing his forearms. That was dangerous territory.

"Oh, that whole thing?" Helen knew everything. Judit needed backup and she didn't want to give Rohan and Patrick another reason to fight. She tipped her head from side to side. "I mean, it's complicated, right?"

"Yeah, but I feel weird about it."

"So, like, apologize. Talk to him like an adult."

"I know, I know." She grimaced and lowered her voice. "But also, he was a dick to Cazzi so maybe I shouldn't be, like, nice to him?"

Helen pressed her lips together in thought. "Fair point. Also though, Cazzi's not here and, not to be selfish, but we're gonna be stuck on a bus together so maybe you need to put that aside for a few months." She shrugged.

"I feel like a bad friend though."

"Have you talked to Cazzi about it?"

"She doesn't know about that night at the party and—"

Helen waved her words away. "Not that. But like, she knows you're both here right?"

"Yeah."

"So, you guys talk about that?"

Judit looked at the ceiling. "I was maybe avoiding her a bit cuz I thought she'd try to talk me out of going on the fest."

Helen poked Judit's foot. "Text her."

Judit groaned.

Helen poked her foot again. "Dooo it."

"Ugh, why do you have to like, know things, or whatever?" Judit pulled out her phone.

JUDIT

> Would it be breaking the friendship code if I wasn't a total asshole to Patrick? We're still mad at him right?

Cazzi's text bubble appeared. Disappeared. Appeared. Disappeared. Then:

CAZZI

> What happened was between him and me. You don't have to let it make things awkward on your trip.

JUDIT

> Yeah, but he was an asshole who ghosted and jerked you around!

CAZZI

> I know what happened.

> I'm not happy with him. But we have... history. If he makes an effort to change I'm willing to forgive him.

> So don't be an asshole to him just cuz of that. Feel free to be an asshole to him if he's an asshole to you though

Dammit, that meant Judit should apologize to him, didn't it? She showed Helen the text exchange just in case there was an out somewhere.

"Nah," Helen said. "You gotta be an adult, sorry."

Grumbling, Judit burrowed into her bed and glared at the back of Patrick's head until the movement of the bus lulled her into dozing off.

6

> *"You're hoping*
> *You're thinking*
> *I might explain*
> *Make it all make sense*
>
> *There's nothing I can say*
> *I wish I could*
> *Wish I could*
> *But my lips are sewn shut*
> *I can't pull these stitches out*
>
> *You don't get it*
> *How could you?*
> *You're too well-adjusted*
> *You think I can be trusted*
> *You dream me*
> *As I could've been*
> *That's why you can't understand*
> *Why"*

— "Stitched Lips" by User-Friendly Omega off of *Suicide King*

Judit was shitty at pep talks—especially when she didn't mean them. But her nerves were frayed just by a few hours of trying to ignore a man who was clearly ignoring her. Something needed to be done.

"Okay," she told herself in the tour bus bathroom mirror. "You're okay. He's a *reasonable* human being and you have a right to be here. Everything's gonna be fine."

"Everything's fucking fantastic, now get out of the damn bathroom," someone, it sounded like Leo, yelled through the door.

Judit sighed, took one last look at her make-up, and opened the door.

"*Thank you*," Leo snapped, slamming the bathroom door behind him. He looked like he'd heard nothing but bad news during their drive to the first fairground venue somewhere in the Inland Empire of SoCal where they'd meet the rest of the fest. The bus ride had certainly been a quiet one.

She shrugged off his rudeness and left the bus with Helen, heading for the mess tent. The crew got there ahead of them to set up and the festival was half-built, skeletons of stages and booths casting long shadows in the dying light.

It was still hot as fuck, the air like a dry fist around her, hazy with dust kicked up by the construction. She fished her mask out of her pocket, putting it on. It cut the dust but didn't make her feel any less like she was melting. Her hair stuck to her neck and face and the cotton of her dress clung to her in a way that made her wish she'd worn a darker color.

"I'm starving," Helen said, apparently unbothered by the heat or the dust. "Do you think the food will be decent?"

Judit shrugged, glancing at the line of porta potties off in the distance. If the food wasn't good then, well, they'd all be miserable. That would probably make Patrick sooo much more charming. Ignoring each other for two months of sharing a bus couldn't last. Sooner or later everyone would notice and then the uncomfortable questions would start and who knew what he'd say.

"Hey," Helen said, catching Judit's mood. "It'll be fine. I'm sure he won't be an asshole."

Judit took a deep breath. "I hope so."

Helen slung her arm around Judit's shoulders. "If he is, I'll kick him in the balls—with my cyborg foot." She grinned. "Completely by accident, of course. These things happen."

Judit laughed. "They are tragically common."

"Such a shame." Helen laughed as they walked into the open side of the tent—straight into a long ass line.

It took them a good fifteen minutes to get their food, which didn't bode well as only about half the acts were here. But the food, when they got it, looked good and featured actual vegetables.

Even better, the minute they got out of line Rohan gestured them over to his table with Benji. Judit sat next to him, Helen on her other side. Rohan beamed at them. Benji looked distracted, fanning their face and scanning the other occupants of the tent.

"Hot as hell, isn't it?" Rohan remarked cheerfully.

"It'll get hotter," Benji replied darkly. Then they focused their attention on the table. "I'll make an announcement to the rest of the team later but I've got a stash of water, sunscreen, and baby wipes if anyone runs out. Don't tell the other acts."

"Baby wipes?" Helen asked.

"We're only in hotels once a week," Benji said.

Judit blinked, nonplussed.

Rohan groaned. "Oh shit, I didn't even *think* of that."

"Yep," Benji said, sighing. "I'm going to have a hell of a time keeping my make-up from melting off my damn face."

"How'd you do it on Warped Tour?" Rohan asked.

"Baby wipes mostly, but when we went back with an actual tour bus, we just splashed ourselves in the sink. The damn shower never actually worked."

Judit's brain clicked into gear. "Wait, aren't there showers in the campgrounds?"

"Yeah," Benji said. They stabbed their fork into their food, hard. "In my experience, there are usually about four working showers in a campsite. The fest is going to be nearly two hundred people, give or take an act or five. You do the math."

"Fuck," Judit hissed.

"I hope you brought flip-flops." Benji gave her a slightly frightening grin.

"Chill, Benji." Rohan patted their shoulder. "It'll be fine. You'll just have to lower your standards to where they were in your early twenties."

"In my early twenties, people thought I was a man," Benji muttered, their black hair falling over their eyes.

The entire table paused, everyone's brain visibly examining the statement and trying to find the best thing for a cis person to say to that.

"Well," Judit hazarded, "no one would make that mistake now."

Benji looked up, cocking an eyebrow that said *what the fuck do you know?*

Judit wilted. Damn, she should've just shut up.

"We've got your back," Rohan said, quietly. "We'll be just as filthy as you are, so you may not want us standing too close to it, but we'll be there. Whatever you need."

Helen nodded. "Hundred percent."

"Yeah," Judit said, trying again. "We can have melted make-up together. I'll let you know when you need a touch-up if you do the same for me."

Benji's mouth kicked up a bit at the corner. "Your lip stain is smudged."

Judit checked her reflection in her phone and fixed it. "Thanks. You have mascara under your left eye." She smiled when Benji dabbed it away.

"So." Helen fairly vibrated with excitement. "You were on Warped Tour?"

Benji's smile got bigger. "Twice. Once when we were small and once when User-Friendly Omega was at its peak."

"Daaaamn," Judit said. "I always wanted to go." But her mom never would've let her spend a whole day in the sun like that. It would've triggered a migraine or something and she'd have been sick halfway through it anyway.

Helen nodded along. "What was it like?"

Benji spent the rest of the meal regaling them with Warped Tour stories. Judit saw Patrick, Leo, and Patrick's band sat at a separate table even though there was plenty of room. She could tell by the strain in Rohan's smile he noticed it too.

When the meal was over, Rohan and Benji asked them if they wanted to walk the grounds. Helen happily agreed. Judit wanted to but Patrick got up from his table and left the tent and she had to—something. Talk to him. Make this right, somehow.

"I'll catch up with you," she said. "But I think I forgot to put on sunscreen and I'm starting to feel it."

"Sun hats," Benji said, snapping their fingers. "We're selling hats at our merch table. Hats are now part of your sellers' uniforms."

"We have uniforms?" Helen asked.

"Yes," Benji said. "Wear hats, remember your passes, and cover your nips."

Judit was still chuckling at that when she caught up with Patrick as he walked back towards the bus.

"So, I think we should talk," she said before mentally rolling her eyes. Smooth she was not.

"Not now," he said.

She blinked. "Seriously?"

"Dead fucking serious. I have nothing to say to you."

She snorted. "I doubt that."

"I just can't—" He made a frustrated sound. Patrick rounded on her, stopping so abruptly she skidded, throwing up a cloud of dust around them. It haloed him like he was standing in the wreckage of something. The brooding villain. Or like the Death card, he was so skinny. He stared at her, jaw set.

She'd read about intense stares like this, seen them in movies. They'd seemed so much better through a screen.

She narrowed her eyes. Crossed her arms. Tapped her foot. The dust settled around them and his silence was denser than the heat, the dust, the last of the sun.

She could wait him out, no problem. Sure, her hips hurt and she was getting increasingly thirsty but—

"You lied to me, you knew exactly who I was," he hissed. "You knew I wanted to talk to her—"

"What's up?" Leo appeared next to him. "You two piss each other off already?"

"Patrick and I were just talking," she said. Maybe she could get Leo to go away so Patrick could get whatever speech he stored up out and she could apologize and they could be all good.

Patrick's eyes narrowed, his glare getting sharper, and she realized she'd only ever heard Cazzi call him by his full name.

Whoops. So much for all good.

Leo crossed his arms. "Uh-huh."

"We're done." Patrick spun on his heel and walked away with the fluid grace of someone who used to do complicated choreography for a living.

"Welp, I dun't know what you did, but good luck," Leo said sympathetically. "Rick can hold a grudge for literal years. Also, I'm always on his side so—" He bowed with a flourish. "Fuck you very much. Have a nice night."

Great. Now she had twice as many enemies.

7

"Girl, I can tell you're trouble
Got him thinking you're nice
But I know your type

Baby, you're trouble
Capital T, nothing left but rubble
Baby, you're trouble
Just like me

He thinks he's got a good thing
He thinks he's on stable ground not
A bit of boredom away from heartbreak

He doesn't know you'll leave his lap
Come meet me around the back
Like calling to like

Baby, you're trouble
Capital T, nothing left but rubble

Patrick sat with Sabrina on the bus couch, jamming on "Caretaker's Blues" with their instruments unplugged. Kevon sat next to them, drumming on the arm of the couch with his sticks. The three of them weren't quite cohesive yet but they had only managed to practice together twice since Patrick joined the lineup.

"I think there's room for a bass solo after the bridge if you want one," Sabrina said, strumming the chords of the middle eight bars on her teal tabby-striped PRS guitar.

"I'm here to showcase you," Patrick pointed out. Plus, a solo? He hadn't soloed live on any instrument since he played double bass in high school band class.

Leo leaned on the arm next to him and leaned back over the group. "Selfie time! Look cute!"

Sabrina and Kevon grinned at the camera. Patrick tilted until he was out of the shot. He was no longer contractually obligated to be in social media pictures.

"Oh come on, don't be camera shy." Leo pouted at him.

"Ashamed of being in my band?" Sabrina joked but there was something off about her tone.

"No, I just wasn't feeling a picture," Patrick said. "Besides, you want people coming to your shows for you, not for me."

Sabrina rolled her eyes. "You're not *that* famous anymore."

Patrick shrugged. Out of the corner of his eye, he could see Helen in her bunk, rubbing Judit's shoulders. Judit rubbed her friend's knee above the prosthetic. As if sensing his gaze, she looked up. Patrick glanced away.

From the front of the bus, Benji clapped their hands.

"What?" Leo asked, raising an eyebrow.

Benji ignored him. "All right folks, I'm not your camp counselor and I don't do icebreakers but we need to function as a team and we can't do that if we're all doing our own thing all the time. Let's do a record pull."

Patrick and the other musicians perked up. Oh, shit, Benji might not be his favorite person right now, but he loved a record pull. The new music, the deep cuts, the inspiration... he did one with every band he produced and it always helped them figure out the sound they're looking for.

Helen raised a hand. "Excuse me, um, what's that?"

"We sit together and each of us plays a song after first talking about why they like it," Kevon explained.

"So, it's an icebreaker?" Judit asked.

Benji sighed. "It's cooler than that, okay?"

The girls looked at each other, shrugged, and got out of their bunks. Leo sat on the floor in front of Patrick, the girls sitting across from their group.

Battle lines. But no, there was no battle in a record pull. As if to demonstrate that, Benji sat in the aisle, connecting the two camps.

"I'll go first." They grabbed their portable speakers and hooking up their phone. "I really got into Dessa during lock-down. I love the production on this song, the samples and the vocal treatments create all these little details to text paint and frame the lyrics well. Also the imagery in the lyrics? So good. Anyway," they said, seeming to catch themself geeking out, "This is '5 out of 6.'"

Patrick immersed himself in the song, letting the loops, high-hats, and the rapper's voice build to the chorus which expanded over him like a wave. Dessa could sing too, damn. The others listened in silence, Judit and Sabrina had their eyes closed, and Kevon tapped along, but no one was on their phone.

Sabrina was next to them so Benji tapped her to go after the song ended. She scrolled for a moment on their Spotify. "So with this song, I love the idea of liquifying music and getting drunk on it? Such a great image. I wish I'd thought of it myself. Also the energy? On point. This is 'Liquify the Music' by Eat the Cake Band."

The song was a bop, Patrick remembered it from the record pull they'd done for Doc Conjure's album. It was an indie track and the production had some small flaws he itched to fix but it was compelling and the song itself was great.

After the track finished, Kevon cracked his neck and picked a song in less than ten seconds. "This band blows my mind as a percussionist cuz they don't use the traditional methods of percussion like drums but they create it through samples." He mimed his head exploding with a grin. "This is kinda a creepy cut but man, the percussion is lit as fuck. Yeah, anyway, this is 'Body & Blood' by clipping."

The song was its own little horror movie built out of liquid sounds and a story about a cannibalistic female serial killer. Kevon was big into alternative percussion and had brought a different clipping track to the Doc Conjure record pull. He'd gotten Patrick hooked on the band too.

Patrick could see Benji bobbing their head to the track. Yeah, this would be up their goth kid alley. Kevon grinned at Benji but after a long moment, they looked away.

The song ended and Judit picked up the phone. She frowned as she scrolled, focusing like it was a test she planned to ace. Finally, she picked.

"I'm a total romance lover." She looked around, catching the reactions around the room. "And I will fight you if you give me shit about it."

Patrick remembered her demanding to talk to him, braced to fight. Yeah, that tracked.

Helen nodded. "She will."

"Anyway," Judit said with a nervous laugh. "Conan Gray is amazing at songs about longing. I heard this the other day and it nailed exactly how I was feeling about being single. This is 'People Watching' and it is fantastic for belting out when you're alone and emo."

Judit rocked in time with the song, mouthing along. Conan's mournful voice filled the bus, the sparse piano almost lost to the hum of the engine. The space in the track and the breathy emotion in his voice gave Patrick chills. Judit's face reflected the changing landscape of the song as if she was really singing along, really performing, really feeling everything in the lyrics.

Then abruptly the song ended. Judit's anguished face disappeared and Patrick blinked. Oh no, had he been watching her the whole time? He wrenched his gaze away.

Helen grabbed Benji's phone. "Okay, I'm gonna bring up the mood a bit. This is my current favorite rah-rah song, it's such a banger. We had so many quarantine dance parties that started with 'Kill This Love' by BLACKPINK."

By the end of the militaristic trumpet intro, Helen pulled Judit up to dance with her. Leo immediately stood too, dancing in place and pointedly not looking at or dancing with Judit.

Patrick smiled at Leo for being petty for him and began scrolling to put his song pick in as the song came to a close but Leo snatched it away. "No, we're keeping this party going. This is a bit of a throwback but a friend of mine did an amazing drag performance of it right before we left on tour and I'm obsessed."

He pressed play and the complex percussion of "Get Ur Freak On" by Missy Elliott filled the space, the impressive number of samples coming together to undergird Missy's rap.

Sabrina hopped up, Kevon on her heels. They busted out

dance moves they'd clearly practiced together. Leo extended a hand to Benji.

So much for being petty to all Patrick's enemies.

Benji hesitated.

"Stop thinking," Leo said. "You wanted us to bond right?"

Benji stood, without taking his hand. Their dance moves were rusty and self-conscious. Judit and Helen were worse, though. Holy shit, neither of them had rhythm nor did they seem to care.

Were they confident or delusional? Patrick couldn't tell. It was kind of mesmerizing to watch though.

The song wound down and everyone turned to look at him, crouched with the phone in his hand. Well, he could read a room.

"Gotta keep the party going," he said and turned on the Weeknd's "Blinding Lights."

A cheer went up from the rest of the group. He straightened and bobbed his head, enjoying the earworm.

"Nuh-uh." Leo grabbed his hand. "We all know you can dance better than that."

He spun Patrick like they were in a ballroom, forcing everyone to the edges of the lounge and then he started into something that looked like it had been choreographed ten years ago. Patrick rolled his eyes. Of all the choreo they'd memorized, this was the one Leo picked?

Good thing his muscle memory was still good. Patrick matched Leo's movements, trying to fit them to the mostly similar rhythm of the song.

Helen screamed in pure fangirl joy. "The 'Trouble' music video dance!"

Patrick tripped over the raised edge of the aisle and laughed as Leo nearly took out the table. The friends grinned at each other. Behind Leo, Patrick could see Judit watching him, looking bewildered but smiling like she couldn't believe what was happening. Like for a shining moment, there was no feud between them, no bad decisions or anger.

You could make that happen, said a voice in his head.

But if he just let everything go, would he be caving like he had for so many years as a Beatboy? Would he lose the agency he was trying to carve out for himself?

8

Dearly beloveds, welcome to the first issue of the must-read newsletter of the tour! I, your wise and omniscient narrator, will bring you the latest in the best goss, parties, and calls for help. Bring me your tidbits, your event pages, your lost and found oddities, and weird tour poetry! Share it with your friends, share it with your enemies, just don't share it with the press.

Remember kittens, what happens on tour, stays on tour.

With love and judgment,

LS

—Tourgasm Vol 1

Patrick lay in his bunk, staring at the faint outlines of the ceiling. It was dark and nearly everyone was asleep, their breaths and restless shifting a chorus of small sounds around him. His mind flitted around, trying to find something to spiral on.

Cazzi—

Rohan—

Leo—

Martin—

Angela fucking Alice—

73

Judit—

He cut each thought off, dragging his attention back to the sounds around him, timing his breaths until they were even. His breathing was a metronome, tying the chorus together, backed by Sabrina's restless shifting, Kevon's slight snoring, the wind outside...

Patrick hovered right above the threshold of sleep, unable to cross. He tried to keep his mind clear but just trying sent a cluster of thought fragments tumbling in his head, breaking the careful rhythm of his breaths. The sounds around him became a cacophony.

He grimaced in the dark, covering his face with his hands. Dammit, this used to work! He wouldn't have been able to get through years of touring if it hadn't. But now, nothing worked. Not for the last week. He'd resorted to smoking pot in the middle of the night, sitting by his pool like some kind of LA cliché but even that was spotty, at best. Usually, he maxed out on three nights of insomnia before his body gave in and forcibly made him sleep but his anxiety had leveled up. The exhaustion of the heat and the unexpected dance party hadn't been enough.

Go him.

Fuck.

Maybe he could sneak out for a walk around the grounds. He weighed the danger of that and of the questions he'd inevitably get if he woke someone up. With his luck, it'd be Sabrina or worse, Judit.

Judit who called him by his full fucking name like she had any right. Overly familiar, Nana would call her.

He turned on his side and glared at Judit's bunk just because he could. Might as well find some silver lining to having to sleep across the aisle from her. She slept turned away from him, curled into the covers, her dark hair spilling over the white pillow as it caught the light from under Leo's door.

Judit with her faux-niceness and her dorky unself-conscious joy, pretending not to know who he was. Trying to force a conversation probably so she could say some fake-ass apology and call him unreasonable if he didn't accept it. Judit, protecting Cazzi like she was fragile.

Like he used to. Like he protected Cazzi from his feelings, from any explanations—

Not the point.

Judit, thinking she could just smooth things over somehow. Like he could forgive her.

For what? Witnessing your weakness or taking care of you, jackass?

She'd only taken care of him because she had an agenda, just like every other fucking leech in Tinseltown. He should've known better. He'd been at an industry party, after all.

God, that was depressing. Sometimes he missed his optimism, the naivety he'd had when he was younger. He couldn't quite remember when he'd lost it. Sometime around what happened to Tanya and getting famous. It was amazing how fast fame disillusioned him. It would never leave him. His name, his face, his life, his talent were all useful to people, whether he liked it or not. It should've felt good but it just made his lungs lock up and his eyes burn.

Men don't cry, his father barked from his memory.

So he never did. Some days he thought he physically couldn't.

Judit chose that moment to turn over, her eyes half open.

Patrick froze. Maybe she was asleep. She probably couldn't even see him anyway, it was pretty dark.

Leo decided to open his door and go to the bathroom— leaving the door open. There were murmurs of protest, Benji's "close the damn door or I'm going to take your fucking bedroom privileges" rising above them.

Judit's eyes fluttered open, squinting against the light. Her nose scrunched and it was... kinda cute? That couldn't be right. She was the enemy. She had no right to be cute.

As if she'd heard his thought—hadn't Cazzi once told him she was a psychic? Wait, *could* she hear his thoughts?—her gaze latched onto him.

He went rigid, willing himself to look away, look away, look away—

She blinked slowly at him, still clearly half-asleep. Her mouth opened but no sound escaped. Her lips moved. They looked soft.

The lights shut off to a chorus of relieved groans.

"Fucking finally," grumbled Benji.

Patrick wasn't listening. He rolled over, just in case, his mind buzzing as it replayed the image of her lips. What had she mouthed? He was no lip reader but he was almost certain she'd mouthed his name.

He lost the rest of the night debating if there was any significance to that.

THE NEXT MORNING, Judit walked the grounds alone, wearing her new NoN hat. Helen was still asleep and the fest didn't start for several hours but Judit's joints were stiff despite her stretches and she needed to move. It was nice out too, despite the ever-present dust. The temperature wasn't actively trying to kill her yet and the sky was a clear blue with a few adorably fluffy clouds.

She took a selfie to show off her hat and feed the algorithm on her social media accounts. She didn't like to post a lot of pictures of herself, her following was just big enough that somehow every selfie attracted random men who felt no shame in making creepy comments. Unfortunately, social media was still the way most people found her and her online reading offerings. So now she had to tell the internet she was on tour so they'd come get readings from her at the booth.

She put the phone away so she didn't waste data checking her likes.

Stages were going up all around her, filling out from the skeletons they'd been when the NoN bus arrived yesterday. She counted two main stages (LadyWater and Greenbrew—though she wasn't sure which was which yet), two smaller stages, and dozens of booths interspersed with villages of porta potties.

Judit waved at a few crew people working on the setup. She didn't know anyone but surely that would change.

Why they didn't start the tour in LA didn't make sense to her, but then how many big ass empty lots were in a city like that? Probably none as cheap as this one in this suburb she'd never heard of. She wondered if she'd remember it when they left in two days. Would the whole trip be like this? She hoped not. She hadn't traveled much out of state and it would be kinda depressing to just see the suburbs of America.

Oh well, travel was travel. It'd be an adventure either way. Judging from the weird newsletter she'd gotten this morning, she suspected this would be interesting.

A figure in the distance caught her eye.

She hadn't planned on seeing Patrick. She'd wanted to give him space. Also, she was semi-certain she'd woken up in the middle of the night to him staring at her. All good reasons to avoid him but her feet guided her unerringly and suddenly there he was, in front of her. He sat on a mostly constructed small stage, head bent low as he tapped on his phone. He hadn't seen her yet, thank goodness, and it gave her a minute to steel herself.

He's just a man. A grumpy, semi-famous, (kinda pretty) man but a man all the same. Even so, she wished her feet had found her literally anyone else. She considered just walking away while she could. But, she was a psychic and she knew a sign when she saw it.

She climbed the stairs and walked up to him. "Hi."

He didn't look up. "I'm busy."

I can see your screen, jackass. "I'm sure those cat videos can spare you. Talk to me." She bit her lip. "Please." *Also, were you staring at me while I was sleeping? Cuz I don't know how I feel about that.*

"I don't want to."

"What are you, five?"

"Yes. This is child abuse."

She snorted. "It's child heckling at worst."

He scowled, finally looking at her. "You think you're clever."

"As much as I enjoy bantering, and I do, I really do, I am trying to have a serious convo here."

He sighed and stood with ease and fluidity she envied. As it was, she ached. That tour bus bed wasn't exactly ergonomic. "What do you want?"

"A truce."

His eyebrows rose.

"We're on this tour for like, two months. That's too long for us to be dicks to each other."

"I'm not seeing anything in this for me."

"Less tension, stress, hatred, and annoyance in your life is nothing?"

"You vastly overestimate how much stress, tension, and annoyance you cause me."

"Dude, we live together! How does that not stress you out?"

He shrugged.

Judit sighed. "Look, I didn't know who you were when I first found you. You were just someone who needed help. Yes, I eventually figured it out, but would you have wanted me to stop and be like, 'Oh hey you're Ricky Rick, can I get an autograph?'"

He leaned forward fast enough that it was nearly a lunge. It was all she could do not to lean away. "You knew who I was talking about. You knew I wanted to see her and you talked me out of it."

"If you were in my position and someone was trying to get to your sister or your friend and was acting like you, don't you think you maybe would've steered them away until you knew if they were cool?"

"You know I'm her best friend. She talks about me, I know she does. She told me about you before—" There was a wavering of uncertainty under his words.

"Before you ghosted her again?" Judit took a breath. *She also fucking cries about you. Do you know how frightening it is to see the Queen of Masking cry?*

"She does talk about you. But I don't know why the hell you'd think I'd be Team Patrick after the way you treated her." She crossed her arms. "Frankly, I feel disloyal offering you a truce, but Cazzi isn't here and we have to work together."

"Fuck off. You don't know me. You don't know our relationship." He turned back to his phone.

"No," Judit snapped, her patience with this man-child evaporating. "But I know Rohan and Cazzi's and I like it better, seeing as it's actually healthy." She spun away and stomped towards the stairs. But not before seeing his expression.

He looked like she'd punched him in the stomach. She refused to feel bad about it.

9

"Going to Endfest? Come say hi to the Now or Never Records team at our booth across from the @Greenbrew Rock stage! We got all your merch-related needs... and maybe one or two Beatboyz 😊"
—@NoworNeverRecords

Judit stood under the shade of the merch tent and watched Benji demonstrate the cash register and card app (again).

"I think we got it," she said with her most trustworthy smile when they finished.

Helen nodded. "We both survived the retail trenches. We got this."

Okay, *survived* was a strong word. Helen was fired from her job folding T-shirts when she slipped and accidentally put her prosthetic through a display window and Judit quit her bookstore gig because they wouldn't let her stay off the floor when the early morning sun shone straight into her eyes at the cash register and caused her daily migraines.

But really, how hard could this be?

Her answer came about an hour into her shift when Benji

let Helen go to rest for her evening shift and then got called away to deal with something themself. Judit was left alone with what looked like no customers but what almost immediately became a swarm of increasingly pissy festival goers.

It wasn't a line. A line she could've dealt with. It was a seething mass of people yelling and thrusting their fingers in her face, pointing at the merch they wanted, and then arguing with the person also waving their arm in her face that *they were there first, fuckhead.*

She tried yelling, waving her arms, anything but the only thing that seemed to work was selling the damn merch as fast as she could.

Then she ran out of size small RK shirts. She stared at the empty box like more might magically appear. Maybe there were more on the bus, if Benji had told her there were she couldn't remember. She sent them a text that was far too calm for the sodden mess of panic that was her brain. She called Helen repeatedly.

No one answered.

"What do you mean you're out of size small?" The question was more of an accusation, at this point.

"Try back later," she kept saying.

"We also have medium," she kept saying, trying not to hyperventilate through her mask.

The card reader crashed. When it booted back up it wouldn't scan anything. She called Benji but they didn't pick up which was probably good because she definitely would've burst into tears. Instead, she punched the numbers in by hand, her fingers and wrists cramping.

Her shirt stuck to her back. The waistband of her shorts dug into her belly, starting a deep ache in her pelvic muscles. She really, really had to fucking pee.

No one would pick up their damn phones.

The crowd got bigger, the mass billowing as far as to the

stall across the wide lane, overshadowing the ones on either side of her. The woman in the charity tent next to her kept shooting her glances like she was afraid Judit was about to drown.

She wasn't wrong. Judit hadn't sat down in what felt like forever, her head pounded, and she was about one more angry customer away from crying.

Then she saw him.

Patrick strolled by, anonymous in his mask and sunglasses. He paused, clearly seeing her. Then he kept walking.

Un-fucking-believable.

She hip-checked the cash register closed so hard it almost fell off the table and most definitely bruised her hip. Judit felt like screaming. The man was either so disconnected from reality he was unable to comprehend what a fucking disaster this was or he was a complete asshole and didn't care. She wasn't sure which was worse.

"Alright!" boomed a huge voice. "Form a line. An orderly line!" Leo appeared from nowhere, rising above the crowd like a benevolent giant. Using his shovel-sized hands like a traffic controller, he turned her unruly mass of customers into a meek line in thirty seconds flat.

A woman burst into tears at the sight of him. Judit sympathized, she was close to tears herself. Leo paused, offered her a fist bump, and then a hug when she needed more. He said a few words to her, before posing for a selfie.

Then he ducked into Judit's stall, grinning. "You looked like you could use a bit of help."

"You're my gorgeous, glittering hero." Judit swallowed a sob of relief along with the urge to throw her arms around Leo's neck and cling. This was what a decent person did, not walk away with a shrug like Patrick.

"I get that a lot," he said and started grabbing merch for her to ring up.

It wasn't exactly smooth. He didn't know where things were and inevitably every sixth customer was an (occasionally crying) fan who wanted a signed shirt and a selfie, but damn it was a hundred times better than doing it alone. Plus, any time the line deviated from a manageable shape, he jogged out and conducted them back.

Finally, Benji came back as the line began to die down. "I heard you needed help?" They looked quizzically at the dwindling line.

"You missed the worst of it," Leo said, signing yet another shirt. "I swear we're out of half of everything already. We're popular!"

"There's more in the bus," Benji said distractedly. "Damn, I didn't think it would be busy so early." They looked at Judit. "Why are you typing those card numbers in? I showed you how to use the reader."

"It crashed and now nothing scans."

They frowned and took the tablet after she was done with the transaction. They fiddled with it for a minute and handed it back. "Try now."

She let the next customer tap their card. It worked. She blinked, not sure if she was relieved or ready to scream from frustration.

"Quirk of the reader," Benji said, their expression warming with sympathy. She must really look like shit. They showed her the trick and she did her best to insert it into the steaming mess of what was left of her brain.

"Hey!" Rohan jogged up. "Here to help!"

Benji sent him and Leo off to go get more boxes from the bus. "I'm sorry I didn't come sooner," they said when the other two had gone. "I was dealing with the promoter. I'll try to hang around the merch tent more when I have other business."

Judit mustered a smile. She had visions of Benji hovering over her like a worried wraith and it wasn't as hot as she would've liked. "I think as long as we have two people working we'll be okay." She ran off to the bathroom before anyone else could come try to rescue her.

When she got back Helen was there and apologizing for not feeling her phone going off. Benji extracted a promise from both of them that they'd be glued to their phones, sound on, before sending Helen away again. Judit sat, finally, gloriously, into the nice padded chair reserved just for her. The last of the customers trickled away and she sighed, closing her eyes.

Benji sat in the camper chair next to her. "I'm going to recruit more people for this."

"Hire people?" Judit opened her eyes in surprise. She didn't think NoN had the budget. Hell, she was pretty sure Rohan bought this chair for himself.

Benji shook their head. "Back in my early UFO days, we sold our own merch. Doc Conjure can do the same."

Judit snorted before she could stop herself, her filter annihilated by three hours of retail hell. "I don't think Patrick will do it."

Benji gave her an assessing stare. "Whatever relationship you two have, I doubt you know him as well as I do."

Judit straightened at their cold tone, barely managing not to squirm. She'd crossed the line. It was too early to alienate her supervisor. "You're right. Sorry."

Benji nodded, regarding her before turning away like they had lost interest.

By the time her shift was over, Judit felt utterly depleted. Popping a CBD gummy, she dragged herself to the mess tent and sat, spacing out over her food.

"You look like you need a drink." Leo sat across from her. Or rather Steph Infection did, the former Beatboy was in full drag. Steph was a good six inches taller than Leo, her face contoured with green tinges that made her look witchy and monstrous yet glamorous. She put down two paper cups and pulled out a flask with a wink, tossing long green hair behind the shoulder of her ruffly green-black iridescent dress. She had to be sweating her ass off but Steph looked barely bothered.

At Judit's nod, Steph poured each of them what was probably a double shot. "Hope you like vodka."

They tapped their cups together and threw back the liquor. Judit barely managed to breathe past the smooth burn of good booze but Steph didn't even look phased. She smiled. "So, that was a shitshow."

Judit groaned and dropped her head into her arms on the table. "Completely."

Steph patted her hand, carefully avoiding scratching Judit with her long pointed acrylics. "We all bomb, honey. Benji shouldn't have left you alone."

"Does this mean you like me now or are you just pity drinking with me?"

The drag queen laughed. "Like I need an excuse to drink with anyone. Besides, I've had my fair share of bombs. You haven't truly bombed until you've been booed off stage at a leather bar in the middle of fucking nowhere and have to flee town."

Judit giggled.

A chair scraped and Rohan sat next to her. "That bad, huh?"

"Before Leo rescued me, I thought I was gonna be murdered by people because we were out of small shirts with your face on them." Judit hid her face again. Oh god, he was going to fire her.

Steph and Rohan laughed. "That takes me back," Steph said. "Remember that time we nearly had a riot on our hands because merch ran out of babydoll shirts?"

Rohan snorted. "I thought it was tank tops."

"Either way, we had to come out and sign shit for an hour

because the venue was worried about property damage, and the label thought we'd get bad press."

"Was that the time that fan got us all to sign her arm and got it tattooed the next day?"

"You say that like it only happened once."

Judit peeked up at them. "Just how many people have your signatures tattooed on them?"

Both singers hummed uncertainly. "A lot?" Rohan finally hazarded.

"Yeah, we thought it was pretty cool at the time," Steph agreed.

"And now?"

They both shrugged.

"I'd still do it," Steph said.

"Yeah, probably," Rohan said. "I just make sure it's pretty." He glanced at his smartwatch. "Shit, I gotta go. Hang in there, Judit. It'll get easier," he said, leaving with a kind smile.

Judit straightened, covering a flush of annoyance with a smile. He didn't know what it was like to expend so much more energy just to function. To constantly tune out pain and smile as her muscles strangled her nerves until they screamed.

Steph poured herself another shot. "First show's always the worst. At least you didn't trip on your dress and fall face-first into a lesbian wearing a spiky bra. Remember when those were a thing? Well, this one time I was playing this tiny queer club in New York..."

Judit peered up at Steph. The CBD and the booze were kicking in concurrently and things were lighter, easier. "I thought you were siding with Patrick," she blurted out.

Steph blinked at the interruption. "Honey, who do you think told me to come rescue you?"

Judit gaped at her. "What?" That was Patrick? Fuck, that was... was... aggravatingly kind of him. In a cryptic, round-about way.

"Rohan and Benji too, I'm sure." Steph shrugged. "I don't know what's up with you two..." She gave Judit a look. "Unless you want to tell me?"

Judit shook her head, not trusting herself to speak. So, was this Patrick being nice to her? Was he accepting her truce?

Steph sighed. "Pity. I'll just have to wring it out of Rick. That'll be a pain in the ass." She threw back her shot. "He's good people, Rick is. That's hard to find, especially in this industry."

Judit made a non-commital noise, her mind still whirling.

Steph tapped own her nose with a slightly wobbly finger, somehow managing not to poke her eyes with those frightening nails. "You'll see, baby girl. You'll see."

Judit smiled politely. Frankly, she had no idea what to think.

PATRICK STOOD BACKSTAGE, bouncing on his toes. Even though he had performed thousands of times, his stomach was in knots. He gripped his bass tight, his fingers slippery. It had been so long since he'd been the one in the spotlight, and even longer since he'd played an instrument in a live show.

"Nervous, Pat?" Sabrina asked, obviously enjoying his discomfort. Behind her, Kevon twirled a drumstick with a grin.

"No," Patrick said in a quelling tone.

"You sure?" Kevon held up a flask.

James, the Beatboyz's old manager and Rohan's stepdad would've slapped that right out of Kevon's hand if this had been his band. Patrick just shook his head. Booze just gave him acid reflux these days and boy, did that make him feel fucking old.

The warm-up song ended and Sabrina ran out, followed by

Kevon. Patrick took a breath and ran after them, taking his place in the middle quadrant of the stage, to Sabrina's right. It had been a long time since he'd played a show without a backing track to cover any mistakes.

"Hello Endfest!" His sister called out to the ten people in the audience, the various people working the booths near the stage, and the few curious passersby. "We're Doc Conjure, and this is 'Caretaker's Blues'!"

Kevon counted them down. Patrick had four seconds of nauseous terror before his bass part came in. Muscle memory took over and the music embraced him. He put his head down, letting his loose locs cascade over and cover his face.

By the third song, he relaxed into the groove, living in it, in the high of performing. By the fifth, he looked out at the crowd and realized there were a good sixty people out there. Right up against the stage. He couldn't remember the last time he'd played a venue where people were allowed that close to the stage. Most of the audience bobbed their head to the music— with the occasional bout of under the influence dancing. There was no one screaming, crying, or otherwise losing their shit the way Beatboyz crowds did.

Patrick never got used to the way their fans used to completely break down at the sight of them either on stage or out and about. It felt extreme, almost frightening, the amount of importance and love the fans had given the band.

He'd been relieved to fall into obscurity, though he doubted he'd ever be totally unrecognizable. Right now, he could see at least three people staring fixedly at him. What surprised him was sometimes he missed that unabashed love. Once when he'd been too sick to do a show on a tour, a contingent of fans camped outside their hotel and chanted, "Get better soon, Ricky Rick!" for an hour. It had been both wonderful and overwhelming. When he'd waved at them from the window, half the crowd broke down into hysterics, screaming their love for him.

If that ever happened again he'd probably hate it but sometimes he thought back to that night and smiled.

He let his gaze travel over the crowd, trying to parse who was here for the band and who was here for him. His eyes snagged on the NoN merch booth across the dusty walkway. Judit's friend was now working the cash register, Benji sitting in the chair behind her, their face obscured by an NoN hat.

Leo let Patrick know Judit had made it through the rest of the rush with help from him and Rohan. Patrick felt guilty not helping himself, but he knew from experience if he'd gone into fan interaction autopilot he'd have been an exhausted puddle by Doc Conjure's evening show time. Rounding up everyone else to go help her had been a hundred times more helpful. Besides, he doubted Judit would want his help anyway. Not after the way he'd been an asshole to her.

Worse than that, she'd been right. She'd been caught between him and Cazzi and done what she thought would protect her friend. That Judit thought Cazzi needed protection against him when he had protected Cazzi for so long—

I don't know why the hell you'd think I'd be Team Patrick after the way you treated her.

He clammed, hitting the wrong string twice. Sabrina missed a chord on her guitar and Kevon went off-beat. Patrick's brain refocused instantly, the music taking over and filling his mind until he was back in the groove, bringing everyone else with him. He could overthink later. The show deserved his best, the band deserved his best, the audience deserved his best. Always.

10

BBfangurl92: *OMG with Martin Mejia coming to Endfest, does that mean we'll get a Beatboyz reunion??*
CapitalTtrouble: *Nah, the band can't stand each other. If they start fighting, I NEED someone to film it okay?*
Beatbabez456: *I have a BBz fanfic you might like...*

Judit sat in her bunk, a ring light vibrating with the bus's movements next to her as she took pictures of the Wednesday Worries Tarot card spread sitting on the lap desk in front of her. The spread was one of six social media posts, each themed for a day of the week, she was scheduling out—or would when they reached a hotel after the next fairgrounds in New Mexico.

The bus technically had Wi-Fi but it only worked decently if no one else was on and they weren't in a dead zone, and those stars weren't aligning too often in the week they'd been traveling through the desert.

The bus lurched and her light tipped, making a dive for the floor. Helen caught it from her bunk before the light ripped itself out of the socket and handed it back up. "I think you need a better method," she said.

Judit sighed, looking out at the lounge where Leo sprawled across most of the couch, doing something complicated with a spreadsheet on a laptop, his feet on the small table. Patrick sat next to him, crunched into a ball, reading on his phone. Sabrina and Kevon were already down for the night in their bunks but Benji sat up front talking to the driver, Toni. In short, no fucking room for photos unless she braved the gauntlet of Patrick and Leo to try to use the little table in front of the couch.

She considered the floor. It was an indeterminate possibly brown color that made it hard to tell if it was clean. She'd seen Toni sweep it but not in a way that particularly inspired her to sit on it or lay her cards there.

She looked again at Leo's feet on the table. It wasn't a nice background but she could spread one of the pretty pieces of fabric she'd brought over it and the light probably wouldn't fall as much. But... that would mean telling a former pop superstar and current drag star to move his feet. She fidgeted.

Be assertive, she told herself. Leo was nice enough. He'd probably roast her but he wouldn't be that much of a diva about it, right?

If she didn't think about how Patrick was right there, it wouldn't be an issue. (She hoped. He helped her, he couldn't hate her that much.)

Gathering up her cards, she climbed carefully down from her bunk, holding on tight when the bus hit a pothole. Walking in a moving vehicle still took some getting used to but she managed well enough.

"Hey." She tapped the table. "Do you mind if I use this?"

Leo blinked, squinting and refocusing from the computer. "What? Oh yeah, sure." He pulled his socked feet down and let them dangle off the end of the couch.

Well, that was easy.

"What are you doing?" he asked.

"Posing card spreads for socials," she said.

There was mischievous troll energy in his smile. "Right, you're an Insta witch."

Patrick snorted, still looking at his phone.

"I'm a psychic who uses Instagram to promote my work, yes," Judit said patiently.

"Are you good?" Leo asked.

"What's good?" Judit replied. "Accurate? Actually psychic? Knowledgeable?"

Leo sat up all the way, interest sparking in his eyes. "Are you tarot only? Do you incorporate numerology or astrology?"

Judit blinked at the shift in conversational energy. "I divine with just about anything if I try hard enough but it's mostly intuitive. I track astrological stuff to some degree but on a casual level. As for numerology, I use Crowley's deck but I'm not dipping into the *777* or anything. Are those practices you're into?"

"Well—" Leo leaned forward, looking excited.

Patrick put his phone down, a fond smile playing on his lips as he looked at his friend. That was all the warning Judit got for the sudden lecture on the world history of using numbers to divine and how it was used in everything from the I Ching to Vedic astrology to English Qabalah. Judit let it flow over her, knowing it was way too much math for her to possibly retain. She hoped her face didn't betray how hopelessly lost she was.

Maybe it did because after giving her an appraising look, Patrick nudged Leo with his elbow. Leo glanced at his friend and cut himself off mid-sentence. "I take it you're not a math person," he said to Judit.

Judit grimaced wryly. "I'm really fast at retail math these days, but no I'm not about to go do math for fun."

"Fair."

"Is that what you're doing with your spreadsheets?" Judit asked. "Occult math?"

"If that's what you call accounting," Benji said, breaking off their conversation with Toni. They sat next to Leo. "He does our books. Now or Never is a collective, we all wear many hats." They glanced at Patrick and away.

Patrick stiffened, the hand on his phone tightening until his knuckles went pale.

Leo glared at Benji. "Who does HR again?"

"Me," Benji said.

"Mm-hmm," Leo said.

Patrick closed his eyes and took a deep breath.

Benji narrowed their eyes at Leo. "If you're trying to imply something, spare us all the shade and just say it."

Aw hell. Judit wondered if she could get out of this by just backing away slowly.

"Leave it," Patrick said, opening his eyes.

Leo sputtered. "Someone should—"

"*Not* you." Patrick glared at his friend.

Leo huffed. "I'm just trying to help."

"That's not the help I need."

"It's not like you actually ask for help when you need it."

Benji rolled their eyes.

"Can we not do this here?" Patrick asked.

Leo sighed. "Fine." He turned to Judit. "Tell my future, psychic."

Judit blinked. "Um..."

"Start pulling cards or I will interrogate you about your content monetization, investment plans, and retirement accounts."

If Judit's mother didn't handle billing and accounts for a dental office, Leo's words might have scared her. As it was, Mom didn't understand being a psychic as a career choice, her way of trying to relate was to constantly try to find ways Judit could monetize her hustle and invest smartly. Though Mom immigrated to the US in her twenties, she proudly did her and Judit's taxes every year. Judit was forever grateful someone else handled her hodgepodge of 1099s even though it gave Mom hours to tut about her job choices and suggest several office jobs with benefits. So Leo trying to weaponize that shit against her like just because she was broke she didn't know how money worked? Yeah, fuck that.

Judit crossed her arms. "Ask me nicely. Like a real person, not your peon."

Benji laughed. "Oh shit."

"Shut up, HR," Patrick growled. (Damn, that growl should not sound so good.)

Benji pressed their lips together, nostrils flaring.

Leo stood, looming over her. Then he slow clapped. "I knew you had a backbone somewhere."

"Don't play this like you were testing me," Judit snapped. "None of you are coming out on top in whatever shit you have going on here." She waved dismissively at the lot of them. "You want a reading?"

She pulled out three cards and slapped them in a rough line on the table. She flipped the middle card: five crystalline cups intertwined into an inverted pentacle and "Disappointment" written at the bottom. "This is all of you now. You're festering with old resentments but still intertwined. You need a fresh start, to cauterize your wounds with honesty."

She flipped the first card: eight stacked swords glowing against the purple and red abstract background, with the subtitle "Interference." She tapped it. "This is your past. Your old convictions, patterns, and limitations clashing with each other." She glanced at Patrick who glared back.

"Cute parlor trick," he said.

"I'm not done." Judit flipped the last card. The Ace of Cups with its psychedelic sky beam exploding out of a blue double-handled cup. "You could have the new start you all need but you need to be open and tell the truth, both to yourself and each other. Take in what you need and let go of what you don't. Apologize, be sincere because you're all interconnected, whether you like it or not." She swept the cards back into her deck and bowed. "Ask and ye shall receive." She straightened and made deliberate eye contact with each of them. "So, be careful what you ask for."

Spinning on her heel she walked away. Helen gave her a high five. Judit climbed into her bunk and shut the curtains.

Dammit, now she was stuck here until everyone else went to bed. (Had she really told off no less than three famous people? Oh god.)

She hadn't even been able to use the table either. She'd just gotten on to somewhat decent footing with Patrick and Leo and now she'd pissed them off all over again and added her boss in for good measure. If any of them bad-mouthed her online or in the industry... she muffled a groan in her hands.

Some victory this was.

SITTING ALONE at a table in the mess tent the next morning, Patrick felt hungover. Not physically. He hadn't even smoked up last night. But fuck, was his head fuzzy and full of static. He, of course, had barely slept so he'd spent the night thinking about what Judit said yesterday. He'd thought up a thousand comebacks since then but they all fell flat even in his head. Who the fuck did she think she was anyway? He'd never had such an aggressive reading in his life, not to mention one with cards.

If he'd ever thought Judit was nice, he knew better now.

At least it was quiet. It was too early for most people, including him. He'd given up on sleeping earlier than usual. He shoved another spoonful of cereal in his mouth and forced down another sip of tea. The bacopa in the herb mix made it earthy and bitter but combined with the yerba mate, it should make him at least semi-functional.

Benji sat next to him, looking far too put together for this hour. They sipped their coffee from a travel mug that read "NO" in colorful, fancy script. It popped against their all-black outfit. They were dressed somewhere between business and punk with a short-sleeved button-up, skinny tie, pencil skirt, and a good hour's worth of make-up and hair.

"We have to talk," they said.

"As long as it's not about Judit's little show last night," Patrick said. After she'd stomped off, he, Leo, and Benji had sat there awkwardly. Leo had giggled and Patrick had been tempted to join in but it was clear Judit took her whole spiel very seriously—also, alarmingly, she hadn't been wrong. He'd elbowed Leo until the bigger man shut up. Then they'd all wandered off, not making eye contact.

Benji shuddered. "God, no."

"Good. I'm here. Talk."

"So is Martin." Rohan sat on his other side. "In about an hour."

"Shit." Patrick drank his tea faster.

"We need you to actually be a part of this label and help us run interference," Benji said. "I don't trust Nicky to keep Martin away from Leo."

"Please," Rohan added. He sipped something that smelled like chai from a plain metal mug and took a bite of muffin.

Patrick swallowed the reflexive anger at Rohan for thinking he had the right to ask him anything. Dealing with Martin would take all of them and probably more if he got into it with Leo.

"Yeah," he said. "I'll be there."

Benji stood, looking at their phone. "There is now."

"That fucker would be early," Rohan grumbled.

Patrick drained as much of his tea as he could without getting a mouthful of the bacopa powder at the bottom. Then he downed his cereal. "Anyone got eyes on Leo?"

Rohan nodded. "He's on the bus."

Patrick shook his head. "Leo's still gonna find him."

"Why do you think we need you? You've had the best track record with him," Rohan said.

Patrick grimaced. The track record hadn't been exactly easy or painless to come by.

They left the tent, following Benji's directions to the massive fleet of tour buses and semis, all parked and shut tight. As a group, they stopped several yards away, around the side of Rohan's bus. They weren't spying exactly, just watching from a distance.

Right in front of the fanciest bus stood Nick Sullivan, coffee in hand and the other fiddling with the keys clipped to his cargo shorts. He looked out of place: not clean-cut enough to be a suit, not enough presence to be a performer, not purposeful enough to be crew. His small crowd of assistants fidgeted nervously.

"What do you think the odds are Martin will just stay in his bus like a good little diva?" Benji asked.

"None," said Patrick and Rohan at the same time. He could see Rohan looking over to share a grin, but Patrick refused to acknowledge it.

"What if we locked him in the bus bathroom?" Benji mused, inspecting their nail polish.

Leo loomed over them out of nowhere, startling all three of them. "I'm here for that, but only if we set it on fire with the little twat still in it."

Patrick squelched the very undignified urge to yelp. He

glared up at Leo, who gave him an unrepentant grin. He had dressed to look his best, his clothes emphasizing his muscles and his make-up subtle but purposeful. Patrick sighed.

He'd be fucking ecstatic the day Leo got over the mess that was Martin.

"Shoo," Benji said. "We don't need a scene. Not in front of the promoter."

"Fuck no." Leo visibly planted himself. "He needs to know he's on my turf."

"Go piss around the grounds then," Benji said. "Leave the twat to us."

"DO NOT run around pissing everywhere," Rohan cried, clearly remembering the Brisbane incident.

Patrick winced at the memory.

"Bitch, please, I'm a lady." Leo touched his collar like he was looking for pearls to clutch. "You gotta pay extra for piss play. A lot extra."

Patrick faked a cough. "Brisbane."

Leo didn't even bother to feign ignorance. "You know I was off my head on—"

The doors on the biggest, fanciest bus opened. Nick straightened and handed his coffee off to an assistant.

"Okay, remember kids, we are adults. Professional adults who have to pay back any damages we incur," Benji said. "Especially those made in front of the *fucking promoter*."

"Fuck off, *Mom*," Leo said.

Benji turned their full glare at him. It was rumored their glare alone once made several execs at a certain multinational record label hide under a table and whimper.

Patrick and Rohan leaned away. Leo wilted and mumbled an apology. Patrick never got over how scary Benji could get in the blink of an eye. The only person who scared him nearly as much was Angela Alice.

Patrick settled in for the wait and people started exiting the bus. Martin could never resist a flex. He'd be the last person to leave the bus and it'd be a fucking exit.

"What is this, dueling entourages?" Benji wrinkled their nose. "Does Mejia really pay all these people?"

"Nick should've brought more people to try and outdo him," Rohan said.

"That would just give him a bigger audience," Leo said.

"You're right." Rohan looked at Leo. "Leo, why don't you head out? A small audience will make him look like an ass."

"If it looks like an ass and sounds like an ass..." Patrick muttered.

The entourage lined up on either side of the door like this was a choreographed exit they did regularly. It probably was. They looked so damn serious.

Nick tried to subtly check his watch.

"Nice try, Ro," Leo said. "I'm staying. This is my tour—"

Rohan sighed. *"My* tour."

"It's neither of your tours," Patrick muttered, watching Nick. The man smiled blandly but couldn't seem to figure out what to do with his hands. He crossed his arms, uncrossed them, fiddled with his keys, glanced at his nails, literally anything but check his watch again.

Leo ignored him. "—And I'm not gonna hide like I'm afraid of him."

"Toxic masculinity alert," Rohan mumbled. It sounded so much like something Cazzi would say that Patrick lost his breath for a second.

"Oh fuck off," Leo said. "Are you gonna hide when Angela Alice's broom lands?"

"No, but I'm not going to start a turf war about it," Rohan said.

Benji snorted.

The double line of people turned their faces to the open

bus door. They raised their arms like supplicants awaiting a god in some shitty movie.

"Oh hell, here we go," Rohan said, rolling his eyes.

Leo started humming "God Save The Queen."

Martin descended like the royalty he sure thought he was, nodding to his people as they clapped. His casual workout gear looked like the tags had just been snipped off and his limited edition Jordans were blindingly white. Were those diamonds in his sunglasses?

Patrick fought the urge to sarcastically clap along. Nick looked like he was reaching the end of his patience, his smile slipping and his hands clenching and unclenching by his sides.

"Just to be clear, this is a completely healthy, able-bodied man being applauded for exiting a bus?" Benji asked. They must've never met Martin before.

"Yep," Rohan said.

"Wooow." Benji laughed as Martin approached, his entourage falling into formation behind him.

Martin looked as sleek as ever. He was cut like a dancer and polished like an Instagram influencer, even more than he had been in Beatboyz. He put on a humble celebrity smile and put his palms together to give them the real-life equivalent of the prayer hands emoji. "Hello all." He looked at Nick then turned his attention to the four of them, standing like idiots around the corner of their tour bus.

He winked.

Good lord, how had the guy who had once sent back a bottle of Crystale because it wasn't cold enough gotten even more insufferable? Patrick glanced at Leo. He was stone-faced. Rohan looked done already. Benji looked like they were suppressing both laughter and some very cutting remarks.

Nick copied Martin's prayer hands, bowing awkwardly. "We're honored to have you on our tour," he said. "I'm Nick Sullivan, let me know if you need anything and I'll cover it."

Martin smiled benevolently at Nick's ear. One of his entourage stepped up. "We told you explicitly in the rider that no one was to make eye contact with Mr. Mejia."

"Your rider said crew—" Nick sputtered, his face turning rapidly red.

Martin laid a hand on his entourage member's chest and pushed him back. His smile never changing, he turned to Nick. "My people get overzealous. But in the future please address any requests to my assistant. Good day, Mr. Sullivan. I will not keep you any longer."

He turned his back on Nick and walked right up to Patrick and his labelmates.

Benji copied Martin's prayer hands, their eyebrows jumping mischievously. Patrick wondered if Martin was too far up his own ass to realize Benji was fucking with them.

"Benji Omega," Martin breathed, saying their old stage name in a weirdly intimate way. Patrick was willing to bet it was entirely to piss Leo off. Martin always thought he was so fucking subtle. "I'm honored."

Benji smiled frostily, "I'm sure you are."

It was all Patrick could do not roll his eyes. Behind him, he could practically feel Leo stiffen. The longer Martin ignored him, the angrier he'd get. They all knew it.

Martin's smile cracked and reformed. "You're cute, even after all these years."

He was using Flirty Smile #2, as Rohan and Patrick had dubbed it one boring day traveling between venues. Even as a teenager, Martin had come equipped with a whole arsenal of practiced facial expressions. They had, of course, named them all. It had been Patrick's pet theory for about four years that Martin was secretly a robot the label was testing to see if they could make an artificial boy band without anyone noticing. Rohan maintained Martin was a cyborg at best, maybe a pod person. Then they'd gotten high and watched some *Star Trek:*

The Next Generation movie on hotel cable and decided he was Borg.

That was before Leo started hooking up with him. Then it became pretty obvious Martin was just as human as the rest of them.

Benji's smile was all teeth. "Take a walk with me."

"I would love to see the festival layout," Martin said. "Seeing as I'll be back."

"Perfect," Benji said. Something about the way their eyes gleamed would've made Patrick worried if he liked Martin at all. Luckily, he didn't care. "Let's go."

The two of them walked off and Patrick was about to congratulate Leo on keeping his cool when Martin turned back and said, "So good to see you, L. I'm so impressed you got as far as you did on that drag show. You really lived up to your potential." He turned away.

Patrick felt Leo move and didn't stop to think. He turned around and drove his shoulder into Leo's stomach, putting his whole weight into it, toppling them into the dirt. Leo landed on his ass and Patrick landed across his legs, taking two kneecaps to his ribs. He couldn't move for a moment, his body absorbing the shock of impact.

He looked up just in time to see Martin smirk in triumph.

"You've done enough damage," Rohan hissed, stepping in front of them to block Martin's view. "Try to be the better man for once."

"Whatever." Martin turned to Benji and offered them his arm. "My tour?"

Benji looked over Patrick's head in the direction of Nick and made an angry noise deep in their throat. They turned to Martin and crooked a finger, not taking his arm as they stalked off, the dipshit trying to walk fast to catch up without looking like he was hurrying.

His entourage stampeded after him like they were afraid if

they couldn't see him Martin didn't exist. Or, more likely, that if he didn't see them, he'd forget their existence.

Leo tried to stand but Patrick dug his elbow into the muscle right above the other man's bad knee. Leo's harsh gasp told him he'd hit his mark. "Can't you fucking trust me? I wasn't going to——"

"You should be thanking him, Leo." Rohan turned around. "Get up, you two. He's gone." He offered Patrick a hand but Patrick ignored it. Though he was trying to put away his anger, he wasn't there yet. Patrick stood on his own.

His ribs ached, so did his shoulder, and his knees and hands where they'd hit the dirt. At least he didn't have to look camera-ready at the drop of a hat anymore.

"Hey, boys." Nick and his assistants had arrived. "What was that about?"

Leo stalked away without saying anything. Nick watched him go and looked at Patrick and Rohan. "Well?"

Patrick snorted. "You have to know our band history."

Nick squinted at him, tapping his chin. "You were all in some boy band? Beak Boys or something?"

Patrick couldn't help it. He glanced at Rohan, just to see if this conversation was for real. Did this asshat really think any boy band would be called Beak Boys or was this some petty powerplay?

Rohan's face went incredulous right before it smoothed into a polite mask. "Beatboyz," he corrected Nick, far too nicely. His training must be kicking in. "We were in the Beatboyz."

"Yeah, but you guys broke up like ten years ago."

"Five." Patrick leaned on his own training to keep his voice even. "Leo and Martin had a falling out. Feelings were hurt."

Nick shrugged. "Fine, whatever. It's not my problem until it's my problem so don't make it my problem, got it?"

"Yep," Rohan said, popping the 'p'.

Nick looked at Patrick until he nodded too. "My guys!"

Nick clapped them both on the shoulders. "I'm counting on you!" He pointed finger guns at them as he walked away. "Our sponsors want a good clean fest and we'll give it to them, amiright?"

Patrick gave him a weak thumbs up as he disappeared. What a fucking prick. "Which sponsor are we trying to keep squeaky clean? The bullshit healthy energy drink or the tasteless hard seltzer?"

Rohan sighed. "I'm over this already."

11

Bad news bears, kids. The dickheads are descending. By that of course, I mean our illustrious temporary headliner and the collective attached by the lips to his well-buffed ass. Ew, that sounds like a human centipede thing... eh you get the picture. Too much of that overly maternal Cancer energy in those people. So enjoy the mediocrity and as always, let me know if you see anything juicy.

Shuddering but still love you,

LS

—Tourgasm vol 2

Judit took another round around the grounds, reminding herself she'd spend most of tomorrow in the bus not moving. They were only spending a day in New Mexico instead of the two they'd spent in Arizona and SoCal. She felt decent enough this morning but a day of sitting would inevitably wreck her. The looser she was now the less it'd hurt. Plus she had a call to make.

She waved at one of Rohan's backup dancers as the other woman jogged by. It was nice out anyway, not too hot yet. Judit took a breath and dialed the number for the gynecologist specializing in pelvic pain her doctor referred her to back when she had health insurance.

She kept her breathing steady as the nice receptionist took her information and scheduled her an appointment for the day after the tour ended. She double-checked the copay then hung up.

You need this appointment, she reminded herself. *You'll have money from the tour if there are any unexpected bills.*

She'd been hit by enough surprise bills to last her a lifetime and they scared the shit out of her. Every test, every visit had the potential to punch her in the wallet when she least expected it, no matter what the doctor or the front desk said things would cost.

Let it go.

Her long exhale made her bangs brush her eyelashes and she made a mental note to trim them at the next hotel.

She focused on the scenery around her. The dry earth, the endless sky, and scrubby plants all a backdrop for the festival around her. It was still strange this whole ecosystem of stages, concession stands, port-a-potties, photo booths, and performer's tents would soon disappear and reappear in another city to plant the flags of Green Brew Energy and LadyWater Hard Seltzer.

At least it was early still and they hadn't opened the grounds for the public so it was pretty empty. No weird dynamics she was roped into and didn't understand, no grumpy hotties, or people giving her occult purity tests. Nobody to see her stress about possible future bills.

She hadn't spent this much time with so many other people in close proximity since the pandemic. It wore on her.

She rounded one of the main stages and noticed Benji coming towards her, looking sharp as hell. They looked so good she almost didn't see who they were with. When she did, she nearly fell on her face.

Martin Mejia walked towards her.

Marty fucking Mac in real life, not on one of the posters she'd tacked on her wall in high school. He looked like he'd stepped right out of a publicity shot along with a small crowd of hot people who were clearly here for him.

Could life get any more surreal?

She nodded at Benji like they were colleagues. (What was she going to do, wave?) Benji nodded back with a tight smile and Judit enjoyed the thrill that ran through her.

Martin Mejia smiled at her. She smiled back like this happened to her every day. Helen was going to lose her shit when she told her. She already swapped shifts with Judit tonight so she could see him live, never mind ten feet away and smiling.

Benji said something to him, a wicked gleam in their eye. Martin stopped... and walked towards her! Judit had the brief impulse to run. Sustaining a conversation with Martin Mejia felt beyond her.

He's just a human being, she told herself as she popped her earbuds out. *Like Rohan.* Except Rohan was dating one of her best friends so he was real to her. *Fine, like Patrick.* Patrick was an asshat but somehow that was reassuring. Asshats she could handle. She'd worked retail, she'd driven a bus, hell, she read cards at a shop in a strip mall. Asshats were nothing new.

"Hello Judit," Martin said her name like a Spanish speaker, and the familiar inflection, the same one Papi used, soothed her nerves. The rest of his words were California-plain but it made her feel weirdly close to him. "Benji Omega tells me you're a psychic."

Judit glanced at Benji. Their make-up was on point, their expression pleasantly neutral, but Judit got the feeling they were cultivating a deep disdain for the man next to them. She wondered if anyone else could tell or if it was just one of those feelings that always turned out to be right.

Benji shrugged, their face unreadable. (Maybe that disdain wasn't just for Martin. Maybe it was for her. Oh god, had she pissed them off with that reading last night? Is this where they threw her under the bus and killed her career?)

"That's true," she said carefully. She was having a hard time getting a read on Martin. She felt like if she reached out, her touch would slide right off of him. It was unsettling.

"I take it you're good or you wouldn't be here," Martin said.

"Well, I'm not going to say I'm not." She laughed. Did he not know she worked the merch table? Had Benji told him about last night?

Martin chuckled politely, the sound oddly rhythmic. Like he was on a talk show and the only one who knew it. "Why don't you come by at..." He glanced back.

The man directly behind him looked at his phone. "You have a fifteen-minute opening at 11:20 am."

Martin looked back at her and said, like that interaction had never happened, "Eleven-twenty."

The man with the phone was already typing furiously.

Judit was about to say yes when Benji said, "Is your schedule clear at that time, Judit? I know you're pretty busy these days."

She blinked at the pointedness of the question. Did they not remember she'd switched shifts with Helen?

"She's very in demand," Benji told Martin. They winked at her behind his back. (Maybe they weren't *that* mad?)

She made a show of checking her completely empty calendar app before saying, "Looks like I can squeeze you in then." She winced internally, hoping he wouldn't think she was dissing him.

Instead, Martin nodded and walked away, his entourage trailing behind him. Benji chuckled, following.

Judit stared after them. What the hell just happened?

. . .

At 11:15, Judit stood in front of the bus one of the roadies had directed her to (she thought his name started with C, maybe Chad? Chet?). She was five minutes early and she wondered if that had been a bad idea.

Fuck it. She knocked.

The door was opened by a woman she recognized from earlier. "Name?"

"Judit Kemenes. I'm the psychic?" She wished it hadn't come out as a question.

"ID?"

"Seriously?"

The woman's face told her she was indeed serious. Judit handed her the crew badge she'd been issued. The woman inspected it like she was checking a diamond for flaws before handing it back. "He's on a phoner right now. Wait out here."

Judit was proud of herself for not giggling at the word "phoner" until the door slammed in her face. She was pretty sure this was an insult but she waited anyway, leaning against the bus as best she could without getting road dirt on her dress.

Someday, she'd be successful enough no one would make her wait outside their trumped-up StarWagon. This was just a stepping stone. One that would hopefully lead to some cash. Not that she wanted to be super famous or anything. Frankly, that didn't sound great, and the grinding she'd need to do to get there would probably destroy her physically and mentally. But to be established enough that she'd get some fucking professional courtesy would be nice.

She wasn't going to delude herself. She liked his music and she still couldn't believe she was going to spend time with *the* Martin Mejia, at his request, no less, but he probably expected to get a full reading for free. People usually did. Especially people who thought they were important, like local politicians.

Those were the worst and Sacramento was full of them. Sometimes she obliged them if she thought they'd get her good word of mouth or something. But she only did it one time. Only her friends got free readings more than once.

Just as she was responding to another text from Cazzi mentioning oh-so-casually that the tour would intersect with Angela Alice soon, the door opened. "He's ready for you."

Like he was a doctor or something. She stifled a sigh before putting on a smile and climbed into the bus. There had to be twenty people in the front of the bus alone, on their phones and lounging about. They were all pretty in a skinny, conventional way. She wondered if that was calculated to make normal people feel insecure. (It was working.)

"Judit!" Martin called, opening his arms like she was his long-lost daughter even though she wasn't nearly that young. He sat on a stationary bike bolted to the floor of the bus, pedaling like he was on the Tour de France.

"Martin!" She mimicked him, playing along.

"Come in, come in." He beckoned her closer and pointed at a couch next to him. The five people crowded on it dispersed.

She made her way towards him, ignoring the dirty looks she got every time she accidentally bumped into someone. The minute she sat down, he pounced. "What type of psychic are you?"

Oh boy, twice in less than twenty-four hours? Just her damn luck. She smiled. "Intuitive. I've been divining since I was a child."

"Using what methods?" His questions were rapid-fire, like he had a list in his head and meant to check off every one.

"Cartomancy, mostly." It'd be overwhelming if she hadn't spent the last few years doing readings at every occult shop she could commute to.

"Tarot, oracle, Lotería, playing cards?"

"Tarot mostly, though given enough familiarity I can use most decks."

"Rider-Smith-Waite or Thoth?"

"Thoth."

"With what success rate?"

Along with the skeptics getting their first reading, inevitably, there was always some dickhead who tried to trip her up and "reveal" her as a fake. Either that or they thought they were experts and wanted to show off and make sure she knew they were way above her but still deigned to consult her. The occult offered people who felt like they weren't getting their entitled respect a thousand ways and titles to make them feel special. The ones who were really special rarely showed that shit off.

She figured out he'd probably read a few beginner witch books and was trying to apply them to make sure she wasn't a fraud. Her back ached from sitting twisted to face him. That, compounded with the nasty looks she was getting from the hangers-on, ate at her patience.

"Why don't you let me demonstrate?"

"What are you going to use?" He leaned over the console of the stationary bike eagerly.

"How about we start with a classic?" She pulled her deck from her pocket, unwrapping her cards, and placing them on her lap. "Hold your question in your mind."

"What? No candles or chanting?" One of the skinny minions asked. "No crystal ball?" The crowd around them oh'ed and giggled.

She pinned them with a look, concentrated, and pulled a card, showing it to them. The Nine of Swords, broken, dripping blades pointing down to the title: "Cruelty." She didn't use the titles when she read but they had their uses.

Martin craned his neck to read the card and cackled. It was a much realer laugh than the one he'd used before. "She nailed you." He grinned at the speaker then pointed at Judit. "Read me."

She did a basic three-card reading, laying the cards on the wide arm of the couch. He didn't tell her his question. She didn't ask. The outlook wasn't good.

"You have to change your approach," she told him, "or you'll destroy what you're trying to save."

Martin nodded but said nothing.

One of his entourage approached and dipped his head in a near-bow, a phone in hand. "Your eleven forty-five is on the line."

Martin didn't acknowledge him. He looked at Judit and smiled like he was on TV. "Thank you for your time."

She was escorted out without so much as an allusion to money. She rolled her eyes as the bus door closed behind her.

"Making friends?" Patrick asked, strolling by.

"That's what happens when you're nice to people. Try it sometime," she snapped, her annoyance at Martin finding a new target.

"Nice is fake. Trust me," he said, his eyes narrowing at the bus.

"Fine," she said, because the more she knew people in this industry, the more she found that was true. "Kind then. Try being kind. Like Benji, they helped me set this up."

His nostrils flared. "If you think that's kindness, you don't know Benji."

She hesitated. "What?" Had Benji set her up to fail? Were they taking revenge for the whole Tarot incident last night?

Patrick sighed. "Forget it. I'm probably off-base."

But, she couldn't forget it, what if he was right? What if she couldn't trust her boss to look after her? (Not that she hadn't had some shit bosses in her time, but still.) She headed for the booth where Benji was scheduled to be.

Patrick frowned. "Where are you going?"

"I need to know."

"Just let it go."

"No. If I let it go, it'll fester." Like her last relationship had festered until she nearly suffocated. She was not doing that here, not when she'd be stuck with it for the rest of the summer.

He followed her. "Look, I was just talking out of my ass."

"No, you said it for a reason and you know them better than I do."

He grimaced.

She examined his expression, intuition ticking away, putting it together with the conversation from last night. "They screwed you over, huh?"

"I'm not talking to you about this."

So, that was a yes, at least in his mind. That explained a lot. Ugh, celebrity drama was a lot more annoying when you actually lived it.

"You're not going to stop, are you?" he said as she approached the booth. Benji was on their phone in their chair.

"Nope."

Patrick mumbled something under his breath but kept pace with her as they approached the booth.

"Hi," Judit said to Benji, suddenly at a loss for how to do this diplomatically. She really didn't want to be kicked off the tour in the middle of the desert.

Benji nodded at her, not taking their eyes off their phone.

Judit fidgeted, the hot sun beating down on her neck. Helen gave her an inquiring look. Judit shook her head at her friend and took a breath to try again.

"Did you really sic Martin on her?" Patrick said—no, demanded. All the annoyance he'd been directing at her directed at Benji.

Helen's eyes went wide.

Benji looked up slowly. They blinked at Patrick then at

Judit. "Hello to you too. I gave her an opportunity. How did it go?" They asked Judit.

"Good, I think?" Judit said, off-balance. She glanced at Patrick, glowering next to her. Was he going to take over? Would she have to fight to redirect the conversation from whatever was going on between the two of them?

But he just nodded at her then at Benji. (Was he being supportive? Was this a setup?)

Benji cocked their head at her. "Did you have something you wanted to say, Judit?" they purred, sounding scarier than if they'd yelled. (Damn, why couldn't they have yelled? She knew how to handle yelling.)

Judit inhaled hard. "Yes. I appreciate the opportunity. Thank you."

Next to her, Patrick deflated. He shook his head and walked away. It shouldn't have hurt.

Benji smiled. "You're welcome." They watched him go. "I did sic Martin on you." They looked at her. "But I figured after your demonstration last night you could handle it."

"That's kind of fucked up," Judit blurted.

Benji chuckled. "Old habits die hard. I'll do better next time." Their phone rang. "We good here?"

Judit nodded though she was still reeling. Benji got up and answered the phone, strolling back behind the booth.

"What was that?" Helen hissed.

"I don't know?" Since they had no customers, Judit flopped in Benji's chair. "There's a bunch of drama I don't understand."

Helen patted her arm. "Me either, but we'll figure out how to navigate around. Tell me about meeting Martin though!"

Helen quizzed her about meeting Martin until the knot in Judit's chest she hadn't even noticed dissolved.

"You look better, less freaked," Helen said later, gesturing at her own face. "Did you sleep at all after last night?"

Judit shrugged. "I'll nap later."

"You're adapting fine, though? Besides the drama shit, I mean."

"I'm getting through it. You?"

Helen shrugged. "Trying to put it all in the 'Not my problem' box and compartmentalize."

"When you're a famous designer they'll all be begging for your looks anyway."

"Damn straight. And when you're psychic to the stars, Martin will have to beg you for a reading and then you'll overcharge him by three hundred percent."

Judit laughed.

"But for serious," Helen said. "How are you holding up? What are your pain levels?"

"I'm all right. It's an adjustment and that tour bus bed is probably going to be the death of my back but I'm managing. And I doubt I'll ever be far from a supply of pot with this crowd. How are you?"

Helen grinned. "Dude, barring our bus mates killing each other, and the dust in my prosthetic, I am enjoying life. I am *living* for Benji's style, though I'm not happy with them putting you in the middle of their feuds. Would you be mad at me if I asked them to do a TikTok?"

Judit shook her head. If Helen could get some good celebrity content out of this tour, Judit wasn't going to stand in her way.

Helen craned her head back to look at Benji as they paced. She ran a popular fashion channel on several platforms but conquering TikTok was her summer challenge. She and Judit were planning on putting together a tarot-themed line of accessible clothes together in the fall with their fest paychecks. "Oh, and I've got something for you."

Helen opened her sketchbook to sketches of flattering but non-constricting dresses she was designing with Judit in mind and handed it over. Judit paged through, her eyes growing misty. "Oh Helen," she sighed. "These are *perfect*."

"I know, right?" Helen gave her a quick side hug. "I can't wait to get my hands on my sewing machine." Judit smiled at the thought of Helen's lime green sewing machine with its disability justice stickers. Helen's work was garnering interest and she already sold most of the sample line she'd debuted in the spring. She wanted her own fashion house someday and Judit was entirely certain she would have it. She didn't need to be psychic to predict that.

Judit just wished she was as confident in her own future. At this rate, she'd be fired halfway through the tour.

THAT NIGHT, Patrick watched fog roll over the LadyWater stage, billowing around the dancers' feet as they leaped, swirling and accentuating the figure at the center. Martin sang, hitting notes that had been out of his range five years ago. He danced, flirting with the crowd. The set built up and fell around him and his people, telling a story in gorgeous and expensive detail.

In short, he was showboating. The crowd loved it.

Patrick had to admit: it was impressive, even from backstage. It was also ten times more expensive than the RK show budget and Martin had to know it. He was showing up Rohan on what was supposed to be the RK comeback tour. Patrick bet it was on purpose.

Rohan was probably trying to figure out how to stress-bake in the bus microwave while crying to Benji. Or Cazzi. Leo shut himself in his bus bedroom after his show and assured Patrick he would not come out unless "that little twat actually did catch fire."

Patrick grit his teeth. The shitshow was nearly done, thankfully. Martin would fuck off tomorrow morning, splitting off to his own tour until he rejoined them again on a couple more dates. One down, two to go.

And that wasn't counting the impending doom of Angela's arrival at their next stop.

Patrick realized Martin was doing his outro, thanking his band and dancers like he thought they were actually real people. So he did know he was supposed to treat employees like human beings. Shocking.

Patrick's phone buzzed.

LEO

Why is Martin following our little Judit?

Since when was she theirs? Or little, for that matter? Then again, everyone was little to Leo.

PATRICK

Get off social media.

LEO

I'm not on social. At the booth. Judit's freaking out.

PATRICK

Problem?

What an opportunist, falling in with someone like Martin. Couldn't she see what little dickweed he was? Patrick shook his head. She certainly hadn't been able to hold her own with Benji today. Though, now that he'd cooled down, he felt bad about pushing her. He'd been inspired by her nip-it-in-the-bud confidence and then to see her deflate when the time came? He couldn't just stand by. But he'd forgotten in the moment Benji was her boss, her HR, the person deciding her schedule.

Sabrina had given him a tongue-lashing when she'd heard about it. "Just because you want to quit doesn't mean you should get some poor merch girl to do it for you!"

Apparently, word got around because Leo had already rolled his eyes at Patrick for it too.

Whatever. They were right, which was fucking annoying. Maybe tomorrow he'd apologize if she'd even accept it.

He was trying to be better about the apology thing.

You mean like you've apologized to Cazzi? You're only apologizing to Judit because you can't ghost her. Cazzi's probably glad you're staying away—

He shut the thought spiral down, forcing himself to focus on five things he could see (the roadies, the stage, the dancers, his phone, Martin), four he could hear (the calls of the crowd, the synth player clam as he played under the backing track, Martin still talking, one of the speakers buzzing), three he could smell (pot, spilled beer, the inside of his mask), two he could touch (the grit between his fingers—hell the grit on his whole body, sweat sticking his clothes to him), one he could taste (more fucking dust)—

LEO

Maybe come over here.

Patrick took that as his excuse to get the hell out of there. If he was running it was only so he could beat the crowd. No, fuck it. He was worried. Martin had a big following and just mentioning a small account like Judit's could blow it up—and not in a good way. If Judit locked up in front of Benji, he could only imagine the overwhelm a landslide of followers and comments would bring.

When he got there, Judit paced behind the booth, staring at

her phone and muttering to herself. Leo handled the steady trickle of customers.

Patrick slid into the booth next to him. "I thought you were locked in your room."

Leo shrugged. "I was bouncing off the walls. Benji made me cover their shift. I think they're scoping out Martin's show."

Patrick hadn't seen them but that wasn't surprising given the size of the crowd.

"Is she okay?" Patrick nodded at Judit. Her mask hung off one ear and he could see her breathing from here.

Leo shrugged again. "Can you walk her through the basics of protecting your account when it goes viral? I keep getting random rushes."

"Sure." Patrick frowned. He approached Judit slowly. "Judit?"

She jumped and looked up. "Oh, uh, what?"

"Breathe."

"I'm breathing," she said, voice pinched with the tell-tale signs of not enough air.

"Good. Give me your phone." He held out his hand.

"Why?" She pressed it to her chest. He did his best not to dwell on how the gesture pushed her breasts up against the neckline of her dress.

"Are your mentions, DMs, and notifications off the charts? Is it making you anxious?" He could hear it buzzing incessantly against her breastbone. Hell, it was making him anxious.

"What do you care?"

"Look, it's going to take me two minutes and then you can go back to working your shift instead of stranding Leo."

Judit blinked and looked over at Leo and the customers he was trying to pose with while swiping someone else's card. "Shit. Fine." She handed Patrick her phone and came around to peer over his shoulder, putting her mask back in place. Her skirt brushed his bare calf like a caress.

Nope. He stopped that line of thinking in its tracks.

First, he turned off all her social media app notifications, holding up a finger at her protest. "Trust me."

Then he closed her DMs, wincing at the quick glimpse of what he saw there. He handed the phone back. "Don't check any of those until the morning. Keep your DMs closed for at least a week. Notifications off permanently if your follower count stays up."

She nodded, sliding the phone into her pocket. "Thank you."

He met her eyes, searching what he could see of her face behind her mask. "Did he give you any warning?"

"Martin? No."

"That was thoughtless of him."

She shrugged. "Maybe he was trying to be nice?"

"Maybe. Don't answer any press inquiries if they ask about it. They'll just twist shit."

"Is him following me actually news?"

Patrick shrugged. "What passes for it these days, for some people."

"Was everything you did this closely monitored too when you were famous?" She pressed her fingers to where her mouth was under her mask. "Sorry, that was prying."

"It was that bad," he said, remembering how trapped he'd felt. How everything he posted was scrutinized for secret meanings and scandal.

"Oh." She reached for him then thought better, her fingers falling away just before they brushed his arm. "How awful."

He turned away from her compassion. It made him feel too raw, too seen. "Yeah. Anyway, talk to Benji if you need any more guidance on that stuff. Or Rohan or Leo."

"Or you?"

"Or me."

They looked at each other for a long moment.

"I'm sorry," he said. "I shouldn't have interfered, earlier."

She shrugged. "It's okay. You were trying to help, I could tell."

"I was projecting."

Judit snorted. "No, you were right. Benji admitted it."

Patrick nodded. "That tracks."

She looked at him like she could see exactly what they did to him. "I hope you two can get past whatever happened between you."

Patrick remembered the determination and anger on Benji's face as they invoked his contract to keep him on the label long enough to finish Rohan's and Sabrina's albums. *"I'm protecting my interests,"* they'd said, *"You think I'm easy to employ?" They spread their arms, the flourish encompassing all the layers of identity they didn't bother to lay out. "This is my soapbox too, my platform, my risk."*

"Hey, can I get some fucking help here?" Leo yelled, dispelling the memory.

Judit swore and scurried over. "Anyway, thank you!" She called again over her shoulder at Patrick, her eyes smiling.

It was a small gesture, but it warmed him all the way back to the bus.

12

"Platinum pretty
Cut me baby
I bled gold
Don't pray for my soul
It's already sold

I'm a sellout sweetie
Made money so I wouldn't starve
Hate me, honey, I'm popular
Bitch Queen superstar
Superstar, superstar

I aim for arenas
You can't see past the old scene
You bragged about me in the record store
Now, they play my shit in the grocery store

Satan's princess went mainstream
Fanatics get in line to scream
I'm gonna laugh from my money throne

> *Watch the haters scrape and groan*
> *Beg, cry, howl*
> *How did I climb this high?*
> *Beg, cry, howl*
> *How far can I go?"*
> — "Platinum Pretty" by Angela Alice off of *Bitch Queen*
> *Cometh*

"I hear Angela Alice is coming in tomorrow," Judit said, trying for casual, a week later in Florida. "Anything I can do to help?"

She'd been sitting in the mess tent first, reading while eating when most of the Beatboyz and Benji sat next to her. If she thought too hard about it, it felt like a fanfic, except in a fanfic she would've showered more than once in the last week. They'd been on the road for over two weeks now and occasional hotel (okay, motel) stops were already becoming crazed as the fest collectively raced to get to the hot water before everyone else used it up. Leo, Benji, and Patrick seemed to be over the Great Tarot Reading Incident but she still felt like she had to make up for lost goodwill.

Rohan grimaced at his lunch. "Did Caz put you up to this?"

"No." Though she'd mentioned it several times with increasing worry. Rohan and his ex hadn't been in the same room together since her break-up album dropped.

"I'm fine," Rohan said. "She'll barely be here. We probably won't even run into each other."

"Are you looking to buy real estate in that delusion or just renting?" Benji asked, without looking up from their phone.

I must be feeling more than the heat today cuz, damn, their voice. They sounded like a hot villain who would be redeemed and become the love interest everyone would be rooting for in the inevitable love triangle. They weren't even trying. Goodness, to have a voice like that. People must eat out of their hands. Hell, *she'd* eat out of their hands, if they asked.

"You going to start another Twitter battle with her?" Rohan shot back, breaking her train of thought. He had a lovely voice too but it lacked the bad-but-you-want-them-anyway quality of Benji's. He sounded like what he was: a nice guy who, she'd found out, brought an Easy Bake Oven with him on tour so he could bake for people. She bit into the cookie he'd handed her when he'd sat down and smiled. Coconut chocolate chip, Cazzi's recipe, she'd bet on it. He must be missing her.

"I have not communicated with her in any way since before the pandemic," Benji said primly.

"I take it the two of you are just going to be fighting the White Witch of the South the entire time she's here," Leo said. "Should we bring popcorn or is this going to be more of a dinner theater kind of engagement?"

Judit laughed.

"She's Satanic white trash from Florida. Don't try to make her sound special," Benji said. "Rohan, don't forget about your phoner in five."

"Oh hell," Rohan said and finished his meal in record time, before dashing off. He doubled back and pointed at the last bite of cookie in her hand. "What do you think?"

She smiled. "Just as good as Cazzi makes 'em."

His grin was pure dorky sunshine. God, she wanted someone to love her like that.

"So." Benji put their phone away and fixed their gaze on her. "You want to help."

"Rohan said he was fine?" Dammit, why had that come out as a question?

Benji folded their hands on the table in front of them. "Rohan is a lovely man with one very large blind spot. Her name is Angela Alice."

"Ah," Judit said, not entirely sure this was the case. Judit had met her fair share of Satanists and "dark" magic practitioners. They'd never been especially frightening. Well, most of them hadn't been. There were always a few that were worrisome. Plus, Rohan seemed pretty competent. (And you know, a full-grown adult.) But then, Judit had never had a famous ex, let alone one that had made an album about their break-up.

"This is why you texted me, isn't it?" Leo said. "'Come have lunch with us, Leo. It'll be fun, Leo.'" He shook his head. He didn't seem surprised.

"We kept you from being a complete dipshit and some probably nasty assault charges. It's time you repay the favor," Benji said, unperturbed.

"I told you I wasn't going to do anything. I'm not going to beat on my ex. Rick knocked me down because he's a worry-wort. Where is he, anyway?"

Benji grimaced. "I'll talk to Rick separately. When I can track him down."

Leo shook his head. "That's what you get for siding against your friend."

Come on, come on, Judit thought, *have the hard conversation you need to have!*

Benji's eye twitched. "I had a friend on each side. Please fucking explain to me how I could have possibly avoided pissing off one of them."

Leo smiled. "The trick is that Rick will hold a grudge forever. Rohan's too much of a nice guy not to forgive you eventually."

Judit deflated. Welp, there went that opportunity. Maybe she spent too much time with people who narrowly avoided becoming psychologists. Her demi-sister and Cazzi would've inserted some insightful guiding questions or something and gotten them to open up.

"What a sound basis for deciding who's right. Why didn't I

think of that?" Benji rolled their eyes. "And people call me cold and calculating."

Thinking of the way they'd put her in the crosshairs of someone known to be an asshole, Judit said nothing.

They certainly calculated out this whole "Keep Angela Alice Contained" plan, she reflected later as she sat in what would be the front row of Rohan's show, watching him do his rehearsal and sound check. Benji wanted her to keep an eye on him. She'd feigned interest in the behind-the-scenes aspect of his work as if she hadn't seen half a dozen soundchecks on the stage across from their merch booth. Granted, most bands didn't get a soundcheck so the only acts she'd seen was the big heritage rock band who closed that stage every night.

As it was, it wasn't bad, sitting here watching dancers in plain clothes and Rohan in shorts run around and mimic the show she'd seen just a few nights ago and would probably watch again tomorrow. The music starting and stopping was getting old but at least she didn't have to stand.

"Where'd you get the chair?" Asked a voice as the music cut off yet again. Ugh, she really needed to get some alone time because even his voice was doing it for her. Not that it was a bad voice, low and smooth and—*omigawd Judit stop it!*

She looked at Patrick, standing next to her, and hoped her face was not as red as it felt. (The chair, he asked about the chair!) "Cedric brought it for me." It wasn't as good as the chair at her booth but she appreciated it nonetheless.

"Cedric," he repeated. "The roadie?"

"Cedric is an up-and-coming lighting expert." She waved at the man in question. He was on the catwalk, disturbingly high up, but he let go of the light he was adjusting to wave back. He was a lovely man who'd helped them set up the merch booth a few times. She'd given him a free reading when he'd asked about the sign she and Helen made once Benji approved her giving readings during dead times.

"You like to sit," Patrick observed, as the music started again. It wasn't at full volume so they could speak without yelling.

"It's a calling," she said lightly like she could stand all day if she wanted.

"Benji put you up to this."

"Sitting? No, I'm just an avid fan."

"Running interference. I'm on Rohan duty too."

"They didn't want you siding with Angela Alice?"

Patrick snorted.

"Is she that bad?"

He nodded. "How are you doing with the whole being viral thing?"

"I haven't looked at my notifications since the last hotel. Told myself I was conserving data. That's healthy, right?"

He laughed and it took her right back to that night in LA. The memory felt soft-focus, wreathed in fairy lights like they had both been someone else for a few hours.

She looked at him. Really looked at him for the first time in days. He looked steady, calm. She knew with familiar certainty this was a front. He felt like the cliff ledge, sharp and danger-ous. He was teetering and he would fall sooner than later. It made her want to take his hand, ground him to the earth.

The short hairs on the back of her neck rose, her entire back tingling. Was it because her instincts were rejecting the impulse or—

She turned around.

At the top of the aisle delineated by caution tape and cones stood a woman. She was alone, which was exactly what Benji was trying to avoid. Angela Alice, though not in her usual bridal white and thick make-up, was hard to mistake for anyone else. She was tall, even without the boots, the stark black tattoos on her hands, arms, chest, back, and neck standing out against her pale skin. She strode down the aisle, her hip-length white blonde hair streaming out behind her, her black-rimmed eyes fixed on the stage.

It was impossible to look away. Yes, she was pretty, she was striking, but there was something more. Judit grabbed her deck in her pocket and squeezed, trying to ground herself. She wished for something protective, a stone, an amulet, a weapon, anything.

A soft cloth thing dropped into her free hand. No wait, there was something stick-like inside. She tore her gaze away from Angela Alice and looked down. A flannel bag lay sewn closed in her palm.

"Angelica root," Patrick said. "It helps. Ironically."

"Thank you." Judit slipped it into her pocket and stood. "We should probably do our job now."

Angela Alice drew even with her chair and gave the two of them an assessing look. If people thought Benji was cold and calculating, they'd never met Angela. Her pale eyes were too far away for Judit to pick out the color but they felt reptilian all the same.

Rohan had to know she was here. Surely everyone could feel the wash of *something* rolling off her. The very air vibrated with anticipation so fraught it would make Dr. Frank N' Furter proud.

"I'm going to distract him," Patrick said, low and close to her ear. She shivered but nodded.

Judit braced herself and said in her best fangirl voice, "Oh my god, it's Angela Alice! I'm such a fan!" She forced herself to rush forward, Angela's presence growing more overwhelming the closer she got.

The other woman stood still, taking her in. Then she broke into a benevolent smile.

Judit, who had never swooned in her entire life, who had never heard of anyone swooning outside of a period piece, nearly swooned. Good fucking lord, what was this woman? She kept nattering like it was a defense. "I swear I never do this, but can I get an autograph?" She brandished the notebook and pen she'd brought just for this.

The root in her dress pocket bounced against her thigh and clarity surfaced.

"Of course." Angela Alice took the notebook. Her voice was sex in motion, low, slightly raspy but still smooth. Honed, like a weapon. If she and Benji had a conversation in front of her, Judit would have to take a very cold shower. "Who should I make it out to?"

"Oh, um, Judit?" Dammit, now she sounded like she was lying, or worse, didn't know her own name.

"Judit," Angela murmured, flipping the notebook open and writing.

"Angie." Rohan stood at the edge of the stage, looming over them. The lights threw his face in weird shadows and split his actual shadow into misshapen pieces. For a moment, he didn't seem so nice after all. Patrick stood behind him, looking exasperated. The dancers had disappeared.

"One moment, Ro. I'm with a fan." Angela didn't look up.

Rohan met Judit's eyes, giving her a look that told her he knew exactly what she was doing and didn't appreciate it. Aw man, she didn't want Rohan mad at her. Fucking Benji, putting her in the middle of all this. Where the hell were they and Leo, huh? Clearly not doing their part of the plan.

Angela finished her autograph with a flourish, handing the notebook and pen back with another knee-melting smile. Judit clapped her hand over the angelica root in her pocket instinctually to stay upright. Angela tracked the movement and her smile got complicated, tangled with emotions Judit had no idea how to parse. But she didn't let go of the root.

"Wasn't Leo supposed to be giving you a tour?" Patrick asked. He edged around Rohan as if trying to get in front of the other man.

Angela put on an air of confused innocence like it was a sweater. "I'm not sure. I went out for some fresh air and heard your rehearsal." She clasped her tattooed hands in front of the skirt of her black sundress. If someone was looking at a picture of right now and not looking too hard, maybe it would be convincing.

Rohan sighed. "I thought we were past this."

"Why Ro, are you suggesting we should be friends?" Angela arched an eyebrow.

Patrick looked braced for something, anything.

"Yes," Rohan said.

"What would that little wannabe shrink of yours think?" Angela asked and then looked at Patrick. "Or was she yours? I was never quite clear on that."

"She's not property," Judit snapped, then realized her mistake when Angela looked at her with new, razor-edged interest. "Whoever she is."

"You're right." Angela stared at her. Judit fought the urge to squirm. "Our Cazzi is a woman in her own right." She looked at the men on the stage. "Do tell her hi for me, whichever one of you is still speaking to her." She swept away, looking every inch the Bitch Queen she'd dubbed herself.

"Damn," Judit exhaled, Angela's presence receding like a loosening corset.

Benji emerged from backstage. "There's someone who didn't work on herself during quarantine."

Leo loomed behind them.

"Where were you?" Patrick demanded. "Did she sneak past you? Her?"

"Disturbingly, yes." Benji's gaze was fixed on the corner Angela disappeared around. Their interest was palpable but Judit wasn't sure what kind it was.

Rohan frowned and pinched a necklace under his tank top like it gave him strength. "I told you I didn't need help. If you treat Angie like a problem, she'll become one." He glared at Benji.

"Leaving a cancer unattended won't make it heal miraculously," Benji said, unperturbed.

"For the thousandth time, she is a human being, not evil incarnate." Rohan stalked away.

Benji and Patrick exchanged a glance.

Leo dropped off the stage like it wasn't a four-foot gap and stood by Judit, watching. "Better view," he whispered, loudly.

Judit nodded, mostly because she didn't know what else to say. A low ache started in her back and hamstrings. She bet Angela Alice didn't hurt at all at the end of her show, let alone from standing a little too long and sitting in a shitty folding chair. She knew it was internalized ableism, but it frustrated her that functioning like a normal able-bodied person left her in daily pain.

She sat, pulled out her deck, and asked herself a question. A quick shuffle and the answer was in her hand. She hummed to herself and asked a follow-up question.

"Well?" Leo asked when she'd drawn again. "What does the future hold?" There was a mocking edge to his tone.

She looked up to see everyone watching her. Great. "Rohan's right. The more you fight her the more complicated it'll get. The more you'll get entangled." She looked directly at Benji. The cards couldn't name names but they'd given some pretty broad hints and her trusty feelings filled in the rest. "You have to decide how tangled up you want to get."

13

"Poor lil rich shit
Having kids
Was just a societal itch
They scratched and never looked back

You want them to see you
You spill your guts
Wreck your car
Offer up your insides
With all these little suicides

They pay your bills
Take away your pills
Put you away secured
For your 90-day cure

Poor lil rich kid
You cry for help
For more than the money you're dealt
All you get is guilt"

—"Every Last Breath" by User-Friendly Omega off of *Suicide King*

Judit definitely wasn't watching the Doc Conjure show for any reason besides the fact it was right in front of her (well, more like to the left but directly diagonal to her). Besides, the merch booth was slow. She needed a distraction from the pain between her eyes and the way all her clothes stuck to her skin along with what felt like any dirt within a mile radius. Even Leo, next to her, looked wilted in the heat.

The music was good. Like a bluesy sort of punk. Sabrina was a great performer, dancing and working the crowd until they were singing along to songs they probably didn't know five minutes ago. Kevon was a great drummer, playing so hard she worried he'd get heatstroke. And sure, yes, Patrick somehow managed to make standing in one place, holding down the rhythm with easy confidence look... kinda hot? Judit wasn't sure how, given she was too far away to quite make out his face and he was barely on the big screens where they broadcast the shows, but something about his stance, at the shape of his long limbs in his loose tank top and shorts (since when were men's shorts sexy?), and the way his locs were tied back—

"Hi, are you the Tarot reader?"

Thank goodness. Judit tore her attention away from the stage and to her first Tarot client in Florida.

The woman was about Judit's age, smiling hopefully. She was dressed with care: cute shorts, a clinging barely-there top with a nice bra, fantastic make-up, an adorable backpack, and badass boots. The humidity and heat didn't seem to bother her though it was making Judit feel like a half-melted candle.

The client was also trying not to cry. She was good at masking but Judit used to live with Cazzi, and once you'd seen the master at work, every other performance was easy to spot.

Judit gentled her smile.

The woman took a deep breath and spilled her question all in one exhale. "All my life I've been told I need to be extraordinary, that I will be extraordinary. But the truth is, I'm not. I'm not and I never will be and that truth is killing me slowly. What do I do? How do I save myself?"

The question hit Judit square in the eyes. The reunion email scrolled in her mind.

She glanced away, catching a glimpse of Benji in the crowd by the Doc Conjure stage, watching the show with... was that Angela Alice in a brown wig? She was getting distracted.

Judit held a deck of cards in the middle of fucking Florida, sunburnt, and courting a headache because she wanted to be more. Bigger, louder, better than the future people saw when they realized how much pain she was always in.

But she couldn't think of that now either. Instead, she shuffled her deck and desperately hoped for an answer, for herself and her client.

The cards she pulled made the tears the other woman had been holding back fall silently. Judit pushed the box of tissues at her elbow to the woman without a word. By the end of the session, the client smiled, thanking her, clutching the notes she'd taken to her chest.

The spread did nothing for Judit.

But it put her in a fucking mood, long enough that even she was getting sick of her thoughts. She stood. "I need to stretch my legs quick."

Leo shrugged. "Go for it."

"Back in five."

She walked into the crowd, curious. Was that really Angela Alice she'd seen next to Benji?

Doc Conjure was playing a slow song she didn't recognize, quiet enough she could actually hear the conversations around her like—

The woman next to Benji saying, "So, I'm distracting you."

Yup, that voice. It was Angela, for sure. Did Benji need backup? Should Judit make her presence known?

Benji didn't move. "You're not as special as you think you are."

They seemed fine? Maybe she should just go. But she didn't move, curiosity getting the better of her.

"How strong you are. Poor little rich kid putting up with the likes of me."

"Your words, not mine."

Judit caught the edge of Angela's half-smile as she turned and resisted the dueling urges to run away and smile back. "Not just mine. I'm offering up my insides."

Benji straightened. "No, you're regurgitating mine. If you're going to quote my songs at me, at least do it correctly."

Angela clasped her hands together and tipped her head back like she'd won something. A nearby man looked over and stared, his mouth half-open. Not like he recognized her but like he couldn't help it.

Judit couldn't blame him, she couldn't look away either.

Angela hummed something, loud enough to be heard as the Doc Conjure song faded out. Was that User-Friendly Omega's "Every Last Breath"? Holy shit, what a fangirl!

"Your vocals on Ro's new album are phenomenal," Angela told Benji.

Benji nodded.

"You should put something new out," Angela said.

"I don't want your advice," Benji snapped.

"I'm just saying—"

"Child, I was a platinum artist before you were legal. You don't get to 'just say' anything to me."

"Not true. I was perfectly legal when *Suicide King* went platinum. I bought it with my own money and everything." There was an odd note in her voice and Judit shivered with the crowd as the temperature seemed to dip for a moment. "Besides,"

Angela went on like nothing happened. "You and I are only five years apart. That's nothing."

Benji looked down their nose at her. Somehow. The two of them were nearly the same height. "If five years is nothing then I matured much faster than you did. You're still a child to me."

Angela laughed in their face. Judit found herself smiling. Benji held themself rigid.

Angela's laughter died and so did Judit's smile. "You really don't like me do you?" Angela asked.

"Am I supposed to feel bad about that?"

"No," she murmured. "I wanted to know where I stood." She turned to look at the stage.

After a moment, Benji did the same.

A new song started and Judit escaped as sneakily as she could. Hoo boy, those two... those two were a whole thing she didn't even want to touch.

But when Benji asked her to keep an eye on Angela Alice at Rohan's show she said yes, even though it meant she'd have to buddy up with Patrick again. Better her go than Benji fuel Angela's weird obsession with them. It wasn't like Judit could talk to them about it either, she didn't want to fess up to eavesdropping and Benji seemed pretty touchy about the whole Angela thing.

And well, Patrick was kind of okay now. He seemed to be getting over the whole LA thing, anyway and maybe that meant he'd let Cazzi go too.

Not that Judit had any horse in that race. It would just be... nice. Less stress for everyone.

Yep, that was her story and she was sticking with it.

PATRICK SCANNED THE CROWD, looking for any sign of Angela Alice. She'd slipped away after her soundcheck and he was certain she was in here somewhere, watching Rohan's show.

"Any luck?" Judit appeared behind him. The crowd bumped her against him, her collarbone against his arm, softness pressing against his bare skin on either side—

Nope. Don't get distracted.

He shook his head, stepping away so they no longer touched.

She yelled something about Angela in his ear but was drowned out by a swell of music. The sound didn't mask the sensation of the stray tendrils of hair tickling his face as she teetered on her toes to reach him. Or the warmth of her as she swayed close enough to touch. As usual, she wore a loose flowy dress, and, as usual, the heat stuck it to her body in places that he was finding harder and harder not to notice.

Instinctively, he reached out and steadied her with a few fingers on her upper arm. She blinked up at him and he realized he hadn't touched her since that night in LA. Did she still think about that night? Did she remember it the way he did?

She stumbled and almost took them both down.

"Hold on." He set her on her feet and leaned down, curling his body towards her. "Say it again."

Maybe that was too close because her eyes got wide and she swallowed hard. "Angela wore a wig at your show."

Well, that explained why he didn't see her white hair. But she was on after this. Surely, she wouldn't still be wearing it?

"How the hell does she hide? I should be able to feel her across the whole grounds. She—" Judit waved her hands about like she might catch the word she was looking for. "—exudes."

Patrick frowned as a new song started, one from the new album with his production. It was hard to concentrate when the music—his riffs and samples—begged for his attention. Even with earplugs in—especially with earplugs in, cutting the feedback and excess noise—the performance called to him. It was weird hearing them live outside the studio, then even after two weeks of this, it was still weird to hear anything live and in-person these days. But it felt good. He wanted to bathe in it, let the music wash through him, and quiet the static in his head.

"She's like a reverse empath," Judit continued. "I've never felt anything like it."

He should say something to that, shouldn't he? But the music called to him. How could she think when the performance was thrumming through the audience and they were singing along? He'd forgotten how good it was to be in the crowd, watching them lose their inhibitions and just move however the spirit took them. He couldn't remember the last time he felt free enough to do that, especially in public.

"Oh dear." Judit stared at the stage as the song ended.

Patrick followed her gaze. Angela Alice was on stage in full all-white regalia and ghostly make-up. She had a mic.

"This could go badly."

Patrick pulled out his phone and hit record.

"What are you doing?" Judit frowned at him.

What was he doing? He almost put the phone down. But no, what if something happened and he missed recording it? That's what they were doing here, right? Keeping an eye on Angela?

"Benji will wanna see this." So would Cazzi. Not that he had the right to show it to her, but still. He wasn't thinking about her incessantly anymore but a good friend would let her know, right?

No. He didn't need to insert himself in their relationship anymore. It wasn't healthy.

But he didn't stop filming.

"Angie and I aren't together anymore," Rohan said, "But as she's here, I couldn't resist a throwback moment."

"The Dark Lord knows I love a throwback moment." Angela's laughter rippled through the crowd.

Rohan laughed too. "On that note..." He nodded at the band and they launched into the opening chords. "They say we're strange bedfellows," he crooned.

"Well," Angela cocked a hip and gave him a challenging look. Her voice rolled over the crowd and grabbed them. "Opposites attract. We're proof of that."

"We fit like puzzle pieces," Rohan sang back.

"Your crazy matching mine."

Patrick would never like Angela, but he couldn't deny she was a fantastic singer and clearly in her element on stage.

"They can't pull us apart," they sang together. Their voices blended beautifully, Rohan's clear, golden voice highlighting her ragged darkness. Patrick found himself leaning forward.

It was a good duet, obviously unrehearsed but they were both pros who improvised well, revolving closer and closer together until they were nearly nose-to-nose by the bridge. They looked about to kiss. Patrick gripped his phone tighter. This was what he was filming for. He'd have to send it to Cazzi if that happened. He couldn't live with himself if he didn't.

Rohan backed off, finishing the last chorus farther away. Patrick let out the breath he'd been holding.

The crowd exploded when the song finished. It was a good encore gimmick and if Rohan was thinking like a performer he'd try to make sure he ended every show he could that way.

Patrick stopped recording, tucking his phone in his pocket.

"Wow," Judit muttered, rubbing her face. "She's—They —Wow."

He turned to leave. The video was burning a hole in his pocket. He needed to think.

Her hand caught his shirt, tugging him back but carefully not touching his skin. He remembered the way she touched him in LA. Her touch had been warm then, comforting, a caesura in the whirling fractional notes of his thoughts. He wondered briefly if touching her right now would let his mind breathe again.

"Be careful with that," she said.

"What?"

"The video." She looked into his eyes like she knew exactly what he planned. He certainly didn't.

"I know what I'm doing," he lied.

"It's not going to go the way you want." Her all-knowing tone grated on him. He didn't know what he wanted. The minute he felt like he was moving on, something sucked him back into the maelstrom of emotions. It was fucking exhausting.

He shook his head, words jamming in his throat. She didn't understand.

"Tell me, Patrick." It was still weird to hear his full name on her tongue. No one but Cazzi and his family called him that. It spun an extra awareness around the word, a certain frisson. "Do you love her or do you just think she should love you the way she used to?" The question cut through him and he knew it would keep echoing because it sounded so much like the things he asked himself late at night.

If it hadn't been love what had he been doing for the last year and a half? Why had he put himself and his best friend through hell? If it hadn't been love, had Cazzi kissing him made him the cheater he'd been afraid he'd become since the whole Grandpa Pat scandal?

Why couldn't he just let this shit go?

He deadeyed Judit. She stared right back.

Someone in the leaving crowd jostled her, breaking her grip on his shirt. She glanced away at them and Patrick took the opportunity to flee.

Ducking backstage, he flinched as he opened his chat with

Cazzi, seeing all the texts he'd ignored over the last year. Damn, he was an asshole.

Before he could overthink it, he sent the video to Cazzi. Whether Patrick was in love with her or not, she had a right to know what her boyfriend was up to. If something happened with Rohan and Angela, he'd never forgive himself if he'd stayed quiet.

No one gave Nana a heads-up that her husband had been cheating on her for years. Instead, she'd been humiliated when it came out at a party with her family and friends to see. Patrick wasn't about to repeat that pattern.

THE MINUTE JUDIT'S phone rang on the way back to the tour bus, she knew Patrick sent the video. She picked up without looking at the caller ID. "Hey, honey."

"Okay," Cazzi said, her voice dead around the edges the way it was when she'd used too many of her coping mechanisms all at once. "I heard your voice on that video so I need you to tell me if I'm overreacting."

"You're overreacting. They're not getting back together."

Cazzi exhaled hard. "You'd tell me though—"

"I'd tattle on your boyfriend any day. Even though he's signing my paychecks."

"Fuck. Shitty question, I shouldn't have asked." Judit could practically hear Cazzi taking apart the power dynamics in her head.

"Talk to Rohan, Caz."

"I will. I will. I just wanted to get the panic out first."

"I'm honored."

"You should be. It's just, Judy, it's *Angelica*." Her voice climbed a little higher under the deadness. It was a weird combination, one Judit was pretty sure wasn't seen in nature.

"Yeah." Judit blew out a breath. "I've met her."

"So, you get it."

"I mean, yes, but I don't know how anyone spends more than five minutes in a room with her, let alone lives with her for years."

"She's still intense, huh?"

"My god, Caz. What *is* she?"

"Hell, if I know. Something dangerous."

"Dangerous?" Judit stopped walking. "Do you think she wants to hurt him?"

"It's... hard to know what she wants." Cazzi paused. "She tried to clear the air for the whole break-up debacle about six months ago."

"Angela Alice said *sorry*?"

"Well, no," Cazzi huffed. "She sent us a card that said 'I'm over this and I bet y'all are too.' Ro called her immediately and we had this super awkward conference call. But the bottom line is she said regretted all that shit she pulled. But seeing them together on stage again—"

"I don't think he wants her back," Judit reassured her. Frankly, she didn't think Angela cared about Rohan much anymore. (Though why had she been so spicy when she arrived? Was she just fucking with them? Ugh, what was with this lady?) Angela had a new target: Benji but Cazzi didn't need something more to stress about. "But I do think he misses you."

"You got a feeling about it?" Warmth and life leeched back into Cazzi's voice.

"More than a feeeeeeling," Judit sang, just to make her laugh. "He made your cookie recipe in his Easy Bake today."

Cazzi laughed, trailing off with a happier sigh. "Thank you, Judy. I'm in lesbians with you."

"I love you too, Scott Pilgrim," Judit replied.

They hung up laughing.

Judit climbed the bus stairs emotionally wrung out and bodily aching. She texted Helen.

JUDIT

Tell me something good.

HELEN

You packed our copy of Grosse Pointe Blank.
And half the bus is hanging at the booth.

JUDIT

Thank the goddess.

She lay down on her bed, setting up the beat-up portable DVD player her cousin passed down to her on her chest and popping the movie in. There was something so soothing about John Cusack as a fast-talking hitman going to his high school reunion.

Which reminded her anew that *her* ten-year reunion was coming up. Fuck. Ten years. When did that happen?

That fucking email. She'd been doing so well not thinking about it but between the movie and the client she'd had today, well, that scab had been ripped right open.

Sitting on her bunk with the DVD menu looping thirty seconds of soundtrack she opened the email again. Her wrists ached, her ovary burned a slow hole through her flesh, and her tight neck muscles were threatening a headache. She popped a CBD gummy and stared at the date. She had five months to become amazing or at least passably impressive. This tour would make her interesting, right?

No, said a nasty voice in the back of her head, *you've been struggling for ten years. You should be successful by now.*

Be compassionate, she reminded herself as she started the film. *Worse comes to worse you can tell people you murdered the president of Paraguay with a fork.* Maybe someone would get the reference.

"Reunion anxiety?"

She looked down to see Patrick standing by her bunk like he'd just come out of the bathroom, which is really the only way he could've snuck up on her in this damn bus. Reading over her fucking shoulder because he was tall and the bunk was not. He nodded at her email. She locked the screen and dropped the phone on the bed. "I know what you did."

"Last summer?" His lips twisted in something close to a smirk.

She closed the player. "Yeah, lockdown like the rest of us. No, you asshat, Cazzi called me."

He stilled. "Is she—?"

"She's fine, no thanks to you. But I'd duck when you see Rohan because she called him next."

He nodded. "Good."

"Good? *Good?* Are you fucking kidding me? Where do you get off trying to sabotage them like that?" She got up on her knees, trying to loom over him.

"I-I—" He swallowed. Shook his head. "It's none of your business."

"She is *my* friend. I was there when you ghosted her both times. I helped her put herself back together. Don't fuck with her just because she's with someone actually emotionally available."

"I know her better than you'll ever know her."

"No. You knew her. I know who she is now."

"Maybe, but I did what I thought was right." His jaw clenched.

"Yeah but—"

"I don't have to justify myself to you!" He snapped.

"No, but you need to have some responsibility for your actions!"

"Not to you." He stalked towards the exit.

"You are such an asshole sometimes!"

He flipped her off without turning around, his hand the last thing she saw as he disappeared into the night.

Screw whoever the president of Paraguay was. She was real tempted to go after Ricky Rick with a fork. That is if she had anything that wasn't a biodegradable spork. She could just see the headline now: *Crazy Psychic Stabs Former Pop Star with Spork.*

Talk about interesting. She rolled her eyes at herself and started the movie. Better to leave the forking to John Cusack.

14

Hi everyone! I've gotten a lot more followers in the last few weeks (thanks for the shout out @theRealMartinMejia) so I thought I'd reintroduce myself. I'm Judit, a Tarot card reader and psychic, currently on tour, selling merch and doing readings at the @NoworNeverRecords booth at #Endfest. I love campy movies (and quoting them), clothes by @DesignedByHelen, pet pictures, and trying new food. Come say hi if you're at Endfest or hit me up any time if you want a reading. Internet is spotty out on the road but I'll get back to you as soon as I can. Thanks for following! :]
—@JuditReadsTheFuture

The next morning, Patrick ran around the empty festival grounds, listening to the beat of his feet against the packed dirt. If he listened hard enough maybe he wouldn't think.

Cazzi hadn't replied. It had kept him up half the night. Had he done the right thing? Judit certainly didn't think so.

He spotted Rohan walking towards him on an intercept

path. Patrick ran faster, veering away. They hadn't hit each other in a while but last time it had been about Cazzi too.

Rohan raked his fingers through his hair as if weighing something. Then he sprinted.

Shit! Patrick forgot how fucking fast he was. Rohan'd always been speedy, lapping him during training even when they were teenagers and the extra inch he had on Patrick seemed to increase that exponentially.

The grounds were ringed by unoccupied stages. The public wasn't here yet, and wouldn't be for hours. The tour bus was out of reach. Cazzi still would've rabbitted but Patrick—well, it all seemed futile. He stopped.

Rohan skidded past and turned around, facing him. He breathed in a fast, angry tempo and his expression matched. For a long moment, neither of them said anything.

Then Rohan said, "Were you trying to upset her?"

Patrick shrugged. He felt hollowed out, tired. "The performance got weird. She had a right to know."

"It was just a performance. We've both moved on and you *know* me. You know I don't cheat." There was hurt in Rohan's eyes.

Patrick did know, but he'd trusted Grandpa Pat too once. He'd thought his grandparents' relationship was the gold standard for love when he was growing up. He'd held on to that belief even as the industry showed him a million ways people could betray each other. Look where it had gotten him.

"Sure." He turned to walk away.

"Stop fucking with her head," Rohan said. "It's not fair to her. She still cares about you."

"I care about her," Patrick snarled, whirling back. Anger was loud and white hot in his head. "I wouldn't have sent it if I didn't."

"How come every time you show her how much you care

you hurt her instead?" Rohan snapped back. "And then I have to pick up the pieces."

Patrick's fists clenched. He wanted to slug Rohan, to run away, to wretch, and—most unforgivably—to cry.

"Let it go," Rohan said. "For all our sakes. Let her go." He walked away and Patrick could see his fists were clenched too.

I'm fucking trying, he wanted to yell. *You think I want this?*

Instead, he let the words simmer in him as he walked off toward the far corner of the fairgrounds. There were plants there, bushes, and things other people would consider weeds. But Patrick knew all their names. He crouched down running his fingers over the local variant of Plantago Major—also known as plantain, though it was in no way related to the banana-like fruit. The small plants with their wide round leaves and seedy stalks grew pretty much everywhere, especially along the sides of the road like this. If it wasn't so close to the pollutants of the fest, he might pick it for a poultice if someone had a nasty splinter or something that needed extracting.

Stroking the leaves soothed him, his knowledge of the plant and its uses circling in his head until it drowned out the overwhelm swamping him.

A hand touched his shoulder, tentative. Gentle. The relaxation faded. He looked up slowly.

Judit stared at him through her sunglasses. "Did you hear me?"

He shook his head.

"You okay?"

He blinked. The question seemed absurd. Of all the condescending—

"Because I've been trying to get your attention for like *minutes* and I think that leaf isn't going to make it."

He looked down and realized he'd shredded the leaf in his fingers. Regret crashed over him. "I'm sorry," he whispered to the plant, detaching what was left of the stalk gently and placing it on the ground. He looked at Judit.

She gave him a sympathetic smile.

He looked away, embarrassed. More people were milling about, getting ready to open for the public. How long had he been here?

"Maybe it would be a good idea to go back to the bus? I think they're gonna start letting people in soon."

Fuck, the last thing he needed was a crowd. He stood.

"I'll walk with you," she said. "I'm heading that way."

"Why?" The word came out croaky and he cleared his throat, noting with professional interest the phlegm and constriction that hadn't been there before. He swiped a hand over his face, relieved to find only sweat, no unconscious tears. The idea of crying without knowing it felt like a living nightmare.

She shrugged. "Leo and Sabrina would kick my ass if I left you here and you got carried off by a fangirl mob."

The idea he was still a viable candidate for that surprised a laugh out of him. It had been a good few years since he seriously feared being stampeded by excited fans.

She smiled, blowing her errant bangs out of her eyes. "Is that a yes?"

"Sure," he rasped, falling into step with her. It was easier this way. Maybe talking to Judit would let him forget what he'd done for a while—

Yeah, no. Fuck. He'd thought he was doing the right thing last night but in the harsh morning light, it was clear he was just falling into old patterns gouged by his dead grandfather's bullshit.

A pit opened in his chest. How could Cazzi possibly care about him after all he'd done? After all the ghosting, the asshole moves? The suffocating urge to cry swelled in his throat, behind his eyes.

"Hey." Judit laid a hand on his bicep. Patrick realized his hands were tight fists and he'd stopped moving. He relaxed them, focusing on Judit's face. The sympathy in her eyes over her sunglasses made him want to collapse and run away at the same time.

"Hi," she said. "There you are." She smiled and it was the nicest thing he'd seen in a while.

"Why are you being nice to me?" he rasped, his voice even worse than before.

Her mouth twisted and she sighed. "Man, I don't know. I guess I'm just really bad at maintaining grudges in the face of obvious misery."

"Damn, say what you really mean."

She rolled her eyes and started walking again. "Come on, asshat. I've got to get back to the booth."

"I don't need a babysitter." He stomped after her.

"Fine with me. I've never been good with anyone childish."

A door opened and he realized they stood in front of their tour bus. Sabrina stared out at them, her hair still in its bonnet. "What's up?"

Judit looked at him. "I'm fighting with your brother."

Sabrina looked from him to her. "What else is new?"

Patrick rolled his eyes.

Sabrina's eyes narrowed but she looked away, turning to Judit. "Aren't you on shift at merch?"

"Yep." Judit didn't give him a second look before turning away. It hurt more than he expected.

"Was she bothering you?" Sabrina asked. "I can make her life hell."

Patrick shook his head and climbed into the bus. "I can handle it."

Sabrina sighed. "You don't have to, though."

Patrick smiled, patting her shoulder awkwardly. They

weren't especially close in age or temperament but Sabrina was all right as little sisters went. "I appreciate it."

"Do you? You never take me up on anything."

He shrugged. "It's the thought—"

"No, that's not what counts," Sabrina interrupted him. "And don't give me any of that 'men don't accept help because we're men' shit. I know you got it in stereo from Dad and Grandpa Pat—"

They both paused, his name hanging in the air between them.

Sabrina pulled in a shaky breath. "—But you *know* better. I don't want to keep watching you suffer in silence, okay? It's not fun for anyone."

Patrick dropped onto the couch in front of her, thinking. This was another thing he'd internalized from Grandpa Pat. Another fucking thing to unpack from a dead man. "He fucked us up good, didn't he?"

Sabrina sat next to him. "You more than me. You were his favorite." She shrugged. "I used to be so jealous but now I think I dodged a bullet."

"He wasn't—There were good times," Patrick insisted, remembering the way Grandpa Pat would delight in showing him old music and listen with interest as Patrick grew older and showed off his newly discovered favorites. Later, he would be the first person to listen to Patrick's original work, the first person he called when he was cast as a Beatboy, the first call he made when the band imploded... Somehow those glowing memories got muddled with the bad shit—when Grandpa's mistress came and exposed his giant lie, the way he'd shut down Patrick's vulnerabilities with pronouncements about what men did and didn't do.

"Yeah," Sabrina said. "He was complicated." She leaned her head on his shoulder. "It gets me randomly like I'll hear a song and think 'Oh, Grandpa Pat would love that.' Then I'll have this whole tangled mass of feelings about it."

Patrick nodded. "I'm still so angry at him," he whispered.

"Me too," Sabrina whispered back.

They sat like that until they were almost late for their show.

JUDIT WAS NEARLY BACK at the merch booth when someone almost as big as Leo jogged up. They looked vaguely familiar. Judit thought she'd seen them somewhere backstage.

"Hi," the stranger said with an easy smile, white teeth flashing against brown skin. They were built like a linebacker in a short skirt. The look made Judit happy. "You're Judit, right?"

Judit put on her best customer service smile. "So they tell me."

"I'm Danielle, most folks call me Dani. She/her." A hand was thrust towards her and Judit shook it automatically. "Look, we're playing tonight and she'd like a reading."

Judit blinked. "Who?"

Dani snapped her gum in surprise. "Oh, sorry, usually people know I'm a Siren." She grinned like that was in any way helpful.

"Um." Judit's mind scrambled, trying to find some bit of information that made what Dani said make sense.

Dani laughed. "Not a fan, huh? That's cool. I'm one of Angela Alice's backing band. We're called the Sirens. Sirens of Scream if we're feeling fancy."

"Oh. Oh!" Judit said. "Wait, Angela wants a reading?"

"Yup." Dani snapped her gum on the 'p'.

Damn. Damn. Dammit. How did she say no to Angela Alice?

Her follower count was still uncomfortably high since Martin followed her and she felt newly self-conscious about everything she posted now. How many of them would actually stick around for her when Martin's glow was gone? Also, why did so many of them feel the need to comment or slide into her DMs? They were mostly nice but the creepy was definitely on the uptick. How much weirder would it get if Angela Alice fans joined in?

"So here's the thing," Judit started. "I kinda came down on the Rohan side of the divorce, if you know what I mean."

Dani grimaced sympathetically. "She has ideas for your business too. Tips and shit. She's good at that stuff, ya know."

Judit started to argue and then thought about it. "If I say no, will she keep asking?"

Dani shrugged. "You interest her."

"Oh," Judit said faintly. That was good? Maybe?

Dani put her arm over Judit's shoulders. "She's really not as bad as everyone makes her out to be. Trust me, I've been in her band forever."

"If I asked you to let go, would you?" Judit asked. "Or are you planning to drag me there?"

Dani's arm lifted immediately. "It's all up to you. No pressure."

"Tell me something," Judit said. "Are you the biggest person on her team?"

Dani nodded, her eyes narrowing like she expected this conversation to get uncomfortable real fast.

"That's pressure," Judit pointed out. A girl didn't spend years living with a pair of sex educators not to be well-versed in various types of coercion and consent.

Dani squinted at her. "Would you prefer Ang came herself?"

"See that's also pressure. Given the way she is."

Dani chewed her gum thoughtfully. "This doesn't sound like a battle I can win." She turned on her heel and left.

"That's it?" Judit called after her.

She turned back with a grin and a wink, then shook her head. And walked away.

JUDIT WAS at dinner when the next attempt arrived. It was in the form of Gemma, a tiny butch Black woman who introduced herself as "Dani's girlfriend and the guitarist."

"Nice to meet you," Judit said, not sure what else to say.

"Can you please tell me why you don't want to talk to Angela?" She folded her hands in front of her and smiled pleasantly.

Judit sighed. These people were seriously single-minded. "True consent is not having to justify your 'no' to anyone. No is a good enough reason by itself."

Gemma considered this, smoothing her edges. "Good point. You're not that shrink, are you?"

"Which shrink?"

"The one that stole RK from Angela."

"One." Judit held up a finger. "Cazzi did not steal anyone and she's a sex educator, not a shrink. Two." She held up another one. "Clearly not. I'm a fucking psychic."

Gemma raised her eyebrows. "So you couldn't be a shrink?"

Judit stabbed her spork into her pasta with unnecessary force. "My god, you Sirens are irritating."

Gemma smiled. "Being an asshole is part of the job description."

"Only way to survive whatever Angela puts out?"

Gemma's face went all serious. And intense. Real intense. "Don't you shit-talk her."

The hairs on the back of Judit's neck rose and Gemma

turned towards the entrance. In fact, everyone in the tent turned in that direction.

Oh hell, Judit thought, grabbing for the root in her pocket. She hadn't been without it since Patrick gave it to her.

"Hey, Gemma." Angela Alice sat next to her bandmate like she was a normal person doing a normal thing instead of whatever the hell she was. She had grabbed a tray of mess tent food. It was decent food, but it wasn't *that* good. Not celebrity good.

She was even dressed casual. No disguise or stage make-up, just 'look I'm a regular person who wears regular jeans and T-shirts.' Judit wasn't fooled. Those jeans were probably designer. That Alice Cooper shirt had to be pre-distressed, not old. Her deep purple lipstick probably cost more than Judit's part of the rent.

"Hey Angie," Gemma said, unphased. Judit wondered if she had her own shielding method or if the Siren had just built up a resistance to Angela over time.

Judit was too annoyed to be awed. She just nodded and kept eating. The faster she finished the faster she could get out of there.

"So, I was thinking," Angela said, picking up a bite of food. "I should do a cameo on your social media. Something easy, general." She popped the bite in her mouth. "I already followed you."

Judit nearly choked. She'd been sparing on her social media usage thanks to Patrick's advice. It was a nice break, both for her brain and her data usage.

"I'll also name-drop you and your handle on my social media. We'll do a selfie or something." Angela waved the details away. "Then you give me a private reading."

"What?"

"Well, I realized I should've offered you something.

Summoning you like that was—" Angela paused, smiled. "—high-handed."

Judit clutched at the angelica root in her pocket. It was hard to think with that smile directed at her. She realized she was smiling back.

Someone pulled out the chair next to her. Next time, she'd sit at a table with only one chair. Or maybe hide somewhere.

"Are you fucking with my people, Angelica?" If Judit thought Benji sounded dangerous before, they sounded positively frightening now, their voice deeper, smoother, darker. Their face was deceptively calm and they hadn't even bothered to pretend they were having a meal.

"Is that what the kids call helping these days?" Angela leaned forward and turned her attention to Benji. Being out of her gaze let Judit relax until the other woman continued. "Or would an old geezer like you even know?"

Judit braced herself. Gemma watched the exchange with interest.

"Play your games somewhere else." Benji leaned back and crossed their arms. "Leave my people out of it."

Angela leaned even farther forward, her eyes sparkling with interest. "You just love foiling my evil schemes, don't you?" She lowered her voice and Judit found herself inching closer to hear. "You wanna know what I was planning to do to her?"

Benji gestured for her to go on. They looked bored. Judit didn't believe it for a minute.

"I was going to help her. Lift her up, one woman to another." Her teeth flashed in a split-second grin. They looked sharp. "Support her career. Dastardly, aren't I?"

Benji looked at Judit, turning away from Angela like she wasn't there at all. "Did you want her help? Was I interfering?" They looked like they genuinely cared about the answer.

Judit now felt like a giant dickhead when she said, "No. I don't feel comfortable accepting help from her."

Angela leaned back, heaving a dramatic sigh. "Is this because of the break-up? Did you not see the show last night? We're all good now."

"Even if Cazzi wasn't my friend, I still wouldn't appreciate your methods," Judit shot back. She stood, taking what was left of her food. "I won't waste any more of your time."

Benji stood with her, their slender frame curving towards her protectively but not touching her.

Angela stayed seated and shrugged. "Your loss." Next to her, Gemma shook her head.

Judit walked away before they could say anything more.

"Well done," Benji said, heading off their own way once they were out of sight.

"Thank you for stepping in," she said. "But you're getting entangled." It was the closest she'd gotten to bringing up the exchange she'd eavesdropped on yesterday.

Benji scoffed.

"I don't think I was what she really wanted," Judit spoke from the feeling in her gut.

Benji stilled.

"Not to be your stereotypical psychic, but be careful with that one."

Benji nodded. "Noted."

They left and Judit headed for the bus. They were in the middle of Florida and there was no way she was leaving the festival grounds when there were alligator warning signs all over the place. Plus she needed a nap. If she didn't get one she was liable to snap at the next person who got on her nerves.

"You just keep making fun new friends," Patrick said, coming out of the dining tent behind Judit. Dammit, that sounded funnier in his head.

"Oh, for fuck's sake!" She snapped, stomping away.

He considered giving up on the conversation but it felt bad to leave it like that. She had been kind to him. Well, after being justifiably pissed at him.

"That came out wrong." He kept pace with her easily. "I'm not judging you."

"You most certainly are." She wheeled around and stabbed a finger into his chest. He halted, struck by the tiny point of contact. "I don't know what high horse you think you're on, but I'm getting really fucking tired of it."

"I'm sorry." He leaned in, his chest curving against her finger. His hand came down on the crook of her pointing arm just... holding it.

What was he doing?

She tilted her face up, watching him. He couldn't stop looking at her lips. Her breathing picked up.

What would it be like to kiss her?

Her gaze caught his.

What would it be like?

"What...?" She murmured.

What was he doing? What had he been saying? He barely knew. Fuck, what was happening to him?

He tried to drag himself into what remained of their conversation.

"I'm trying to protect you," he said. Well, shit, that sounded weird and possessive. Where the hell was all his boy band charm now? He really needed to stop staring at her. But something about the sunlight skimming along her soft cheeks...

"Why?" She wasn't looking away. Did she feel this too? She flattened her palm against his chest, her arm tensing like she might push him away.

But she didn't.

"I-I—" What had they been talking about? Did it matter? What would she do if he dragged her closer? If he—

"Well—" She seemed to grasp for words. "Don't. Don't try to control me. Don't tell me what to do. You have no right. No say." Her hand curled into a fist, crumpling his shirt. His grip on her arm tightened slightly. She had to lead here. If she pulled him towards her—

She pushed him back, breaking both their grips. He stumbled, but only for a step.

Message received.

She looked away from his face. But her gaze tracked all over him.

It didn't mean anything. Weird things happened on tour. He'd seen it a thousand times, he was just usually better about not getting caught up in them.

"I'm not trying to control you," he said, trying to salvage this. Piecing the conversation back together, ugh, he sounded like an asshole. Again.

"Yeah? Neither is Martin, neither is Angela, neither is Dani or Gemma. They just get real upset when I'm not as grateful for their 'not controlling me' as they think I should be." Judit shook her head, not looking at him. Writing him off and putting him in the same category as Martin, no less. "You're just as bad, sending that video."

"That was a mistake. I'm not them." He said, voice rough. Probably from the heat. Sure, it was wet heat but—fuck don't think about wet heat.

"No," she agreed. "You're your own brand of problem."

She walked away.

"I'm trying," he said. "I'm trying to be better."

But she gave no sign of hearing him.

15

Welcome to Satan's Armpit aka Florida in July
There is nothing quite as horribly humid as the home state of the Florida
Man in the middle of the summer. **So** *glad we have two whole stops here!*
In case anyone didn't notice the disturbance in the force, Angelica "Angela"
(creative stage name there) Alice has been swanning around our little
mobile community stirring up trouble as only a friend of the devil can. Fun
fact: She's from Florida! (figures)
We can only hope today's summer storm washes her away (and doesn't
turn into a hurricane).
Another fun fact: Florida is the lightning capital of the country, so if
you've always wanted to be electrocuted, this is the place to do it.
Stay electric my pretties,
LS
—Tourgasm vol. 3

"And then I just left," Judit whispered to Helen at the merch booth as they packed it up the next morning on yet another travel day. The booths around them were mostly stripped down and the wind was picking up, but who knew who might be around. "Like one minute he's super helpful

"

then he's a dick and now, what? He's into me? What the fuck is happening, Helen?"

"Besides a really intense story for your future memoirs?" Helen said. "Sounds like either the lead up to some good hate-fucking or that non-concordance thing you were telling me about? Where the genitals and the brain don't agree?"

"Arousal non-concordance?" Judit mulled it over, trying to remember one of the many times her sister and Cazzi discussed the concept. They explained it as the genitals react to everything sexual while the brain is more selective and the two agreed a very small percentage of the time. Which was normal and nothing to worry about. "Maybe. But I think my brain was kinda into it too? Even though I really don't want to be."

"I mean, I don't blame you. It's conflicting. He's hot but also he needs to get his shit together. I watch Doc Conjure's shows all the time because *oh my gawd* his forearms when he's playing bass. Hellooo!" Helen moaned and then caught herself. "But yeah, he's a hot and cold mess."

Judit laughed, flapping her shirt against her chest, wishing it was less humid so she could sweat. It was seven in the morning but she was already sticky and too warm. She never thought she'd miss the dry sweaty heat of the deserts they'd left. "Right? Even anger-fucking would be a disaster because of the whole Cazzi thing."

"I'm pretty sure anger-fucking is always a disaster of some magnitude. But yeah, this would be epically bad."

"So what do I do?" A drop of rain conjured itself out of the humid air and fell on Judit's forehead. She glanced at the ominously purple clouds sitting overhead. Yikes, those looked nasty.

Helen shrugged. "Avoid him? Or at least never be alone with him? He seemed to feel it too, right?"

Judit tore her eyes away from the clouds. "I think?"

"Definitely avoid him." Helen looked around the empty

stages that were already partially packed up by the crew. "I'll stick to your side as much as I can but maybe you should hang out on Rohan's bus for a while. I bet if you asked to ride with him he'd let you."

Judit shook her head. "I'm not leaving just cuz I had intense eye contact with someone."

It was sprinkling now.

Helen swore. "I'm gonna run the stickers and electronics over to the bus before the rain gets worse. Will you be okay?"

"Yeah. Ask them why the hell no one's brought a bus around yet too while you're there."

"We need walkies or something." Helen checked her phone. "I have no bars in this swamp."

Judit looked at the sky. "Call in reinforcements too. It's way too gloomy out here."

"You got it." Helen took off at a jog.

Judit focused on packing as fast as possible. She could fix stuff later. A bad feeling took root in her stomach and she did her best to breathe through it.

Out of nowhere, Patrick appeared. He grabbed a box next to her and started throwing shirts in. "Hey, I heard you need help."

Judit stifled a groan. Of all the people... but she couldn't turn down help right now. "Thanks," she said grudgingly.

They worked without speaking as the rain picked up, filling the silence between them. Making the ground muddy then slippery then—

"Holy shit." Judit looked at the mud, which was covered in water, soaking her shoes and rising fast. "It's flooding."

Patrick swore under his breath. "Where's the fucking bus?"

Judit glanced around. The stages were almost all packed away in the semis they were stored in and the fairgrounds were flat as far as she could see, except for one or two trees. The other crew were wearing rubber boots and running as fast as they could in the water. She glanced down at her old, very soaked, running shoes. She suddenly remembered Leo's most recent edition of Tourgasm (the man really hated Florida) and his super reassuring factoids about lightning.

The semis were the tallest things around here, right? Taller than the tent for sure.

The world flashed bright as if on cue. Not more than a second later thunder shook the earth, making her stumble and her teeth click together.

She'd never heard it so close before.

"Oh no," Patrick said.

The bad feeling in Judit's stomach twisted and dropped.

"Should we go back to the bus?" she asked, lightning and thunder cracked almost right on top of each other. The water was now ankle-deep, warm, and still rising. If lightning touched down around here, would they get electrocuted?

"I think it's too late for that." He pressed his lips together, looking grim.

"W-what do we do?" Fear and adrenaline thumped in her head like a headache, making it hard to think. Please universe, let Patrick know what to do because she was blanking on everything she'd ever known about storms.

PATRICK HAD no real answer to Judit's question. He had the very unhelpful urge to Google it though he had no bars and hadn't gotten anything even close to 3G let alone 5G in the days since they'd been here.

He took a deep breath, focusing. This was an emergency. They didn't have time to panic and by Judit's wide eyes, she was already halfway there.

Okay, think. The bus was a ten-minute walk in good conditions, less if they ran, but could Judit keep up? Would it be more dangerous to run in these conditions?

The world whited out then shook in a wall of sound. When it cleared, the nearest tree was on fire and the semis were all closed up, the crew piling into the cabs. There was no more room in there.

The tent creaked ominously leaning until a stake came out of the ground. It wouldn't hold much longer. They needed to get out of there. Now.

He grabbed Judit's hand and tugged her towards the storm. "Come on!"

She didn't move. "Out there?" She looked scared and distrustful. He couldn't blame her.

"I won't let anything happen to you. No matter how pissed we are at each other." He held her gaze.

She searched his face and nodded.

He dragged her out in the storm in a doubled-over run.

"Where are we going?" She yelled over the wind, following him.

He had no clue. A ditch seemed like a good idea but it'd be full of water and that couldn't be safe. In the distance, he spotted one of the cinder block bathrooms that were sometimes in this type of fairground.

He pulled her in that direction, going as fast as he could while staying low. She stumbled behind him but managed to keep up.

He slammed into the men's bathroom door just as another double whammy of thunder and lightning overwhelmed his senses. When it was over, he realized two things. One, the door was locked, in fact, it was covered in caution tape. Two, Judit was huddled against his back.

She was warm. Soft, the bare skin of her arms brushing his. Her breath on his neck.

He shook the feelings off.

"It's locked!" he yelled over the wind.

She tugged his hand and led him to the women's restroom. He hesitated. Women's bathrooms were a shelter and he felt like an intruder.

"Come on," she insisted, tugging his hand again and opening the thankfully unlocked door.

He took a breath and followed her in. Desperate times and all.

It was... a bathroom. Gray walls, no lights, no urinals, and maybe slightly cleaner than the men's bathroom would have been. He thought about the caution tape and revised that thought to *much* cleaner.

Judit took a shaky breath, letting go of his hand.

The wind heaved against the walls like it was trying to knock them down, making sounds he couldn't even begin to describe. Thunder shook them again, lightning flashing through the windows but he finally felt kind of safe. He swiped water out of his eyes.

"Thank you," Judit said, not looking at him. "I think I panicked back there."

He shrugged off her thanks. "It happens."

"I wish we'd been able to save the merch though."

"Fuck the merch. You alive is more important any day." His voice sounded harsh bouncing off the cinder block walls.

Her eyes widened. "You're right. But um, will the lost stuff come out of my paycheck?"

Patrick shook his head. "Benji wouldn't do that. Even if they tried, I wouldn't let them."

Judit blinked. "Oh... well thanks. Again." She laughed awkwardly, flicking wet hair out of her eyes. She took her NoN hat off and flipped her hair to the side, squeezing it out, not looking at him.

He couldn't seem to stop looking at her, though. Her dress

was soaked, sticking to every curve and her make-up was smudged around her eyes, making her look vulnerable.

She looked back at him. "You're staring."

"My bad." He tore his gaze away, remorse setting in. *Don't be a creep, Patrick!* He wasn't her employer. He was barely part of the label anymore but still, there was a power imbalance there.

Silence descended, leaking into the areas between the sounds of the storm.

JUDIT DIDN'T DO WELL with awkward silences. Never had, never would. But she wasn't going to break this one. She glanced at her phone. No bars and a visibly declining battery. She put it away hurriedly. The bathroom wasn't especially interesting, not even any inspired graffiti in the stalls or the walls.

She ran the air dryer on as much of her dress as she could, even sticking her head under it though the angle was even more awkward than the silence. (How did she even notice it this much when the storm was so loud?)

"Bored?" Patrick asked when she finished.

She shrugged, looking over at him. He was on her left, leaning against the wall and staring at his phone. "Any reception?"

He shook his head and put it away but not before she saw the picture on his lock screen.

"Aw, is that your cat?" The words popped out of her mouth before she could consider if she wanted the answer.

But the way he smiled shyly and pulled out his phone to show her made her decide maybe she did. "Yeah, that's Scoot."

She peered at the adorable tortie kitty sprawled in what

had to be the world's dorkiest position on her back, paws in the air, apparently asleep. "She's so cute! Does she always sleep like that?"

He chuckled. He had a nice laugh, quiet but deep. Like he was shy about it. "She picks the least comfortable-looking ways to sleep. Sometimes I swear she does it on purpose." He pulled up more photos, flicking through them as Judit made unintelligible squeals, the only appropriate reaction to so much cuteness.

She didn't know how long they spent scrolling. "Is your whole photo roll Scoot pics?"

He chuckled. "Most of it. Is that weird?"

"No," Judit said. "If I had a pet I'd be the same. An embarrassingly large part of my data storage is pictures of other people's pets."

"You want to see something funny?"

Thunder rumbled over them and Judit inched closer to his shoulder. "Um, yeah."

He flicked to a video. "My dad is pet-sitting right now. My Nana is out of town with her new boyfriend."

"Aw, cute! I love older folks dating."

His expression was slightly pained. "It's not as cute when all their dates are in your pool."

"You live with your grandma?"

"Yep, my house is big enough. Sabrina too."

"Cool." She couldn't imagine having a house that big. Or knowing her grandma that well. "I'm kinda jelly. Mine is back in Hungary. I haven't seen her in years."

"Oh," Patrick said. "My mom's mom is kind of distant. Not as far, East Coast, but not big on connecting. Being in a boy band wasn't her definition of successful."

"Rude," Judit said. "Mine's supportive, it's just—" She shrugged. "An expensive flight."

"Fair. I like Nana much better anyway." He pressed play.

In the video, Scoot sat on what looked like a kitchen floor, staring at the camera holder with her big, adorable, round eyes.

"Proof of life, Scoot," said a deep, serious voice from behind the camera.

"My dad," Patrick whispered.

Scoot stared at Patrick's off-screen dad blankly.

"Come on, Scoot, we practiced this. Proof of life."

Blank stare.

His dad sighed. "Okay, fine." A hand picked up a kibble from the bowl next to the cat, holding it up. "Proof of life."

Immediately, Scoot stood on her hind legs, looked into the camera, and made several yipping mews like a tiny coyote. The sound was so unexpected Judit burst into giggles.

"Yes! Good girl!" Patrick's dad threw the kibble and the cat snatched it out of the air with both paws. The video ended.

Patrick sighed. "He always teaches her the worst tricks. Now, she's gonna yell at me every time I go by her food bowl." But he grinned.

"Your dad trains your cat?"

Patrick laughed, the sound echoing gloriously around them. "He tries. I'm pretty sure she's training him though. Scoot knows her own power. I swear she tests out new sounds and looks to see what's most effective."

Judit couldn't help laughing again. "Your tiny Machiavelli."

"Yeah." Patrick smiled. Oh man, she was really starting to like his smile. "Good thing she was born a cat."

Judit realized she was leaning into his shoulder and had been for who knows how long. She could pull back but she didn't. It was a tiny surrender, a momentary truce. He was warm and despite the humid heat, her damp clothes were giving her a bit of a chill. It didn't mean anything.

"Your dad sounds cool," she said.

He stiffened. Shit, she'd stepped on something there. "It's

complicated." He put down his phone but didn't move away from her.

"Understood," she said. "My dad situation is complicated too." The familiar hurt and irritation flashed through her at the thought of her feckless bio-dad, probably out teaching New Age bullshit that bordered on predatory. It was shocking that he hadn't started his own mini-cult but then again he hated feeling tied down to an ideology, let alone people. His beliefs shifted with the wind, the politics, the algorithm... Yeah, there was a reason she blocked him on socials. That and the anti-vax misinformation he was spreading lately.

Patrick sighed. "Parents are weird."

Judit chuckled. "Don't even get me started." She put up her fist. "Daddy issues club?"

"Daddy and granddaddy issues," he said but bumped her fist.

"Way to one-up me," she said, laughing.

"I win?" He made a face halfway between a grimace and a smile.

"Yay?"

They chuckled wryly then lapsed into silence. Comfortable silence. The near-constant wind changed directions and heaved against the door, rattling the frame and causing a draft. Judit shivered in the sudden chill.

"Cold?"

She shrugged, raising her head to look at him. Her neck was stiff from the angle. "You're not?"

He shook his head.

"Lucky."

He glanced away. Bit his lip. Looked back at her. "I'm... um, this is maybe weird but..."

"But?"

"I'm not coming on to you but..."

"*But?*"

He opened his arms. "Do you want to borrow my body heat, in the least creepy way possible?"

She blinked. That had to be the most awkward way to say that. Another draft cut through the building and she felt her muscles tightening in the cold. Did she want to be held by him though? Weren't they like, enemies? *Were* they enemies? She wasn't sure anymore.

Fuck it.

She stepped into his arms. He closed them around her, his touch light. They stood stiffly, barely touching. Damn, this was awkward. She shivered again.

Lightly, he rubbed her shoulder blades.

Slowly, slowly, she relaxed against him, damp clothes against damp clothes but ahhh, he *was* warm. Her arms wrapped around his back. She lay her head against his chest. Ever so tentatively, he rested his cheek against the top of her head, the beginnings of stubble catching in her hair.

The door rattled again and she burrowed deeper against him. His arms tightened and she sighed. How did she feel so comfortable here? She couldn't remember the last time she'd been held. The last time she'd been cuddled. Sometime before her last relationship probably. Maybe during aftercare after a scene, not that she'd participated in many of those. She'd dabbled mostly, occasionally playing but mostly feeling like a tourist. It was hard to let go when you were there with your demi-sister's coworker, even if she was your friend and (former) roommate too.

She pushed Cazzi out of her head before the guilt could take root.

This was nothing. This was platonic. Shared body heat in a way that didn't feel as awkward as she thought it would. (No one needed to know how good it felt, how good he smelled, how her nipples had brushed his chest and sent shocks through her nerves, how she was resisting brushing her lips against his throat.)

At some point, they'd started swaying gently. Like they were slow dancing to the storm.

She closed her eyes and let the moment wash over her. She could figure out what it meant later.

16

"Hello there sailors! This is Steph Infection and you're listening to 105.9
FM. Stay sandy, Miami Beach!"

The storm died down, the daytime darkness slowly lifting.
Patrick had to let her go. She felt so—what? Right? No, that couldn't be. His muscles locked in protest but he forced his arms open, dropping them more abruptly than he'd meant.

She opened her eyes, looking at him in confusion. He gestured at the clearing skies outside of the high, opaque windows. She nodded, stepping back.

The feeling of her soft body against him lingered like the floral scent of her shampoo.

Together, they stepped tentatively out of the bathroom, squinting in the sudden sun. Well, Patrick squinted. Judit pulled out her ever-present sunglasses. They covered her expressive eyes and for some reason, broke the spell of their storm bubble.

Distance yawned between them as they trudged through the mud to the wreckage of the merch booth.

172

Shirts, hats, stickers, and bits of exploded boxes were scattered around, beyond repair. The tent was backed against one of the semis, twisted in an unpromising pretzel. The tables and chairs were scattered about.

Without speaking, Judit began picking up the remains of the merch. Patrick dragged the tables and chairs into a group then regarded the tent with a grimace.

Footsteps squelched up next to him.

"Do you think it's salvageable?" he asked.

"I don't care." Benji grabbed him into a fierce hug. "Tents can be replaced."

"Holy shit, you scared me!" Sabrina slammed into him from the other side.

"Same," Rohan said, putting a hand on his shoulder. "I'm really glad you're okay."

"Out of my way, assholes!" Leo swooped in like a bulldozer, knocking everyone back to lift Patrick into a bone-crushing hug. "You're a fucking dipshit, staying out in that storm!"

"*Dying*," Patrick wheezed, exaggerating only slightly.

Leo laughed and swung him one more time before putting him down. Judit was being bombarded by Helen who shook her friend's shoulders gently and seemed to be vacillating between laughing and crying at her. Judit's gaze caught his, and she wiped a tear from under her sunglasses. But she smiled at him.

It felt like the sun coming out all over again.

THE NEXT MORNING, after they'd dug the buses out of the mud and rode through the night to make up for lost time until they go to their proscribed stop, Patrick sat in his bunk with the curtains drawn and wondered what the fuck was going on with him. When Judit looked at him like that he'd lost any sort of sense and wanted... Well, he had *wanted,* and that shook him more than anything. He hadn't wanted anyone in a long time. His therapist said that was a symptom of not picking himself, said that he didn't know his own needs because he wasn't connected to his body.

Sure, he'd spent ten years at the whim of the label. The only real rebellion he'd had was Cazzi. He'd always told her everything even when it was hush-hush. Almost everything.

He'd been unmoored when Martin left and the band fell apart in his wake. He'd taken the gigs his agent got him. Taken Rohan's stepdad's advice as well as his parents'. Then Hazel came along and dating her meant he didn't have to think too hard about what he wanted. But he'd known it was a mistake. Maybe that's why he hadn't told Cazzi he wasn't single until it was too late.

He remembered the way Cazzi looked that night in the dark, lit only by the lights in his pool. It was right before The Kiss, her laughter and easy banter making him feel lighter than he had in months. He shied away from the memory. It was the last time things were fully good.

Had it really been years ago he'd felt that alive? That couldn't be accurate. He remembered dancing with everybody at the record pull, laughing with Judit after Rohan's release party, holding her—see? He could enjoy shit.

Fuck you, anxiety.

He was in therapy but knowing why his mind was fucking with him didn't always make it easier to accept. Cazzi always accepted him. Until he'd pushed her too far and she'd kicked him out of her life.

If he was a responsible, reasonable adult he'd make that phone appointment his therapist wanted him to make and talk about all this.

He looked at his phone. But if he talked about it, it'd be real. All these weird moments with Judit, how constantly tired he was, how hard it was to let go of Cazzi even though he was trying.

A shadow loomed by the side of his bunk and his curtain drew back. "Am I interrupting your emo moment?" Sabrina said, sounding a lot more casual than her tight expression. She was worried about him. Again.

"Knock, will you?"

"On a curtain?"

"I'm trying to have some illusion of privacy here."

She barked a laugh. "Good luck."

He rolled his eyes at her. "Did you need something, Briny?"

She stuck her tongue out at him. "Don't call me that."

"Don't be annoying and I won't."

"Ugh! You're such an ass." She crossed her arms. "Your white giant is asking if you can come out and play. He doesn't wanna come back in because he's afraid the A/C might make him 'sweat more when he goes out.'" She snorted.

He got up, not because he wanted to talk to Leo but because if he kept brooding, he'd never stop.

Sabrina lowered her voice. "You sure you're okay? Sitting in the dark is..." She grimaced.

"I'm fine."

"You can talk to me, you know."

"I'm talking to you right now."

"You sound like Dad when he's being all man of the house."

Patrick frowned. "Not true. I talk a lot more than he does." Dad had loosened up over the years but he hadn't been ready for kids when Patrick came along and thought the best way was the strict way. The way Grandpa Pat raised him. Dad let go of that view as Sabrina grew up but Patrick had already left to join the Beatboyz by then. Sometimes, it felt like Sabrina had gotten off easy.

"Barely." She frowned. "Especially lately."

He shrugged. "I'm just not used to touring. I forgot how exhausting it is."

"You should come to some of the afterparties sometime."

"What part of *exhausting* says I need more shit to do?"

She wasn't listening. "Or maybe we should get out, explore the local scene."

He sighed. "No, Sabs, seriously. I do not need to get out more. I've been out. I spent ten years touring."

"And you did lots of crazy stuff, blah, blah, blah. Yeah, I know," Sabrina rolled her eyes.

A knock sounded on the door. It opened and Leo called, "You coming or what?"

Patrick sighed and edged around his sister. Leo brightened at the sight of him. He'd been clingy since the storm yesterday.

"What's up?" he asked.

"I needed to talk to someone who wasn't an up-and-coming comedian," Leo said, shaking his head. He'd picked up a couple of fans in the local comedy duo Nick booked on this leg of the tour. They were an odd addition to the lineup but as long as they didn't try to talk to him, Patrick didn't care. "Those two think they're so funny."

"They're all right," Patrick offered, strolling away from the bus. He caught bits of their show and it was reasonably entertaining.

"Exactly," Leo said, following him. "All right is all they are. But they think they're the funniest thing since sliced bread."

"You have to admit slicing bread is a laugh fest."

"Oh, no doubt. A dangerous amount of laughing happens around sliced bread," Leo said like this was a normal thing to say. "Probably more than happens around those two."

"Ouch," Patrick said. "Shady."

"I know, I know." Leo sighed. "They're just getting on my nerves."

They fell into companionable silence.

"So what's with Judit?" Leo asked. "Do we still hate her? Because I'm getting mixed messages."

Patrick schooled his expression. "You make it sound like we're some high school girl clique."

"Oh yes, I forgot you were too straight for girly shit."

"You know that's not how I meant it." Patrick frowned. "I didn't hate her."

"Oh? You've changed your mind?"

"No, I was just very irritated with her."

"But now?" Leo was looking far too invested in this.

"Now..." He wasn't sure. Being near her had a reverb, a shivering awareness. That moment, when she touched him and everything disappeared but her finger on his chest, her palm, her fist... When she leaned against him during the storm, her frizzing hair tickling his cheek when she said sweet things about Scoot. When he'd held her... "It's different."

"Different, how?" Leo was completely focused on Patrick. "Give me the tea. Don't be all cryptic."

Patrick shook his head. "She's Cazzi's friend. I don't think we'll ever get along."

"Even if you patch it up with Cazzi?" Leo cocked his head. "I thought that was your endgame."

Patrick shrugged. "I think Judit's opinion of me is set." He refused to think about the way she'd snuggled into him, almost nuzzling his neck, her breath warm against his skin, her fingers tracing his ribs—had she known she was doing that?

"Hmmm." Leo regarded him.

"What?" Patrick bristled. He didn't like the way his friend was looking at him, like he was a project.

"Does that bother you?"

"What? The way you're taking my measurements with your eyes?"

"Well, I have to. You're so skinny. I like to make sure you don't waste away. You've never even been gay chubby have you?" This from the man whose biceps threatened to eclipse his head.

"Fuck off." Sure, there had been once or twice during the grind of touring and practicing and recording where he'd been too stressed to eat to the point of almost fainting onstage but that was long ago. He made it a point to eat regularly these days.

Leo waved that away. "I'm kidding, I'm kidding. All bodies are beautiful and Rick, you damn well know you're hot."

Patrick ignored this. "What were you hmmming about?"

"What?" Leo squinted, thinking back. "Oh yes! Does it bother you Judit may never like you?"

Yes. "No. Why should it?"

"Uh-huh." Leo's gaze searched his face, looking for the truth. But he'd never been as good at reading him as Cazzi had been.

The thought of her was a dull stab in his stomach.

Leo pointed at his face. "I saw that, you liar. You do care!"

He shook his head. "I was just missing Cazzi."

Leo frowned. "You're going to have to get over her if you're even thinking about being with someone else."

"*What?*" Patrick squawked.

"Oh, we're not there?" Leo rubbed his nose in embarrassment. He grimaced ruefully. "A friend told me recently that I jump to romance way too fast. Maybe he was right."

Patrick patted Leo's shoulder. "You fell for him?"

Leo's grimace deepened. "I was getting there. I bought him flowers and he shut me down real quick."

"Ouch." Patrick winced in sympathy.

Leo shrugged, old misery making his words brittle. "At least I didn't get in too deep before we figured that out."

Patrick patted his shoulder blade awkwardly. "You'll find your future husband someday."

Leo blew out a breath. "I sure hope so, you know I just want to retire and be a trophy wife." He laughed.

Patrick smiled. "I know. I've seen the shirt."

17

Post Tour, Post NoN Ideas
Score that indie film (the depressing one or the buddy comedy? both?)
Do album? Covers? Tom Morello-style collabs?
~~Endorsements?~~
~~Get a real job~~
—Patrick's Notes App

Judit was having a strange few days. Angela Alice and Martin Mejia were gone, the fest was on the move to the next spot, but there was still something strange in the air. She noticed Leo and Rohan talking at the motel they'd stopped between venues but when she joined them they obviously changed the subject. They hadn't looked like they'd even showered yet and Judit knew for a fact Leo had a fit if he couldn't get a hot shower. She later saw Rohan and Benji whispering and looking at her. She tried not to freak out about it. She was probably just reading too much into coincidences.

She had been doing a good job of avoiding Patrick, at least. Though, she wasn't at all sure that she was the only one doing the avoiding. She'd caught him edging out of rooms she'd just entered and taking sharp turns when he'd seen her.

Ugh, he gave her whiplash. One minute, he was holding her like he never wanted to let her go, then the next he was a foot away looking like he never wanted to touch her again. Fuckwittage, as Bridget Jones would say. Yeah, no thank you. She didn't need that in her life, even if he was nice to look at and even nicer to feel and...

Nope. Nope. Nope.

Now, they were in yet another freshly thrown-together festival ground. She was fairly certain they were in Georgia somewhere but her grasp on where they were was fraying. The festival layout was always the same. Walking the grounds, she squinted at the trees and the surrounding areas. Except she didn't know a damn thing about trees. It was still humid though. Georgia was humid, right?

She stopped at the Green Brew stage and waved at Cedric as he set up lights with the other techs. She was learning their names. They were learning hers. They all waved back. It was almost like a family slowly forming around her. They weren't friends but if she had a problem, she knew they'd help her and vice versa. She didn't hate it.

Rohan jogged by. He'd already lapped her twice but she waved anyway. He ran backward for a second to flash her a thumbs up. By the grin on his face, he was counting down the days until Cazzi arrived, on a detour from some conference she and Eva were attending. It'd be nice to see them.

If Patrick didn't make it weird.

Footsteps trudged next to her and for a split second, she thought she'd summoned him. She turned to see Sabrina walking up, her hair caught in a fluffy ponytail. She nodded at Judit, in the walking part of a jog, judging by her bright blue workout gear.

Sabrina popped out an earbud. "Morning."

"Morning," Judit replied, wondering what she wanted. People who joined her on these walks inevitably wanted something. Yesterday, the guys from some band called Creepmother pressed a flier for some afterparty into her hands and told her to "bring all her hot friends."

Why was it so hard to have a normal conversation with someone who just wanted to chat? Well, there was Helen but they had opposing schedules. Rohan was nice but he was too busy to hang out. The dancers had formed a clique, the comedians were annoying, the musicians were all partiers or introverts who needed to show you how deep they were, Leo was Patrick's, and Benji was busy as fuck. The crew, though friendly, seemed divided from them all by some invisible line.

Sabrina kept pace with her and regarded her through her sunglasses. Judit let the silence stretch between them.

Sabrina sighed. "Don't tell me you're not a talker. I couldn't handle another strong, silent type."

"I'm just not sure what you want," Judit said.

"Oh," Sabrina said, brightening. "That's easy. I'm trying to figure out what the hell is going on with you and my brother."

Judit frowned. "Nothing."

"Really? I thought y'all were cool after the storm."

Judit shrugged. "Sort of? I'm Team Cazzi. Rohan got me in the divorce."

"You're tied up in that whole mess?" Sabrina frowned.

"Unfortunately."

Sabrina shook her head. "Cazzi's all right but she's making my brother miserable."

Judit bristled. "I think the feeling is mutual."

"It's that twin flame bullshit." Sabina sighed. "They need to get over it."

"Oh, one hundred percent. But you know, that shit's obvious from the outside. Not really from the inside," Judit said, remembering all the people who'd warned her about moving in with her last relationship. It was incredibly annoying, proving them right.

Sabrina nodded. "True. True. Hey, what happened the other day when you brought Patrick back to the bus?"

"You'll have to ask him about that."

Sabrina groaned. "Come on. I'm worried about him. There's no talking to him. He talks almost as little as our dad does sometimes and there are dead people who talk more than Dad in quiet mode." She paused and reconsidered. "Except when he's lecturing. Then you can't shut him up."

"If I found out he was a danger to himself or anyone, you'd be the first person I'd call," Judit said. It was what she'd want to happen if she was in Sabrina's place and Eva was worrying her.

Sabrina nodded. Her breathing went ragged for a second and she swiped her cheek. "Thanks. Means a lot."

"Of course," Judit said, resisting the urge to hug her. They weren't there yet. "Are you worried about something?"

Sabrina shrugged. "I don't know. He's so closed off and sometimes I just get in my head, worrying, you know? Like, I'm the reason he's here. What if that's making him worse?"

Judit nodded. "That's a lot to put on yourself. I mean, he's a grown adult who chose to be here and he's choosing to stay, right?"

"True."

"If you want, I can do a quick reading for you about it."

"Maybe." Sabrina smiled. "Thanks."

They spent the rest of the walk chatting about everything but Patrick. They parted ways at the bus when Sabrina decided to go for another lap. It was nice.

Judit climbed aboard, ready to read for a bit before her shift. She heard Patrick's voice a second before she saw him. He stood in front of Leo's door, talking to him while the other man lounged in his doorway.

Patrick looked good. More than good. Uncomfortably good, with those taut shoulders, his narrow waist, and the cascade of neat locs drawing her eye to the muscles of his back. Every nerve turned on and she stopped dead.

"Hi Judit!" Leo called, too loud for the enclosed space, waving madly. Was he warning Patrick she was here? (Did he think Patrick didn't have eyes?)

She waved back weakly.

Patrick turned, looked at her, and glanced away immediately. He gave her an awkward nod, his gaze somewhere past her left shoulder.

Whatever, at least he wasn't staring at her. Oh, the way he had looked at her in that dingy bathroom... the way he held her... (ugh, shut up brain.)

She shucked her shoes, and climbed into her bunk, shutting the curtains as hard as she could close curtains. But she still had to put in her earbuds to drown out the rumble of his voice.

PATRICK WAS GETTING SETTLED backstage when he heard it. Judit. Talking to his sister. He listened. They were laughing. Their conversation sounded comfortable, easy-going. That was new.

Well, Sabrina had always been better at flirting with girls than he was.

He saw them coming around the corner and realized Rohan was with them. They squished together and took a selfie. Probably some social media shit. Patrick had been avoiding that all tour. He did his obligatory social media maintenance but the sheer number of people who still liked, commented, and DM'd him was unnerving. He didn't like strangers in person. Why would he like them better on the internet?

A reminder buzzed on his phone, the same one that'd been coming up every day for the past week or so. *Schedule appointment.*

He ignored it, opening his notes app and staring down at his post-tour, post-NoN project idea list. He was in talks to score another indie film but that was a charity project. He liked composing film scores and supporting creative projects outside of the big industry machines.

Maybe he could open his own production studio. He made a note to check with his lawyer about the non-compete clause in his NoN contract. Benji was way too thorough to be fucked with. Not that Patrick wanted another label. Hell no. Too much admin. But music was his calling, his talent, and the only thing he felt qualified to make money off of. That big house he owned wouldn't pay its own mortgage and though his mother had helped him invest his money, he didn't feel comfortable going without income.

Sure, NoN didn't exactly pay the bills—the investments covered those—but he felt more stable knowing there was a paycheck coming, especially supporting his Nana and sister. They made their own money but they didn't pay rent and he never wanted to be in a position where he had to charge them. Though, if Doc Conjure took off, Sabrina might be living somewhere else sooner rather than later.

The thought made him glance at his sister—just in time to see Sabrina grin at Judit. It'd been a while since he'd seen her look at someone like that. Sabrina hadn't had any big heartbreaks he'd heard about but a long series of disappointments had shrunk her smile more and more. Was she crushing on Judit, now? Why her, of all people?

Judit grinned back. Rohan had slipped away at some point after the photo and stood a ways away, on the phone.

Patrick couldn't stop looking at Judit. She hadn't smiled at him like that even before he'd been an ass to her. She probably never would.

He hated how that realization felt like a loss. He didn't need to be liked by everyone. But Judit wasn't everyone. She was kind, probably to a fault. Funny, pretty, strong—

Oh hell, he really was attracted to her, wasn't he?

Her gaze flicked in his direction and Judit saw him. The stillness took him, quieting the fizzle and pop of his nervous system. He didn't know what to do with the fact that she stilled every time now too.

This time she was the one to turn away.

THEY HAD DONE SO WELL at avoiding each other but now he was everywhere and Judit couldn't understand it. Didn't they have a good staying-away thing going? Why did he have to go and ruin it?

He passed by when she worked in the booth, helping Benji carry something.

He ran by her with Leo while she did her daily walk.

He ate lunch at the same time, dinner at the same time, sometimes even breakfast.

And he stared. Every time. He had the fucking *gall* to look shocked every time he saw her. Who did he think he was fooling?

She wanted to confront him but what if he looked at her like that again and she um, did something regrettable?

It was almost a relief when she opened up the booth and it was just him waiting there.

"What are you doing here?" He asked as if her name

hadn't been on the roster like everyone else's. Well, not his, not for this shift.

"I work here." She was tired and crampy. She'd hoped with her erratic IUD-blocked menstruation she'd skip the whole period thing this summer but *nooo*. If he wanted a fight, he'd come to the right place. "What's your excuse?"

"Leo asked to switch shifts with me so he could hang out with a friend."

Judit shrugged, wishing someone fucking warned her.

"We keep running into each other." He sounded puzzled. Did he think she was stalking him or something?

She snorted, booting up the tablet. "You're the one who stopped avoiding me." It wasn't until she heard the hitch in her voice that she realized, him avoiding her had *hurt*.

He jerked his gaze away from the boxes where he had been checking their stock, taking her in. "I thought you were avoiding me too," he said quietly.

"I was. But only because you started it." Her throat constricted. Oh fuck, now was *not* the time for her period to wreak havoc on her hormones. Because that was the only reason she was having this much of a reaction. She didn't care what he thought about her. Or if he did, at all.

He took a step towards her. Hesitated. Reached out—

She turned away. If he touched her, she'd cry and that was not how she wanted to start her shift.

"I'm sorry," he said. "I'm still processing—"

"It's fine. How are you with ringing up?" He'd worked shifts with Helen. Her friend hadn't complained so Judit figured Patrick could hold his own.

"I can do it but you want me to do the people stuff."

She turned back to look at him. "What now?"

He smiled tentatively. "Trust me."

She blinked because *holy shit*, she was having flashbacks to the poster above her dresser in her childhood bedroom where

Ricky Rick had shyly smiled at her for years. "Um." What the fuck was this? He was barely smiling! She shook her head and snapped her mouth shut because yeah, she'd been that embarrassingly stunned. "Okay, fine. Whatever. How are we on smalls? I don't want to run out again."

He turned to check but not before she saw his smile get real. Just a glimpse but fuck, how had she forgotten his signature boy band smile had nothing on Patrick actually smiling. Good thing he was so grumpy.

Not that any of their customers would've guessed. Fans were treated with firm respect and manners that would make any mother proud. Normal customers were charmed by his practiced smiles and easy banter. He was *good* at this. People bought extra and were distinctly happier when they came to check out.

"Are you a changeling?" she asked during a lull.

He bounced on his heels and chuckled. "This is nothing. You should've seen me ten years ago."

"Sit." She patted the chair beside hers. "We still have three hours. I don't want you getting heat stroke. You're too tall to drag back to the bus."

He shook his head, taking a sip of water. "If I sit down I won't get up."

She shrugged. "Suit yourself." She appreciated he wasn't actively being an asshole but the energy he threw off made her antsy.

Leo stopped by a while later and gave Patrick an incredulous look. "Are you in full Ricky Rick mode?"

Patrick bowed with a flourish like he was on stage.

Leo laughed. Then he leaned over to Judit and whispered, "Keep an eye on him. He's going to crash hard. Call me if you need me to carry him."

She thought Leo was joking but when they packed up the booth and headed back to the bus the hyper customer service vibe faded. His steps dragged, his shoulders slumped. He hauled himself straight into bed, falling into his bunk like dead weight.

"You good?" she asked, after watching him lie there unmoving for a full minute.

"Fine," he mumbled into the pillow.

Sabrina came out of the bathroom, hair wrapped, and looked at her brother. "Did you give yourself heatstroke?"

"No," he told his pillow.

"He was very social at the booth?" Judit said, annoyed at her tentative tone. "Leo called it 'full Ricky Rick' mode."

Sabrina sighed and poked his shoulder. "Go wash your face and wrap your locs, you'll thank me in the morning."

Patrick grumbled, curling into the covers like a recalcitrant kid, shooting his sister a dirty look from between the bars. It was kinda cute and Judit suppressed a giggle. He dragged himself out of bed and to the bathroom.

Sabrina looked at Judit. "You know why he did that, don't you?"

Judit shook her head. She was a card reader, not a mind reader.

Sabrina sighed, leaning her head on Judit's shoulder. She turned out to be one of those touchy-feely friends. Judit didn't mind. Being single always made her skin hungry. "You know who's coming tomorrow."

Yeah, sure Eva and—

Judit's eyes widened. Of course, it hadn't been about her. It never was with Patrick.

Patrick woke up groggy with the all-consuming knowledge that Cazzi was coming to the show tonight. That he slept at all was an exhaustion-induced miracle, one he had worked his ass off for.

She was coming and he had no idea what to do or say. No one would tell him when Cazzi was coming in. No one would've told him she was coming at all but she'd texted him.

He reread the message. *I'm stopping by the festival tomorrow. We can talk if you want. Cool if you don't.*

She was trying so hard not to put pressure on him. Like he was delicate or something.

Okay, he'd texted back, for the first time since their fight. *Tell me when and where. I'll be there.*

The thing was, he wasn't sure he really wanted to see her, but he couldn't stop thinking about it. If he skipped seeing her, he'd regret it.

He spent the day a nervous wreck.

At breakfast, Leo pulled him aside. "Do you need anything? I can loom menacingly behind you if you want."

"What? Why?"

"You're gonna go hash it out with whatsername, your secret best friend you never told me about until she broke your heart."

"You're still salty about that, aren't you?" Patrick said, trying to not think about the fact she hadn't even texted him back yet.

"Absolutely. I take all the secrets you don't share with me deeply personally. Not the point though. In all seriousness, do you need support?"

Patrick forced a smile. "I'm fine."

"Yeah, sure. Text me when it's over, okay?"

"Mmhmm."

Sabrina cornered him on the bus as he was getting ready

for their set. "Hey, I just wanted to say: I'm here if you need me."

He didn't bother pretending ignorance this time. "I'm not as fragile as everyone seems to think I am."

She flinched. Then her lips pressed flat and she said, "Don't snap at me. I'm trying to be a supportive sister and shit."

He gentled his tone. "Sorry, I know I've been kind of all over the place about this."

She raised an eyebrow.

"But," he continued. "I'm trying to move past what happened." He realized this was the first time he'd admitted it out loud. "I'm not trying to get her back or anything."

"You sure?"

Maybe. Probably. Out of the corner of his eye, he saw Judit passing the bus, beelining it for the booth, the wind plastering her dress to her front and her long skirt billowing behind her.

"I'm sure," he said.

Replacing one girl for another? Asked a nasty voice in his head.

He shut the thought down. His attraction to Judit wouldn't go anywhere. It was safe like that. Even if she had sounded hurt that he'd been avoiding her.

"I hope so," Sabrina said. "See you backstage."

Sabrina, who Judit was definitely more into than she was into him. Right.

He finished putting the finishing touches on his stage outfit after Sabrina left. He'd started out with skintight jeans and an assortment of flattering shirts. The heat and the much lower standards of the other rock bands had been a bad influence on him. Now, he wore a still-flattering tank top, decent enough shorts, comfortable shoes, sweatbands on his wrists, and a bandana to keep the sun off his head. And nobody fucking cared. What a revelation.

Despite everything happening today, he looked forward to

the set. It would be a relief to get lost in the music and the controlled chaos Sabrina brought to the stage.

He was about to head out when his phone buzzed. Just the reminder again. He cleared it. If he could figure this out, maybe he could stop going to therapy. Sure, he was still planning to detonate his professional life the minute the tour was over, no matter how his feelings shook out, but that wasn't something he hadn't survived before.

He'd bounce back again. Probably.

He played his set, he waited backstage, he wandered the grounds. Fans recognized him and he did the selfie thing, pulling on the dregs of his social reserves.

Then the text came. He followed it and waited. Leaning against the back of the empty LadyWater stage. Early. That was okay. There wasn't another band playing here for at least an hour, no roadies around. Just him, the humid air, and the magnolia trees.

He tried to rehearse lines like he knew what he'd say but mostly he tried to keep his head above the memories.

Cazzi daring him to do the talent show that he got scouted at.

Cazzi in his arms at the beach, broken and scared after what happened to Tanya.

Cazzi telling him he had her favorite voice of all time when he doubted his talent.

Cazzi kissing him. Her face when he had to tell her about Hazel.

Her smile when he FaceTimed her for the first time after ghosting her.

The taste of the coconut chocolate chip cookies she always baked when he was in town.

Him kissing her and her eyes going dreamy like she'd gotten everything she'd ever longed for.

Her trying not to cry when she banished him from her life.

Her in the distance, straight-backed and masking her emotions on Rohan's arm at the release party.

The way she was looking at him right now.

18

"We don't need ghosts here
The hate, the love, the arguments
Have soaked in
I taste them in my sleep
Along my skin they creep
In this empty house

It's a hundred outside
But in here, it snows
My teeth chatter
Like it matters
I sit here
I did this
I carved you in
I pried you out

I echo in the halls
I am the only one who calls
It just keeps ringing
The only thing singing

To me

The pity of silence
Is my only guidance
As I scrub you out of
My empty house"
— "Empty House" by Angela Alice off of *Romance Inverted*

Cazzi stood in front of Patrick. The lines of her body were taut, her eyes wide, the few freckles that survived adulthood stood out against the paleness of her skin. If he moved wrong she'd bolt.

He straightened slowly, remembering the way she used to flinch when he moved too fast. That was right after what happened to Tanya but she looked just as skittish now. The realization squeezed his heart until it felt like it would stop.

"Hey Caz," he said.

"Hey Pat." Her voice was breathy and rough. She'd cultivated it to be smooth and soothing over her years in grad school but that was just another mask.

He didn't know what to say, how to start. "How was the flight?"

She shrugged. "Flying's weird now."

"Yeah."

They fell silent. He couldn't stop looking at her. What if he glanced away and she was gone? Would that hurt or would it be a relief?

"I missed you," he said. That, at least, he knew to be true.

She choked on something that sounded like a cross between a laugh and a sob. "You missed *me*?"

"I know, I know." He scrubbed his hand over his face. "It's my fault. It's all my fault."

She made a hurt noise in the back of her throat. "Maybe we can start over, Pat. Be friends again?"

He looked her straight in the eye. Her pupils were huge, something she'd always told him signaled attraction. Her breath came rabbit quick. He took a step towards her.

She touched one of the sigils tattooed on her arms and stabilized herself, her breathing evening out. He remembered when she'd gotten into sigil magic in college, how she used to send him pictures of what she'd drawn on her arms to tell him how she was doing today by how many she needed. Now, they were all tattoos, marching up her forearms. She tilted her chin up, not like she wanted a kiss but like she wanted a fight.

He stopped. "Can I hug you?"

She considered the request. Her eyes were clearer, her pupils smaller. Angela might be the scariest woman he'd ever met but Cazzi was steel when she needed to be. She had to be or she'd have fallen apart years ago. "Let's talk first," she said. "Clear the air."

He nodded.

"This unfinished conversation is killing me," she said. "I need to close it. I don't want to lose you but I can't—" Her composure slipped, her expression crumpling. She touched another sigil, the ritual grounding her, smoothing her face. "I can't keep doing this. It's untenable, not just because you're my best friend, but because we have too many people in common."

"Okay," he said, gathering himself.

"Okay? Okay, what?" She demanded.

"Okay, I'm sorry."

"What..." Her voice cracked along with her composure.

"I'm sorry. I-I thought I loved you. Could love you, that way."

Her fingers moved up to the last sigil on that arm. Her face went smooth, masked. Her voice was dead-sounding when she said, "Did you think I wanted to talk to you alone to see if you loved me the way I used to love you? Is that why you agreed to see me?"

The way she put him in the past tense was both painful and a relief. He shook his head. "I've been struggling with this."

"Yeah, well, join the club." She snorted. "I'm head over fucking heels for Rohan. I'm *marrying* him. I don't need your angst, your pining, or your unrequited love. I just want to know if there's any chance we can be friends again."

"I don't know," he admitted. "I think kissing you might be my biggest fuck-up." He wanted to take them back the minute the words left his mouth. They were too true, too raw.

She made a small sound like someone had punched her in the solar plexus, taking all her air. The fingers on her arm dug in, contracting like claws. "Right back at you. Why did you kiss me?"

This was where he could tell her, where she'd understand. "It wasn't about you, Grandpa Pat cheated on Nana and—"

"And, what, you were using me to prove you weren't him?"

The words hit him like a slap. His ears rang, his stomach dropped. For a second he couldn't see, couldn't breathe. It sounded so shitty when she said it aloud.

"Not consciously—"

"So, I was an afterthought?"

"You were an obsession! You've been haunting me for years and I just want it to stop!"

"Right back at you, asshole! I hate thinking about you!" She covered her mouth like that would help anything. "Fuck," she said through her fingers. "How did we get so good at hurting each other?"

He shook his head helplessly, afraid to speak. Words slipped out anyway. "I'm sorry, Tawny."

She sobbed and he moved without thinking, gathering her to him. "I'm sorry, I'm sorry," he whispered over and over into her hair.

She clutched at him, burying herself in his embrace like she used to when the world and her trauma overwhelmed her. She cried silently, the way she always did, but he could feel the fine shudder of her shoulders, the way he always could.

He hated to let her go, but could they even be friends if all they did was hurt each other without trying?

THE MINUTE JUDIT SAW CAZZI, she knew. Her friend had that emotionally fucked-up look even her masking couldn't cover.

"Saw Patrick?" Judit asked when Cazzi came to stand next to her and Eva in the VIP tent running next to the side of the GreenBrew stage. Rohan was due on stage any minute.

"Yes." Her eyes were red and bloodshot but she seemed sober. Judit was betting on tears over pot anyway.

Eva sighed. "Did it help?"

Cazzi considered it. "Maybe," she said, sinking into the chair behind her (the VIP tent had chairs! Also, a bar but it only served GreenBrew and LadyWater).

Eva shook her head. "Twin flames. I'm telling you. Just let him go."

"I'm not in love with him," Cazzi said defensively. "I just don't want to give up the person who's always understood me."

"Doesn't seem like he's understanding you now," Eva muttered.

Judit shook her head.

"You gonna tell Rohan?" Eva asked.

Cazzi exhaled hard. "Yes. Later. When I've processed it."

"Just promise me you won't ruin a good thing over that asshole," Eva grumbled.

Judit found herself bristling. Why? Because her demi-sister

was calling Patrick something she'd called him a thousand times in her head?

"Fuck off," Cazzi snarled. "You know me better than that."

Judit blinked. It was always weird to hear Cazzi snap. She was so often even-keel. But then again, nothing and no one made her defensive like Patrick.

Eva shut up with an irritable sound.

The undercurrent of tension stretched through the show even as they clapped, screamed, and sang along. Rohan was on his game and with every love song his eyes lingered on Cazzi. She glowed under his gaze, seeming to forget her hang-ups on Patrick. If she was anyone else, Rohan would've probably pulled her up on stage and kissed her at the end of the show, he had that look in his eye.

He settled for sweeping her off the minute the encore was over.

Judit and Eva walked the grounds, watching the crowds stream out now the headliner was done.

"That Patrick is such trouble," Eva said, shaking her head.

Judit made a non-committal noise. She wanted to agree but somehow she couldn't. Yes, Patrick and Cazzi should never be together. Yes, he constantly pissed Judit off. Yes, he was grumpy, annoying, prickly, and... yet.

"How's the conference?" Judit asked.

Eva shrugged. "It's a general university-level conference so everyone is freaking out about the state of education and funding. Throw COVID into all that and it's a hot mess. Most people don't know us but the people who do either love or hate us." She sighed. "Honestly, it would've been more fun to spend the day here." She launched into a story about some asshole who decided to tell them off for corrupting the children during his question to their panel. "It was more of a comment than a question," Eva said with a laugh.

Judit laughed with her. "How about the Condom Pixies

program? Any issues there?" she asked as if Eva didn't text her about her work all the time.

Eva smiled. "Nah, we're still throwing condoms at students. The local naysayers have moved on. I hear the dance department was putting on something mildly scandalous."

"Nice, nice." Judit was grasping at straws, looking for something to distract Eva from the eventual big sister concern she'd pull out in three, two——

"How's the tour going?" Eva looked at her in concern. "You holding up? I hear these things can be pretty grueling."

Judit shrugged. "It's good. I'm fine." She knew Eva meant well but Judit was used to handling herself. She was an adult, dammit. She was flailing a bit but still.

"You're taking care of yourself?" Eva pressed. "Don't do that overworking thing artists love to do. That work all day, party all night shit isn't for you."

Judit bit her tongue against her first response. "I'm taking care of myself," she said, "You know I couldn't party all night if I tried."

Eva chuckled. "Fair. Just remember, your health is worth more than this gig."

"I *know*."

"Okay, okay, I'll lay off." Eva raised her hands in defeat. "No, wait, I lied. Did you start on that five-year plan thing your mom is making you do?"

Judit groaned. She hadn't thought about it at all. Well, not since her mom brought it up during their last call.

Eva patted her back. "You've got time to figure it out. You can always bounce ideas off of me. I bet if we structure it right, we could figure out how to make your reading profitable enough to get her off your back."

Judit grabbed her in a one-armed hug. "Appreciate you."

"You better," Eva said with a wink.

They walked until Judit had to sit. Eva headed back to her

hotel. Judit sat on the empty bench after her demi-sister left, taking in the silence. There was no silence on the bus, let alone privacy. She stared at the stars.

There were more here than she could usually see in Sacramento. It was lovely to be out at night and feel safe. She'd missed that about living in Clementine. Midtown was great—during the day. At night though? She hadn't been prepared for the badly lit streets, the number of people wandering them, or the shit they got up to in the alley behind her apartment. But here on tour, now that the audience was gone, she knew pretty much everyone within their little fenced-in circus.

Someone sat on the other side of the bench. She tensed, startled. He sighed and she knew him without looking. So she didn't look. She tensed for an entirely different reason.

"How is she?" he asked after a while.

"Stay away from her," Judit said, disappointed but not surprised. Of course, he'd ask about Cazzi.

"Planning on it," he said.

"What?" She gave in and looked at him. His locs were down, despite the lingering heat, shrouding his expression. He sat, head bowed, hands clasped.

"It's over, I think. Whatever was left."

Shit, what do you say to that? Judit reached out, hesitated, mentally shrugged, and patted his shoulder with the tips of her fingers. Once. Twice.

He shot her a wry look.

She gave him a "what do you want from me" shrug.

The side of his mouth tipped up in a sad smile. "I know you're happy about this."

"I mean, I think it's for the best." She shrugged again. "It's hard to watch both of you suffer."

"I'm surprised you haven't written me off yet."

She snorted. "You underestimate the softness of my heart."

"You don't have to feel sorry for me just because you're into my sister."

"I'm—what?"

"It's cool. I have eyes."

"But, I'm not—We're not—" She liked Sabrina. She was gorgeous and sweet but Judit's feelings were friend-love not romantic or sexual. Not that it was his business.

"Oh." He ducked his head and Judit bet if she touched his cheek it'd be scalding. "Awkward."

"Did she—"

"No, no, I jumped to conclusions."

"Oh. Cool."

"Yeah."

They sat in uncomfortable silence for a while.

"I should probably get some sleep," Judit said.

"Yeah, me too."

Neither of them moved.

"It's so quiet out here," he said.

"The bus is so loud," she said.

He sighed. "I'm so tired. All the time."

"Same."

"Merch is hard."

She echoed his sigh. "It's not just merch."

"Yeah, I didn't miss touring and this hasn't changed my mind."

"I think I could've liked it if I wasn't in pain every day." She regretted the words as they left her mouth but she was at the honest point of tired.

He furrowed his brow at her. "Old injury?"

She shook her head. "No injury and no diagnosis. Don't have the money to get one and didn't have insurance when I was back home."

He was quiet for a moment. "Have you tried herbalism?"

She groaned, fuck being polite. At least he hadn't told her to try yoga or prayer but jeez.

"I'm a certified herbalist," he said.

"Wait, what?" She stared. That explained the root.

"I don't practice on anyone but friends and family and I don't think I can cure you but I could help with the pain if you're interested."

She considered. Maybe she could stop rationing her CBD gummies. A memory poked at her: Cazzi's extensive tea collection. Didn't she say...? She closed her eyes, trying to capture the memory: Cazzi inhaling tea steam and getting teary-eyed.

"You made Cazzi's teas?"

He nodded. "I won't charge."

She searched his face, but he looked sincere. He *felt* sincere. "Thank you. I'll think about it."

Her phone buzzed and she glanced at it. Who the fuck texts someone this late asking whether you'll be at a reunion a full season away? "Ugh."

"Hmm?"

She shook her head. "Post-tour bullshit."

"Lay it on me."

"Really?

He shrugged. "I need the distraction."

"If you insist," she said and way too many words spilled into the night. "My high school reunion is at the end of the year and I'm not weird, successful, or interesting enough. I didn't even start a fucking vanlife cult. I don't have enough time, money, energy, or spoons to do all the things I'm supposed to do to perfect my platform, brand, or network. I can't even make a five-year plan to get my mom off my back."

"Huh," he said. "Are your classmates on tour with the biggest moving festival since Warped Tour?"

She made a face at him. "Stop being reasonable."

He chuckled. "We can always start a cult if you want. I bet Leo would be down. We already live on a bus."

She laughed. "Oh shit! You're right!"

He stood with another chuckle. "I need to go pass out in said bus." He held out his hand.

She frowned. "Don't baby me just cuz I'm in chronic pain."

"You helped me, maybe I just want to return the favor."

"Fine." She put her hand in his. It was warm, his long fingers wrapping around her palm.

He hauled her up, surprisingly strong. She found herself less than an inch from him, looking up.

What would it be like to kiss him? The thought lodged itself into her brain and she couldn't look away from his lips. If she just stood on tiptoes...

He looked down at her, so close she could hear how shallow his breath was.

He cleared his throat, let go of her hand, and took a step back.

That was that.

19

Five Year Plan

~~*In this five year plan, I will …*~~

Year 1: Find a job with health insurance (full-time? Are there part-time jobs that provide benefits? Can I get an office job without a degree? Would it destroy my body? Places are still work from home right?) Boost social media without being creepy to all the celebs I now know, get to over 2k followers on at least one platform, do 3+ online readings a week? (Is that enough? Should I make a monetary goal? Shit, do I need to make a budget? Should I start an LLC?)

Year 2: Is it too late/sketchy to work as a phone psychic? (Look up)

Year 3: ??

Year 4: ??

Year 5: Success (WTF does that look like??)

—from Judit's Note app

The next morning was better than he expected. He felt… lighter. Freer maybe. Which also gave him a twinge of guilt but he pushed it aside. He was moving on, dammit. By the end of the summer, he'd be uncomplicatedly single and striking a new direction in his career. A whole new leaf, even if it scared him.

The reminder to call his therapist buzzed on his phone and he stared at it. Maybe he didn't have to do this alone. He probably couldn't get in before the end of the tour anyway, the way she was booked up. The thought was weirdly comforting. He dialed.

Like most ridiculously hard things, it was easy once he forced his brain to do it. The call was over in five minutes and his appointment wasn't until post-tour but maybe he wouldn't need it by then.

Patrick puttered around his hotel room, glad Kevon was off somewhere. Though maybe it would've been better if he was here...

He glanced at the alarm clock between their twin beds. When they'd stumbled off the bus and into the hotel in the middle of the night, Judit stopped him in the hall and told him she was interested in trying herbalism. She'd be here in less than an hour. Would it be weird to be in a room together? Especially one with beds...

He shook himself. He was not going to creep on her just because she was attractive and he couldn't seem to stop having these weird staring moments. Today, he was a healer and that was a sacred duty.

He showered and set about the ritual of making tea in a hotel room, glad to be back on the road again. A hot sticky weekend in a tour bus with a crapshoot of camp showers no one wanted to use got gross fast. It was enough to make him miss the days when Beatboyz were in five-star hotels every night. He hadn't loved being famous but it had its perks.

As it was, he was brewing tea in a coffee pot. He unzipped his bag of tea blends and contemplated the glass jam jars nestled within. Each contained an herbal blend he'd crafted himself. After all his classes, certifications, and learning from Nana he still felt like he was scratching the surface of the wealth of plant knowledge out there.

He toyed with his options. Sometimes the first cup of tea was the best part of his day. He had blends for tiredness, inflammation, to boost his immune system, to warm him, to cool him, to balance him, to calm him, and for pain.

As if on cue, there was a knock on the door. A strange nervousness kindled in his stomach. He'd just seen her at the sad excuse of a continental breakfast not two hours ago, why was he be nervous now?

Goddamn beds.

He shot them a dirty look before shrugging off the feeling and crossing the small room to open the door.

As expected, Judit stood outside on the concrete walkway. She wore one of her light cotton maxi sundresses, this one patterned with starbursts of orange and yellow against a dark blue background. It skimmed her curves and did, um, nice things for them. He wrenched his gaze away and stood aside to let her pass. "Come in."

She did, taking her sunglasses and tucking one folded leg into the front of her dress. He glanced away. As had become the norm lately, he was hyperaware of her and her body. Cool. Great. Just what he needed.

He gestured for her to sit on the one chair in the room. He'd set up the desk next to it with his mobile herb kit. It was limited to the basics like yarrow, lavender, peppermint, ginger, chickweed, wild lettuce, damiana, chamomile, marshmallow root, angelica root, and a few more but it was a start. Unfortunately, there wasn't a green space around the hotel far enough from the roads and their pollution that he could look for anything local that might supplement his supply.

When she'd sat and he'd washed his hands, he asked, "Is it okay if I touch the pulse points on your wrists? I have some ideas of what I want to give you but pulse-testing helps."

"I don't know what that is, but okay." She held out her wrist.

He took it gently, searching out her pulse until it thumped against his fingertips. Holding it for a few minutes, he tracked the beat—it was fast. Really fast and not slowing down. Her breathing was quick too.

"You okay?" He asked.

She nodded, her lips pressed together.

"You're panting."

She took a deep breath through her nose. "Sorry, doctor visits sometimes stress me out. Well, the insurance issues afterward mostly."

He let her wrist go and knelt in front of her, not too close. "I'm not going to charge you anything. Not now, not ever."

Taking another deep breath, she nodded. "Okay, okay." She held out her wrist.

Standing, he took it, tracking her pulse as it slowed and steadied into an even rhythm.

Picking up a pinch of the first herb he placed it in her palm. Her pulse jumped erratically and didn't calm down until he brushed the herb into the trash can.

"I know you do tea but for some reason, I thought you'd use pills or something," she said.

He shook his head. "I only use herbs I know the source of, and preferably, grow. Supplements are badly regulated and sketchy, at best." He'd read a scathing article about it recently and felt very validated looking out at his and Nana's herb garden. Of course, given his remedies weren't FDA-tested, he didn't think the doctor who'd written it would feel the same. His anxiety and interest meant he kept on top of any quality studies on herbs, but they weren't as frequent as he'd like.

He put a lid on the jar and moved on, seeking herbs that

calmed her pulse from the selection of anti-inflammatory ones and pain relievers he had. As he did, he asked questions, clarifying symptoms and pain spots. She answered with the rote ease of someone who had done this far too many times. It made him ache to think she had so much pain but no medical help or support outside of his skills.

When he was done, he wrote down the list, instructions, and the proportions then made a mix that would last her a few weeks. It took out his supply of wild lettuce and burdock but he might be able to harvest some on the road if he was lucky.

Handing her the jar and list, he said, "This should help but if you're feeling any unpleasant side effects, stop and come see me."

"Thanks. You sure you don't want me to pay you?" she asked, a trace of nerves in her face like he might change his mind and demand money, despite his reassurances.

He shook his head. "You're helping me by letting me stretch my skills."

"Oh, well, you're welcome?"

He smiled, then, before he could think better of it, said, "I was just about to make myself a cup of tea if you want to join me?"

Before she could answer, his phone rang. A call from Dad. "Never mind. Rain check? I should take this."

She smiled and left. He answered the phone.

"I have your cat," his father, Edward, intoned in greeting. "Cooperate or you'll never speak to her again."

Patrick resisted the urge to roll his eyes. His dad had a very dry sense of humor and presenting all his updates on Scoot like he was a catnapper for some reason amused him. "She doing good?"

Dad turned the camera on, showing him Scoot asleep with three paws in the air all pointed in different directions. "I have concerns."

"She always sleeps weird. Or is there something else?" Patrick quelled the rising tide of anxiety at the thought of anything happening to his cat.

"No. She's well." He paused. "Who's this girl Sabrina keeps taking selfies with?"

Patrick reoriented, used to abrupt subject changes with Dad. "One of our merch girls."

"They dating?"

"That's Sabrina's business."

Dad turned the camera so his face was visible and gave Patrick a stern glare. He was wearing a button-up and a tie, his fade impeccable as always, though the effect was slightly marred by the clump of orange-black cat hair on his shoulder. Patrick squirmed, knowing Edward could outstare him any day.

"That's Sabrina's business, sir?" he tried.

Edward kept staring.

After what felt like an eternity, Patrick huffed. "No, they're not."

Dad nodded, his glare dissipating. "Thought so. Seems like more your type."

Patrick sputtered. "What? I don't have a type."

Dad shrugged. "I don't care who you date as long as you stop moping after that Cazzi. You have your Nana worried."

"I—what?" *They knew? How did they know? When had they figured it out?*

He shook his head. "A man handles his shit, Patrick. Own it and move on." He hung up.

"I'm trying," Patrick told the empty room. He dropped the phone on the bed with a sigh. Sometimes he felt like Dad's image of him had frozen the day he'd left home as a fifteen-year-old to go live in the Beatboyz bootcamp house. It didn't matter that he owned his own house and for now, a share in a business, or that he hadn't been in the tabloids for doing something scandalous, label fabricated or not, in years.

Then again, Patrick had kind of been drifting through life since the band broke up. Doing what other people told him was the smart thing to do. Yeah, well, that was going to change soon enough.

20

BENJI

I'm just saying it works in books

and movies

ROHAN

I'm just saying it's manipulative

LEO

Or is it romantic? Have you seen the way he looks at her?

BENJI

Or the way she looks at him?

ROHAN

It's not our business though. It's between them

LEO

Don't get all goody two-shoes. It'll make your life easier. Hell, it'll make MY life easier. I'm so over this feud. I want you both to be happy

BENJI

Just think of it as an experiment. It'll work or it won't

ROHAN

I guess… is it bad I've kind of enjoyed this?

BENJI

On tour you make your own fun

—Texts from Benji's phone

When she got back to her room, Judit drank a whole cup of Patrick's tea. It was the best tea she'd ever had, earthy with a hint of spice, warming but not too much, and deeply satisfying. She'd never heard of half the herbs in the list he'd written. (He had neat handwriting though, kinda fancy even.)

She wasn't sure if it was the tea but she wasn't as stiff or achy as she expected to be the next morning. With a smile, she set about getting everything together to leave again.

The whole festival was in the process of packing and loading themselves back onto the buses when Benji found her.

"Good morning," they said. It was a perfectly normal greeting but she knew they wanted something.

She returned the greeting with a smile. It made her feel special somehow, to know them this way, even if it wasn't more than as a boss. Like their fame rubbed off on her a bit.

"I need a favor." They leaned towards her like they were about to tell her a secret. Maybe they were. A girl could dream.

"Okay." She leaned forward too, trying to figure out how they'd done the gradient effect of their silvery blue eyeliner. She noticed they minimized their make-up and femininity on the road but it was still as masterfully done as their full-blown looks when the festival was in bigger cities. "What's up?"

Benji frowned. "I really hate to ask this but—" They hesitated and their frown deepened. "You can drive right?"

"Yesss," she said, not sure where this was going.

"We ran out of small shirts completely and I had them delivered to this motel but they're running late. Nicky agreed to loan us one of the roadie cars, can you please stay and get them? They should be here soon so you should be able to catch up with us, easy. I know you're not a roadie or anything but we're kinda short on time and—"

"I'll do it," she said. An afternoon to herself to read and not have to be on a bus crammed with people? Hell yes.

"Thank you!" They smiled.

She stared. *Pretty.*

Chill out Judit, she scolded herself.

"I'll send you the info and the directions to the next hotel." They handed her a set of keys. "Oh, and Patrick is going to help you. There are a lot of boxes. Thanks!"

She snapped out of her daze. "Wait, what?"

"You'll need the second pair of hands, trust me," they said, already leaving. "I'd bring an extra pair of clothes in case you need to stay the night. I'll cover it if you do."

"Stay the night?" she repeated faintly.

That was how she found herself clutching an overstuffed tote bag and sitting in the tiny lobby, next to Patrick. Well, next to was an exaggeration. They were sitting on opposite sides of a small couch, the space of one indeterminately blue-gray cushion between them. She had her nose in the paperback she'd found in a little lending library at the last hotel. She stared at the words. Something was happening in the book, she was sure of it. She just wasn't certain what it was.

He wasn't sitting much closer than he did when they were in their respective bunks and he wasn't doing anything. Just sitting there, on his phone while everyone left. It wasn't like they hadn't touched, he'd held her for like, ever in the hurricane, for fuck's sake. Nothing happened. Nothing would ever happen.

(But what if they had to stay the night somewhere? Alone.

What if an only-one-bed situation happened? Was that nearly as common as romance novels made it seem?)

One of the comedians joked as he walked by that Judit and Patrick looked like a couple right before a divorce. She'd stopped bothering to figure out which was which. They both answered to Mitch anyway, for reasons no one had quite figured out.

She gave the duo a weak smile. Patrick didn't bother looking up from his phone.

Leo blew them kisses and yelled, "Play nice, kids!"

Sabrina and Helen gave her hugs. Sabrina poked her brother until he stood and gave her a faux put-upon hug.

Through it, Patrick didn't say a word. Didn't seem bothered. Meanwhile, Judit mangled the pages of the already well-loved book in her hands.

Slowly the lobby traffic drained away and even the desk attendant faded into the back to do whatever she did while not at the desk. Judit and Patrick were alone. She felt nearly as awkward as she had in his motel room, his fingers burning deliciously on her wrist.

"Why did Benji pick us for this?" she wondered aloud to the empty lobby. The motel had looked at the color of the couch and fallen in love. Everything was shades of blue-gray from the light blue-gray floor to the dark blue-gray desk, to the middling blue-gray walls. It felt dreary and medicinal. She suppressed a shudder. At least it didn't smell medicinal.

"They want me to pull my weight but haven't worked up the courage to say it to my face," Patrick said. "I'm not sure what you did."

"I said yes," she said.

He looked surprised. "You did?"

"I mean, I thought it'd just be me—that sounded worse than I meant."

He frowned. "You thought Benji was going to leave you

alone somewhere you've never been to haul a bunch of merch by yourself?"

It was her turn to frown. "I guess I didn't think about that." Now that she was, it worried her. What state were they in again? Tennessee? Or was that yesterday? All these small states were hard to keep track of for someone from a state it took two days to drive across. "Have *you* been here before?"

"It's possible. I've been a lot of places." He stood. "Come on, let's get something to eat."

"What?"

"I saw a cafe around the corner and I need more than that hotel 'breakfast.'" Somehow, his sarcastic air quotes looked very serious.

"What about the shirts?"

He walked to the desk and tapped the bell. One loud clear note rang out. The desk lady appeared. He smiled. She straightened and smiled back, tilting her face to display what was probably her best side.

"If our delivery gets here before we get back, is it okay if it stays here for a bit? We're just going around the corner to get food."

"Not if you're going to that cafe around the corner," she said, "You'll wait forever and the food is—" She lowered her voice. "crap. Go down a block and across the street. Melissa's Cafe. Best in town."

"Melissa's? Got it." Patrick nodded. "And the packages?"

"Will be just fine here, so long as they're not waiting more than an hour or two."

"We'll be back before then," Patrick promised.

A few minutes later, Judit found herself sitting in a cracked vinyl booth. Melissa's was small and offered somewhat basic American breakfast/lunch fare. The place was empty except for them and the waitress/hostess but the kitchen smelled like melted butter and strawberries. The radio was playing some kind of sports game but the volume was too low for her to make out much.

She stared at the laminated menu, fiddling with its curling, split edges, and debating how much she could afford to spend. The place was cheap but Judit wasn't about to spend much of anything if she could help it.

"I'm paying," Patrick said as if he'd heard her thoughts.

"No, I'd rather we went dutch," she said, hating herself. The hotel breakfast had evaporated an hour ago. She'd been planning to subsist on the weirdly-gendered-but-kind-of-tasty GalEnergy bars she'd been hoarding from Grocery Outlet and hotel mints until she caught up with the tour.

He gave her a long look over his menu. "I won't expect anything from you. I have money. This is nothing to me, but it's something to you. Please, let me do this."

She snapped the menu closed. "Why?" He'd been nice to her for the last few days and she hated being suspicious but with his track record, would it last? Was he just doing it out of some misplaced idea that she needed help because she was in pain all the time?

He sighed. "Just take the free meal, okay? It's not a trap."

She opened the menu again, cheeks hot. Maybe she was being too sensitive. "I didn't think it was."

"Then why are you treating it like one?"

"You're the one who keeps blowing hot and cold. I'm just trying to keep up," she said into the menu.

"I told you, I'm trying to do better."

She closed her menu. "This isn't some help-the-poor-invalid thing to make you feel better about yourself, right?"

He blinked. "Is this because you told me about your pain and I made you tea?"

She hid behind the menu again. "Maybe."

"Judit." He pushed her menu down with a finger. "You are

too much of a weird, kind, lovely, perplexing person for me to reduce you to your symptoms. Okay?"

"Okay," she mumbled, her face hot and a smile tugging at her lips. *He called me lovely. Omigawd is he into me? He's attractive but am I—? I can't—right?*

"Are we friends now?" She blurted out.

That seemed to stump him. "I don't know. Should we be?"

"If we're going to be nice to each other and you're not gonna keep making my friend miserable, then why not?"

He considered this. "I'm not sure that's the right term," he said after an unflatteringly long time.

"Okayyyy," she said. She'd thought they'd made progress but now she wasn't so sure. "What's the right term?"

His eyes got wide and it was his turn to bury his head in the menu. "Still figuring that out."

She stared at the menu in front of his face. Was he embarrassed? Shy? It was kind of cute and the possibilities of what he thought they might be if not friends... her heart sped up. She tried to keep all that out of her voice and said casually, "Well, all right then. Be pedantic about it."

He lowered his menu. "We're cool though, right?"

"I mean, that's what I was trying to get at."

"Good." The menu went up again.

"As long as that's settled, oh, not-friend of mine."

"I'm still paying though."

She gave his menu a bemused smile. "Knock yourself out." Truly, she didn't understand how his mind worked sometimes. But that didn't bother her as much as she thought it would.

She turned her attention back to the food options. Best not to think too hard about what was happening between them or her feelings about it. Even if she could feel them churning right under the surface of her thoughts.

Lᴜɴᴄʜ ᴡᴀs sᴜʀᴘʀɪsɪɴɢʟʏ ᴏᴋᴀʏ. Patrick hadn't been expecting much but the food was decent and Judit seemed content to read when he ran out of social energy. She didn't even seem to be too weirded out by his awkwardness earlier. Why couldn't he have just said yes to being friends? It would've been so much easier and less embarrassing than the truth: he wanted her and it was a bad idea.

There was no way he could think of to say that elegantly.

The shirts were waiting for them when they got back to the hotel. Eighteen boxes were stacked next to the front desk. Judit's eyes went wide and honestly, Patrick was shocked too. Were they that popular or had the storm done that much damage?

Judit muttered something about bringing the car around and left. Patrick put on a smile for Beverly, the woman at the desk, and picked up the first box. It was surprisingly heavy. Damn, maybe it was time to get back to working out. Playing bass clearly wasn't a replacement.

He put the box by the curb. Beverly came out behind him with another box. He smiled again, mostly because it didn't seem right to stop now.

He heard the crunch of tires and turned in time to see Judit backing up a big black Lincoln SUV. She drove like a truck driver, one hand on the wheel, one arm resting on the open window. She gave him a thumbs up and popped the trunk.

Together with Beverly, they filled the trunk. Patrick thanked her and stood in front of the passenger door, girding himself. He wasn't driving but he hadn't been in a car not driven by Mike since the pandemic. That was the way he liked it.

The engine turned on and the window in front of him rolled down. "I'm a good driver," Judit said.

"That you feel the need to tell me that worries me."

She sighed. "Just trying to ward off any bad female driver stereotypes you might be having."

"It's not you. I don't like being in cars." He said it quietly, hoping she couldn't hear him.

"Fair," she said, damn her ears. "I'll make it as smooth as possible."

He wished he'd thought to grab his safe driving charm from his bunk on the bus. He couldn't keep standing here. He was breathing in enough fumes to make his nose burn as it was.

He got in.

"Can you navigate?" she asked. "Would that help?"

"I can," he said, pulling up the directions on his phone. In the back of his head, he built a protection spell.

She drove well, confidently but not overly casual or aggressive. He set up the directions, his phone barking out orders to get them on the freeway they'd spend over a hundred miles on. As it did, he pulled out one of the angelica roots from his bag, along with a few protective herbs and a couple iron nails. He put them all in a travel mug with a piece of the receipt for lunch on which he'd drawn a sigil Cazzi had once made for him. He said the words she'd made the sigil out of under his breath. "It is my will to be protected from accidents, attacks, and police officers."

He repeated the words in his mind, capped the mug, and focused his intent on it until the anxiety dissipated. He breathed a sigh of relief. It was a rough charm, built out of the contents of his backpack but it felt right.

"Hoodoo?" Judit asked after a moment.

"More of a kitchen witch, if that. My Nana's the hoodoo worker."

She smiled. "I knew you were magick."

He huffed. "Handing out roots does kind of give it away."

She laughed. "Just a bit."

"What do you practice?"

She shrugged. "A mish-mash of things. Whatever resonates with my gift, you know?"

He nodded. "Does it run in the family, your gift?" He regretted the words as her face scrunched up. Why had he asked? He knew her family was a potential sore spot. Even if they hadn't joked about the Daddy Issues Club in the storm, they spent too much time in close proximity for him not to have seen her have strained phone calls with her mother.

"I hope not," she said. "If my dad's got any sort of gift, I can't imagine he's using it for good."

"Oh," he said, not sure what to say.

"He's not a *bad* person—ugh, I don't know why I'm defending him but he's not a great person, you know?"

"Sure." The industry, hell, the world was full of people like that. And worse.

She sighed. "It's complicated like you said. He was the first adult to believe in my precognition and he fought for me when my mom didn't but he also didn't stick around very long after that." She shrugged. "I had a better father figure in my mom's ex, ironic, I know, and my bio-dad had been flaky before so I can't say I was super surprised by the time he fully ducked out, but it still hurt. I'm not sure if it's better or worse he's basically a low-level New Age grifter. Yeah, okay, that was TMI. Sorry." She shot him an apologetic grimace. "My family is a weird ass mess but it works, mostly."

Patrick didn't know what to say and silence seemed like the worst option. "I feel that. We're messy too. Just... different."

"Gotcha," she said too brightly. "Okay, totally natural subject change, um, er, oh god, my brain is not wording."

He chuckled. "I definitely feel *that*."

"Words are *hard*." Judit groaned.

"We don't have to talk."

"I know, I just thought since you're uncomfortable in cars I'd distract you—dammit, I'm fully failing, aren't I?"

"You're good, you don't have to." He looked around the nearly empty road. "It's not so bad right now."

"Anything I should avoid? Sharp turns or stops?"

He shook his head. "It's fine." There had been no single big trauma that stopped him from driving. Rather it had been a build-up: fans swarming his car until he couldn't open the door let alone move the car, being pulled over a concerning amount, LA drivers who thought they lived in a road rage video game, a number of small accidents—some of which had been intentional on the other driver's part once they'd seen who he was, his father's voice in his head getting angrier every time Patrick made a minor mistake at the wheel...

Yeah, it added up.

"It's just anxiety," he said.

"That's still a thing though," Judit said.

"I don't like to make a big deal about it." He had a driver who he trusted implicitly, it was fine.

"Okay." She shrugged again. "I don't mind if you do though. If we're going to be friendly, your demons will eventually meet mine."

He snorted. "I think they're pretty well-acquainted."

She grinned. "Oh honey, you ain't seen nothing yet."

21

Doc Conjure Casts a Spell on You

*The line-up for Endfest is admittedly pretty epic and eclectic but it was one
of the smaller acts that really blew me away. I was sitting in some shade,
waiting for Creepmother to play when this badass punk band came on
stage. Doc Conjure fucking rocked the fest, rocked the stage, and rocked my
brain. They're funky, hard-edged, and fire—and my girlfriend loved them
because their singer is a chick! Honestly, it got me thinking: I could stand to
see more chick singers at big fests like this. Endfest has maybe one. Two, if
you could Angela Alice's dates. Do better, organizers. I can name at least
three chick singer bands, four now that I'm a Doc Conjure fan.*
—Epic Ass Music blog

I t was nice to drive again. Judit hadn't driven long distances
like this in a long time. Neither she nor Helen could afford
a car but she'd had a brief stint as a bus driver. It'd been a
strange gig, exhausting and full of odd, sometimes erratic
people but well-paying. Unfortunately, the long days of sitting
and being on high alert wracked her body. Too bad. She
enjoyed driving.

The highway went through big stretches of green. So much

green! And not even farms or anything either. Trees and rivers and swampy-looking places. She wished they could explore. But they'd probably be trespassing on someone's land and that sounded like a one-way trip to trouble.

They'd been going for a few hours now and the gas gauge was dangerously low. She should've filled up by the motel but she hadn't thought about it. She didn't relish stopping at one of these turnoffs marked by falling down buildings and dubiously accurate signs, but there wasn't anything big for miles.

Patrick pointed at a sign up ahead. "Last gas in twenty miles," he read.

Judit swore and took the turnoff.

Against the protests of the GPS, she pulled into a gas station in a place not even Google could find on a map. She didn't like the look of it, small, shabby, and a brand she didn't recognize, but she liked the empty tank light even less.

Patrick filled the tank as she popped into the tiny market to pee. She looked at the two guys at the counter and hesitated. They looked like evil hillbilly twins out of a slasher film, trucker hats, and camo overalls included. One of the hats was red with white lettering but she couldn't tell what it said. She was almost certain they had a basement and it was a murder basement. The trees that looked so nice from the road seemed to close in on her.

One of them smiled at her. It looked like a leer.

But fuck, she'd had to pee for the last twenty miles, and holding it too long pissed off her pelvic muscles. She ducked into the bathroom, keys between her fingers. She was out again in record time, encouraged by the small hole in the wall of one of the two stalls.

She hurried back to the car. "Don't go in," she told Patrick. "It's creepy as fuck in there."

He looked over at the market with a frown. "How far is the hotel?"

"Two hours, according to Google."

He looked at the sky. It was still light out, thankfully, and probably would be for hours. Despite the sticky heat, she was very happy it was summer.

He finished filling the tank and they got in. She turned on the car. The check engine light turned on and stayed on. She swore.

He saw the light and his eyes narrowed. "Drive a bit. Maybe it'll turn off."

Well, she certainly wasn't staying here. She could see the twin with the red hat looking at her through the window. She peeled out of the lot and back onto the highway. The car was sluggish, the accelerator reluctant.

The light stayed on.

"The car sounds rough," Patrick said.

She concentrated and heard an unevenness to the rumble of the engine. "Bad gas?"

"Wouldn't be surprised."

"Fucking hell."

"Probably cut it with water or mixed types or something."

"Damn it." Judit sorted through her random bits of car repair knowledge. Water in the gas tank was bad, but there must be a way to fix it, right?

"I'll call Sabrina, she took autoshop in high school," Patrick said.

He called and outlined the situation to his sister. Judit could hear the other woman cursing even though she wasn't on speaker. Then she settled down and started issuing rapid-fire instructions. Patrick nodded and wrote them on the back of a receipt spread against the dashboard. He hung up. "We need an auto store."

He rerouted the instructions and an hour later they found themselves in front of an auto store in another small town.

"I am so out of my comfort zone," Judit said. The town

had two stoplights and was named after a Confederate general. She'd never been on such high alert. If there was another set of creepy twins in there, she was done.

"Tell me about it," Patrick said, tying his locs back.

"Would it be better if I went in alone?"

"I have no idea," he said.

In the end, they went in together. Again there were two white men at the counter, but these guys smiled in a way that didn't creep her out and were actually helpful. When they told them what they needed, one of them said, "Oh yeah, that happens. One of those middle-of-nowhere stations? They had about five teeth between them?"

Judit nodded. "They were horror movie creepy."

He laughed. "I bet. There are some sketchy stations out here. They probably siphoned gas and stored it wrong. Something like that happened to my wife and me a while back when we were driving to Vegas. Same kind of thing out there in Nevada. They know they got you on account of all that desert." He handed them the gas tank cleaner they needed.

After administering the cleaner, they were back on the road. The engine sounded better but Judit was still on edge. It was creeping closer to night and their detours put them out of the way of the hotel by an additional hour.

Her back ached and her neck was stiff. Steel clamps slowly formed around her skull. She wished she hadn't run out of CBD in a state without legal weed. It wasn't like she could brew any of Patrick's tea in the car either. "I take it you don't drive at all," she said, between bites of energy bar. It was getting close to dinner time.

Patrick went stiffer than her neck. "No."

"Okay," she said. "No worries."

"Are you getting tired?" He looked guilty.

She shrugged. "I like driving but my body doesn't."

He nodded. "Has the tea been helping? I know it's a bit soon to tell."

"Maybe?" she said. "You're like, pretty professional as an herbalist. You never wanted to be licensed?"

"No," he said. "Licenses are public record, and I'm... shy about anything public record." He grimaced, clearly remembering something.

She vaguely remembered some of the super invasive stories that ran about him and his band. "Fair. It's cool you keep studying, though."

He shrugged. "I do them when I feel like I need to fill a knowledge gap."

"So, you have a bunch of degrees?"

"Only one degree. Lots of certificates though. I like to know things."

"I might go back to school and get some business courses, someday," Judit said. "I feel like you can't go wrong with business learning. Or at least that's what my mom says." Her mother had been hot on the topic in their last call. She'd wanted Judit to go to Clementine University and get a Bachelors (at least). The idea of going to school where her demi-sister and friend worked gave Judit mixed feelings though. Also four years of business classes? No, thanks.

"Do you want to turn your readings into a big business? Get famous?" he asked.

"Didn't you when you joined Beatboyz?"

He shook his head. "I just wanted to make music."

She snorted. It sounded like a line out of one of those earnest "behind the scenes" band documentaries.

"Yeah, yeah," he said. "I know. But I was an awkward teenager who was good at one thing and hated high school. Beatboyz meant I got to do that thing all the time and quit school."

"Win-win," Judit said.

"Pretty much." His shrug, from what she could see out of the corner of her eye, was less than convinced.

"Man," she said. "I feel like one of the only people who enjoyed high school."

"You *enjoyed* it?"

"*Enjoyed* is a strong word, but I didn't hate it, you know? I wasn't popular or anything horrid like that but I had the most friends I've ever had in my life. I miss those people. We all had so much potential, we were all going places."

"We're going places right now." He squinted at the address on his phone. "The Celebrations Motel and Suites. Hard to get fancier than that."

Judit laughed. "Point, but I don't feel like I've accomplished anything. I know I'm playing the long game but I don't get a lot of clients, my social media following is laughable, and I'd just like a real tangible win."

"What do your cards have to say about that?"

"Stuff I don't want to hear," she replied with a groan.

He nodded. "I get that. It's hard for me to hear anything but the shit in my head." Out of the corner of her eye, she could see him clutching the travel mug.

Her phone rang from the cupholder.

Patrick picked it up. "Hi Benji. I'm putting you on speaker."

"Hey all," Benji's voice filled the car, low-res and tired. "They double-booked the fucking motel. We're going straight to the fairground, I'm not sure where we'll park since our reservation isn't for another day but that's not my problem. Nicky's going full Karen on the motel staff."

"How long's the drive?" Judit asked, dread forming a stone in her belly.

"Another five hours," Benji sounded vaguely murderous. "I'm sorry."

"We can't drive that tonight," Patrick said. "We had car trouble and we're too far out."

Judit breathed a sigh of relief.

"Grab a room somewhere," Benji said. "The label will reimburse you. Enjoy an extra night of showers." They lowered their voice. "I gotta go. Nicky's looking fit to throw things. Apparently, we need an adult."

Patrick rerouted them to a hotel in the nearest city without comment.

By the time they parked in the hotel parking lot, Judit's head was full of pain. It only increased as they got out, all the attention she'd paid to the road now freed up to point out just how much she hurt. She knocked back an Excedrin Migraine with the last of the water and what was left of the energy bar.

Thankfully, Patrick handled the room arrangements and she was able to just exist, which was effort enough. He led her to the rooms, plastic keycards in hand. The carpets were diamond patterned, gray, and green. Like scales or a chain link fence.

"Judit?"

She blinked and accepted her key. "Thanks. Which one's mine?"

He looked concerned. "There's only one room. Two beds," he added hurriedly. "They're booked up for some local event. Don't you remember? I asked you if that was okay?"

"Oh." She vaguely recalled agreeing to something. This was bad, but she struggled to remember why. "Okay."

"Judit."

"Hmm?"

"Your pupils are different sizes." That explained the blind spot.

"Happens. Head hurts."

"Migraine?"

"Oh yes." She slid her keycard into the door but it didn't seem to be working.

He took it, turned it right side up, and slid it in. The little light turned green. She shuffled into the room, focusing on the floor because the light from the hallway was just too much.

The bed called and she answered, collapsing face first. If she was lucky, she'd fall asleep before the nausea kicked in. Clutching a hotel toilet was even less appealing than clutching her toilet at home. She shucked her shoes and crawled under the covers.

"What can I do?" Patrick asked.

"Let me sleep," she said. Her stomach tightened. "And get me some crackers, please."

"Okay." The door opened and closed.

Thank goodness she wasn't alone or this would be so much worse. (Thank goodness it was Patrick, who already knew her pain and didn't pity her. Who had taken care of her before without any dramatics or expectations.)

She groped her phone out and put on music, volume low. She'd love to listen to her book but she couldn't concentrate on anything that complex.

She drifted in the soundscape of FKA Twigs' album *Magdalene*, time expanding and contracting with the waves of pain and consciousness.

22

"You take care of me
I care for you

It's all we can do

No one else will fight for us
No one else knows
They don't get how these things go

I hurt when you hurt
I'm cursed when you're cursed
We're in community
There's no excluding, see?
We're in community
It's more than you and me"
— "In Community" by Doc Conjure off of *Grandma's Spells*

Patrick stood in front of the vending machine, turning over everything he knew about migraines. They were tricky and could be caused by a variety of things, resulting in a cornucopia of symptoms, none of them fun. From what he'd observed, Judit was dealing with pain in her head and neck, light sensitivity, and possible nausea. She'd taken painkillers on a mostly empty stomach, which wouldn't help the stomach stuff.

He grabbed a Coke, some water bottles, two bags of crackers, and a couple energy bars for himself.

The room was dark when he got back, faint music emanating from the bed. He paused when the door closed, getting used to the dark. The bathroom was to his left, divided from the beds by a wall. Judit had taken the bed right next to it.

"Is it okay if I turn on the bathroom light?" he asked.

She mumbled, "Yeah." So he did.

She didn't protest so he left it on, getting to work in the diffused light. Humming along with her music, he opened the crackers and coke, kneeling by the bed. "Eat a cracker for me?"

She fumbled for it without opening her eyes and he placed it in her palm. She ate.

"Coke?"

She grimaced, but sat up a bit and drank some. Then she slumped back into the bed with mumbled thanks. The shadowy light softened and obscured her. Strands of dark hair were stuck to her cheeks and her forehead was creased in a frown. He fed her another cracker then placed the coke, a bottle of water, and the crackers on the bedside table.

She burrowed into the pillow and groaned, her shoulders hiking to her ears, and her face scrunching. It hurt to look at her but when he ran through all the treatments he knew, he didn't have half of what he needed and he wasn't sure about the interactions with whatever painkiller she'd taken.

She groaned louder, the sound breaking off into a sob as she curled tighter into herself. His hands knotted into fists, he felt helpless.

He hated feeling helpless, it was a sickening echo of the feeling he'd gotten fifteen years ago when Cazzi called him half out of her mind because of what happened to Tanya. He would've done anything to have been there, to have stopped it from happening. As a teenager, he thought it would've been so much better if he'd been the one with the blood on his hands, not her. Of course, it would've turned out worse for him.

Judit sobbed again, wrenching him out of his memories.

"Would it help if you held my hand?" he asked.

She opened her eyes, squinting at him. Tears leaked onto the pillow and starred her lashes. "You don't have to fix me."

"Would it help?"

She sighed, her eyelids fluttering closed. "Maybe." But her hand emerged from the covers.

He sat on the edge of the bed and interlaced their fingers. Her skin was soft against his. And now he couldn't move without disturbing her. Not his smartest move.

She sobbed through her teeth, her body curling around his back, her forehead digging into his leg. Without thinking, he reached down with his free hand and smoothed her hair back.

She sighed and relaxed against him. He stroked her head again. She turned into the caress. So he kept doing it, murmuring to her as she writhed in pain and humming along with the music until she fell into a restless sleep.

He looked at the clock and realized he'd sat there for nearly three hours. He felt empty in a peaceful way, tired out. His back complained so he stood, slipping his hand out of her grip.

After a quick stretch, he turned off the light and lay in the other bed, watching her. Well, mostly listening. The room was too dark to see much beyond the red numbers of the radio clock hotels of a certain price point always seemed to have. Whatever music she'd been playing long ago ran out so he listened to her breathe, monitoring it to make sure she wasn't still in pain, that she wasn't waking before the painkiller finally did its damn job.

Her breathing felt both familiar and alien. He'd spent so many years listening to Cazzi breathe over phone lines, over video, in real life that if she called him right now from a blocked number he'd know her from her first breath. He'd been listening to Judit breathe for most of the day but the nuances were different, as if he could hear the shape of her echoing in the air of her lungs.

Cazzi breathed with deliberate slowness, some part of her always monitoring and measuring until her control slipped and everything became quick and ragged. Judit breathed several different ways: quiet and calm when she was okay, long and deep when she was trying to control her pain, short and jagged when the pain took over, in quick bursts when she was stressed or scared, slightly open-mouthed and gasping when they had those intense staring moments...

Now, she breathed so deeply he could barely hear her. He found his inhales matching hers.

Patrick fell asleep without meaning to, their breathing in time.

JUDIT WOKE up in a new world, fresh and nearly pain-free. When she was younger, waking after a migraine was an almost religious experience, her whole body feeling bright and rejuvenated in comparison with the pain. Now, as she approached thirty, she got fewer migraines but the morning after was less glorious, less fully recovered. She sat up slowly, still stiff, the threat of a headache still lurking at the base of her skull. It made her feel delicate, like fine china balanced on the edge of a table.

She looked at the other bed. Patrick lay on his side, sleepily watching her. She remembered abruptly she'd fallen asleep curled around him with one of his hands in hers and the other stroking her hair. The murmur of his voice was on loop in her memory like a song stuck in her head: *Sleep, sleep Judit. Sleep, sleep.*

"Feeling better?" She couldn't read his expression. (Did he feel as off-balance as she did?)

She nodded, gingerly. Her brain felt wobbly but functional. She took a sip of flat coke, the caffeine clearing some of the cobwebs from her head. "Thank you for um…"

He nodded. "It's nothing."

(Didn't feel like nothing, but whatever.)

She looked at the time. "Did we miss breakfast?" Maybe if she acted normal, neither of them had to acknowledge how good it felt when he held her or how often it seemed to be happening.

(Would it be so bad if they did, though?)

He seemed to agree with her because they didn't talk much past confirming they could still get breakfast. He didn't speak again until they were on the road.

"Do you get those much?" He asked out of nowhere.

"I used to, but I got better at catching them early as I got older. I haven't had one this bad in a while." She grimaced, piecemeal flashbacks of past migraines flickering in her mind. She pushed them aside.

"Do you know what triggers them?"

She shrugged. "Muscle tension, stress, not eating enough, not drinking enough, the sun hitting my eyes at the wrong angles, weather changes, sinus pressure… You get the picture."

"That explains the sunglasses."

She touched the pair on her face. "Yep."

"What triggered the last one? How long ago was it?"

She almost didn't answer. It really wasn't his business, but then she remembered him stroking her hair in the dark and something in her softened. "A break-up. Almost a year ago." (Had it been so long already?)

He made a sympathetic noise.

"I was the dumper," she said, the words spilling out. "It was a stress headache from the anxiety of doing it. I was living with them. I had to move during quarantine. I thought we were in love but I was just a band-aid disguised as a sex toy." She shook her head, trying not to remember how they found ways to punish her every time she didn't want to have sex when they did.

"That's rough."

She nodded. "I'm never going to be a third in a marriage again, that's for sure. Not one that didn't start with me in it." She watched him out of the corner of her eye to see how he reacted. It was a test but she did it anyway.

His eyebrows jumped but he boxed away the emotion before it could show any more. "Understandable," was all he said.

She shrugged. "In hindsight, moving into the carriage house of a couple I'd met at a play party three months before wasn't my best move. If I'd been rational about it then I'd have realized they didn't actually want to be a throuple, they wanted to use me to fix a marriage that wasn't working. Then the pandemic started and we were suddenly all home all the time." She shook her head. "It got clear quickly I needed to get out of there."

"I bet." He sounded stunned but not judgy. Which was good. If he'd been judgy she'd have been tempted to leave him on the side of the road.

"Yeah." She thumped the steering wheel, all the anger she

had about that time rushing back. It made her feel overheated and antsy. "I was being fucking stupid."

"Everyone's stupid when it comes to love." He said it like a mantra, like a core truth. It raised her hackles. *Of course*, he'd believe that. Was he lumping her into his old fixation? (With Cazzi—oh shit, Judit wasn't jealous of her, was she?) "My grandpa Pat used to always say that," he said quietly.

She chewed on her thoughts, sorting through her mess of feelings on the subject. After all they'd been through he deserved more than her kneejerk rage.

"I used to think that," she said finally. "I think I used it as an excuse to ignore the red flags I knew would come back to bite me in the ass."

Shit, was that too pointed?

He was quiet for so long she had to swallow down a dozen different apologies. She already thanked him for his help at breakfast, but she couldn't get the way he'd held her or his voice murmuring her name out of her head. It'd been a long time since she let someone take care of her like that. Hell, it'd been a long time since someone volunteered.

"I know what you're getting at," he said finally, his voice pensive.

"Do you?" she asked. Ugh, why was she poking at this? He'd been kind to her.

"You're not exactly being subtle," he said.

"Sorry, I mean, I just feel like it's related is all."

"Yeah, to something—and someone I'm trying to get past." He inhaled sharply. "I'm not sure what you want me to say. I fucked up. So many things fell apart over the last few years. All I knew how to do was react and I hurt a bunch of people I loved. I have to live with that."

Judit pressed her lips together. She'd pushed too hard. (He said loved—*past tense!*) A feeling tugged at her. (Don't say it.) "Maybe," she said, the words coming whether she wanted them or not. (Shut up. Shut up. Shut up!) "Obsessing about her didn't so much feel right as it felt familiar."

Silence.

She risked a glance. He was stone-faced, unreadable. Uh-oh.

After a while, he said, "I'm over her, okay?"

She really wished she could get a better look at him, gauge his reaction. As it was, she could only go off his flat delivery and the tension vibrating in the car. "Sure, yeah. Shutting up now."

"Thank you." But he didn't say another word for the rest of the trip, no matter how much she tried to get him to talk.

Welp, fuck.

23

Darlings, we've hit the doldrums of the tour, we're low on merch, and I'm low on tea! Help a girl out, will you? Find or do something scandalous, else I might expire like a Victorian lady trapped in a tragically banal marriage!

Also, happy Leo season! Be sure to celebrate me,

LS

—Tourgasm vol. 6

They arrived to chaos at a truck stop not far from the next festival campground. Roadies and PAs roamed around the buses, up and down the hallways created between them, congregating in anxious knots with some of the performers.

Benji called it a truck stop on the phone, but really, it was an oversized gas station. Towering awnings stretched over dozens of diesel pumps and a sign claiming there was a shower were the only things making it nicer than your average Arco. Patrick supposed this was cost-effective, or maybe just the only option after the pandemic closed so many motels, but he still didn't like it. He'd stayed in worse places when Beatboyz was still not making enough money to warrant much of a budget, but back then he'd been a teenager. Now, he was too damn old to think it was exciting.

He headed off to track down Benji, who wasn't answering their phone, and figure out where the hell he was supposed to store all the boxes. It was better than dwelling on the frustrating conversation they'd had in the car. He'd had eight different pissed yet articulate conversations with Judit in his head but his brain was too tired to make those words come out coherently. So they just swam in circles, spiraling while he stewed.

There was a tug on his shirt.

"They're this way." Judit pointed in the opposite direction. There was a semi truck and a random Indian restaurant over there but not much else. Not that there was much anywhere. The truck stop was an oasis in a sea of dusty fields.

"One of your feelings?"

She nodded.

He shrugged her off and headed into the knot of gossiping crew. Nick Sullivan had to be in there somewhere. Patrick hadn't spent much time with him, partially out of avoidance and partly because he didn't need anything from the man. Patrick was low maintenance on tour, something that always endeared him to past tour managers, especially in comparison with Martin and Leo.

He saw Judit shake her head and follow her feeling. Whatever. She was probably right but he'd had enough of her damn feelings in the car. It hurt that she'd been the person he'd talked the most to about what he was going through and she still didn't trust him. Even after all they'd been through.

He grabbed the first roadie he could find.

The man shrugged when he asked. He never worked on the Doc Conjure shows so Patrick hadn't bothered learning his name. "All I know is Sullivan's MIA and the Bitch Queen and

Marty Mac are gonna show up any second." He didn't know where Benji was either.

Patrick thanked him and swore under his breath. He called Sabrina and got her take on the gossip, which was everything was going quickly to hell.

He took a deep breath after he hung up and called Rohan. No answer.

Irritated, Patrick found a knot of roadies in front of the fast-food joint sharing space with the truck stop, talking and laughing. Helen was with them, flirting with Judit's roadie friend Cedric.

"What's going on?" he asked them.

Cedric shrugged and Helen rolled her eyes. "Ask Leo. He came back to the bus with a black eye last night."

Patrick sighed. "Okay, can you unload the merch from the car? I need to figure this shit out."

Helen nodded and he handed the keys to her. She looked at the roadies around her and said pointedly, "Later guys."

"Need help?" Cedric asked.

"It's eighteen boxes, yes, she does," Patrick growled, staring them down until a few broke away to help Helen and Cedric.

Then he set about finding Benji, Leo, and Rohan, checking on the NoN folks as he went, not by design, but because they kept coming up and asking him shit. He warded off their questions as calmly as he could and worked his way around the truck stop. Everyone had their own idea of what happened and they all sounded ridiculous. Brawls, love triangles, embezzling, broken bones, murder plots, running away—every story was different.

The bruised faces and split lips of the comedy duo did support the brawl story. But of course, they chose now to finally shut up. They refused to talk to him, invoking the fifth like he was law enforcement.

Benji and Rohan were nowhere to be found. Leo was

reportecly shut in his room with the words FUCK OFF scrawled directly on the plywood. It was ominously silent in there.

After about an hour, he stood facing the Indian restaurant. It was called Taste of India, the building squat and the windows dark tinted. If Benji and Rohan were hiding in there, he was going to drag them out by their ears the way his grandmother used to drag him out of places when he was being bad.

The bell above the door jingled when he entered and an Indian woman his mother's age hurried up to him. "Table for one?"

"I'm looking for some friends…" he trailed off, seeing them in the corner booth with Judit. "Excuse me," he said to the hostess.

Judit saw him first, her eyes widening. She shook her head like she was telling him to calm down. Fuck that.

"What the hell are you two doing hiding here? It's a kicked anthill over there!" he demanded.

"I know." Benji didn't even have the grace to look surprised, they dragged a hand over their face. "Martin is thirty minutes out and our favorite hellion isn't far behind him. Nicky's dick got hard for one of the comedian's groupies and he and the comedians got into it last night. No one's seen the little shit in hours."

Judit shook her head in disbelief. It was hard to tell if it was because of Nick's behavior or if she was shocked the comedians had groupies. Patrick was torn between the two.

"They got into a brawl," Rohan said. His eyes were ringed with shadows and he looked like he hadn't slept. "Leo—well, tried to help."

"Shit." Patrick dropped into the seat next to Judit. She looked surprised. "Is Leo okay? He won't come out of his bedroom."

"Oh, Leo's fine," Rohan said, "but Nick's got a broken arm on top of being MIA, and both comedians look fucked up."

"Is Nick gonna press charges?" Patrick asked. It didn't matter who started it, any judge would look at Leo and know he finished it.

Benji shook their head. "No, but it took some doing."

"And money," Rohan said.

"We need to go back out there," Patrick said. "People are freaking out. I calmed them down as best I could but they're drawing their own conclusions. I heard about sixteen different theories about what happened."

Benji and Rohan stared at him.

"What?" he snapped.

"He's right. You two need to be seen," Judit said.

"It's not our tour," Benji pointed out.

"We're the biggest names here until Marty and Angela arrive," Patrick said. "We've gotta put on a good face, keep people from running off into the fucking cornfields." He looked at Rohan. "It's like the time Beatboyz headlined that pop festival and the whole place got flooded overnight, remember?"

Rohan nodded. "It ruined half the equipment the acts stored there. We organized a lending program and the show went on." A smile ticked up the corner of his mouth.

Patrick looked at Benji. "Don't tell me you haven't been keeping an eye on Nick's shit."

Benji snorted. "So what, you want us to take over the tour? We don't have the cash."

Patrick shook his head. "We just need Nicky functioning well enough to get through the rest of the run."

Benji tapped their fingers on the table, the pattern like a guitar strum. "Okay, get to Nicky, prop him up, and/or whip him into shape until he can handle managing this monstrosity again. No problem." They rolled their eyes. "Why didn't I think of that?"

"What about his assistant?" Judit asked. "He has to have one right?"

"Drove him to get his damn arm set," Rohan said. "I heard a rumor that they've been back for a while but good luck getting on that bus. They won't talk to either of us." His lips twisted. Back when they were Beatboyz, Nick would've bent over backward for them.

"What if we got Martin to help?" Judit ventured. "Don't look at me like that! Leo told me Nick was all over Martin when he was here."

"Might as well ask Angelica to huff and puff and blow his damn bus down," Benji muttered.

Rohan shook his head. "She might have a point. Hate to say it but, Martin is bigger than all of us."

"I'm with Benji," Patrick said, "I'd rather have Angela tear his bus apart."

Rohan snorted. "She hasn't done that in years."

"Why not hedge your bets and ask them both for help?" Judit asked, making everyone else grimace. "What? You're all worried about the tour falling apart. I think they'd be invested too."

They paused to digest this.

"Stop being right," Patrick grumbled, scrubbing a hand over his face.

"Don't send me to talk to Angelica," Benji said. "I'll take Martin over her any day."

"Fine," Rohan said. "I'll talk to Angie. Patrick?"

"I'll go with you," Patrick said, already regretting his plan.

"Annnnd, he's here," Benji said, looking at their smartwatch. "Okay," they stood. "Come on, Judit, as punishment for your good idea, you're helping me." They paid the bill on their way out, Judit trailing them. She glanced at Patrick before she left.

Rohan sighed. "Something always has to go wrong on these things, don't they?"

Patrick crossed his arms. "You two hiding doesn't help things."

"We weren't hiding," Rohan snapped. "We were having lunch and calling our legal and accounting folks to see how fucked we are if this tour combusts."

"And?" Patrick braced himself for the answer. "What did Leo and Tasha say?"

Rohan ran his fingers through his curls. "Leo is non-verbal but Tasha thinks she could get the fest to pony up if they don't declare bankruptcy. We'd survive—barely."

Patrick grimaced. "I feel like we've been barely keeping our head above water since we started."

Rohan shrugged. "You haven't been helping that."

Anger surged up Patrick's spine, venom filling his mouth as feedback screamed through his thoughts. But Rohan was right. He hadn't been helping. He breathed, counting each inhale.

"Not that I blame you," Rohan continued. "I probably would've done worse in your position." He sighed and looked at Patrick through the fringe of curls flopping over his eyes. "I'm sorry for what it's worth. I want—I'd like us to be friends again. Someday. I know Cazzi does too."

Patrick mulled it over. Rohan had been one of his best friends for over a decade before this happened. Cazzi loved Rohan. And... Patrick didn't love her, not like that. It hurt a bit less every time he thought it. He could believe it more. He felt like he was reconfiguring his reality with each repetition.

Cazzi probably had some neurological data to back that up. The thought made him almost smile.

But did he want to stay with NoN with the specter of all that happened hanging over them?

"Maybe," he said, finally.

Rohan's watch dinged and he stood, clapping Patrick on the shoulder. "Let's talk more later. We're long overdue."

Patrick grimaced but nodded. It was probably better to quit in person than over email anyway.

24

"Everything I put my hands on turns gold
But everybody I touch turns cold
My statues and me sitting home alone
Only business calls my phone

I've got that Midas touch
Except for love
I've got that Midas touch
It's not enough

Is it me or is it you?
I don't know what to do
There's no one who can hold me
No one to hold on to"
—"Midas Touch" by Martin Mejia off of *This Endless Road*

Martin glared at the truck stop through his bus window as he pedaled on his stationary bike. "This is unacceptable."

"That's why we'd like your help talking to Nick Sullivan,"

Benji said, looking about as humble as Judit had ever seen them. It was a brittle front and she wondered if Martin could see through it as easily as she could.

Martin waved their words away. "My manager is already calling him."

"I doubt he'll answer," Benji said. "Rumor has it he's holed up in his bus nursing a broken arm and a broken heart."

Martin scoffed. "I once did a whole show on a broken ankle."

"Wow, that's commitment," Judit said, hoping she wasn't laying it on too thick.

Martin sniffed. "Exactly."

"That's why we need your help," Judit continued. "He's being a child but... I think he'll listen to you."

"I don't need this festival." Martin shook his head. "I should just leave. If he wants me, he can beg."

"What about the rest of us?" Benji snapped. Their humble mask crumbled, the anger flashing in their eyes. Judit resisted the urge to lean away, put some space, any space between her and that anger. She abruptly remembered Angela Alice wasn't the only one known for tearing apart a tour bus or two.

Martin crossed his arms, nostrils flaring. "What about it?"

Benji threw up their hands and turned away. "Fucking pop divas."

A feeling bloomed in Judit's mind, a whisper of intuition. "Look, I know he gave Leo a black eye—"

"He what?" Martin demanded, his knuckles whiting on the handlebars of his bike. His whole focus shifted, zeroing in on Judit. She fought the urge to shrink beneath it.

"Leo was trying to help and Nick..." Judit shrugged, mostly because she had not a damn clue what happened.

Martin hopped off the bike, grabbed a towel from his PA, and stalked out of the bus. Benji and Judit exchanged a glance then rushed after him, elbowing through the crush of entourage members trying to do the same.

They got out of the bus, reaching Martin. He whirled around and barked "Stay!" at his entourage.

A chorus of protests rose but his people stayed. Benji rolled their eyes.

"Which bus?" Martin demanded.

Benji pointed at the ultra-deluxe bus parked at the far end of the lot, backed nearly into a field.

"Fine," Martin said. "You're taking me to Leo when I'm done."

"No," Benji said.

"We can't promise you that," Judit said. "But we can ask if he'll talk to you. No guarantees."

Benji shot her a murderous look but Judit held firm. Someday those two would have to work out whatever was between them. She'd only seen them cross paths in passing and she could tell there was history. Why not now? The fest was in the middle of nowhere and going to shit anyway.

"Good enough." Martin stalked towards Nick's bus, leaving Judit and Benji hurrying in his wake. Another fleet of buses pulled in, crowding the packed lot.

"Are those Angela's?" Judit nodded at the fleet. There was nothing that made them stand out, no band name, none of the advertisements that were plastered over some of the buses and vans of smaller bands.

Benji checked their smartwatch. "With our luck, yes."

Martin reached Nick's bus and pounded on the door. "Nick Sullivan, open up!"

"Hoo boy," Judit murmured.

Benji grinned, the expression sharp-edged and wicked. They were a jagged blade with a smile next to her, making adrenaline prickle along her skin.

Martin got his phone out and snapped at someone. He hung up without saying goodbye and glared at the door.

People in the maze of buses surrounding them were poking their heads out, watching from a distance.

Martin tapped his foot, peering up at the windows.

"Any luck?" Benji asked.

He shook his head and banged again, this time on the luggage compartment, making the whole bus boom.

"Neat trick," Judit said, hoping nobody noticed she'd flinched at the noise.

Martin pried at the door, trying to break the lock. "Nick Sullivan, it's Martin Mejia and I demand to see you!"

"Wow, he went from zero to sixty didn't he?" Angela Alice stood next to Judit like she'd been there forever. Her shimmery lips were turned up in a half smile but the rest of her face was bare. She wore black yoga pants and an oversized Ghost T-shirt hanging off one shoulder.

Judit tried not to stare. Remove the tattoos and—No, Angela would never pass for normal. But she seemed almost approachable.

Benji jerked their gaze to Angela and exhaled hard. Angela's breath caught, so quietly Judit would've never heard it if she wasn't within touching distance. Judit drew her hands closer to herself. Her whole body was a mass of prickles and goosebumps. She very much wished she was anywhere else than between them.

"Is it my turn?" Angela asked, her voice low and eager.

"Oh hell." Patrick arrived, Rohan at his heels.

Rohan sighed. "Can you do it?"

Angela cocked her head, studying the bus. "Let's find out." She sauntered forward and leaned down to whisper in Martin's ear when he pulled back his leg to kick the doors. He paused, putting his foot down.

They sized each other up like two cats on the prowl and smirked at the same time.

Angela turned back to their group and winked. Judit shivered, unable to stop herself, and grabbed the root in her pocket. It wasn't there. She'd left it on the bus. She rubbed her arms, chilled despite the muggy heat.

Angela circled the bus like a shark, gaze trained on the windows, Martin watching her curiously. She stopped in front of the doors again and tapped, the noise loud in the sudden quiet. "Nicky," she called, her voice cajoling, a half-step off from friendly. An uncanny valley of tone, just wrong enough to be disturbing. "Nickyyyy, it's Angieeee. Come out, come out."

Silence. Judit gripped her arms tighter.

Angela looked at the crowd and pouted, her eyes bright. She looked like she was enjoying herself, playing it up for the watchers. "Nickyyyy," she called, louder, eerier. "You know I hate it when you ignore me."

Judit felt her shoulders creeping up to her ears, her whole body tense to the point of pain.

Something small and hard pressed against her spine. Her shoulders dropped, the chills abruptly fading. She looked behind her to see Patrick pressing an angelica root to her back, his arm awkwardly extended.

"It's the only one I have on me," he said apologetically. (Maybe he'd gotten over their convo in the car?)

She smiled and took a step back so his arm could relax at his side but still keep the contact against her. He traced it across her back, following the curve of her ribs. She stopped breathing, unable to focus on anything but the slow progress of the root over the fabric of her dress. She leaned into it, she couldn't help it. It had been so long, too long.

He traced it down her arm, the rough texture of the root and the warmth of his skin just out of reach drowning her senses. He placed the root in her hand, resting his fingers on it so they shared it without touching.

Angela rattled the lock on the bus, snapping Judit out of the sensation of almost holding hands with Patrick.

The singer pulled a card out of the pocket of her yoga pants and slid it along the crack of the door, humming something just loud enough to hear but not to identify. There was a click and the door gapped but didn't open.

"Two locks?" Angela laughed, the sound too bright and tinkling, bouncing off the maze of buses around them until it seemed to come from everywhere. "Don't you trust me, Nicky? Or is it everyone else you're worried about?"

"Can you unlock it?" Martin asked.

Angela shook her head but crooned, "Nickkyyy, come out and play. Remember what happened last time you wouldn't come out?"

Nick Sullivan slammed up against the clear glass of the folding door like a jump scare monster in a horror film, staring at her with wide eyes.

Judit flinched back even though she was several yards away. Patrick's shoulder bumped her and his fingers flexed over hers, giving them a brief reassuring squeeze, but even he looked perturbed.

Angela leaned closer to the glass. "Hi Nicky, I missed you!" Now, her voice was girlish, excited.

"You swore," he hissed. "You signed a goddamn NDA!"

Angela shrugged. "Who knows what I'll do? I'm that freaky little bitch remember?" She bared her teeth at him. "We freaky bitches are unpredictable. Now, *open up Nicky*, the nice people want to talk to you."

Nick shrank back from the glass. He stared at her for a long minute, as if gauging her seriousness. She held his gaze, looking like she was dying for an excuse to repeat whatever happened between them.

Nick's shoulders slumped and he opened the door.

"There, there," Angela said. "That wasn't so bad wasn't it?" She smiled at Nick. A full smile, a real smile. Even with the root in her hand and only catching it from the side, Judit couldn't stop staring. Nick just about turned into a puddle, smiling back and nodding like a bobblehead.

Rohan and Benji surged forward, ready to make use of Nick's defeated state. Judit and Patrick were left, not quite touching and not sure how to stop.

25

About the last few days…

Look, we all make mistakes that sometimes result in breaking the wrong
people's arms, causing all kinds of accidental chaos, and some regrettable
Sharpie use that is now being taken out of our earnings. Hypothetically.
Anyway, I heard a certain pair of bad actors are still at large so be careful
tonight and don't get lost in any corn fields or whatever is growing around
here. Soy? Rice? I'm not a farmer. I'm just a simple soul who likes to sing
and looks damn good in women's clothes.

Keeping it cute,
LS
—Tourgasm vol. 7

What disturbed Judit the most about the all-day breakfast buffet the next morning, wasn't the mass of jiggling scrambled eggs sitting under a heat lamp for god knows how long. It was that, of all the people who'd decided to dine down in the tiny off-brand Denny's serving as the unofficial mess tent at this truck stop, Martin and Angela were sitting at the table near hers. She couldn't hear what they were saying, but they were having far more fun than anyone had any right to have at seven am. (Taste of India didn't open until eleven or Judit would eat there instead.)

It was infectious too. She kept smiling without meaning to and that only disturbed her further because the food she half-heartedly plopped on her plate wasn't worth smiling about.

Benji sat next to her, their back to the disturbing duo. Under their make-up, Benji looked wrecked. "I don't know what's going on over there," they said quietly. "But I don't like it."

"I'm not sure anyone does," Judit replied, glancing at a posse of Martin's entourage at a table across the restaurant who was side-eyeing Angela with an increasing lack of subtlety.

"Those dipshits are going to get their asses handed to them if Angelica decides to pay attention to them," they chuckled, the sound raspy. "That'll be a good show."

"Why do you call her Angelica?" Judit asked.

"What?" Benji's toast stopped halfway to their mouth.

"You call her Angelica, not Angela."

"Oh," Benji took a bite. Chewed. Swallowed. "Because Angelica is her real name and I want to remind her she came from somewhere." They paused. "Also, every time I call her that, I picture her as that brat Angelica in *Rugrats*. Keeps me from losing my shit when I deal with her."

"She keeps looking at you," Judit said. It was true. Angela (Judit couldn't quite bring herself to think of her as Angelica) had been watching Benji out of the corners of her eyes since they'd entered the room.

Benji's shoulders went taut. "I know. She's my least favorite fangirl."

"Is she harassing you?" Judit asked.

"I don't know what she's doing." Benji looked grim. "That's what worries me."

Judit pushed some pale fruit around on her plate. "Why are they here? Shouldn't they be meeting us at the fest grounds?"

Benji shrugged. "I hear there's a shortage of hotels around here. The pandemic killed a lot of them. Better to camp a tour fleet with a fest than alone, lets you blend in and be less of a target."

Leo set a plate next to them with unnecessary force, making the food on it jump. He glared at Angela and Martin. Martin gave him a finger wave. Leo's fingers tightened on the plate.

"If you're going to sit at our table without asking, at least fucking sit," Benji snapped, not looking up.

Leo sat, turning his glare to Judit. His black eye was ringed in defiant glitter. "You want me to talk to that twat?"

"We just said we'd ask you to," Judit said, "We didn't promise anything."

"It worked, didn't it?" Benji said.

"Hmph." Leo glowered at Martin again.

"You're just giving him what he wants," Benji said.

Leo transferred his glare to Benji. "What do you know?"

"Just what you're making obvious." Benji pinned Leo with a narrow-eyed look. "Are you going to be able to hold it together or do I need to assign you a wrangler?"

Leo looked away. "I'm fine."

"You better be," Benji kept staring at him. "You've caused enough trouble."

"I just don't like them together," Leo said, looking back at the duo.

"Nobody does," Benji muttered. "They're plotting something, I just know it."

"Maybe they actually like each other," Judit said.

She was hit with a pair of baleful glares.

"Enough with the glaring," she said. "They're human beings. Most human beings need friends. We're social animals and all."

"Martin doesn't have friends," Leo said at the same time Benji growled, "Human? Angelica?"

Angela and Martin chose that moment to burst into gales of laughter. It sounded real to Judit, but then they were professional performers so, who knew?

Benji and Leo swiveled towards them.

"Don't look at them," Judit said. "You're just feeding the beast."

Leo turned and pointedly stared at her, his yellow-green eyes boring into her. "All right, then. Good morning Judit, how are you?" He smiled at her with far too many teeth.

Benji rolled their eyes and made a show of paying attention to their food.

"Ready to be on the road," she said.

"Judit," Benji said oh-so-casually, "How did your side quest with Patrick go? Merch all in order? Car okay?"

Judit felt her face heat. "The merch is fine. The car might need looking at, though." She proceeded to give them an unnecessarily in-depth retelling of their car troubles, leaving out her migraine and Patrick taking care of her. Those memories felt... precious.

She didn't want Benji or Leo to jump to any conclusions about that.

LEAVING the truck stop was a relief. However, it left Judit plenty of time to overthink what to tell Eva when she texted for an update. She barely knew what to tell Helen about her side trip. Did she tell them about the whole Patrick being nice to her thing? Could she tell them he was moving on from Cazzi? That seemed private.

Plus, Leo kept coming up to her bunk and lingering in a way that she knew far too well. He wanted a reading. (Funny how people suddenly respected her gifts when they needed something.)

She didn't need her cards to tell her he wouldn't like any reading she gave him. She really didn't want to make a man nearly two feet taller than her mad. She caught Helen's eye and her friend started an impenetrable wall of questions and fangirling.

Leo didn't work up the nerve to ask before they arrived at the campsite. Judit shot out of the bus the minute it parked, her blue Converse kicking up clouds of dust. Helen would keep Leo busy for at least another five minutes. She was happy to have any excuse to talk to him.

The fest was somewhere on the eastern seaboard now, in one of the small states that wasn't New York. It was pretty up here, and blessedly, a handful of degrees cooler and less humid than where they'd just been.

Judit wished she knew more about geography but they hadn't taught it in school and she'd never been very motivated to read about it. Maybe she should remedy that. This might be the only time she got to travel like this.

Her body certainly couldn't take doing this too often. She grimaced at the thought and shunted it aside. It was a reality she couldn't face right now. Not when she fizzed with anxious energy. Instead, she struck off to find Benji, following the tug under her sternum.

She found them in a knot of roadies and stage managers. She waved at Cedric and the folks she knew. Half the knot waved back at her, catching Benji's attention.

"Oh good," they said, "You're here." They seemed to pick up on her manic need to move and put her to work building the merch booth with Helen, taking pictures for social media, then doing inventory on the booth during her shift.

Every time she finished a task, there was another until about an hour after her shift when she was dispatched to go rest and eat with strict instructions not to help for the rest of the day. She crashed for twenty minutes, ate as much food as her anxious stomach could handle, and braved the dregs of the crowd to take a lap around the fest.

Then she called Rohan, asking to be put to work.

"No," he said. "Benji told me you were banned from working until tomorrow. They're looking after you. That's rare on tour. Take it."

"I'm feeling good today," she replied. She felt like she needed to keep moving or she'd drop, hard. "I need to use it while I have it."

He sighed. "Come hang out then. I need a distraction."

She arrived at his tour bus only to find him, Benji, and Patrick sitting in lawn chairs looking exhausted. She sat in the last open one. It was next to Patrick, which sent a frisson of awareness through her.

The chair was too big and the angle too steep to be comfortable but her tired body collapsed the moment she reclined. The last of her energy fled. She groaned. "Dammit Rohan, now I'm never getting up."

"Join the club," he said.

"That's why we're here," Benji said. "We can't get out. They're trap chairs."

Patrick laughed softly.

Rohan and Benji glanced at him in surprise.

"Is Nicky still being squirrelly?" Judit asked, staring out at the trees peeking out between the buses, stages, and fences. Big, lovely old-growth trees.

Benji barked a laugh. "Not while the Doom Twins are here."

"God, Angie and Martin, I can't even..." Rohan mumbled.

Judit would be glad when they were gone. While every

other act that wasn't part of the core tour seemed to be at the fest as little as they could be, those two lingered like a bad stain. Probably because they headlined two alternating nights each this time around.

"Why did we work with Nicky again?" Patrick asked

"He came highly recommended," Benji said.

"By who?" Judit asked. "Someone with no groupies on their tour?"

"God Killing Devil Spawn," Benji said.

They all paused to digest this.

"Family-friendly band, are they?" Rohan asked.

"Christian country pop, actually," Benji joked.

That got a laugh and they settled into companionable silence for a moment.

"How the hell do those dickhead comedians have groupies?" Judit wanted to know. She immediately looked around in case they could hear her. You never knew with everyone wandering everywhere.

The others shrugged. "People think they're funny?" Rohan hazarded.

Benji hummed thoughtfully. "They've opened for tons of bands. I can see why Nicky picked them."

"I want groupies," Judit decided. Groupies would be a nice distraction from whatever was happening with Patrick. Not that merch girls got groupies outside of jackasses leering from the line for the drinks tent.

"No, you don't," said Patrick and Benji at the same time.

"I don't mind groupies," Rohan said with a smile. "They're very sweet."

"What about that time six of them showed up on your doorstep?" Patrick asked.

Rohan's smile dropped. "That was less sweet."

"Just don't get a rep for sleeping with groupies," Benji said.

"Why? Cuz I'm a woman?"

"No, because then everyone you turn down will get upset you don't want to sleep with *them*," Benji said. "The number of 'it's not you, it's me' conversations I've had over the years is ludicrous."

"Just date Angie," Rohan said. "I don't think I got a single come-on while we were dating. Thought I was losing my touch."

"Don't worry," Benji said. "You're still hot."

"Agreed," Judit said. "Completely platonically."

"I'm not into you," Patrick said. "Not my type."

"Damn," Rohan said. "So close to unanimous hotness." He didn't seem bothered. It probably didn't hurt that there was talk he was in the running for *People*'s Sexiest Man Alive this year.

"I always thought you were hot." Martin's voice made Judit sit up as far as she could in her deathtrap of a chair.

Martin and Angela stood to the side of the bus. They were holding hands. *Wow, Angela's a lot taller than Martin, is she in heels?* Judit tried to peer inconspicuously at the other woman's feet but the hem of her dress skimmed the ground.

"You took the words right out of my mouth," Angela said. Her tone could best be described as simpering, amusement sparking in her eyes.

Next to her, Patrick was alert and upright. Rohan was upright too but he looked more bemused than anything. Benji stayed reclined, their eyes half-lidded and unimpressed. They looked damn good, and they knew it.

Angela's attention zeroed in on Benji. The air crackled with her interest. Martin seemed to be enjoying himself with sadistic glee.

"Oh good," Benji muttered. "The wonder twins are here."

"Making the rounds?" Rohan asked. He, at least, was trying to be pleasant.

"Enjoying the night air," Martin said.

Patrick caught Judit's eye and rolled his eyes. She suppressed a grin, the tiny gesture filling her chest with bubbles and heat.

Oh dear. She knew what this was. This was crush territory. Fuck. This would complicate things and that was the last thing she needed.

"Can we help you with anything?" Patrick's voice was flat and smooth, so like Cazzi at her most masked that both Judit and Rohan did a double take.

Angela's eyes narrowed. Martin grinned.

"Oh no," Martin said airily. "We just wanted to stop by and say hi." He smiled at Angela like a newlywed on his honeymoon.

Her answering half-smile was a twisted mirror of his expression, her eyes too wide, her mouth too tight. Judit couldn't tell if that was on purpose or if she just wasn't sure how to look genuinely happy.

Judit glanced at Rohan but he still looked bemused. Benji modeled apathy while Patrick impersonated a blank slate.

"You two are so cute together," Judit said because she'd reached her fuck-it limit and wanted to see what would happen.

Martin and Angela looked at her, assessing her sincerity. She kept her expression light and smiley. Their combined attention had an almost physical weight. Their expressions seemed pasted on.

Seconds stretched and Judit wondered if they were going to be here smiling at each other for eternity.

Benji stood in one fluid, hateably graceful motion and walked away.

Angela's gaze snapped away, narrowing at their back. Martin sighed, so quietly Judit saw rather than heard it. "Thank you, Judit. You're sweet." He glanced at Rohan and Patrick. "It's nice to meet someone genuine in this business."

Rohan and Patrick stared back at him, stone-faced.

"Come on, Angela." Martin tugged her hand, steering her away until they rounded the corner and disappeared.

The minute he was far enough away, Rohan and Patrick burst into laughter.

"What the actual fuck was that?" Rohan chortled.

Patrick snorted, shaking his head. "'Someone genuine in this business' that's rich, coming from him."

Benji stuck their head out of the bus. "You know they're just gonna go find Leo right? If they haven't already."

That sent everyone scrambling out of their chairs.

26

PARTY WITH CREEPMOTHER!!!!
MUSIC! FUN! BOOZE! PILLS!! MORE!!!
WHERE: OUR BUS
WHEN: EVERY SATURDAY ALL TOUR LONG! 8 PM
BRING YOUR HOT GROUPIES!!

Patrick shot out of his chair like a rocket, his tired mind suddenly very awake. He should've been on Leo despite his exhaustion. Leo and Martin were like the worst kind of missiles, always homing in on each other when they were in range.

Judit stood with him, extracting herself from the chair with care and not a little stiffness. She put her hand on Rohan's shoulder when he started to rise, stopping him. "Somehow, I don't think having you there will help." She looked at Benji on the stairs of the bus. "You definitely can't come."

Benji frowned but didn't argue.

"He's at some party. He invited me. The guys who go on

after Doc Conjure are throwing it." Patrick wracked his brain trying to remember where it was or what the band was called.

"Creepmother?" Judit set off quickly like she knew exactly where she was going.

"Did they invite you?" He suppressed the urge to run. He wasn't sure she would be able to keep up.

"Oh yeah." Her mouth flattened into a line.

"What?"

"They're very... twenty-one."

"Meaning?"

"Enthusiastic and not too bright."

"Ah." *Great.*

Judit led them in a straight line, only deviating from her path to circle stages and cars. Her confidence was unnerving, given they'd barely been here a day and he was fairly certain she'd never gone to any of the afterparties. "You know where you're going?"

She nodded. He bet they were following one of her feelings. That he was starting to trust her intuition the way he trusted Nana's felt strange. Whatever they were following brought them across the grounds to what was indeed a party.

He heard it first, pumping bass that overwhelmed any musicality and was tinny to boot. The party spilled out around Creepmother's bus, lit by a floodlight that probably shouldn't have been there. Half the crew and talent seemed to be in attendance. With the number of red Solo cups and the clouds of weed mixing with cigarette smoke, it looked like a college party collided with a tour bus. Patrick felt old just thinking that. Sure, he'd gone to parties like this when he was younger but it was mostly out of social obligation and the idea that he should be having "fun." That he should have crazy stories.

He hoped tonight's story wouldn't be crazy at all.

Leo was easy to spot, head and shoulders above everyone else, and wearing a shirt entirely made of red fringe.

Martin and Angela were nowhere to be seen. Patrick let out a breath. Maybe they were wrong and the two headliners weren't conspiring—

Nope, there they were, coming around the corner out of the shadows.

He looked at Judit only to realize she'd already inserted herself in Leo's conversation group. Though how anyone could have a conversation with all this bass was beyond him. Patrick followed her, tracking Angela and Martin. He was very aware of the angelica roots in his pocket. The crowd slowly turned towards the couple as they approached the edge of the light.

Why? Why did they have to team up? They weren't having enough fun fucking with everyone on their own?

Patrick reached Leo's side just as his friend started turning with the crowd. Leo paused, catching the expression on Patrick's face. "What? What's up?" He bellowed over the music. If you didn't know him, you wouldn't notice the faint blush in his cheeks or his slight slur.

Shit.

Leo's eyes focused. "What?" he repeated, his voice more urgent.

"I don't know what they're doing," Patrick said, as quickly and quietly as he could while still yelling. He didn't dare turn his head but he could tell they were getting closer and closer. "But I don't think it's real. Don't give them the satisfaction."

"Oh hell," Leo said. "I'm not going to like this, am I?"

"Nope!" Judit yelled.

Leo turned his head, Judit following suit. Patrick watched Leo. His friend was an open book, but still managed to keep secrets. It involved compartmentalization and hurt him every time. It was one of the reasons Patrick hated Martin, for making Leo keep all those damn secrets, diminishing him for all these years.

Everything seemed to go slow, sounds taking an underwater echo.

Leo's face went from drunk and guarded, to shocked and hurt, back to guarded, anger quick on its heels. He crushed the cup he was holding in his fist, something neon and sticky sloshing over his hand. Patrick wanted to punch Martin for Leo, but as it was, he braced himself, ready to tackle his friend.

"Didn't we just see you?" Martin shouted, a smirk in his words.

"Small fest," Judit said sweetly.

Martin smirked at Leo. The drink dripped from Leo's hand. At Martin's side, Angela sized up the situation.

She frowned.

Around them, the crowd went tense. Conversations stuttered. The volume of the music dropped, like whoever was running a playlist and calling it DJing suddenly realized shit was going down.

Judit bit her lip. Patrick could almost hear her thinking, trying to find a way to intervene.

"Holy shit!" A white guy with dyed black hair, at least six silver rings in his face, and the prerequisite punk pop skinny jeans—heat be damned—appeared, clutching his black beanie like it might fly away. Patrick was fairly sure he was the singer of Creepmother. "Angela fucking Alice is here. Guys!" He turned, yelling into the crowd, his voice over loud in the sudden quiet. "The fuckin' Bitch Queen is at OUR FUCKIN' PARTY!"

"Dude!" Another guy popped his head out of nowhere, joint in hand. "Holy fuck, man. I'm such a big fan." He was tatted from the neck down like a wannabe Travis Barker so he was probably the drummer. His cut-off shirt and ropey arms supported that.

"We all are," a third white guy yelled from farther back. He looked like someone put Pete Wentz of Fall Out Boy in a blender with a member of Insane Clown Posse and called it a bassist. Gold chains, gold teeth, and an emo hair flip of the kind Patrick hadn't seen since 2010.

Angela half-smiled like this was her due and she was used to it. Martin smiled too but Patrick could tell he was quietly steaming. When was the last time Martin had been upstaged?

Creepmother tried to whisk Angela into their circle, beckoning and grinning.

"No," she said.

"Aw, come on," the singer said, "Have a drink. On the house." He winked.

Angela showed him her teeth in something that could be called a smile if you'd only ever heard of a smile in theory. "You don't want me to have a drink."

The bassist and the drummer drew back but the singer was definitely drunker than them. "We've got weed too." He leaned in like he was about to let her in on a secret but didn't lower his voice. "And pills."

Patrick was almost certain Angela would unhinge her jaw and rip his head off.

She showed even more teeth. People backed away. Patrick wanted to back away. There was something scary in her eyes, a dead, flat light that said, *Not only have I seen some shit, I've done some bad things.* After yesterday, he believed that.

The singer put his arm over her shoulders. Angela watched him like a spider watching a fly fall into her web.

Patrick grimaced. Judit covered her mouth. Leo swore under his breath. Even Martin took a step back, dropping her hand.

Creepmother's singer yanked her towards him.

Angela swiveled her head like a horror movie doll and then everything moved so fast Patrick had to reconstruct it in his head afterward.

Angela drove her palm into the singer's chest, slamming

him into the dirt. His beanie went flying. Patrick could hear the breath slap out of his lungs. She knelt on his chest, not letting him catch his breath, one hand pressed against his throat. She hooked a finger in the biggest ring on his face.

"Touch me again," she growled, her voice low but pitched to carry. She sounded demonic, tenuously in control. "I dare you."

Her long white hair curtained her face but judging by the singer's expression it was as frightening as her voice. He shook his head frantically. The finger looped in his jewelry moved with him. She probably didn't want to rip it out just yet.

She leaned closer. The singer tried to lean away but the ground was too firm. There was a long, loaded pause where it seemed like she was saying something but Patrick couldn't hear what.

"Uh-huh," the singer mumbled.

"Promise?" she rasped. The baby hairs on Patrick's neck stood on end. He couldn't look away. Dread churned in his stomach.

The singer nodded desperately.

"Good. Remember this." She unhooked her finger and stood, leaving the kid wheezing in the dirt. "Take me home, Marty." She held out her arm.

Martin looped his arm in hers, looking disoriented. The crowd parted before them. No one wanted to be anywhere near touching her. As the shadows swallowed them, her laughter rang out, joyous and free.

"Holy shit," Judit mumbled, hands covering her mouth. Her eyes were huge over her fingers.

"Well," Leo said. "That was not how I expected that to go."

"Somehow, I don't think that's how Martin thought it would go either," Patrick said, glad he was able to keep his voice dry. He'd seen that kind of reactive violence before but not in a long time and never so forceful. Cazzi had done her best to train that out of herself. But damn, Angela looked like the scariest possible version of Cazzi during a trauma response.

27

"Know how you see me
Not quite right
Don't fit your list
Exactly the wrong kiss

You're wrong, wrong, wrong
If you'd just look, look, look

Lemme show you, baby

I'm your missing piece
The bad you can't quite face
Lemme show you
It's not all tragic on the wicked side"
— "Lemme Show You" by Beatboyz off of *Trouble*

Still dazed by Angela's freak out, Judit found she agreed to let Patrick walk her to the bus.

"I don't think she's prowling the grounds looking to attack people," she pointed out when he brought it up.

He glanced at Dylan, the singer of Creepmother, sitting in a folding chair like his dog had died, been resurrected, and tried to kill him. His band had pulled him upright. He'd brushed them off, loudly declaring he was "fine" but he hadn't said a thing since. Judit was pretty sure Angela broke something in him and it wasn't his sternum. He hadn't drunk or smoked since and he even turned down one of the pills he'd been so excited about.

Judit still couldn't believe what she'd seen. She wasn't exactly sheltered. When you lived in the janky part of a city like Sacramento and rode (or drove) public transit you saw some crazy shit but that... that had to be both the coolest and freakiest thing she'd ever witnessed.

"It'll make him feel better," Leo stage-whispered. He was on his way to another bus with a roadie.

Patrick shrugged in agreement.

What the hell. She'd said yes, and here they were, walking through the shadowy festival grounds in silence.

"Thank you," he said.

She startled. "For what?"

"For your help."

She stared at what she could see of him in the dark. "You're welcome?"

"What you said in the car—"

"I'm sorry. I shouldn't have pushed so hard I just—"

"No, it's okay. You were right."

"I-I was?" She gathered herself. "I mean, thank you."

He nodded and heaved a breath. "I needed to process it but I couldn't find the words to tell you that."

"Oh." She blinked, rearranging the memory of his silence in her mind. "I can give you more space next time if that helps."

"Maybe, yeah."

"I get it. I hate when people harp on shit I know they know

I know if that makes sense." She laughed.

He smiled. "I feel you."

"Anyway, I know better and I'm sorry I did it to you."

"Thanks." He stopped, turning his face to the sky. "Look."

She looked. Stars spangled the sky like a sea of distant fairy lights. More than she'd seen, maybe ever.

"Whoa," she breathed.

"Yeah."

They stood, taking in the view. She felt small, unmoored, but weirdly connected in a gooey New Age way she didn't want to examine. Like, they were the only two people in the universe. Just her and Patrick, standing so close she felt the heat from his arm next to hers.

She missed being held. On the tour, she'd tried to avoid touching people besides Helen or Sabrina, mostly because she didn't feel like she knew them. But the way he held her before called to her.

She leaned into him.

He stiffened. She almost pulled back but then he softened and leaned into her. His locs bumped her shoulder. Old Spice, shea butter, and lavender washed over her. It was lovely but it made her want more, too much more. But she couldn't pull away.

She shivered.

"You cold?" he asked.

She shrugged, using the motion to pull herself away.

She moved to keep walking but he said, "Are we good?"

"I don't know, are we?" She turned to face him but caught the toe of her sneaker on a dip in the dirt and flailed, almost falling. He caught her, his warm arms holding her lightly, her hands landing on his broad shoulders. She stared up at him, barely visible and backlit by the stars. She couldn't make out his features well, but she knew at that moment she could've drawn him accurately from memory (if she knew how to draw).

A sense of rightness hummed through her. A feeling. A strong one. This was exactly where she needed to be.

(Oh fuck.)

"Half of me wants to be friends," she said, letting the words spill out even as her stomach swooped and her brain freaked out.

"And the other half?" He breathed, his voice quiet and endlessly deep. She could feel it vibrate in his chest against her nipples. Every nerve in her body turned on.

He leaned down. She went on her toes, pausing a breath before his mouth. "Yes?"

He nodded.

His head dipped, hers went up and... their lips met. Every nerve went electric.

She looped her arms around his neck, grinding closer, his embrace tightening. He licked her bottom lip, and she opened for him, nipping his top one. He seemed to like that because he cupped the back of her head and his breath went even more ragged.

She didn't know how long they kissed but it felt like forever and not long enough. She couldn't remember kissing like that since secret make-outs in high school. Desperate, foolish, and electrifying.

When they broke for air, she clung to him for balance. "Whoa."

He chuckled, the sound running through her body, wreaking all kinds of havoc. "Yeah."

No wonder Cazzi had been so hung up on him.

Oh hell. Cazzi.

He seemed to have the same thought at the same time because they pulled apart almost together.

"We shouldn't have done that," he said. She was thinking the same thing but it still hurt to hear.

"Yeahhhh," Judit sighed. "But we're single adults. We just let off some steam. It's been hectic. It was stress relief."

"No one needs to know."

"It was an anomaly. We're not run by our desires. I'm sure it'll be the last time." (Did it sound like she was lying? It felt like she was lying.)

"Too bad," he murmured almost too quietly for her to hear.

"Don't do that," she said. "Don't fucking tempt me."

She could only see the edge of his smile in the dark but it was wicked. She shivered again, though she felt overheated and needy. She wanted to grab him back, kiss him more, fuck him right here in the dirt. Too bad it was a terrible idea on several fronts.

"You're right," he said, his voice serious. "It'd be too messy."

Thank goodness he was on the same page as her. (Now, if she could only stop wanting to shake him for being so damn reasonable.) She couldn't get off with him anyway. She'd never be able to face herself after, let alone Cazzi.

Dammit. She turned back towards the bus, determinedly counting her steps to calm her mind and body. He kept pace with her, silent but still oh-so-tempting as they reached the other tour bus area, the lights bringing his features into view. God, he was gorgeous.

A gorgeous mistake. One she wouldn't make again. The guilt was already creeping in, but she refused to let it taint the moment.

They arrived at the door and she said, "Let's be friends?"

"Sure." But the way he looked at her made her want to throw herself at him again.

28

Hey Cazzi, funny story, I kinda kissed Patrick?
Hey so, you're over Patrick, right? Cuz we might have a thing
I kissed Patrick (we kissed each other) Patrick and I kissed
Is it weird if I date Patrick? We kinda have a thing...
Oh god, i did a thing dont hate me
—Judit's deleted texts

P atrick was distracted over the next week. He forgot things, consulting his to-do list more times than he probably ever had in his entire life. It didn't help that he was rusty on the admin tasks he'd let slide over the last year. But now that Nicky was basically useless he couldn't just stand by, even though he'd dropped his phone so many times Leo asked him if someone lubed it up. Even now, despite his best efforts, the cracks of his case were still encrusted in mud from the rain that morning.

It would bother him more but all he could think of was Judit's body—her lips—against his in the dark. She played like a sensual melody under his thoughts, interfering and popping up at the worst time until he stuttered and clammed and looked like he was fucking unprepared.

Rohan and Benji kept looking at each other every time he did like they knew something he didn't. Leo kept laughing at him. Sabrina straight up asked if he was okay.

Judit seemed to be everywhere: on the bus, working the booth, in the dining tent, chatting with Rohan or Benji, hanging out with the roadies or Sabrina and Helen. At least she wasn't riding with them on Rohan's bus right now, talking business. Everyone seemed to fucking like her, even Leo now, but then what was there not to like? They didn't even know how she could make you lose your mind with a kiss.

They didn't know—right? Well, Leo definitely didn't and Rohan never cheated once in Patrick's entire time of knowing him despite ample opportunity. Patrick looked at him over Benji's shoulder, flopped across the bus's couch, dead to the world, his phone pressed to his chest. That he was probably waiting for a text from Cazzi when she got off work in an hour was a vague irritant. Judit hummed through his mind, a competing melody. She was only a friend, a distraction, but even so, it relieved him that Rohan wasn't likely to hurt Cazzi just to poach Patrick's friend again.

Would Benji? Judit did seem awfully friendly with them...

Patrick looked up from double-checking the schedule on the next stop near Minneapolis to consider the enby sitting across the bolted-down table from him. Benji bent over their phone, the reading glasses no fan would ever see perched on their nose. Curls flopped over their forehead and a frown creased their brow. Patrick personally didn't find them attractive but he could tell his was the minority opinion.

"Stare all you want," they said without looking up. "But if you touch, I'm gonna start charging."

"Get over yourself," Patrick replied. "You're in my staring space."

"I'm in everyone's staring space," Benji said, the reflexive brag sounding tired. They took their glasses off and rubbed their eyes. "Ugh, someday we're going to make enough to outsource some of this media management to a team."

Patrick let out a breath. Of course, Benji wasn't running around trying to get into Judit's pants. They probably didn't even have time to get into their own pants. He winced at the image and how off-base his whole line of thought was. Even if Judit fucked half the crew he wouldn't have a right to say anything. Somehow that only frazzled him more.

"How are we doing?" he asked, trying to get out of his Judit spiral.

Benji shrugged. "Well enough. Reviews are mixed, sales are decent, and socials are getting increased traffic. We might be able to put together a NoN-only tour next year."

Rohan groaned. "Don't talk to me about next year."

Benji rolled their eyes. "I'll have you know UFO once toured—"

"For a year and a half straight," Rohan and Patrick chorused. Rohan grinned sleepily and Patrick let himself smile a bit.

"Beatboyz toured for months on end too," Patrick pointed out.

"Stadium tours with fancy hotels," Benji muttered.

"When we were big," Rohan said. "We did our fair share of malls and sleeping in vans. I think we visited every single mall open in the mid-2000s."

"Don't tell me UFO didn't have big ass tours and nice hotels," Patrick said. "You went platinum and headlined a bunch of tours."

"Are we competing on who had the biggest tours or the shittiest?" Rohan rubbed sleep out of his eyes.

Benji shrugged, the gesture making them smaller somehow. Patrick noticed deepening shadows around their eyes under their make-up.

"You good?" Patrick asked.

Rohan sat up, fully awake now. His thick hair was standing at odd angles and Patrick was tempted to take a picture just for blackmail purposes. He stopped the thought before it could sound too fun. That was pre-Rohan stealing Cazzi behavior. Hell, it was feed-the-content-machine pre-Beatboyz break-up behavior. The fans would've loved it.

Benji nodded. "Just tired."

Rohan reached over the back of the couch and patted Benji's arm. "Switch. You nap, I'll look at media shit."

Benji shook their head. "I'm fine."

"Give me something to do," Rohan insisted.

"Go back to sleep. You gotta look pretty for your interview in thirty minutes."

"It's a phoner," Rohan said. "Nice try."

"You know he's just going to keep annoying you," Patrick pointed out. "Might as well give him something to keep him occupied."

Rohan shot him a smile. Patrick nodded back.

"Fine," Benji said. "I'll mark some of the emails we need to respond to in the Now or Never inbox. Can you take care of them?"

"On it!" Rohan picked up his tablet.

Patrick went to the small kitchenette and pulled a mug down. He had his day bag with him so only a few first aid and daily use herbs but—

"Don't make me one of your gross-ass herbal teas," Benji said.

"Shut up. They're good for you," Patrick said.

"You sound like my mother," Benji grumbled.

"It's okay to allow people to take care of you," Rohan said. "Now what do you want me to say to this magazine? They look super small, but I kinda like their style."

Benji answered but Patrick was rooted in place. Rohan's

advice was exactly what Cazzi would've said had she been there. The hurt of that got duller every day, even as it found a new spot to hit him. Maybe, someday, every part of him would be inured to the pain. It made him hopeful.

29

"Never seen anything like
Your hair framing your face
The sparkle in your eyes
How you say my name and sigh

I'm wordless
Fumbling, bumbling
Can't say your name or I'd die
(pretty, pretty)
All I wanna say is

You're pretty pretty
Please
All I'm asking is
Pretty pretty
Please"
— "Pretty Please" by Beatboyz off of *Beatboyz*

Judit hit the motel bed like a ton of bricks. It was a tad lumpy but god, so much better than the bus bunk. Helen had already dropped her stuff and gone to hang out with some roadies. She'd invited Judit but there was no way Judit was giving up the privacy.

She reveled in what passed for silence in a motel: someone showering next door, people talking in the hall, the rest of the tour settling in for the night, and a suspiciously rhythmic squeaking above her. Still, it was quieter than the bus and without the prickling awareness that Patrick was barely two arm's lengths away.

There was a knock on her door. Had Helen forgotten her key? She'd already forgotten her key in their room three times over the tour. Luckily, Judit tended to burrow into the room and not leave until breakfast.

"Coming," she called, hauling herself out of the embrace of the bed. Could she staple the room keycard to Helen's shorts? Maybe that was extreme.

She opened the door, ready to give her shit about forgetting again. The words died on her lips. Patrick stood there, looking as tired as she felt. "Dinner?" he asked. "We're all going to the place next door."

It was only then she realized he wasn't alone. Sabrina, Benji, Rohan, and Leo were all with him.

She almost said no. Patrick looked like he needed sleep more than food, but she wasn't his mother. Plus, she was hungry.

"Uh, sure," she said. "Give me a sec. I'll meet you there."

After a quick outfit change and touch-up on her make-up, she headed for the restaurant attached to the motel. Dimly lit, it looked like it had been built in the 1970s and stayed there while the world moved on. There was a rock wall, a counter at the bar, shiny napkin dispensers, and a mint green and blood-red linoleum-checkered floor. She blinked, taking it in as a waitress about her mother's age with '80s curls speed-walked past, tossing a "Welcome to St. Croix's," at her in a bright cheery voice at odds with the state of the eyeliner bleeding out around her eyes.

"Judit!" Sabrina stood from a table across the restaurant, waving. The rest of the table looked over. Most of them waved, and Patrick gave her a small smile.

Judit wove around the few patrons towards them, keeping a reflexive six feet away from strangers and waving at a group of roadies at the bar. They waved back, and she noted both Helen and Cedric were MIA. Hmmm.

Dinner was nice. The food wasn't anything special but the company was fun. Leo had the table snorting their drinks and dying of laughter with his tales of the drag queen circuit. He could make even the worst show disasters hilarious. His and his fellow queens' tucking mishaps made everyone but Sabrina and Judit cross their legs and do their best not to clutch their crotches in public. Which just made her and Sabrina laugh even harder.

Eventually, his stories gave way to anecdotes from the Beat-boyz days, drawing Rohan and even Patrick sometimes into telling bits and pieces. Patrick tried to cover his little sister's ears a few times during the scandalous stories but Sabrina waved him off, demanding more.

It was strange to see Rohan and Patrick telling stories of when they were friends when it was clear their friendship was still strained.

Would that be me and Cazzi if I date Patrick? Judit thought sadly. No way she'd throw away a friendship over a good kiss (even if it was really, really, ridiculously good). *But I mean, Cazzi's happy with Rohan. Maybe it wouldn't be weird.*

Nah, it'd probably be weird, at least at first. But maybe it could be good, eventually.

Not that she was planning on dating Patrick. It was just one kiss.

After dinner, they ended up in Leo's room. The conversation and laughter buoyed her until she barely felt her exhaustion. Patrick and Leo sat on one bed, Benji and Rohan on the other, and the booze Leo usually stashed in the bus was arrayed in front of the TV, which played some shitty late-night movie no one watched. She curled up on the chair, Sabrina lounging on the arm, her head hanging above Judit's. If things were different, Judit would probably be damn happy about having a pretty girl practically in her lap. But Patrick kept looking at her with warmth in his eyes.

If she was a reasonable woman, she wouldn't stare back at him. If she were reasonable, she'd pick someone less messy, someone open and easy. But she wanted him, the man with the endlessly dark eyes that always seemed to be watching her.

She hadn't drunk much, but what alcohol she had in her supplied her imagination with a thousand ways she could sneak out of this room and he could find her, alone. She felt like she was burning alive under his gaze.

"You alright?" Sabrina nudged her shoulder. "You're quiet."

"Huh?" Judit came back to the moment. "Yeah, fine, just getting tired."

Patrick wasn't even looking at her now and she wanted to drag him into a dark corner. She looked away. She needed to get out of there.

So she did, making her excuses and getting out as fast as she could.

In the hallway, she let out a breath, expecting the tension from the room to dissipate now there was a door between her and Patrick. It didn't.

She headed towards the stairway. She was two floors up and though her hips ached, the idea of waiting for an elevator and then waiting in the elevator made her antsy. Besides stairs were exercise and she practically vibrated with sexual tension.

She closed the door to the stairway behind her. Maybe Helen would be out all night again and—

The door opened again. She turned, her skin prickling. She'd known who it was immediately and there he stood, staring at her like she was everything.

"What's up?" she said, her voice casual.

He climbed the steps until he was eye-level, a few steps below her. "Yes?" The whisper was low, raspy, tortured.

It was exactly what she shouldn't do. It was exactly what she wanted.

"Yes," she breathed.

He kissed her like he was dying, pressing her into the wall but protecting her back with his embrace. Her nerves combusted, bursting into electric fireworks. She clung to him, kissing him back with every needy moment, every conflicted feeling. Her hands went under his shirt, feeling the muscles of his back, the warmth of his skin.

His hands roamed too, mapping her body from face to hips and everything in between, his touch trailing sparks over her skin. Then they hovered over the edge of her skirt, uncertain.

Did he know how much he was making her clit ache? How if he fucked her right here, she'd probably come in two minutes flat?

She gently guided his fingers up. He complied eagerly, tracing her thigh and then over the fabric of her undies. She moaned into his mouth, grinding closer to him until she could feel both his hand and his bulge. He gasped, his hips thrusting against hers, the palm of his hand finding her clit and pressing.

Judit scraped his lip with her teeth, rubbing against him. She was lost, mindless, chasing that feeling.

"Does that feel good?" he rasped against her lips.

"Mm-hmm."

"Can I?" One finger lifted the lacy edge of her underwear.

"Please," she gasped. Then hesitated, feeling the still-tight muscles of her pelvis. "Wait, no."

He paused.

"Sometimes penetration... isn't good for me." When her pelvic muscles were this reactive... yeah, better not.

He nodded. "No penetration, got it. Can I touch your skin? Your clit?"

"Oh, please," she moaned.

He complied, the first shock of his skin against her clit making her drop her head and bite his shoulder.

"A biter, huh?"

"Like it?"

"Yeah." He flicked her clit and she lost the ability to form words. Instead, she groped down until she found him, stroking his dick through his jeans. God, he was *so hard*. He pressed into her touch, just as needy as her. That turned her on almost as much as what his fingers were doing. If they weren't where they were she'd get on her knees and...

His fingers hit her clit just right, her nipples scraped against his chest and her brain melted as the orgasm hit her.

She cried out but he caught the noise with his mouth. She clung to him, losing her mind.

He held her when her bones melted, his lips pressed against the skin of her temple until she came down. She grinned at him and he murmured, "Good?"

"Very." She popped the top button of his fly. She leaned in and whispered, "I'd suck you off, but not here. I wanna touch you though." She put a finger under the waistband of his briefs. "Can I?"

"Please." The word sounded like he'd tried to strangle it on the way out.

"You sure?"

He paused, like he was thinking about it, then: "Yes." He sounded surer so she popped the rest of his buttons and grabbed him. He groaned at her touch, his fingers playing with her nipples through her bra. She couldn't feel much through the thick cups but he seemed to realize that pretty fast.

His hands went under her shirt and popped her breasts out of the cups and then she was the one gasping and moaning. They were so close together and he was revving her up again and it was all she could do not to guide him into her. But she'd never had unprotected p-in-v and she wasn't about to when it would also put her in massive pain later.

"I'm close," he gasped. "I don't—I don't want to mess up your skirt."

She smiled at the thoughtfulness. "Hold on." She pulled a tissue out of her pocket. Well, it was a napkin from the diner, but sometimes tissues were hard to come by. She wrapped the head of his dick, stroked him with the other hand, and leaned in to murmur, "Come for me."

He grabbed her breasts harder and moaned into her mouth. She reveled in it, biting his lip.

He came hard, backing her into the wall and collapsing against her, panting. She held him, his breaths moving against her nipples in a way that made her think reckless things.

"I hate saying this," he said after a while. "But this was a mistake."

"Oh, I know," she said. She'd been thinking the same thing. "But it was the hottest mistake I've made in a while."

He chuckled into her hair. His hips pressed closer to her and she could tell he wasn't all soft yet. "Don't tempt me," he murmured, plucking the now very full napkin from her hand.

"Don't stare at me like you want to fuck me senseless and I won't." The words slipped out of her mouth before she could stop them.

He kissed her then pulled back, examining her face. "I'm not sure I can."

It took all her willpower not to fuck him again right there and then.

30

Bitch on A Beach: NoN is Taking A Day Off!
That's right, beloveds! Our very own Benji is taking us to their friend's
lake house this Wednesday. Keep it on the DL, kittens. This is an NoN-
exclusive so if you must bring a friend or fuck-buddy, swear 'em to secrecy
cuz we don't have room in the van for every Tom, Dick, and Carrie on the
tour. Get your swimsuits, your flippy floppies, be on the bus by 11 am, and
prepare to get Minnesota drunk while pretending that the sandbars of a
lake qualify as a beach (we all know they don't).
—Tourgasm vol. 8

The guilt set in the minute they were apart. *What are you doing?* She berated herself in the shower. *Couldn't think with your brain instead of your pussy?*

It was a great orgasm though. Her pelvic muscles weren't even that upset about it.

That said, she didn't be his rebound, quick fix, or whatever. Plus, Cazzi would probably feel horribly betrayed if she found out. He was right: This had been a mistake.

Now, if only she could be sure it wouldn't happen again the

minute they were alone. She groaned aloud, turning off the water.

Maybe, she thought as she toweled off, *I should just never be alone with him.*

The idea was kind of childish, but it just might work. After all, there were only a few weeks left of the tour. How often would they be alone anyway?

She suspected it would be more than was healthy.

Sure enough, he was the only person when she came down at breakfast. They sat apart but Benji dragged her over when they came down and sat her next to Patrick. She tensed. Had Benji figured out what happened? Had Patrick told them?

But one glance at Patrick told her he was similarly nervous. Not that his face was anything but blank but something about the set of his shoulders and the tension vibrating off him made her sure. He sipped his tea and nodded at her like they hadn't spent an eternal second staring at each other when she'd come in earlier.

"Okay kids," Benji said. "We're in the final leg of the tour and two weeks from now will feature the return of the Doom Twins."

Judit raised her hand.

"Yes, Judit?" Benji asked like this was a perfectly normal way to conduct a conversation.

"Who are the Doom Twins? Is that a band?" Also, wasn't two weeks a bit far out for this sort of planning? She didn't bother asking that though, she knew Benji always liked having a plan.

"No, that's my new name for Angelica and Martin's collaboration from hell, remember?" Benji said.

"Oh, right," Judit said like this wasn't weird at all. "Tell us how you really feel."

Benji waved her sarcasm away. "The last show is at Discovery Park in Sacramento. Lots of local bands. Plus, Nicky has a big afterparty planned. It's going to be a chaotic mess and I doubt the Doom Twins will be able to resist stirring up trouble."

Judit had forgotten the last show was in her neck of the woods. She'd already put Eva on the list. Cazzi was on Rohan's list. She absolutely couldn't be alone with Cazzi. She'd sniff her secrets out in a minute flat. Eva too. Oh fucking hell, she was so screwed.

"What do you need?" Patrick asked, sounding low on patience. Judit wondered if he was coming to similar conclusions.

"All hands on deck," Benji said. "Rick, I need you to keep an eye on Leo. Let me know if he looks like he's gonna go rogue again."

Patrick nodded.

"Judit, I need you on distraction duty. The Doom Twins like you. Keep them out of trouble as much as possible."

"Me?" The word came out as a squeak.

"I'll back you up whatever you do," Benji said. "You seem to have sound judgment and you keep your head around all that celebrity nonsense."

"Me?" Judit repeated, feeling slightly surreal.

"They're right," Patrick said quietly.

Her face got warm and the feeling of unreality intensified.

"You'll do it?" Benji asked.

"I'll do my best," Judit said.

Benji nodded. "We'll help as much as we can. Right, Rick?"

Patrick nodded.

"Good," Benji took a sip of coffee. "Now we're heading to that lake today so—"

"Lake?" Judit asked.

"Didn't you see the latest Tourgasm?" Benji asked.

"Oh." She fumbled with her phone. "I guess not." She

skimmed through Leo's email until she got to the relevant post. "Cool!"

"Anyway," Benji said. "Let's all try not to be assholes to each other, okay? Some of us would like to enjoy our day off." With that, they stood and headed for the exit. "Eleven am sharp, kids!"

"I forgot we'd be doing that today." Patrick scrubbed his hand down his face and took a long gulp of tea. "Fuck."

"This doesn't have to be awkward." Judit sipped her tea. "We're adults and all that junk."

He looked at her. "I'm not worried about it being awkward or us being immature." He raised an eyebrow.

Her face got hot. Her knee bumped his and stayed even though her thighs really wanted to squeeze together. She bit her lip. His eyes locked on the movement and she heard him groan faintly.

The door banged open to admit a couple of bleary-eyed drivers and a cook from the mess tent. Everyone nodded politely at everyone else. Judit tried to pretend it was normal that both her hands were fisted in her lap, not to mention her knee still glued to Patrick's. By the time it seemed like they'd lost the attention of the room, her hands ached.

A warm palm covered her fist. "Relax," he murmured. "It'll sell it better."

"Sell what?" she asked, consciously unclenching her hands. His fingers slipped into her palm but he didn't take them away. Ever so gently, she rested her thumb across his knuckles.

"That there's nothing to see here." His gaze devoured her.

"You not staring at me like you're willing yourself to have x-ray vision would sell it better."

He blinked slowly but didn't look away. "Probably."

"Be careful. I've heard intense staring can be habit-forming."

"Then you're my favorite bad habit." His voice hit a low

note, shivering down her spine, heading for the slow-building ache in her clit.

A gasp caught in Judit's throat. *Holy fuck.*

Rohan set a plate next to Judit with a yawn.

Immediately, Patrick looked away, withdrawing his hand in the process. Judit jerked her gaze away but the loss of the moment left her breathless.

"Morning," Rohan said, around another yawn. "I think I'm getting too old to drink. I'm fucking hungover and I didn't even kill a bottle or switch liquors."

"Kill a bottle?" Judit blinked, feeling slow. "Like drinking it from start to finish?" Two drinks and she was done, she couldn't imagine drinking that much.

Rohan glanced at Patrick. "Is this one of those things we think is normal cuz we're out-of-touch celebrities, but really isn't?"

Patrick shrugged. "Our drinking role model was Leo."

"Oh yeah," Rohan nodded, then winced. "Yeah, that'll do it." He groaned, covering his eyes. "How are you not hungover? You're *older* than me," he whined.

"Uh-huh," Patrick said. "In the wisdom of being a full year and a half older than you, I drank less." He patted Rohan's curls. "Don't worry. Next year you'll get heartburn too."

"Noooo," Rohan groaned.

Judit patted his hand. "If it makes you feel better, I already have the heartburn. I had like, a handful, of Tums last night. It was disgusting."

Patrick chuckled like he knew exactly what she was talking about, his knee pressing into hers.

"Ugh, stop it!" Rohan said.

Patrick and Judit stiffened, their knees springing away from each other.

"Tums are the grossest thing ever," Rohan continued. "How can you affront your taste buds like that?"

"Foodie snob," Patrick said.

"Look," Rohan said, chewing a bite of his eggs with a grimace. "I won a cooking show, I get to be a snob."

"You were competing against other celebrities who thought they could boil water, not actual cooks. Don't get too high and mighty," Patrick said.

Judit almost snorted tea out her nose. That would've been a waste because she was falling in love with the tea he'd made her. The daily ritual was surprisingly comforting and her pain had faded somewhat.

Patrick seemed to notice her mug for the first time. He gave her reusable tea bag an assessing look.

Rohan rolled his eyes. "Just for that, I'm going to burn whatever you order for lunch today. Grill Master's prerogative," he said with a grin.

Patrick narrowed his eyes. "You wouldn't."

"Try me." Rohan locked eyes with him.

"You love food too much," Patrick said, staring back.

"Dammit." Rohan looked away. "You're right."

"Wait, you're cooking for us?" Judit asked. "I thought this was your day off too."

Rohan shrugged. "Cooking relaxes me and frankly, I need grilling practice. There's so much you can do with an open flame and hot coals." His expression got far off and dreamy. It was the kind of look Papi got when he was working out a new recipe.

Judit was hit with a shock of homesickness. She'd see her family soon, with the tour ending in a few weeks. Then she'd go back to... what? Gig jobs and no insurance? If she was lucky her doctor visits would yield some prescriptions she'd then need to hoard once coverage ran out. At least she'll have some savings to cushion her but how long would that last? When she'd first started down the path of trying to cobble together a career as a psychic, she'd had a five-year plan and a fucking checklist. Since the pandemic though, everything had derailed and the tour had only been a stopgap. Her family was right to be worried. Judit was lost. Adrift, she glanced at Patrick, and increasingly confused.

Ugh, why did her mother have to be right?

Her fingers itched for her cards. She stood abruptly, grabbing her tray. "I better get ready."

The boys blinked up at her. "Okay," Patrick said finally.

"See you soon," Rohan said, smiling.

When she got back to the room, she pulled her cards out and sat on the bed, her back propped against the pillows.

Helen emerged from the bathroom, toweling her hair. "Oooh, whatcha drawing for?"

"Me."

"Figured."

Judit shuffled the cards, trying to find the right question. Hell, she didn't even know what spread to use.

"Stressing about the future again?" Helen flopped on the other bed.

Judit sighed, putting the deck back down. "Yeahhhh."

"Cuz the tour's ending soon?"

"Yeahhhh." Judit looked at Helen. "Aren't you?"

Helen shrugged. "I don't know, man. I don't have as much riding on this as you do."

"What do you mean?"

"This tour is your big thing to show off at your reunion, right?"

Now, it was Judit's turn to shrug. "I mean, it was a bonus."

Helen sighed. "I hate to see you like this, you know? You used to be so laser-focused but since that break-up, I feel like you've been doubting your judgment."

"I still trust my judgment," Judit said. "That's like the whole basis of being psychic."

"Your judgment for other people, yeah, sure." Helen sat up.

"But babe, when was the last time you read for yourself? Or the last time you put yourself out there? You used to go to that dungeon all the time and get your kink on but I don't think I've seen you go since you dumped those shitheads."

"I can't go back there! I might see them!"

"Okay, fine, but like, what about dating?"

Judit's knuckles whitened on the deck. "You know dating's a minefield these days, especially for us spoonies."

"Fine, flirting. What about flirting? When was the last time you seriously flirted with someone? You used to love flirting."

Judit's body clenched, kneejerk rage trying to form in her chest at being so fucking *seen*. How dare her friend see her vulnerability and point it out to her? But, Helen was right. Judit had retreated into herself, gotten risk averse, which was the worst thing you could do as a not-at-all established entrepreneur. The tour was the biggest risk she'd taken in over a year. Well, the tour and last night.

"I flirted this morning, thank you very much," she said pertly, then sighed. "But you're totally right. I've been playing it too safe."

"Hold up, go back to the part where you were *flirting* with someone over *breakfast*." Helen hopped onto Judit's bed. "Who was it? Someone from our team or someone else? Guest at the hotel?"

Judit bit her lip, her face heating.

"*Oh my gawd*," Helen crowed. "You're *blushing*. Dude, come on! Spill!"

"It was Patrick," Judit mumbled.

"What!" Helen reared back and almost fell off the bed, pinwheeling her arms to stay upright.

"Shut up."

"No way!" Helen grabbed Judit's shoulder. "Have I been comatose? When did this happen? I thought you were tentative, maybe, friends?!"

Judit shrugged helplessly.

"Oh?"

"I don't know." Judit flopped backward on the bed. "I—we can't be alone."

"Or?"

"Last night, we gave each other handies in the fucking stairwell." Judit covered her face. "Both of us were stone sober too."

"Oh. My. Gawd!"

"I know!"

"You—and Patrick—?" Helen made some very evocative and accurate hand gestures.

Judit covered her face. "Uh-huh."

"And it was good?"

Judit groaned. "Yessss."

"No pain after?"

"No penetration, so no."

"Damn Judy, why is that a bad thing?"

"Because!" Judit sat up. "It was a mistake. We agreed but—"

"But?"

"He flirted with me. Over breakfast and I flirted back and holy shit, Helen, have you ever had someone that hot flirt with you?" Judit fanned her overwarm face, the memory alone notching up her body temperature.

"Uh, yeah, remember Leo got drunk and flirty the other night after his show? I'm not sure it counts cuz he definitely wasn't interested in me sexually but, it's a lot."

"A *lot*." Judit let out a hysterical giggle.

Someone rapped on the door. "Ten-minute bus call!" one of the dancers yelled.

"Coming!" Judit and Helen chorused.

"Fuck." Judit rushed to the mirror, checking her make-up

and dress. Touring lowered her standards on most fronts but she wanted to make a special effort today.

"Packed?" Helen grabbed her bag.

Judit nodded. She'd repacked her bag automatically before breakfast. Helen tossed Judit her bag and she caught it, twinges echoing down her back, shoulders, and arms telling her that would probably have consequences later.

She shrugged the bag on, shrugging off the future. It'd come or it wouldn't. She was determined to enjoy the day.

31

"Hey there! This is RK and you're listening to 101.3 KDWB FM Minneapolis. I'm out on tour but I'd rather Be Home with You."

Patrick sat on an Adirondack chair on the deck of the three-story lakeside "cabin" Benji borrowed from a friend and looked across the sparkling private lake. The closest house was barely visible from the bend of the water and there were old-growth trees everywhere. Humid air pressed against his skin but the temperature was decent compared to some days on this tour.

NoN crew and talent splashed each other in the lake, lay on the sandbar, and picnicked on the grass, eating the grilled veg and meat Rohan happily churned out.

Benji sat in the chair next to Patrick. "Will this all go to hell if I take a nap?"

"Nah," Patrick said. "I'll keep watch."

Benji nodded, pulling their NoN hat down over their eyes. Patrick adjusted his own NoN ball cap, wishing he'd had the foresight to do laundry at the hotel yesterday. He was down to the magenta Lady Water T-shirt a rep had foisted on him and neon Green Brew knee socks that looked ridiculous with shorts but he'd given up wearing jeans halfway through Arizona. Thank goodness playing a sweaty tour in a rock band had much lower standards for stage clothes and fashion than a boy band did. Even his usually meticulous sister now embraced the smudgy eyeliner and tank top look rather than her usual elaborately funky stage persona.

Speaking of, he noticed Sabrina lying on a blanket in the grass, reading a book next to a sleeping Kevon and guarding Helen's prosthetic. She looked tired but happy, in her element. In the distance, Judit floated on her back next to the dock, talking to Helen who dangled her non-prosthetic leg into the lake. Leo tried to sneak up on them, but Judit and Helen splashed him until he gave up, laughing.

"Not feeling the water?" Benji asked from under their hat.

"Maybe later," Patrick said. *When Judit isn't in there looking so goddamn tempting in that polka-dotted high-waisted bikini,* he didn't say. "Who did you say you borrowed this place from?"

"The lead singer of a band who used to open for us," Benji said. "They got big after UFO..." Benji waved their hand vaguely like they didn't care enough to ascribe a verb to their own band's collapse. "They're on tour and she owes me a favor."

Patrick tried to remember any of the acts who opened for Beatboyz over the years, came up with a handful of names and a lot of blurry faces, and gave up. Keeping touch with people had never been his forte, much to James' and his father's chagrin, given how little Patrick cared for networking in the first place.

"I'm afraid to ask what the favor was."

Benji shrugged. "I introduced her to her wife."

"Oh." That was... nice. Patrick was surprised which gave him a flash of guilt. God, sometimes he felt like such a cynic.

Benji chuckled. "Yeah, well, her now-wife was my then-girlfriend."

Well, now. Was Benji trying to be subtle? Fuck it. He took the bait. "You're still friends?"

Benji pushed the brim of their hat up and looked at Patrick, catching the obvious subtext in his question. "It wasn't the same. We hadn't been dating very long or even very seriously. Mostly it was awkward for a while and embarrassing to be dumped. But." They heaved a dramatic sigh. "They're happy together. Unsettlingly so. And, well, the friendship was worth more to me." They dropped their gaze. "It's not the same. "It's just how it worked out."

Patrick chewed this over. "You don't regret it?"

Benji shook their head, staring out at the lake. "It felt... freeing to let it go. I wish it was always so easy."

"So do I," muttered Patrick.

AFTER HER DIP in the lake, Judit was happy to find the lit fire pit inset into the deck. She was less thrilled to see a pair of new faces sitting in the circle around it. She wasn't in the mood for new people.

But Leo gestured her over so she went to get introduced.

"Judit!" he said excitedly, "These are my old friends Lila and Syn! Lila's got weird pain stuff like you."

Judit covered a wince but Lila openly frowned. "Jesus, Leo, weren't you brainwashed better than that in boy band camp?"

"It didn't take." Leo grinned, stood, and gestured at Judit. "Sit."

"Oh, um, okay." She didn't know how to say no without being rude.

Leo grabbed Syn's arm and dragged them up. "Come on, I want you to meet Benji."

"What? Who?" Syn sputtered, trying to smooth their short skirt as Leo propelled them away. They were a solid-sized person but no match for Leo.

"You good, baby?" Lila asked.

"I think?" Syn called back.

"Have fun!" Lila called. "Love you!"

"Love you!"

Judit and Lila watched them go in shared bemusement. "I forgot how not subtle Leo is," Lila said.

"Why does he want Syn to meet Benji?"

Lila shrugged. "They're both enby, probably. Like I said, not subtle." She smiled wryly.

"He's trying to be helpful, I guess," Judit said.

"Yeah." Lila watched Syn disappear. "It would be nice for Syn to have more enby friends. They're not super out."

"Not a great area to be out?" Judit asked sympathetically.

Lila shrugged. "Minneapolis isn't the worst depending on where you live but I think it bothers them to pass outside the house. Bothers me when people think we're a straight couple, frankly, especially in queer spaces." She twisted a finger around her long dark hair. That with her leggings and T-shirt, certainly didn't scream QUEER but then again, why did she have to broadcast?

"I get that," Judit said. "I never know how to be queer 'enough' or whether I'm hurting enough to be able to feel a part of disability spaces."

"Yes, that!" Lila pointed at her. "My body hurts most days and my fucking pelvis is trying to murder me but I don't 'look sick' so you know, I must be fine."

A zing of recognition bloomed in Judit. She'd never met someone with symptoms that were so similar to hers. "Oh man, same."

Lila shook her head. "Getting a diagnosis helped but wow, that was a fight. And getting help? Still an uphill battle."

"You have a diagnosis?" Judit breathed. "I'm sorry, but um, do you mind if I ask what it is? Cuz what you're describing sounds like me."

Lila looked at her. "I'm not a medical professional, you know."

"You don't have to tell me, that's okay."

"No, no, it's cool. I have fibromyalgia and I *might* have endometriosis, that's the pelvic shit. They don't like to diagnose that one—"

"—without cutting you open." Judit sighed. "Been down that road. But with fibro, I thought it was a super intensive eliminate-everything-else testing process." She'd been blocked by more than one doctor telling her she didn't have the insurance to cover all that testing.

"It used to be," Lila said. "Now, it's like a five-minute questionnaire."

"Oh, wow," Judit said. "What the fuck? How is it that easy now?"

Lila shrugged. "Don't know but they don't do much with it. They're just like 'Hey you hurt, we don't know why.' NIH, CDC, Mayo Clinic, they all got maybe a paragraph or two about it online."

"For real?" Judit groaned.

"Yeah, probably cuz even though it's 'very common,' it's mostly in women." Lila rolled her eyes.

Judit groaned again. "Fucking patriarchy! So, not worth getting tested?"

"Oh no, totally worth it. It got me into physical therapy and reasonable accommodations at work plus I got a big fancy word to throw at people when I need help. By the way, PT? Great for the pelvic shit too. Also, anti-ovulation pills help so much if you're like me and get it more around and before your period."

Judit typed all this into her phone. "This is so helpful, thank you."

Lila tapped her lip. "Lemme think if there's anything else."

"Do you get extra pain with orgasms, especially after penetration?" Judit blurted, her face hot. Not that she was thinking about penetration for any particular reason—or person.

Lila grimaced. "I used to. PT helped."

"I can't really afford PT," Judit mumbled.

"Been there." Lila nodded. "Um, my PT said if you put a pillow under your hips and take deep breaths after penetration it might help cuz it gets the blood moving instead of pooling in those muscles. Or something, I'm not science-y."

"I'll try that!" Judit smiled.

"You know there's no cure for any of this?" Lila asked gently.

"I never expected there to be," Judit said. "But you're in less pain?"

"So much less pain!" Lila said.

Judit grinned. "I'll take it."

32

"Don't know what I thought would happen
Don't know how I didn't know
You pull, I push
We won't let go

Baby, we're magnets
I can't resist
Baby, we're magnets
(how do they work?)
Too late for regrets"
— "Magnets" by Beatboyz off of *Keep the Party Going*

Of all the places Judit expected to run into Patrick, the basement of the lake mansion NoN commandeered was at the bottom of her list. The only reason she was here herself was every other bathroom in the place was occupied. Plus, she was still processing her conversation with Lila. It felt at once like the light at the end of the tunnel and a bit of a life sentence to know what she had was probably diagnoseable but also chronic.

"Why are you lurking in the basement?" she asked, shaking the thoughts away. "That seems like more of an Angela Alice thing than a you thing."

He chuckled ruefully, rubbing the back of his neck. "I forgot to do laundry when we were at the hotel yesterday and—"

"There's laundry here?" Judit gasped. "I didn't do laundry either, shit. Do you think it's cool if I do some too?"

"I thought we were trying to stay away from each other." He raised an eyebrow.

"We're adults, right? What's sexy about doing laundry?"

He looked at her. "We're adults. Consenting adults who are very attracted to each other in a private, badly lit space."

She looked around at the leather couches, the string lights, the dark-colored walls, and the high, narrow windows. "It's not *that* sexy here. I believe in us." She grinned. "Also, I really need to do laundry."

Which is how she ended up sitting in a basement lounge with Patrick, listening to the whir of her clothes in the washer and his in the dryer. The leather couch cushions stuck to her thighs and it was dark enough that she didn't care her make-up was long gone and her hair was a stringy mess.

So, of course, all she could think about was Patrick. Right there. Studiously not looking at her. The space between them was so electric she could practically count the inches between her hip and his.

It was awkward as fuck.

"So," she said. "Enjoying the tour yet? Or are you glad it's almost done?"

He was silent for so long she got antsy. "I have mixed feelings," he finally said. "I've done so many of these a large part of me just wants to be done and home with my cat."

"But?" She couldn't help it, she was intrigued. (Also the image of Patrick cuddling Scoot? Too damn cute.)

He looked at her. "Certain things are growing on me." The corner of his lip curled upwards, rueful and soft. She couldn't stop looking at it.

"Yeah?"

He leaned forward. "God, the things I wanted to do to you in that bikini." His voice rasped, shivering against her nerve endings.

She suddenly wished she hadn't taken it off immediately after swimming but she'd lived with two sex educators for far too long to hang out in a wet swimsuit. She swayed towards him. "Maybe, I would've let you."

He tucked a strand of hair behind her ear, his touch sparking against her skin. "And if I asked right now?"

She glanced up at the stairway in the corner of the room, wanting so badly to say yes but— "Someone could walk in."

He followed her gaze and sighed. "You're right. Honestly, I feel weird about fucking around in someone else's place."

"Yes! Thank you! It's rude, right?"

"Unfortunately," he agreed. "Or I'd do unspeakable things to you on top of that dryer."

She blinked, picturing it, hearing the rumble of the vibrations through the wall, and imagining... "Oh damn."

He leaned in close, his voice a low, sensual murmur that frankly, should be illegal. "You've got a good imagination, don't you?"

She swallowed, hard and nodded. Her thighs pressed together against the blooming ache between them and oh my god, if he talked dirty to her in that voice...

A domme once made her cum through dirty talk alone. She glanced at Patrick, trying not to plead with her eyes but also very much wanting to plead.

He looked her up and down, his gaze lingering on her clenched thighs. "Can I?" He looked hesitant but his pupils were huge, his breathing just a bit quick. He wanted this as much as she did. "Just words, I swear."

She nodded enthusiastically.

"Come here." He held out an arm and she burrowed into his side. He dipped his head and his lips brushed her ear, sending a shiver down her spine. "Comfortable?"

How had his voice gotten sexier? She melted into him, letting herself revel in the feel of his warmth, his solid slenderness, the taut muscles of his arm around her, the slight dig of his fingers against her waist. It felt so damn good, just being held like this. "Mmm."

"I'll take that as a yes."

She giggled, wriggling so her breasts brushed his arm, his side. His sharp inhale was everything she wanted. Well, not everything.

"If you were still in that polka dot bikini..." His fingers flexed against her side and her shirt rucked up, exposing bare skin to his touch. It stole all her focus, those few millimeters of touch. That is until he spoke again. "I'd kiss you with my hand up your top, playing with those glorious breasts."

Her breath hitched, her nipples sensitive and aching against the cups of her bra. "Yes."

"Then I would strip you down slowly as you begged me to go faster." He rubbed his thumb down her side, catching it against the waistband of her shorts. She arched so it dipped the barest inch under, sliding against the curve of her hip.

He groaned. "You're not making this easy."

She chuckled. "I thought hard was the point."

"Damn, I just want to slip those shorts off."

"Yeah?" She angled her hips again and his hand slipped a few more inches down the curve of her stomach. She didn't have the brain space to feel self-conscious about it. Every neuron was occupied by the feel of his skin against her, his rapid breathing, the edge they were dancing along.

"Yeah." His seductive rasp was falling apart into a ragged rumble. "Fuck, you're making it hard to think. I want to make this good."

She lost patience, swinging her leg around so she straddled him. "You are." She ground her pussy against the hard bulge of his dick through their clothes.

He grabbed her hair, dragged her down to his mouth, and rocked up into her, swallowing her moan. He was worried about making this good? She was worried he'd ruin her for anyone else and they had barely done anything yet.

One of his hands traced under her shirt, heading for her breasts as he promised while the other cupped her ass, tilting her until their friction was just right. She closed her eyes, lost in sensation. His lips brushed down her neck until he nipped at the juncture of her shoulder. Did he know that was her spot? She gasped and could feel him smile against her skin. Then he bit harder.

"Oh my god," she hissed. "Oh my god, I want you in me so bad."

He stilled. "I don't have anything."

"I do." She shoved a hand in her pocket and pulled out a foil square. "After yesterday..." She shrugged. She'd packed some back in June, optimistic as always but hadn't actually expected to use them, and certainly not with him. After their stairway encounter and flirting this morning, she figured she was better safe than sorry. "I mean, only if you want to though."

"You're amazing." He kissed her roughly and they lost a minute.

Then his hands were on her buttons and hers were on his zipper. Half a minute of awkward struggling later she was back on his lap, her shorts on one leg as she hovered over him. She glanced back over her shoulder at the open stairway.

"Do you want to?" he asked. "Will the penetration...?"

She focused on her pelvis, trying to gauge it. "I think it'll be okay. I mean, we shouldn't..." She bit her lip. "But fuck, I really want to."

"Look at me."

She looked at him.

He smiled. "I've got you. Whatever happens, I've got you."

"Don't make promises. We're too revved up."

He kissed her once, softly. "You're driving me out of my head in the best fucking way but trust me, I don't just say shit to get laid."

"I trust you," she whispered, a little scared to realize it was true.

"I trust you too."

She grinned and sank down, all thought lost in the stretch of slowly... slowly... taking him. Fucking hell, it had been a minute but had penetration always felt this good?

He moaned quietly and bit her shoulder again. She nearly exploded right there. While she was catching her breath, he rocked up in her. She went mindless, riding him as the sensation built and built in her until it took over her senses and everything narrowed to her and him and where they connected.

His hands gripped her bare ass, pulling her cheeks slightly apart and pressing her closer, closer, closer until—

Oh, she was almost there! She slid her hand between their bodies and found her clit, rubbing herself. Every sensation heightened, her muscles tightening as—

"Ohmigodohmigodohmigaaawd—Patrick!" Everything disappeared as pleasure took over and she drowned in the sensation. Fireworks. Everything was fireworks and glorious mindlessness.

Moments, years, days later, she came down.

"You came?" he asked.

"Yes." She rocked against him, faster and faster (damn, he

felt so, so good in her) until he followed her over the edge, the aftershock of his pleasure pulsing against hers. They collapsed together, breathing hard.

The dryer dinged.

Judit burst out laughing. "Your clothes are done."

Patrick chuckled and lifted her off his lap, placing her on the couch next to him so he could clean up. She struggled back into her shorts as he disposed of the condom. Remembering Lila's advice, she grabbed a cushion and put it under her hips. Laying down she took deep breaths, wondering if this would actually help.

He came back after she'd gotten up. She stared at the couch. "You know, we did exactly what we said we wouldn't," she said with chagrin. Reality was intruding but she'd rather focus on the leather couch.

He kissed the side of her head and showed her the Lysol wipe in his hand. He wiped the couch down. "Good as unfucked."

She burst into giggles again. "Dammit, I like you. What a mess."

He sighed. "I like you too."

"What are we gonna do?" Even if the whole Cazzi thing wasn't between them, the tour was ending and he lived in freaking LA.

He put an arm around her shoulders and hugged her to him. "We've got two weeks left on the tour."

"Is this a what happens on the tour stays on the tour situation?"

He looked at her. "If that's what you want."

"Is that what you want?"

He blew out a breath. "It would be simpler, but keeping secrets always seems to bite me in the ass."

Judit exhaled, realizing she'd been holding her breath for far too long. "So, summer fling on the DL but not secret?"

"Are you going to tell Cazzi?"

Judit fiddled with the hem of her shirt. "Let's figure that out together, yeah? I've heard good things about being mature."

He chuckled again. "I'll do my best."

She squinted up at him. "You're not gonna pull the whole, 'I got famous at a young age and therefore my mind is forever frozen at fifteen or whatever so I can't be mature,' excuse, right?"

He gave her quip more serious consideration than she expected. "For the record, I was seventeen by the time we got famous but no, I like to think I've moved beyond that. Being washed up for a while helps." His smile was mischievous, his brown eyes lit with silly glee. Damn, he was lovely when he was all emo but happy Patrick? A few more smiles like that and she'd be a goner.

"Thank goodness." She kissed his cheek. "Because I stopped finding seventeen-year-old you hot a long time ago."

"Wait." He pulled back. "Are you saying you used to find teen me hot?"

She shrugged and let go of his arm, making her way to the laundry room with an extra sway in her hips. With a look over her shoulder, she said, "I may have had a poster over my bed but don't think that means anything anymore."

"Oh no." He laughed, following her. "That means I get to tease you about which of my terrible outfits you liked best."

"That's a lot of swagger coming from the person who is immortalized wearing said outfits." She gave him a slow up-down look.

"Coping through humor," he said, the smile still lingering around his mouth as he pulled out his dry clothes, his hip bumping hers. "It's not like I picked them out."

"Fair," she said, transferring hers to the dryer, making sure to bend at the waist. The look he gave her ass said it was much appreciated. "Okay, I gotta know. What was the worst thing they made you wear?"

He tapped his chin thoughtfully. "Well, there was the time they tried to make me look like Sisqo…"

"They made you blond?!" She almost dropped her clothes, cracking up. "Seriously?"

"We were all blond at one point or another. Come on." He tsked. "I thought you were a fan."

"So, when I said I had a poster of you, what I really meant is my sister gave me the poster out of her copy of *Tiger Beat* because I downloaded 'Remember You Forever' on our joint iTunes account after watching that movie you guys made."

"Oh no." He covered his face with a shirt. "You saw *Boyz in Dublin!?* In theaters?"

"In theaters," she said, grinning. "For a friend's birthday party." He groaned and she cackled. "I feel like this is equally embarrassing for both of us. Not that I'm going to be embarrassed by something that brought me joy."

He put the shirt down. "That movie brought you joy?"

"I got to sit next to my crush the whole time, I was in heaven." She bumped his shoulder with hers. "But also, I still listen to that song. It's fun!"

"Okay, yeah it is, I'll give you that." He resumed folding his clothes. "I don't even hate that one after all the times we performed it."

She watched him fold for a minute. "You didn't enjoy being in the band as much as Rohan and Leo, did you?"

He paused. "One of your feelings?" He shook his head before she could reply. "You're not wrong. I wasn't miserable, and in hindsight, we got really lucky, what with Rohan's stepdad being our manager and protecting us from a lot of the shit other child stars were exposed to." His lips twisted. "But it wasn't me. You may have noticed I'm introverted." He cut her an ironic look.

"You?" she said with mock surprise. "But you're so social!"

"Yeah, yeah. Anyway, it was intense, becoming famous and working to stay famous. Relentless. Ten years of relentless."

She couldn't even imagine, even as some part of her yearned for the grind of doing what you loved while being both in demand and paid well for it.

She lay her head against his shoulder. "I'm glad that part of your life is over."

He pressed a kiss to the top of her head. "Me too."

33

"Never thought I'd meet you
The girl that changes it all
The girl that makes me fall

I still can't believe (can't believe)
I found you (I found you)
Still can't believe (can't believe)
I let you go

I'll remember you forever
My favorite summer
My favorite spring
I'll remember you forever
My favorite regret"

— "Remember You Forever" by Beatboyz off of *Beatboyz*

After the lake excursion, everyone seemed looser. Patrick noticed Benji napped the entire bus ride back to the festival grounds. He spent the ride sitting close but not too close to Judit in the tiny bus lounge, trying to figure out how to get more time alone with her—because holy hell, what they'd done in the basement had to be the best sex he'd had in years. The making out while they did laundry after had been pretty great too. Besides that, he *liked* her. There was no getting around it.

When Leo went to the bathroom and Helen was busy talking to Sabrina and Kevon, Patrick slipped Judit his phone. "Give me your number?"

"Oooh, now he wants my digits." She smiled and wagged her eyebrows playfully as she typed.

Then Leo came back and drew the conversation back to him. It was only later that Patrick saw she'd texted herself: *This is the boy at the rock show.*

He'd smiled even though it meant he now had that one Blink-182 song stuck in his head. He ignored that the lyrics included the words "fell in love with" and texted her back, *can't wait til your parents are out of town.* Then panicked when he realized she might not get the reference.

JUDIT

I'll leave my window open so you can sneak in.

Thank goodness.

He sent her a suggestive GIF and their conversation quickly became a collection of GIFs, jokes, and references bordering on sexting.

They didn't get a chance to talk in private until their shift together at the booth a few days later.

"Well, fancy seeing you here," she murmured when she shimmied past him. She high-fived Helen, relieving her of her shift.

Patrick chuckled to himself as he counted the drawer and gave Benji the extra money so the change drawer was at the bare minimum. He was surprised at how fast he was at it now. Benji took the rest, spiriting the cash to the safe in the bus which they emptied into the NoN bank account every chance they got. When they left him in the booth, he swore he saw them glance between him and Judit with a smile. He shrugged it off. Benji wasn't that perceptive, as much as they might think they were.

Helen left and there was an immediate stampede of Doc Conjure fans. He was, after all, coming off just playing a show. Normally, he'd be embarrassed about being sweaty and gross post-show while standing so close to someone he was attracted to, but literally no one, not even Judit, was fresh three days out from the last time they'd had access to a working shower.

It was muggy and humid today. Leo spent a lot of time this morning squinting at the cloudy sky and rumbling about rain while rubbing his temples. Patrick's app resolutely vowed it would not rain but Leo's headaches tended to be more accurate. If it rained, Patrick was tempted to stand in it just to feel less dusty.

He did the fanservice thing, grateful the balance of Doc Conjure fans were finally tipping from majority 'curious to see how badly washed-up Ricky Rick is' to 'Ricky Rick who?' Sabrina and Kevon hung around for a while, clearly enjoying the meet and greet more. His sister especially was in her element and made him kind of warm and fuzzy to see her surrounded by fans.

"She's gonna be a big deal. Better brace yourself," Judit said, following his gaze.

"Yeah?" His stomach bloomed with mixed feelings. Sabrina deserved to be successful, she was a more talented singer than he ever had been, but being famous had gnawed him down until he was raw bones. He didn't wish it on anyone.

"It'll be good." Judit bumped his shoulder, jarring him out of his thoughts. "She's an adult who knows what she's getting into. And she's got you. And me and Benji and Rohan and Leo and Helen and Kevon."

He smiled at her. "That helps."

She returned his smile. "I'm glad." He couldn't help but melt at how sweet she looked and the sincere confidence in her voice. His fingers found hers under the table and they twined together as much as they could without being obvious. Then a customer came up and he had to let go to man the register.

"You know," he said casually as the customer left. "Most of the bus is going to that party the sponsors are throwing tonight. I hear even Benji is gonna make an appearance."

"You want to go too?" She frowned, pushing stray hair out of her eyes. It just stuck to her forehead and neck. Would it be weird if he tucked it behind her ear?

He shook his head. "The opposite. We could stay in, just you and me. Anything you wanna do."

Her eyes sparked. "Anything?" Then her expression fell. "But Toni—"

"—is gonna be off playing poker with the other drivers. It's Saturday."

She blinked. "It is? *It is*. Hell yes!" She bumped him with her shoulder. "We're gonna have fun tonight, baby."

"Oh, are we?" He dropped his voice to the register he knew she loved.

The way her smile turned hot, made his whole body go tight. He wanted to kiss her right there in front of the whole fest, trail his fingers up under the hem of her skirt and—

The sky opened and dumped a sudden onslaught of rain on the roof of their tent, startling both of them. The canopy held, thankfully, all of Benji's post-storm renovations doing their job.

Judit clapped her hands over her mouth, watching the festival goers race for shelter, some huddling under their tent. Patrick could hear her smothering giggles and smiled to himself.

"Is it weird that I kinda want to go out there?" she asked,

handing him a sticker one of the people taking shelter was buying, obviously out of polite awkward obligation.

"For a free shower? I'd be out there with you," he said, running the card.

She glanced at the few people sheltering at the edge of their tent and back at him. No one was even pretending to be interested in their merch anymore, instead staring out at the rain like they could will it away.

He took her hand and took a step backward towards the edge of the tent. There was a narrow alley between the NoN merch and the back of a local food truck. The dirt there was already soaked. She smiled and nodded.

Together they backed into the rain.

It was like having a never-ending bucket of lukewarm water dumped on his head, cascading off the brim of his hat, rolling down his locs, and soaking through the fabric of his clothes. It took him back to playing in the rain as a child with Cazzi, jumping in puddles and laughing up at the thunder. A bittersweet ache filled his chest at the memory. It had been so simple then, so much easier.

Judit laughed next to him. He tore himself from the past and looked at the way she tipped her head to the sky, eyes closed, grinning like a loon, happy and soaked to the bone. She was so lovely, so full of joy it was infectious.

The ache receded, replaced by something almost as overwhelming but sweeter.

He pulled her to him and kissed her, savoring the taste of rain on her lips and the way she kissed him back.

AFTER SPENDING the rest of their shift damp and grinning, Judit was ready for an actual shower and a nap. She settled for a towel and a cup of one of Patrick's tea blends. The gingery tea alone almost made up for the lack of shower.

"Warming herbs," he said with a smile when she asked. They sat in the bus lounge, chatting as the other occupants got ready for the party.

"Do you have tea for everything?" she asked.

He shrugged. "Only so much herbs can do for some things."

"But that doesn't mean you can't put out your own line of herbal teas." Leo walked over to stand in front of Patrick. "Zip me up."

Patrick rolled his eyes at Judit but there was humor hiding around his mouth as he stood to reach the zipper on Leo's top.

"Good luck convincing him," Benji said, fixing their make-up in a mirror balanced on their bunk rail. "He's very resistant to diversifying his commercial enterprises."

"I don't need to monetize everything I'm good at." Patrick's mouth tightened. "It takes the joy out of it."

"Told you," Benji said to Leo.

Helen came out of the bathroom. "You're still getting ready? We're gonna be late! Sabrina and Kevon are already there!" She winked at Judit, well aware of what she was enabling. She had screamed into her hands when Judit told her what happened on the lake trip and declared herself "cautiously optimistic about this whole mess."

Benji raised an eyebrow. "We may be has-beens but it's still fashionable when we're late."

"Speak for yourself." Leo sniffed. "I'm still very relevant."

"You're gay-famous at best," Benji said.

"It got me my own bedroom, didn't it?"

"Touché," Benji conceded.

"Well, I'm not famous at all and I want to scope out the

hotties before they get sleazed on by that yacht rock band we picked up on the last stop," Helen put in.

Leo and Benji considered this.

"They are pretty smug." Benji zipped their make-up bag shut.

"Smarmy little fuck boys," Leo agreed, slipping on a pair of heeled boots. His head brushed the ceiling. "Do we know any tea about them?"

"No, but I bet there will be some at the party," Helen said pointedly.

Within minutes, the three of them clattered down the stairs, Helen bringing up the rear and throwing Judit and Patrick a double thumbs up when she left.

"She knows?" Patrick asked.

Judit nodded. "I figured having an ally wouldn't hurt. Sorry, I should've given you a heads up."

"She won't tell?"

Judit felt a faint pang of regret that that was even a concern. "Nope, she's good like that."

He shrugged. "Then I'm cool. Don't need someone leaking this while we're still figuring this out." He smiled shyly. "I know this may only be for the tour. I want to hoard my time with you."

"Oh." Judit felt her cheeks heat. "Well, in that case..." She put her mug down and crawled into his lap.

When they came up for air sometime later, crammed together in her bunk, he smoothed down her sex hair and asked, "Do you want to watch a movie or something?"

"That depends," she said, post-orgasm haze dampening her filters. "Do you want to watch my favorite movie?"

"That depends. Will you hate me forever if I don't like it?"

"Probably not, but you'll have to make it up to me." She wiggled her eyebrows.

A slow, sex-drenched smile curved over his mouth. "Then I hate it already."

"No, no, don't prejudice yourself against it." She rummaged around on her bunk shelf, pulling down the DVD player, disc already in it.

"I haven't seen one of these in years," Patrick said, blinking.

Judit flushed, embarrassed. Of course he hadn't, he probably didn't need to watch his data or stock up on used DVDs on the off chance they couldn't pay the internet bill or streaming services. This was Ricky Rick. In her tour bus bed. Oh my god, what was she doing?

Your friend's ex-flame.

Dammit, this was killing her post-orgasm bliss.

He found her binder of DVDs and flipped through. "Damn, this is a great collection."

Warmth lit in her center at his praise. She was a sucker for someone who liked her taste in movies. "Thanks, I grew up on films." Every time she was sick, her mom rented a new movie for her to convalesce to.

"So, you're an expert then. What's your favorite?"

She turned on the DVD player. "Have you ever seen *Grosse Pointe Blank*?"

He shook his head.

"You're in for a treat!" She grinned. "It's John Cusack as a fast-talking assassin with burnout who goes back to his suburban high school reunion to see the old flame he abandoned on their prom night. The script is super clever and it's the best school reunion movie of all time, in my very unbiased opinion."

"You watch a lot of high school reunion movies?" he asked.

She shrugged. "I just want to be prepared—as prepared as movie realism can make me anyway. Did you go to yours?"

He shook his head. "I got a GED when I was sixteen. I didn't have a class reunion to go to."

The reality of who he was slapped her upside the head anew. "Oh, right."

"I've always been curious though. They seem so fraught. Are you looking forward to anything or anyone in particular?" He glanced away when he said *anyone*.

Judit blinked at the lovely curve of his jaw. Was he jealous? Of someone from high school? Did he... did he think there was someone more exciting than him in her class? "I mean, there are some friends I've fallen out of contact with." All of them, if she was being brutally honest. She missed most of them. It made her chest burn to see her old classmates getting married on social media, not that they were getting married but that they were doing it with their high school besties in their wedding parties. Why had no one held on to her that long? How had everyone slipped away? "My school was a joint middle/high school and I think I had the most friends then than I ever had since."

"No long lost loves?"

She laughed. "No. I had a lot of crushes and a few kisses but nothing that had any staying power, you know? I read somewhere that crushes are safe practice for caring for a partner, like an outlet of sorts. Mine definitely were, but not anything more."

He nodded, his eyes on the DVD menu but his attention far away. "I know what you mean. I think..." He frowned as if he was debating whether to continue.

With sudden clarity, she knew whatever he was waffling about needed to be said.

"You think...?" She gave him an encouraging smile.

He searched her face, whatever he saw there causing his shoulders to relax. "I think that was Cazzi and me. I was a safe place for her to put her heart, and... it was the same for me to some extent. But when we tried to make it real..." He shook his head.

She leaned her head on his shoulder. "Sounds painful." It didn't feel much better, listening to it, but her gut feeling said this conversation would work out for the best for both of them. She held onto that certainty even as her emotions pitched towards bitter jealousy at her friend. She would never hold the same amount of space in Patrick's heart as Cazzi did. Not that she should care, but still, it hurt a girl's ego.

"Actually, letting go of that feels good," he said, "Like I put down a heavy thing I've been carrying and I don't know how to balance without it but I've got all this extra energy."

"Totally." She remembered the feeling from her breakup.

"I mostly miss the friendship. She knew so many versions of me over the years and I knew so many versions of her." He shrugged, careful not to dislodge Judit's head. "Maybe that's the problem though, I'm too attached to the past."

"I feel that," Judit said. "Half the reason I signed up for this tour was so I'd have something to brag about to people who I've barely spoken to in ten fucking years."

"What was the other half?"

"Health insurance."

"Damn, I was hoping you'd say me."

"You wish." She poked his armpit.

He yelped and her eyes went wide. He. Was. Ticklish.

"Noooo," he said, seeing her expression. "Don't even think about it."

She lunged at him and the resulting tickle fight nearly made them fall out of the bunk.

When a truce had been called, they were panting on their sides next to each other in the bed, Patrick's long legs hanging off the end. "So who are you going to your reunion with?"

She shrugged. "Maybe Helen if I can bribe her with food."

"When is it?"

"Mid-December."

"You know... I might be free then. I could come with, for science."

Butterflies exploded in her belly. "Why Patrick Jones, are you living vicariously through my high school experience?"

"Hell, you caught me," he said in an 'aw shucks' voice so spot on and unlike him that she howled with surprised laughter.

"Fine," she said, chuckling. "You can come but only if you make me look cooler than the guy who started a vanlife cult."

He grimaced. "I don't know if I have that kind of cultural capital anymore. Can we just lie and say I'm a TikTok dance influencer?"

"What if I tell them you're a DJ?"

"I thought you wanted to look cool."

"Ouch." She laughed. "I'm gonna tell the DJs you said that."

"No, you won't," he said, ensuring her silence with a kiss.

"So," she said later. "What are you doing after the tour? Out of curiosity."

"I don't know." He threw an arm over his eyes. "Quitting NoN but after that, I don't know."

"Quitting? I thought you all were getting along better."

He shrugged. "It doesn't erase the past. Benji and Rohan pulled some shitty things to get me to stay as long as I did."

"Oh." She didn't like to think they were capable of it, but she could absolutely see those two putting Patrick in a bad place to make sure they got their label running. They could be rather single-minded about music.

"Mostly contract stuff, nothing heinous. But it made working with them... toxic." He grimaced, eyes still shielded by his arm. "I don't think I can just let it go."

"Then I'm glad you're quitting."

He peered out from under his arm. "Even if that means I'll be aimlessly underemployed for a while?"

She shrugged. "I think you're rich enough you can float that lifestyle for a while. Frankly, I'm a bit jealous."

He chuckled. "I'm not that rich. More like comfortable."

"See? That's a rich person thing to say. You own a house, babe. There are months where I don't know if I can afford rent." She curled into herself at the words, feeling vulnerable.

He uncovered his eyes fully, but she refused to meet his gaze. "Does the wealth gap between us bother you?"

"Not right now. But in the real world? I don't know."

He rolled over and pressed a kiss to her knuckles. "If we want to extend this beyond the tour, I'm willing to figure it out with you."

She smiled. "We could work out our five-year plans together—not that they have to intertwine or anything. I've never been in a relationship that long, I'm not presuming—"

He laughed. "You're good. I think I know what you were getting at."

She covered her overheated face. "Oh jeez."

His arm snaked around her shoulders, tucking her against him. "The future will come whether we like it or not, let's enjoy what we have right now."

She burrowed into his side with a sigh, the tension of their conversation draining away.

He propped the DVD player on his knees and started the film. As the familiar strains of the Violent Femmes playing "Blister in the Sun" played over the intro, Judit relaxed against him, her biggest concern if he liked the film or not.

34

"Played by my own rules
Cut every class in school
Winged eyeliner, dyed hair
Self-destructive and ready to share
Come on baby, give your heart to me

(Oz from Buffy the Vampire Slayer soundbite: "Who is that girl?")

Manic pixie nightmare
Baby, you think I care? [manic laugh]
Not here for your growth
Could give a shit about your boring life
You want love, I prefer a knife

I may be crazy, but it ain't cute
I may be sexy, but I'll still shoot
I'm erratic, not safe
I'll walk barefoot in the rain
Til my feet bleed"

> — "Manic Pixie Nightmare" by Angela Alice off of
> *Murder Baby*

The next week, Benji sat at the table in Rohan's bus lounge and exhaled hard. "Okay. You can all probably guess why you're here."

Patrick shifted uncomfortably, glancing around. Rohan leaned against the wall behind Benji, hands the pockets of his shorts, Leo sprawled on the couch looking petulant, Helen sat next to Judit, buzzing with excitement, and Judit...

He glanced at her. She looked at him in his position next to Leo, her gaze thoughtful. Did she know how much he wished he was sitting next to her?

She glanced away but a smile curved her lips.

Patrick knew why all of the core NoN team was crammed into the lounge of Rohan's bus and he hoped Benji would be delicate about it.

"The fucking end of the fest party tomorrow..."

Then again, this was Benji.

"...is gonna be a shitshow." Benji continued. "The Doom Twins are gonna run roughshod all over Nicky and we need to protect ourselves."

Leo snorted. Patrick watched him out of the corner of his eye.

Benji glared at Leo. "Especially you."

Leo rolled his eyes but didn't argue.

"So what's your plan?" Patrick asked.

"It's super fucking simple," Benji said, "Stay sober, answer your damn phone, and don't get into any fights or look like an idiot where someone outside of this label might see you."

"And," Rohan added with a smile. "Help out if you see someone who needs interference or support."

"But," Benji leaned forward to speak directly to Leo. "Don't escalate anything."

Red blotches appeared on Leo's cheeks. Patrick nudged him with his shoulder.

"Chill, Benji," Patrick said. "We're all professionals here."

Helen raised a hand but spoke before anyone called on her. "What if we created a group chat and kept everyone posted?"

"I'm not self-surveilling just because I punched a fucking comedian," Leo growled.

Helen wilted. Judit leaned into her, offering silent support.

"You also broke the tour manager's arm and sent him into a depressive tailspin," Benji snapped. "You are our main problem child and you damn well know it."

Rohan stepped forward and put his hand on Benji's shoulder. They clamped their mouth shut, jaw taut with the effort. "We're all under a lot of stress right now," Rohan said soothingly. "Leo's got the worst of it but that's no reason to treat him like a problem."

Benji's nostrils flared but they nodded.

"Just think," Patrick said to Leo, leaning in conspiratorially, "of all the tea we'll collect for the last issue of *Tourgasm*."

Leo's eyes lit up. "Ohmigod, I should've made y'all my spies weeks ago!"

"You already pick our brains for gossip daily," Rohan pointed out.

"That's just how I make conversation!" Leo pressed a hand to his chest, pretending offense.

"I made the group chat. Everyone introduce yourselves," Benji said, their voice bone dry. "Bring on the tea."

Patrick looked at the new notifications already piling up on his phone and fought a grimace. He hated group chats.

"And don't you dare mute it," Benji said, looking directly at him.

Patrick sighed but dutifully introduced himself.

AFTER THE MEETING, Judit took her morning walk. She'd taken to trying to line up her walks with Patrick's almost daily runs but today he was in an interview with the rest of Doc Conjure. So she walked alone. She used the first lap to call a new primary care doctor she'd found to see if she could get a fibromyalgia diagnosis. Well, she'd had to call two because the first was booked up for months but now she was scheduled for a visit a few days after her pelvic pain appointment—in a week.

She exhaled the nerves gathering in her belly. It would be fine. She would be fine.

Judit took another lap, noting the new fleet of buses pulling up across the lot from the NoN encampment. Who was coming in today? She couldn't remember. The list was so long now that they were in the last days of the fest. With a shrug, she made a slight detour, circling the buses as their engines shut down and their generators took over. They were unmarked which probably meant it was a bigger act. She'd noticed only up-and-comers plastered their branding everywhere.

An uneasy feeling took root in her belly, spreading outwards in spirals. It couldn't be, could it? She wasn't due for another day.

The door of the bus closest to her accordioned open and as if summoned by the thought, Angela Alice herself swung halfway out. Her face was drawn, bare of make-up beyond some hastily applied lip shine and her hair was in a messy ponytail that looked like she'd slept on it—face first, judging by the bed wrinkles on her face. She looked straight at Judit and beckoned.

Judit rocked back on her heels. The expression on Angela's face hit her straight in the chest, desperation and sorrow radiating off her in ragged waves that seemed to stick to Judit's skin, weighing her down.

She took a deep breath, knowing her angelica root was in her pocket. She didn't reach for it. She just followed Angela onto her bus.

It was dim in there, the lights off and the tinted windows shutting out most of the sun. The driver, a Latino man about Papi's age, gave Judit a sad smile as he left, closing the door behind him.

Angela stopped in front of one of the couches in the front lounge and toppled onto it like a pile of bricks, face first. Judit stopped several feet back next to what she now realized was a bookcase, a cord securing the books to the shelf like something out of an elementary school library. She ran a finger along the thick cord and resisted the urge to read all the titles.

"You okay?" Judit asked after a long moment of dead silence. Not even the generator was running.

Angela rolled onto her side, the motion jerky like a possessed girl in a horror film, moving in stop motion. She raised an eyebrow as if to say *what the hell does it look like?*

Judit huffed a breath. It felt like she was fighting the heavy atmosphere to inhale. It was honestly over the top. "This is the most emo crap," she muttered, then louder, "I can't help you if you don't tell me what you need."

Angela gave a breathy chuckle. "I don't know what I need."

"You want a reading?"

Angela hauled herself up like the air around them was as heavy as it felt. "Is that how you know what you want?"

Judit shrugged. "Sometimes. Sometimes, I just need to flail until I can figure it out."

Angela nodded. "When I flail, people get hurt. Do the cards."

"I don't have a deck on me."

Angela got up and suddenly was right in front of Judit,

leaning forward with a determined frown. "I know you prefer the Thoth deck."

Judit stumbled back a step. Angela's expression grew teeth, and she plucked a wooden box from the bookcase. She opened it with a tired flourish and presented Judit with a deck lovingly wrapped in brick-patterned satin and dark green ribbons. She sat on the couch.

Judit gently unwrapped the deck. It was the same kind of Thoth deck she owned with the familiar colorful crosses on the back. Didn't feel like her deck though, not at all. She couldn't explain it but she knew she'd never mix up her deck with Angela's.

"Do you want to talk about it at all, or would you just like me to do a spread?"

Angela searched Judit's face and shook her head.

"That's not an answer."

Angela growled, *literally growled,* the sound resonating louder than it should've in the quiet bus.

Judit's hands shook. She balled them into fists and propped them on her hips. "Don't be an asshole. Use your damn words."

Angela narrowed her eyes. "Pull your cards."

"Fine." Judit grabbed the deck, shuffled, and slammed it on the top of the bookcase. "Pick a card." She usually drew for her clients but this wasn't her deck and she wasn't in the mood to provide top-notch service.

Angela raised an eyebrow but pulled a card from the middle third of the deck by what looked like feel. A shiver tickled Judit's shoulder blades.

Yeah, I know, she told the feeling. *She's got power. It's not news.*

Angela handed her the card. Judit placed it face down. "This is all the help I can give you."

"One card?" the other woman said incredulously.

"Under duress."

Angela rolled her eyes. "Yeah, okay, sure."

Judit flipped the card: The Tower in all its flaming Picasso-esque chaos.

Angela inhaled sharply. "It's going to get worse?"

Judit studied the card, letting herself sink into the familiar image and feeling it out. "You are in your fall," she said. "How far you go is up to you. Your choices are your safety net, your self-awareness, your words, and love are your saving graces." She blinked, regrounding herself on the bus, the bookcase cord tangled in her fingers. She let it go with a twang and looked at Angela who was, if possible, even paler than before, the bones of her face standing out and her body taut. "Breathe, Angela."

The singer inhaled, breaking some of the tension in the room. She looked stricken though, fear skittering through her expression.

Judit wanted to put a hand on her arm but somehow touching Angela Alice seemed like something you just didn't do. It certainly hadn't worked out for the singer of Creep-mother. She busied her hands rewrapping the Thoth deck. "It's not a bad thing, in the end. I mean, it'll suck right now, but you'll come out stronger on the other side."

"I'm so tired of learning through pain." Angela put her head in her hands.

Judit's bones felt leaden like she had worked overtime three days in a row and gotten no sleep. She grabbed her root, the feeling fading. She had few enough spoons to have them drained away by someone else's emo moment. "Aren't we all? Look, now is the time for self-reflection. What shit have you been dragging around that you need to let go? All that fun stuff. Talk to a therapist or something. It sounds like you need it."

Angela snorted. "If I had a dime for every time someone told me I needed psychiatric help—"

"Then don't you think that many people might have a point?" Judit interrupted her.

Angela tilted her head from side to side, considering. She shrugged.

"Is there someone I can call to sit with you?" Judit asked, trying to keep her exasperation in check. Her sympathy only extended to a point and she had long surpassed it with Angela.

"I'm fine," Angela snarled. She relented at Judit's look. "Okay, I'm not *fine* but it's better if I don't inflict this on anyone."

Judit continued her stare.

"Anyone *else*."

"Okay." Judit headed for the door. "But seriously: don't do this alone. It's gonna be rough."

Angela leaned over the back of the couch, putting her at face level with Judit on the stairs. She smiled slightly, the effect something like being hit by a hammer through a haze. "Thanks, Judit," she said, her voice soft and husky.

Judit's brain short-circuited. "Uh-huh."

The door opened in front of her and the last thing she heard when she stumbled out of Angela's bus was the singer's deep sigh.

PATRICK COULD TELL something was off the moment he saw Judit walking back to the bus. He got out of the lawn chair he'd been sitting in and went to her with a rushed "Be right back" to his sister and Kevon.

"Hey, what's up?" he asked, jogging over.

She shivered. "Can I get a hug?"

He opened his arms without thinking, only worrying for a

second about being seen as she stepped into his embrace. Then he was holding her and his anxious thoughts were briefly smoothed over by the feel of her soft curves against him. Everything slowed and his breath came deeper, his ambient anxiety dissipating.

"I gave Angela Alice a reading." She sighed into his ear after an indeterminate while. "It was... weird."

"How so?" His mind shifted back into high gear. Angela wasn't due for another day and Nicky might've had something to say about her taking up another act's space if he wasn't so frightened of her.

"She's falling apart at the precipice of something," Judit said. "She wouldn't talk about it but she was more intense than I've seen her. I'm afraid she might have a mental health crisis."

"Fuck," Patrick said, pulling back reluctantly to search Judit's face. "Do we need to call someone?"

"I tracked down some of her bandmates. They said they're keeping an eye on her but they looked pretty wrecked too." Her mouth twisted. "If we tell Benji they're gonna make a thing about it, aren't they?"

Patrick sighed. "Let's talk to Rohan."

Her arms dropped from his sides, breaking the embrace. "Why him?" There was suspicion in her expression. It stung to see it.

"Because he spent four years weathering Hurricane Angela. He'll know what to do."

"Okay," she said slowly.

"Come on." He took Judit's hand and waved at his sister to tell Sabrina he was heading out.

Judit looked at their hands and Sabrina's grin. "Was there a relationship status change I wasn't informed of?"

"Sorry, I just—um, you looked like you needed—I can let go?" He stuttered.

She squeezed his hand. "Maybe just don't hold my hand

where Rohan can see yet. I don't want to deal with the whole 'being intimate with my friend's ex-flame' thing today."

"Yeah, fair." Sabrina wouldn't tell, but how had he forgotten how complicated the Cazzi angle made this? It felt good and weird to realize he hadn't been thinking about Cazzi at all.

He mulled it over while they walked over to Rohan's bus, shooting him a quick text on the way. He knocked on the door, letting go of Judit's hand with a slow lingering touch. She took a deep breath and squared her shoulders.

"Yeah?" Rohan's driver stuck his head out of the door. Patrick couldn't remember his name, only that it was some wild nickname that matched his giant mustache and hard face.

"Rohan's expecting us," Patrick told him. Rohan hadn't responded but he'd see them.

"Let them in, Crusher," Rohan called.

Crusher frowned but stood aside. It was a tight squeeze getting by his barrel chest, even for Patrick. Judit looked at the gap and sighed. Crusher had the grace to look slightly chagrined and press himself closer to the dashboard. He was rewarded with a smile.

Rohan sat on the floor of the lounge, his back propped against the couch and his laptop in his lap. "What's the emergency?"

Patrick looked at Judit. She grimaced but sat on the couch opposite Rohan and explained. Rohan closed his laptop halfway through and buried his hands in his curls, frowning. "Thanks for telling me," he said when she was done. "She didn't seem injured in any way and the bus wasn't torn apart?"

Judit shook her head. "Not that I could see."

Rohan nodded thoughtfully. "If Dani and Gemma are on it, I don't think getting involved will help. I'll reach out to them and let them know we can be back up if need be but that's all we can do. Angie and her band are used to her mental health issues, they have their methods." He smiled sadly. "I'm not sure they'd take our help even if they needed it."

"She took my help," Judit pointed out. "She demanded it."

Rohan bobbed his head from side to side, not quite denying her words. Patrick knew the gesture well. His former bandmate didn't want to burst Judit's bubble but he was sure she was wrong. "I'm not sure she would see it that way."

Judit frowned.

"Does this mean she'll be even more of a problem tomorrow night?" Patrick asked, contingencies already percolating in his mind.

Rohan sighed. "Maybe."

"How do we tell Benji?"

Rohan's fingers were knuckle-deep in his hair again. He groaned. "Benji's grudge... I swear they hate her more than I ever did."

"I'm pretty sure being able to hold a grudge for literal years is required for writing emo-goth rock," Patrick said.

Rohan snorted. "Sure." He let go of his hair. "What if we just didn't tell them?"

"Conspiring against Benji?" Patrick glanced around the bus. "Are you sure they haven't bugged this place?"

Rohan followed his gaze with a lopsided grin. "Mostly."

"Can we just say something vague?" Judit asked. "Like 'Angela seems fragile and weird, keep a closer eye on her but be gentle'?"

"Does Benji know how to be gentle?" Rohan asked.

Patrick remembered their face last January, softening as they ruthlessly kept him from walking away from NoN by dangling his contract and then his sister's success in front of him. He shrugged. "Probably not."

"Ouch, you guys," Judit said. "Give them some credit. I'm sure if we told them to treat her with kid gloves they would, even if it was just because it was strategic."

"You're right," Rohan sighed. "We're being dicks." He pulled out his phone and typed.

Patrick's phone chimed and he pulled it out, noting Judit did the same. That damn group chat.

ROHAN

New intel: Angie is in a bad place. Do not provoke her but keep an eye out.

BENJI

fuck.

LEO

uh oh does this mean benji baby has to be nice to the mean lady?

BENJI

fuuuuuck you

HELEN

It rhymed, it must be true!

ROHAN

i am serious, you know

JUDIT

yeah she didn't look good

PATRICK

^^^

"This is going well," he said out loud.

Judit put her phone down with a sigh.

Rohan looked at his watch, glanced out the window, and snorted. "Yep, they're already on their way."

"Aw man, they're on shift though," Judit said. "I better go help Helen." She got up, hesitated, smiled at Patrick, and left.

Patrick stared at the spot where she disappeared for too long a moment, judging by the grin on Rohan's face. "So what are you going to say to head Benji off?"

"How long have you two been together?"

"Who?" Patrick asked like he was talking to a nosy reporter. "Me and Benji? Not my type."

"Don't use your media training on me. I saw you and Judit holding hands."

"Yeah, right. The windows are tinted."

Rohan gave him a look, knowing he knew exactly how much you could see in a tour bus.

Patrick deflated. "No comment."

"No comment about what?" Benji said from behind him.

"How'd you get past Crusher?" Patrick demanded.

"Who do you think hired him?" Benji raised an eyebrow. "Crusher and I go way back."

"Of course, you do," Patrick muttered.

"What are we doing about Angelica?"

Rohan scrubbed his hands down his face. "Keeping an eye on things. I reached out to her band to let them know we'd help if they needed it."

Benji sputtered. "You *what? Help?*"

Rohan's face hardened. "She's having a bad mental health period. Have some fucking compassion."

Benji glared at him so intently Patrick worried this would escalate.

"Chill, Ben. It's not gonna cause a catastrophe if we're nice to the woman," Patrick said

Benji grumbled but sat. "You're right. I'll keep an eye on her at the party tomorrow."

Patrick and Rohan exchanged a glance.

"I don't know if that's a good idea," Patrick hazarded.

Rohan nodded emphatically.

Benji snorted. "Have some faith in me. I'm a fucking adult and I know more about mental health crises than both of you kids combined."

Patrick rolled his eyes. "Yes, oh agéd elder."

Rohan snickered. "To think, in just one to two years we too will be blessed with such wisdom."

"Not what I meant and you know it."

Both men sobered abruptly, remembering the Suicide King had been a person before Benji turned him into a character in their wildly popular rock opera album.

"I don't think it'll get to that," Rohan said quietly.

"It won't." Benji's tone was final, like they could will it so.

35

So long, farewell…
All right kiddies, new moon in Virgo tonight, so welcome the chaos cuz
we're ending this tour with a bang! Hopefully figuratively. Get sparkly but
put on your sensible shoes and get real with yourself—things are about to
be interesting. It's been an honor, a pleasure, and a calling to be your agony
aunt for the summer. Stay classy, stay in touch, and follow all my socials!
Love and air kisses,
LS

Judit woke up the day of the party and swore she could feel the anticipation in the air. Sure, parties happened all the time during the fest but this was *it*. The last party. The last day of Endfest. She looked over at Patrick, sleeping curled up in the bunk across from hers.

Why couldn't he live in Sacramento? Or at least somewhere closer than 400 fucking miles away. It had been creeping up on her for days, the realization that she wanted more from this. That she could see more with him. But what if this was nothing more than a summer camp romance?

She picked up her deck off her bunk shelf and held it in

her hand, drawing comfort from the familiar cloth-wrapped weight. But she didn't draw a card. She didn't want to know the future yet.

Instead, she reached across the aisle and pushed his shoulder.

He grumbled and burrowed deeper into the pillow. He did this every morning and she now found it cute. Yeah, she had it bad.

"Patrick," she whispered. "Wake up. Time to walk."

He turned towards her and gave her a scrunched grimace, eyes still closed.

"Come on, baby." Everyone was asleep or gone, no one would hear the endearment but him.

He sighed but opened his eyes. "Only because I like you."

"Damn straight, you do." She grinned.

In less than ten minutes, they were walking around the quiet fest grounds, holding hands and leaning into each other. She smiled at nothing in particular, filled with sleepy contentment.

"Rohan has figured us out," Patrick said after a while. "He made some rather pointed comments after you left. I didn't tell him anything but." He shrugged. "He's pretty bright, unfortunately."

Judit snorted at the chagrin in his voice but her good humor didn't last long. "Do you think he told Cazzi?"

"I don't know," he said, his face conflicted. "I don't know if it would be better if she found out from him or us."

Something hopeful zinged through Judit's veins. He wanted to tell Cazzi about them, but he wouldn't bother if this was just a summer fling, right? Sure, honesty was a good policy but would Cazzi need to know if it meant nothing? She chewed on the thought, feeling guilty. "Is this—us—going to go beyond the fest, you think?" she blurted finally. "Like, really?"

Patrick halted, pulling her to a stop next to him and looking her in the eye. "Do you want it to?"

Judit fought the urge to look away, feeling vulnerable. "Yeah, but I've never done long distance and I'm scared. Do you?"

He looked at her for so long without saying anything she thought she was either going to scream or burst into tears, her whole body tensing up in a way that would definitely come back to haunt her in a few hours. Finally, he smoothed his hands over her shoulders, kneading at the knots forming there. "I guess I'm scared too. I really like you and I'm kind of a disaster with a shitty track record in relationships."

"Shitty how?"

He looked away. "Well, there's the whole Cazzi thing. Me and my fucking anxiety caused her a lot of pain. If I had told her I had a girlfriend when she kissed me..." He shrugged. "I try not to beat myself up about it but I feel like a cheater like —" He stopped, pressing his lips together.

"Like?"

Still looking away, he said, "Don't tell Sabrina I told you this."

"Okay."

"Around the time Cazzi kissed me, I found out my grandfather, the guy I'm named after actually, had been cheating on my Nana for decades. His side chick decided she was done waiting for him to leave Nana and told us all. It tore our family apart. Nana wouldn't speak to him. She moved in with me. When Cazzi kissed me and I... enjoyed it, I—" He shrugged. "I know it's not rational or even close to what Grandpa Pat did but..." He stared at the sky, completely rigid except for the tremor of his fingers in hers. "He died last year. COVID. Alone and I never... It was so fast. I wasn't ready. We still weren't speaking."

Her heart *hurt*, god, this poor man, beating himself up for so long for a kiss he didn't even initiate. Suddenly, his hot and cold behavior that messed Cazzi up so bad made more sense.

"Can I hug you?"

He nodded, lips pressed together.

She wrapped her arms around him. "Thank you for telling me."

He nodded again.

"My track record with relationships isn't great either. My biggest one is that utter shitshow I told you about in the car. But..." She hesitated, checking in with herself before she finished the sentence. No, this felt right. "I'm willing to try if you are. I really like you and I think I would never forgive myself if I let you slip away just because I was scared of long-distance or holding a grudge over something you did years ago and are working to get past."

His lips brushed the top of her head, his arms coming up to hug her tightly. "So, we're doing this?"

"Hell yes," she said, reveling in his embrace. "Ugh, I don't know if I'm ready to be back in the real world yet though."

"You'll miss me too much?"

"Well, *yeah*. But also I got a bunch of appointments to squeeze in before my insurance runs out and I think I need to bite the bullet and get a full-time job."

"Like a psychic hotline?"

"Maybe, I don't know? More likely an office job. I need the benefits."

He nodded against her hair. "Let me know how I can help."

"Hold my hand in the doctor's office?" She joked. Well, half-joked. The image of him holding her hand while she fought for whatever diagnosis she could get was comforting.

"If you want me to," he said.

"Maybe," she admitted. "Do you need any help with figuring shit out after you quit?"

"I don't know," he said. "Maybe don't give me any advice unless I ask for it."

She pulled back so he could see her salute. "I'll do my best."

"I know it's hard," he said drily.

"I'll just scream them into a paper bag. It won't be weird at all."

He grinned. "I got really lucky when I found you."

"Technically, I think I found you," she teased.

His laughter rumbled around her, making every nerve hum happily. "Yeah, I'm definitely keeping you, you pedantic nerd."

She laughed. "Asshole, you're lucky you're pretty."

He kissed her. "Right now, I'm just lucky, period," he murmured against her lips.

36

"Are you ready for tonight?
Gonna make your life
Best you remember
So good you can't forget

Yeah, yeah, yeah

It's dark, it's night
Gonna party 'til sunlight
Tonight's the time
Keep it goin', keep it goin'

[crowd chants] Keep that party goin'!

Tonight's gonna make it better
Wash my cares away
Make me forget her
If just for a day"
— "Keep the Party Goin'" by Beatboyz off of *Keep the Party*
Going

Judit and Helen got to the party while it was still being set up, which turned out to be a tactical error. They were immediately drafted into helping.

Nick buzzed around the giant party tent, talking on the phone and managing to sidestep any physical labor. Helen caught Judit watching him and rolled her eyes.

Judit was setting up the bottles Helen hauled to the bar when Patrick and Leo arrived. Set up was mostly done by that point so she ceded the bar over to the Lady Water rep staffing it and made her way over to them. They hadn't seen her yet. She smoothed her one nice dress before catching their attention. Benji helped her refine her make-up, she and Helen fought half the tour for the camp showers, and now she felt fancier than she had in months.

When she waved at him, Patrick stopped, taking her in with that burning gaze. Holy shit, she really did love it when he devoured her with his eyes.

Leo let out a whistle. "Damn girl, love the look."

"Yeah," Patrick said, his voice slightly hoarse. He looked amazing, wearing the hell out of a pair of black skinny jeans, boots, and a half-buttoned sleeveless red shirt. He was probably dying in the evening heat but, *damn.*

Judit couldn't help grinning and by the twinkle in Leo's eyes, he knew exactly what was going on. She didn't even care.

"I'll leave you kids alone," he said.

Patrick tore his gaze away from her and frowned. "Yeah, no. We gotta stick together."

Leo rolled his eyes. "The buddy system doesn't apply here. Relax."

Judit's phone buzzed.

BENJI

Doom twins have been sighted together, on my way to the party.

They arrived a minute later. Alone.

"Where were you?" Leo asked, "Stalking the Doom Twins?"

"Where's Rohan?" Patrick asked at the same.

Benji pointed at Leo. "First off, no. Second." They pointed at Patrick, "He's picking up Cazzi. So." They gestured at him and Judit. "Get your story straight."

Judit had never felt the blood drain from her face before but she already hated it. How had she forgotten Cazzi would be coming tonight?

HE HAD FORGOTTEN Cazzi was coming.

I must really like Judit. That was almost as discombobulating. Sure, he knew he liked her a lot but to like her so much in a summer that she overshadowed someone he'd been pining over for years? It felt wrong somehow, like he was shallow, easily swayed. But also, right.

"Incoming," Helen chirped, her expression more strained than her cheerful tone.

Patrick turned, dread wrapping tight around his stomach. He couldn't face her, he couldn't—

Oh. It was just Angela. With Martin on her arm. His entourage cheered madly like he'd won an award. As they did, Angela gave the party at large an amused look, her gaze staying several beats too long on Benji's blank face. Benji looked through her but Patrick was willing to bet they could tell him exactly how many buttons ran down the front of her blood-red 1950s housewife dress.

"A Real Housewife of Hell and a yacht club Republican

walk into a bar..." Leo murmured, looking derisively at Martin's polo and boat shoes.

"They couldn't look more like a problem if they'd color-coordinated," Benji muttered back.

Patrick watched Leo, keeping tabs on Martin out of the corner of his eye. Leo pretended not to notice his ex while Martin pretended he wasn't scanning the crowd for Leo.

Angela stopped bothering with pretense and stared at Benji. A couple of people nearby followed her gaze. Benji's eye twitched.

"This isn't weird at all." Judit sipped from her Lady Water can.

"Totally normal," Helen agreed, smiling at no one in particular.

More people were turning their way, or more specifically, Benji's way. Patrick was pretty sure Martin had clocked Leo but both men were pretending otherwise.

Half the crowd was now looking at Benji, Angela standing like a puppet master in the middle of them.

"Fuck this," Benji muttered, ducking out of the tent.

Patrick couldn't blame them but hell, this meant he, Judit, and Helen were going to have to deal with whatever Leo/Martin drama came up.

"Yeah same," Leo said, swinging the tent flap open with an attention-seeking flourish.

Patrick looked at Judit. "I've got Leo. Can you two stay here and run interference on any Angela drama?"

She saluted him with a grin and Helen gave him finger guns. "Roger that, big daddy!" Judit said then grimaced. "Forgot I said that last bit. I totally creeped myself out."

Patrick snorted. When he turned to follow Leo he heard Helen say, "Big Daddy is what I called Cedric last night."

Judit's laughter followed him out of the tent.

Now, where the hell had Leo gotten off to?

"Do you ever get the feeling that we're running way too much interference?" Helen asked while the two of them watched Martin and Angela make the rounds, working the crowd like they'd hosted the party themselves.

"Oh, you mean like these people are adults and might act like it if we give them the chance to have the conversations they so clearly need to have?" Judit snorted. "I don't know, seems too logical." She sipped more tasteless Lady Water.

Martin's entourage clapped and squealed at something he said.

"Yeah, true." Helen sighed. "Celebs be crazy, your bae excepted, of course."

"Of course," said a voice beside them in a mocking echo.

Both women jumped, Helen stumbling on the uneven ground. "Jeez, fuck!" Judit gasped, steadying her friend.

Angela gave them an amused look. "Did I scare you?" she asked in a silky voice that begged to be in a horror film.

"What do you want?" Judit demanded, annoyed. She'd spilled Lady Water all over the skirt of her dress. It was clear, but the dirt instantly sticking to the sugary low-proof alcohol sure wasn't.

"Front row seats," Angela said, nodding at the front of the tent.

Judit turned slowly, not convinced she wasn't actually in a horror film. Rohan ducked through one of the half-open tent flaps, holding it open for Cazzi. She caught sight of Judit and waved. She faltered when she saw who was standing next to Judit.

Judit felt the urge to bolt.

There was a crunch next to her. Angela held a Ziploc

baggie of popcorn. Judit stared at her and the other woman offered her some. Helen shrugged and grabbed a handful.

"Look," Angela said. "You did nothing wrong. She let him go. She moved on. Free market and all that."

"Who?" Judit said trying for innocence.

Angela rolled her eyes. "Please, I have eyes. You and Ricky Rick aren't especially subtle."

"Mmm," Helen said thoughtfully. "I feel like you're biased though."

"Deeply and on all things," Angela said around another handful of popcorn. "But in this instance, you know I'm right."

"Devil's advocate," Helen said.

"More of a Lucifer and Baphomet girl myself." Angela winked.

"I can't tell if this is helping or making everything ten times worse," Judit muttered, watching Cazzi and Rohan make their way towards them. They'd been waylaid three times already, people wanting to talk to Rohan and mostly ignoring Cazzi. Exactly the way she liked it in these situations. She wasn't wearing that mask just for the dust or COVID. "Oh god, oh god, oh *fuck*."

"Hey," Angela said sharply enough that Judit jerked her head to look at her. "Chill." The singer punctuated the word with a small, gentle smile.

Judit blinked, the world going into soft focus and her muscles unclenching until she swayed back a step.

"Whoa." Helen sighed behind her.

Angela's face went blank, the smile disappearing like a slammed door.

"Wha—"

"Judit!" Cazzi hugged her, the sudden invasion of personal space almost as startling as whatever Angela had just done with her face. "Sorry for the sudden hug but is she bothering you?"

Cazzi whispered in her ear. "Say the word and we'll figure out how to take care of it."

"No," Judit mumbled, still dazed. "It's fine. Thanks."

Cazzi pulled back, her gaze searching Judit's face. *You sure?* she mouthed.

Judit nodded.

"Hi Angie," Rohan said, his tone pleasant if slightly awkward.

Angela tossed a kernel of popcorn in her mouth, chewed. "Hey, Ro." She glanced at Cazzi. "Sup."

Cazzi let Judit go and offered Angela a tentative smize over her mask. "Angelica. I saw your performance with Rohan. You two were great."

Angela blinked. Ate another kernel. "Thank you."

Uncomfortable silence settled around them.

"Hey Cazzi," Helen said, extending an elbow to Cazzi.

"Oh god, I'm so sorry." Cazzi bumped her elbow with her own. "Long day at work, my brain's fried."

Helen smiled. "No worries."

Before the awkward silence could rise again, Angela checked her Fitbit and sighed. "I gotta go do a thing soon. Can we speed this up?" She looked at Judit.

Judit glared back. "We wouldn't want to make you late, no need to hang around."

"Oh no, being late is the point." There was a wicked gleam in her eyes.

Judit's brain scrambled to make sense of her cryptic words.

Helen's eyes went wide. "Oh shit! Where's Martin?" She whipped out her phone, texting furiously.

Cazzi groaned. "Stirring up drama? Come on, Angelica. Don't you do enough of that online?"

"In-person is so much better," Angela said. She glanced at everyone in the circle one at a time. Rohan conspicuously avoided her eyes. "Oh, come on, you guys. Rip the band-aid off."

"I am not your entertainment!" Judit snarled.

Angela shrugged. "Entertainment is in the eye of the beholder."

"I don't like you," Judit seethed.

"Get in line."

"Angelica, please. Stop." Cazzi put on her soothing 'I counsel college students about sex' voice. "This is not productive."

Rohan stared at the ceiling of the tent, looking like he was asking for patience from anything that would answer.

"Ro," Angela purred. "She doesn't know, does she?"

Rohan lowered his head slowly to meet her gaze. "Angie, this doesn't involve you."

She shrugged again. "So?"

"So, please leave," he said, a hardness Judit never heard before in his voice. "You're being an asshole and you know it." He held her gaze until she looked away.

"Fuck," she muttered. "Fine." She turned and strode out the nearest tent flap.

"Sounds like she and Martin have got something up their sleeves," Judit said, trying to change the subject. "Should we—"

"Judit." Cazzi's tone stopped her words dead in their tracks. "Tell me what she was fucking around about. Everyone here seems to know already." Her gaze cut to Rohan in a way that said there would be a conversation about this later.

He sighed.

"Um," Judit said. Shit, should she wait until Patrick was here? Would it be better if he told her? Was there a *good* way to tell her?

PATRICK FOUND Leo sitting on an empty stage, drinking out of a flask. Roadies and people who wanted out of the crowded hot tent milled around, some of them covertly watching Leo. Patrick stopped in front of him. "You good?"

"I'm not going to embarrass the label," Leo slurred.

"I don't care about that," Patrick said.

"You seem pretty cozy with them." Leo waved vaguely at the party tent.

Patrick shrugged. "I'm still quitting."

"Are we ever going to be all good again?" Leo asked morosely.

"Who? You and me are fine."

"The band." Leo took another swig.

"You want to reconcile with Martin?" Patrick tried for a neutral tone and failed miserably.

Leo shook his head. "The rest of us. I want to all be friends again. I miss us as a friend group. It's all weird, now."

"Oh. Maybe."

Leo grinned.

Benji stomped over to them. "Any sign of the Doom Twins?"

"I thought you had them microchipped," Leo said.

"Maybe we're overestimating this whole thing," Patrick said. "I doubt they care that much."

Benji snorted. "Evil exs like that? Doubtful."

Leo's attention snapped to their face. "What do you know?"

"More than most people give me credit," they said. "But staring like a lovesick dipshit doesn't make it hard." Benji looked pointedly at Leo.

Patrick remembered his conversation with Benji at the beginning of the tour, and yeah, that tracked.

"Pot." Leo pointed at Benji. "Kettle." He pointed at himself.

Benji frowned. "Martin? No, thanks. I don't do douchebags."

Leo rolled his eyes. "There's a fine line between hatesick and lovesick. You know I'm not talking about Martin."

"Are you so drunk you're only speaking in bastardized cliches or is this some new kind of drug I haven't tried yet?" Benji crossed their arms.

"I didn't know there was such a thing." Leo stared over their head.

Benji copied his eye roll. "Yeah, sure, insult me. That'll help."

Leo was still staring over their head.

They snapped their fingers at him. "Eyes down here, you giant bitch."

Patrick turned to follow Leo's gaze. *Oh shit.*

"You are very lucky you're queer and Rohan's friend," Leo growled behind him.

"Hey," Patrick said.

"Yeah, yeah," Benji said. "You're big, it's scary. Blah blah blah. Now use that big head of yours and think about the optics of your giant white ass getting in another brawl on this tour. Especially with someone who looks like me." They gestured at their slenderness, accented by their femme outfit.

Leo grimaced.

"Okay, but seriously—" Patrick tried.

"Yep," they said. "Now, look at me like you don't want to take my head off and maybe we'll get through this party without a shitshow."

Leo heaved a sigh and put on a TV-ready smile. "What if they come to us?"

Patrick gave up. Leo was fucking with Benji now. Frankly, they were being a dick enough to deserve it.

"We'll cross that bridge when we get to it," Benji said.

"Get ready to cross," Patrick said, turning to face the problem head-on.

Martin towards them.

"Hello, Leo." Martin's smooth voice matched his fake smile. Benji turned to face him, laying their hand on Leo's knee and leaning against him and the stage under him.

Did they think they could hold Leo back?

"I need to talk to Leo. Alone," Martin said to Benji and Patrick.

Dammit, Patrick remembered this passive-aggressive bullshit. He looked at Leo.

Sure enough, Leo had his fingers in his ears and his eyes cast up to the sky.

"Not again," Patrick muttered.

"I'm going to guess that he's not into that," Benji said. "Maybe try sending an email."

Martin sighed. "I was promised time to talk to him."

By who? Patrick glanced at Benji. They grimaced.

How dare they bargain Leo's peace of mind like that? And for what? Martin's useless help when Nick locked himself in his bus? This was exactly why he couldn't work with them after the tour. How could he work with a business partner he couldn't trust?

"I didn't agree to that," Leo snarled.

"Something wrong?" Angelica appeared and leaned her forearms on Martin's shoulders.

"I told you it wouldn't work," Martin hissed, overly loud. Maybe he wasn't too sober either. Fantastic.

Angelica sighed. "Darling, let me handle it." She looked up at Leo. Her eyes got big, pleading.

Patrick looked away, grabbing the root in his pocket.

"Leo." Her voice got the perfect amount of sweet, the perfect amount of soft.

Leo blinked slowly at her. "What?"

"Life is short. Talk to Martin." Her expression was haunted, full of regret. Patrick grabbed his root harder.

"Fine," Leo growled, taking his fingers out of his ears.

Angelica leaned against the stage next to Benji. Oh good, that'll go well.

Patrick crossed his arms and stared Martin down.

"You don't need to be here," Martin said loftily.

Patrick looked at Leo.

"It's fine," Leo said, but he took another slug out of the flask. His hand shook.

"I'll stay," Patrick said.

Leo smiled.

"Fine," Martin said through his teeth.

He paused. Patrick could hear Angela and Benji whispering aggressively at each other.

Martin ignored them. "Leo, I think it's time we consider moving past our differences. It will serve us better in the long run."

"Ha!" Leo sputtered.

Did you have a corporate speechwriter feed you that line? Patrick wondered but clamped his lips over the words. If he stirred shit up now it would only escalate. Better to let Martin say his piece, embarrass himself, and leave before he riled Leo up too much.

Martin drew himself up. "It's childish to continue this feud. It's been years and it would be more beneficial to both our careers if you just let it go."

Seriously? If this was him trying to be logical, Martin was being more obtuse than Patrick had ever seen him.

Leo stared at him.

"Frankly." Something about the way Martin said the word

made Patrick certain Leo was going to lose his shit. "It would help your career more than mine."

Patrick hissed out a breath.

"Excuse me?" Leo said, his voice dangerously quiet.

"Leo, no," Patrick said. "He's baiting you." He glared at Martin.

"You know." Angela leaned around Benji, her voice breezy like there wasn't one, possibly two fights brewing in the immediate vicinity. "They were talking about you back in the tent."

Patrick ignored her, focusing on Leo.

"Ro, that one merch girl, your girlfriend, your… is she an ex? I was never clear on that."

Patrick couldn't help it, he looked at the tent. Through the flaps, he could make out their group. It was too far away to read faces but it looked like Cazzi was standing apart from Rohan in a way that looked intentional and angry. Judit was huddled into herself and Helen had a hand on her friend's upper back, supportively.

Had Judit told Cazzi without giving him the option to tell her himself?

His fingers twitched for his phone and he missed half of whatever bullshit Martin was spouting to justify himself.

"No!" Leo bellowed.

Patrick snapped back into the conversation as Leo dumped the remainder of his flask on Martin's head. It would've been more impressive if it had been more than a trickle.

"Fuck you," Leo snarled, stalking away.

Patrick turned to Martin. "That was it. That's all you get. You've done enough."

Martin opened his mouth but Patrick glared at him down. "I know what you did and I have receipts. Don't make me use them."

Martin closed his mouth and nodded stiffly.

"I'll take care of this. Get out of here before the entourage descends," Benji said, stepping up next to Martin. "Here." They thrust a towel in his hand.

Behind them, Patrick could see Martin's entourage running towards them at top speed, weaving through the partygoers. He must've told them to stay.

Already, he could see them glaring daggers at him and some of them following Leo with their eyes.

He hightailed it after Leo.

Five minutes later, Patrick watched Leo pace in front of their bus. The entourage hadn't followed them so Benji must've smoothed things over.

He still had no idea what was going on with Judit or Cazzi.

He clenched his fingers into fists. No one was texting, except Helen whose *you might want to get back here* message was cryptic and useless. Plus, if he looked at his phone now Leo would think he was ignoring him and it would only ratchet his tantrum up to eleven.

"That little fucking twat thinks he gets to just tell me how I should feel and then ask me for a fucking favor in the same breath—" Leo let out a shriek and punched the side of the bus.

"Whoa, whoa, whoa!" Patrick grabbed his arm. There was a slight dent in the fiberglass body and Leo's knuckles were as red as his flushed face. "Hurting yourself is not gonna hurt him, remember?"

"I know," Leo muttered, sullen.

Patrick wrapped his free arm around Leo's shoulders. Leo dropped his head on Patrick's shoulder, the sudden weight and awkward angle making both men stumble. "I hate that he still can hurt me so easily," he whispered.

"Me too." Patrick tightened his embrace, feeling warm tears soaking through his shirt. *Fucking Martin.* He felt like he was back in another unending tour with the Beatboyz dealing with the fallout of yet another *thisisthelasttimeIswear* breakup between Martin and Leo.

"Hey." Judit peered around the bus. "Um, we have to talk."

"I'm in the middle of something." Patrick gestured at Leo. Something about the tentative way Judit held herself spelled trouble. Half of him wanted to soothe her and the other had already reached its emotional labor bandwidth and wished she'd go the fuck away. *Way to be a good boyfriend.*

"Oh Leo," she said. "What happened?"

"Go away," Leo growled into Patrick's shoulder.

"Cazzi wants to talk to you." Judit was trying to tell him something with her eyes but he wasn't the psychic here. Had she told Cazzi? Had she not? Had Rohan? What the fuck was he about to deal with?

"I'm busy," he said, more abruptly than he meant to.

"Let me help." Cazzi stepped around the other side of the bus.

"Oh god," Leo groaned. "The women are multiplying."

Patrick froze. Of course, this was happening. Of course, she was ambushing him now.

"Hi Leo." Cazzi's voice took on the neutrally soothing tone she'd perfected in grad school before she realized she wasn't cut out to be a therapist. She glanced at Patrick, her eyes asking *is this okay?*

What the fuck do you think? He blanked his expression before she could catch the anger and read him like a damn book.

Her lips pressed together, letting him know she'd registered his masking and had thoughts about it. She turned away. Within a minute, Leo sat on the bus steps, telling her a very abbreviated version of his problems while she sat in the dirt next to him. Even emotionally wrecked and tipsy, Leo's PR training didn't fail him. He didn't tell her who his ex was or any identifiable details of their relationship. Patrick wasn't sure if he was proud or slightly disturbed by how well they had been programmed by their management at such a young age.

"Sorry," Judit murmured, coming up next to him. "Angela

tried to expose us and um, I didn't want to be the one to break the news without consulting you. This was the only way I could think of to give you a chance—"

He touched a finger to her wrist, stopping the words tumbling out of her mouth. "It's fine. We'll figure it out."

She exhaled hard, her shoulders dropping. "Okay."

He couldn't help the half-smile quirking his lips. It was okay, wasn't it? It was okay because she was here and for no good reason he had something like faith that they could weather the storm that was already—-

"Oh." It was barely a breath, barely an exhale but after spending most of his life listening to her breathe, he couldn't help but hear it.

He looked up and caught Cazzi's gaze. All the hope and warmth drained out of him at the shock in her expression. The fragility. He had done that to her. Again.

"Oh, yeah," Leo said, looking at Patrick and Judit. "Girl, you missed the boat on that one." He shrugged. "Serves you right for dumping my Rick." He cackled, drunker than Patrick realized.

Cazzi turned her stunned gaze on him. "What?"

Patrick could see her trying to piece her mask back together, trying to keep composed and failing. How could it hurt this much to see? Wasn't he over her?

"Caz?" He whispered, almost afraid if he was any louder she'd shatter in front of him.

Out of the corner of his eye, he could see Judit clasping her hands over her mouth, staring between the two of them. It mattered, it really did but he couldn't stop looking at Cazzi. The way her knuckles turned white when she grabbed the highest-level calming sigil tattooed on her arm. Her raggedly even breathing. The way her eyes wouldn't leave his, clinging like he was the only thing keeping her afloat.

"Cazzi?" Rohan's voice.

She gasped, her shoulders sagging with relief when she turned and saw her boyfriend. "Ro. Hi." She looked at him like a lifeline, like the light at the end of the tunnel.

Rohan took in the scene and her barely functioning mask. "Aw, crap." He rubbed the back of his head with a chagrined 'guess I've been caught' expression Patrick recognized from his old PR shots. Anger tightened Patrick's fists, rooting him to the spot. How dare Rohan use his fucking tricks on her, how dare he manipulate—

"Don't pull that cutesy shit on me." Cazzi lunged upright, her fragility turning into anger. "You didn't warn me. You let me walk in unprepared."

Rohan sighed, dropping the pose. "You wanna do this here?"

Cazzi looked around at her rapt audience. She shook her head. "No." She nodded at Leo. "Seek mental health help and monitor your substance use." Then she looked at Patrick and Judit. "I'm happy for you two. I am. I was just surprised. It would've been nice to know." She shrugged with a brittle smile. "Enjoy your evening, everyone."

Cazzi walked away with her head held high.

Rohan gave them all a sympathetic look before following after her.

"That went well," Leo said, swigging from a nearby cup. Who knew whose it was or what was in it.

Patrick batted it out of his hand. "What the actual fuck, Leo?"

Leo shrugged. "She'd figured it out and I never got to give her a piece of my mind for fucking you up."

"She didn't fuck me up!"

"Could've fooled me. Hell, she's still fucking you up!" Leo yelled.

People were watching them again.

"You don't know what you're talking about!" Patrick hissed back.

"And you didn't even notice that your girlfriend left, like, ten minutes ago."

The bottom dropped out of Patrick's stomach because Leo was right. Judit was nowhere to be seen.

37

"I've had enough
I'm calling your bluff
You said you could do without me
Let's see

I'm walking away
Don't care what you say
I'm walking, walking away
(walk walk walking
Walk, walk walking)"
—-"Walking Away" by Martin Mejia off of *Flying Solo*

J udit sat on her old bed in her old room in her old apartment and finally, *finally* let herself cry. She'd called Helen the minute she'd left the scene of that emotional shitshow. Helen had gotten both their bags (with the help of some of her roadie friends) and they'd left immediately instead of in the morning with everyone else.

Sure, it would've been the mature thing to let Patrick explain himself or even just talk to him, but fuck that. It was hard enough watching the man you love look at another girl with his heart in his eyes. She didn't need to rehash it with him just so they could feel like adults.

God, she'd never felt so invisible in her life.

She'd even swallowed her pride (and tears) long enough to call her demi-sister and ask for a ride home. Not that she wanted to put Eva in the middle between herself and Cazzi but it was that or Mom and there was no way that was happening.

Eva picked them up on the suburban Natomas side of Discovery Park, which was a longer walk but much less sketch than the freeway side with all the discount hotels and encampments. As they walked up the hill towards the park entrance, Judit saw a figure near the trees at the top of the hill.

Angela stood, staring out at the dark street.

Helen and Judit exchanged a glance. They drew level with her and Angela looked at them.

Tears tracked down her face, making muddy trails of her make-up but her expression was serene. Exhaustion radiated off of her. "Didn't go well, huh?"

"Are you okay?" Judit gestured at her face. It felt like such an effort to move.

Angela touched her cheek and looked surprised. She shrugged. "Sometimes the body just needs to cry." She cocked her head. "You look like you could use some tears."

"Does anyone know you're out here?" Judit asked. Helen edged behind her, looking freaked out.

"They know I'll be back. Still got half a tour to do. Can't let them down." She took a step closer, peering at them. "You both are talented. I'll be watching you." Her teeth flashed her smile so fast it barely registered. "In a good way."

Angela turned and strolled back down the hill.

Judit and Helen exchanged a wide-eyed look.

"Is it just me or does she seem like she's about to have a breakdown?" Helen asked.

Judit shrugged, all out of fucks. "She drew the Tower card. She knows what's coming."

They walked the rest of the badly lit route in silence.

Eva took one look at her face and Helen's strained smile and pulled them both in for a hug. "I should've gotten my event covered and come to the damn show," she muttered into Judit's hair.

Judit almost cried then but managed to hold it together. "No way. Nobody gives a condom presentation like you. Those kids needed your guidance."

Eva laughed. "Uh-huh, sure. Get in the car, mija. I'm in a bus lane."

Her sister had been merciful enough not to ask any probing questions. They would come when Eva judged enough time had passed, but who cared about the future when Judit's chest felt like someone had cracked it open and rooted out her heart?

Her heart, god. Her pathetic, breaking heart.

There was a knock on the door.

"Yeah?"

Helen stuck her head in. "The walls are thin. Wanna come sob on the couch? The subletters left half a carton of Lucky Charms ice cream in the freezer. We could have a fully 2000s chick flick break-up montage."

Judit made a face. "That scares me on many levels. Didn't we see them selling that at Grocery Outlet before we left on tour?"

"Yes, and you wouldn't let me get it." Helen pouted.

"Because we were on a bad streak with weird Grocery Outlet food. Remember the Cinnamon Crunch ice cream?"

Helen grimaced. "But this one is free."

Judit went to the freezer. The ice cream had colors not found in nature, was freezer-burned, and looked like it had been eaten with a spoon straight from the carton. She pointed this out to Helen.

"Damn," Helen said. "Somehow, I don't think the freezer kills germs—or COVID." She thought for a second. "I still have a bag of M&Ms from the last gas station we stopped at."

"Sold."

Helen grinned and Judit almost felt like smiling back. That was a good sign, right?

When they got to the couch, Helen opened the M&Ms with a flourish and poured far too many into Judit's palm. The colorful candy tumbled into a heart shape in her hand.

Judit froze, staring at them, breathless. She'd never divined with candy, but holy shit that felt like a message. If only she knew what it meant.

Her phone buzzed in her pocket. It was Patrick. The sight of his name made her chest ache. She wanted to block his number and not read a single one of the multiple texts she could now see he'd sent her.

She looked at the M&M heart in her palm.

Maybe, she could do this.

PATRICK

I fucked up. I'm sorry. Can we talk?

Did you leave?

I guess you left. I get it. Call me?

It's getting late. I'll call you before my flight in the AM.

It's okay if you need time and space. I can do that.

Good night. I like you so much.

Did he though? She kept seeing his stricken face as he stared at Cazzi and she wasn't sure.

"Would I be an asshole if I blocked him for a bit?" She asked Helen.

Helen peered over her shoulder at the texts and shrugged. "What feels right?"

Judit muted him. She wasn't sure if it was right, but she didn't want to talk to him in the morning. She'd unmute him when things made sense in her head.

TWO DAYS LATER, Patrick sat at his kitchen table, cradling a mug of tea in his palms. He was up far too early. The view of the city, half the reason why he'd bought this house, was painted pastel colors by the rising sun.

It was beautiful, glorious even, but he couldn't lose himself in it the way he wanted to. Judit wasn't answering his texts or calls. When he'd texted Helen to make sure nothing had happened to Judit, her friend had told him to fuck all the way off. Which had to mean Judit was fine, right? Physically at least. That's what he'd been telling himself all night.

You should've put her first.

He closed his eyes. Why did he keep fucking up like this?

"Baby, what are you doing up this early?" Nana asked from the kitchen door. She wore her favorite green dressing gown but her short hair was already unwrapped for the day.

"Couldn't sleep." He shrugged. "Still on the tour schedule, I guess."

She pulled out the chair in front of him and squinted at him through her thick glasses. "You're sad. Is it that Cazzi girl again?"

He blinked, remembering how his dad let it slip that the

family figured out something happened with Cazzi. Was he really that transparent? "I'm not sad."

She leaned back in her chair and shook her head. "I thought I taught you better than to lie to me."

"I'm not—" His protests wilted under her unimpressed gaze. "Okay, yeah, I'm not in a good place."

"Girl problems?"

He nodded. "I don't want to talk about it."

"That's too bad because I do."

"Nana—"

"No baby, I can't watch you mope around this house anymore. I should've said something sooner but I know you men like your privacy and I'm just a guest here."

"You're not a guest."

She waved that away like she hadn't been living here and rearranging his kitchen cabinets for years. "What happened with your girl?"

"Cazzi?"

"There's more than one?" She clicked her tongue. "No wonder you're down."

He shook his head. "It's not like that. Not like Grandpa Pa—" He cut himself off abruptly. Nana never wanted to talk about what happened with Grandpa Pat, though it clearly still brought her pain. His death only seemed to make the silence harder to break.

Even now, she squeezed her eyes shut, fist clenching on the table.

"I'm sorry." Patrick sat frozen. It felt like every move he made broke something, hurt someone.

She shook her head and opened her eyes. "Not your fault, baby." She patted his hand. "You're nothing like him."

Patrick swallowed hard but the words spilled out. "Sometimes, I'm afraid I am."

"What do you mean?" Nana's brow furrowed like she couldn't even begin to believe it.

He wanted to stop, to keep it all dammed in but he couldn't. So he told her. He told her about Cazzi kissing him when he still was with his ex. About how he and Cazzi fell apart and how Rohan swooped in. His anger about that and then how he met Judit and thought he was over it but— "Then I saw her and she was so shocked about me and Judit and I... I felt like I was hurting her all over again. Now, Judit isn't talking to me."

"Hmm." Nana sipped the cup of tea she had brewed while listening to him. Ashwagandha and chickweed, her morning blend. "You think all this makes you like your no-good grandfather?"

He shrugged. "Yeah, I guess."

She sighed. "Baby, if your grandfather had gotten that messed up by a little kiss I would not be living with you right now. He wasn't worried about me all those years he cheated. He certainly wasn't worried too much about that side piece he cheated with or he'd have left me years ago. The only person that man worried about was himself and his little friend." She gestured at her lap and Patrick suffered a full-body cringe both at having this conversation with his Nana and at the thought of his grandfather's "little friend." She snorted. "I don't like to speak ill of the dead, but I'm glad I found out before he died."

"I thought you loved him," Patrick said, despite himself.

She sighed. "We had some good times together, don't get me wrong. But now, I question everything. I'm not the only one. She begged me to take him back once."

"What!"

"I said no. What good is a man I can't trust? And that's your problem, baby."

"What is?"

"Your girl, Judit. She can't trust you if you don't trust yourself, if you've still got Cazzi on her pedestal because you think she's some broken girl you've gotta protect, even from you."

"But I keep hurting her—both of them."

Nana shrugged. "Then stop. Pick a girl. I know these are modern times and all but you still can't have both. Not this way." She stood, draining the last of her tea. "You deserve to be happy. We all do, though it took me far too long to see that." She cupped his cheek. "And I *am* happy, what with my new man and getting to live with my lovely grandbabies. I hope you can find your happiness too, whatever that looks like." She patted his cheek. "Now, stop moping and figure out what you want."

He sat in the kitchen long after she left, thinking. Imagining Judit at the table with him, reading a book or creating a spread for Sabrina or Nana, smiling at him every so often. He missed her. So fucking much. Did she miss him too? Could she forgive him?

But he needed to sort out his shit. Prove to her that he could put her first.

Before he could overthink it, he pulled out his phone and dialed.

"Patrick?" Her voice was thick, somewhere between annoyed and worried. He'd woken her, forgetting the time. Before he could beat himself up about it, he reminded himself they had done that to each other plenty of times when he'd been on international tours.

"I think we need to start over."

He heard her breathing change as she sat up. "Yeah, no shit."

He smiled because she sounded so like the Cazzi he remembered, all the professional polish gone. "Can we be friends again?" His voice wavered and he blinked, registering the heat behind his eyes, the fear and hope and pain welling in his chest.

She was silent for a long time. He matched her silence, waiting her out. "Is this because of you and Judit?"

He paused, thinking. "In part. I thoroughly fucked up in that department. I want you and I to be okay again. Go back to the way we used to be before I ghosted you."

She inhaled hard. "We can't go back to that."

His stomach dropped. This was it. He'd destroyed his longest, best friendship.

"Mostly because, I'm not lovesick over you, Pat. But also I need you to get it out of your head that I can't handle—" There was a pause and he could picture her gesturing with her free hand. "—life and shit, you know? I'm a goddamn adult and if we're going to be friends again communication needs to be a two-way street."

"I can do that."

"Can you?"

"I can try. But you have to tell me shit too. No big secrets."

"Once again, not pining after you anymore."

He laughed. "I can tell." He hesitated. "Is it true you're thinking about marrying Rohan?"

"Yeah. Marriage is a big deal to his family and I dunno, I'm not opposed to it."

"You're moving back down to LA?"

"What is this the Spanish Inquisition?"

"Didn't expect that, did you?"

She laughed. "No one ever does."

They talked for a while and it felt almost, tentatively the way it used to, like he was talking to his best friend.

Right before she hung up she shattered the illusion by saying, "So you're going to fix things with Judit right?" Cazzi never asked about his other girlfriends, a big hint he'd studiously ignored before.

"I'm not sure how," he admitted. "She's ignoring all my messages."

"You love her, right?"

"Yes."

"Damn, no hesitation. I like that." Cazzi hummed thoughtfully. "I could call her. We have some shit to hash out anyway."

"What part of you calling her says she comes first and I'm not holding a torch for you?"

"Fair. Well, keep me—" Rohan's low voice filtered over the line. "Sorry, keep *us* posted."

"I'm invested!" Rohan yelled into the phone.

I bet you are, whispered Patrick's paranoia and anxiety. He acknowledged the thought but let it dissipate without giving it too much credence. Rohan wasn't a threat anymore. Hell, maybe someday they could be friends again and this whole thing wouldn't be weird as fuck. But first—

"Hand him the phone," Patrick said, steeling himself. The knot sitting in his stomach since the fest party tightened.

"Yeah?" Rohan said after it was handed over.

"I quit. Now or Never is all yours and Benji's." His stomach knot loosened.

Rohan sighed. "Look, I know it was shitty to keep you in your contract like that but we're working well together now. I think it would be great if—"

"No."

"But—"

"No." Patrick hung up and released the breath he'd been holding for far too long. He felt untethered, free.

Fucking scared, sure, he had spent the time since the band broke up busying himself with projects and certification programs. Now, the future stretched before him with nothing certain lined up and his anxiety shrilled at the unknown. Judit was right though. He had enough financial cushion to take his time to figure shit out. The mental health parts, the career part... maybe even the romantic part.

Patrick stepped out into the backyard and inspected the

garden, his phone on sound. The plants were weathering the heat well enough though it would be time to do some dead-heading soon. He took a lap around the edge of the pool, waiting.

Sure enough, five minutes later, Benji called. Patrick considered ignoring it but they were in town and knew where he lived.

"You can't talk me out of this," he said, picking up. The sudden anger that ignited him was shocking, feeling like it was sucking the oxygen from his brain.

"I know," Benji said. "But what if we renegotiated?"

"Fuck off Benji," Patrick snapped. "The last time we negotiated, you pulled my contract and trapped me for over a year, holding my sister's album hostage. Do you know how shitty and toxic it was to work with you two? How much it ate me up to produce Rohan's records, knowing if I made a wrong move you could take it out on Sabrina?"

Benji inhaled hard. "I would never have taken anything out on Sabrina, you know that."

"No, I don't and I didn't. You damn well know how ruthless you can be. You turned your suicidal bandmate into a symbol of pity and pain, and if Rohan gave you the green light you would've wrecked Angela's career. If I had chosen to fight you would've destroyed what was left of mine."

Benji was silent for a long moment. "I'm not a nice person, I'll give you that."

Patrick snorted.

"I've done unforgivable things. If it helps, I didn't enjoy them. They seemed like the only option at the time. I especially didn't enjoy what I did to you." They paused. "I get that there's no fixing that. I'll email the paperwork you need to leave the label. If you need help in the future, NoN will always be there for you." Another hesitation. "I will too."

"Noted," Patrick said, then forcing the word between his

teeth when his training screamed at him not to burn any bridges. "Thanks."

"Of course," Benji said. "Oh, and Patrick?"

"What?"

"I really am sorry."

"Good." Patrick hung up and threw his phone in the grass.

"Did you really only stay because of me?" Sabrina stood in the window next to the garden. The open window. Fuck.

He nodded. "I wanted to give your debut the best chance to shine I could."

"You thought two people who screwed you over was the best we could do? Hold on." She left the window and opened the sliding glass door. "You can't decide shit like that for me!"

This is why he didn't tell her—

"I'm a grown adult. So are Kevon and Cyrus—don't make that face—and we deserve to know the whole truth about deals we're making."

"This was after your deal," Patrick said. "I wasn't trying to be high-handed, I just—" He shrugged. "—you deserve the best. Benji promised they'd get it for you. Also, I wanted to do the album with you. I'm glad I did. We made an amazing album together. Hell, I'm glad I toured with you. I haven't enjoyed performing that much in years."

"Aw shit." Sabrina covered her mouth. "Are you trying to make me cry?"

Tentatively, he held his arms out. She dove into his embrace.

"What are you going to do now?" She asked his clavicle.

He shrugged. "Take some time to figure it out. I want to stay in music, I'm just not sure how."

"Well, you're a damn good producer. And bass player. Wanna be in a band again?" She stepped back and raised her eyebrows.

He laughed. "I didn't enjoy touring *that* much."

"You sure didn't hate it, though." Her eyebrows went up and down like a suggestive gif.

He frowned. "Don't do that, it's creepy."

"Fiiiine. But you and Judit though…"

He winced. "I fucked that up."

"Wait, what?" Sabrina cried. "Tell me everything!"

He did and then had to duck when she threw pool water at him. It didn't go far but she made her point.

"Damn," she said, shaking the water off her hand. "You did fuck up.".

"I know. I'm just not sure what to do about it. I'm pretty sure she blocked me."

"And you want her, not Cazzi?"

"Yes!" He threw up his hands. "But how do I show her that without turning into some creep from a movie that didn't age well?"

"Hmmm." Sabrina narrowed her eyes in thought.

38

Judit was doing better. Really, she was. Sitting in the bland waiting room of the pelvic pain specialist, she breathed deeply through her nose.

She was fine. Truly. Really.

She held her own hand because, in an effort to be a serious adult, she hadn't asked anyone to come with her. (Who the fuck do you ask for emotional support when you were going to be bottomless anyway?)

Also, because the gyno was in Clementine, Judit was being efficient about her commute time and having lunch afterward with her mom to "talk about her future."

(Thinking about that was *not* helping.)

She fiddled with her phone, too anxious to focus on the book in her lap. Her finger hovered over her text chat with Patrick. She still hadn't responded but every day or so she compulsively checked to see if he had given up on her yet. He hadn't. Every day he texted her little check-in texts, pictures of his garden, his cups of tea, and his adorable cat.

Today, his text said: *Your appointment is going to go great. Scoot and I believe in you.*

The accompanying picture of him with his cat curled up on his chest was illegal amounts of cute. It made her ache. She wanted to be cuddled up with him. If only she had taken him up on his offer to hold her hand through this.

As if he'd heard her, another text popped up. A picture of his hand.

PATRICK

I'm holding your hand in spirit.

Dammit. She had to stare at the ceiling for five minutes so she didn't cry.

After this appointment, she promised herself. *After this, I'll call him.*

They called her name. The appointment went on forever and then suddenly, she was out on the sidewalk with a prescription for anti-ovulation pills, a handout about anti-inflammatory food, and a PT referral she couldn't use until her job search paid off. No diagnosis but if this stuff worked, she wasn't sure she cared.

Dazed, she blinked in the September sun. She was making progress. It felt good, if surreal.

"Judit?"

Judit turned, squinted, and put on her sunglasses. Aw shit. Clementine was too damn small.

"Hi," Cazzi said, biting her lip as she stopped in front of Judit. "Was this a mistake? Should I have pretended not to see you?

"What are you doing here?"

She pointed at the grocery store across the street. There was a reusable bag over her shoulder. "You're not answering my messages." She sounded worried. "Are you okay?

Judit gestured wordlessly at herself.

Cazzi leaned back and studied her, the other woman's gaze cataloging everything. Suddenly, Judit wished she hadn't just invited someone with that many advanced degrees in psychology and sexuality topped off with the knowledge of an old friend to inspect her. She felt all too seen and fought the urge to hug herself, especially when Cazzi's eyes softened. "Can we talk?"

Judit hesitated. This was Cazzi, why was she resisting fixing things with one of her best friends?

Because the boy who broke your heart broke it for hers.

Cazzi sighed. "Let me clear the air. Patrick and I aren't a thing. I am not interested nor am I competition."

"Okay." Judit shrugged. It didn't matter what Cazzi thought, Judit *saw* Patrick's face when he looked at the other woman.

(But the way he texted Judit, that had to mean something, right?)

"Patrick is not in love with me. I don't think he ever was. He just thought he should be cuz we've got history." She pinched the bridge of her nose. "Shit."

"What?"

"Look, am I pissed that you two conspired with my fucking fiancé to keep this from me? Yes, but I'm getting over it—"

"We didn't consp—"

"I know, I know. It just felt like that. So infantilizing." Cazzi shook her head, hugging herself, her fingers skimming over one of her calming sigils. "That Angela, of all people, knew before me…" She inhaled deeply, frowning.

Judit's stomach dropped at her friend's pain. "I'm so sorry. I hated doing that to you. I hated myself for falling for someone who hurt you so bad. I felt like I was betraying you—"

"No—"

Judit held up her hand. "I never would've done anything with him but… I've never felt like this with anyone before—I wanted to tell you so many times. You should've seen all the drafts I discarded but it wasn't just me. We wanted to do it together, and shit fell apart before we could." Judit looked away, pushing aside the memory of that night.

"I get it. I mean, after last year, how could I not?" Cazzi glanced down before fixing Judit with a deeply vulnerable stare. "I just want to make sure you and I are okay. I don't care that you two dated. I'm fucking ecstatic about it. You balance each other well, not that it's any of my business—" She stopped again, screwing up her face. "God, you'd think they'd cover this kind of awkwardness in grad school." She glanced at the sky and sighed. "What I'm trying to say is I miss you." She met Judit's eyes. "Can we be okay?"

Judit let her words soak in, listening to her body's reaction to it and weighing it against her gut feeling. "I want to be," she said finally. "You're seriously okay with us?"

Cazzi smiled. "I'm so happy for you two."

"And… you really think we can work?" Judit hated that she felt the need to ask.

Cazzi's smile grew wider. "Judy, the way he talks about you—"

Judit stiffened. "You two talked about me?"

Cazzi winced. "I can see how that might sound sus but, trust me. Not romantic at all. He's getting his house in order. He quit NoN too."

"Good."

Cazzi nodded. "Rohan's upset but he'll get over it. They needed a clean slate." She waved the words away. "More importantly, Patrick loves you. Maybe text him back sometime soon?"

He loves me? Judit hesitated even though she had been thinking the same thing. "I don't want to be someone's band-aid second choice again," she said.

"Oh, Judy." Cazzi reached out and touched her arm. Judit let her. "Let him prove to you you're not."

Judit stewed on Cazzi's words all through lunch with her mom, through their discussion of which types of office jobs she would qualify for and if they'd let her work remotely. She fiddled with her phone as her mom drove her back home and then made polite chit-chat with Helen.

Finally, her mother left with a promise to forward any job opportunities her way.

After filling her friend in on her afternoon, Judit flopped on the couch next to Helen and stared at his texts.

"Call him," Helen said. "I'm sick of this"

"But, what if he breaks up with me?" Judit passed over the tote of goodies her mother had insisted they bring by Helen.

"As opposed to what? You're current state of together-ness?" Helen asked, rooting through the bag. "Oooh shit, she got us Trader Joe's treats! Did your Papi make those cookies?"

Judit glared at her. Didn't Helen know how fucking bruised Judit felt? How that emotionally bruised feeling made her sleep terrible and her pain worse because of it? (Dammit, how long was she going to live like this?)

Helen shrugged, unrepentant, and ripped open a bag of something chocolatey. "If this was a book you'd be yelling at the page for the characters to 'just have a goddamn conversation already!'"

Judit stuck her tongue out at Helen. "Your logic is not appreciated." She headed for their room.

"Punish me by calling him!" Helen yelled after her.

Judit sat on her bed and stared at the dark screen of her phone. It had been a week since they'd last talked since everything had gone to shit. All his texts were kind, understanding. Fucking reasonable.

She was being ridiculous. Helen was right. Hell, Cazzi was right.

Fuck it.

She called him. He picked up immediately.

"Hi," he said. The word was breathless and cut off like he'd run for his phone and was trying not to word vomit all over the line.

"I don't want to be second fiddle," Judit said because apparently, she was going to babble for the both of them. "I love Cazzi, but if you're still pining for her you need to lose my number because I'm not doing that shit. I can't. I like you too damn much. I might fucking love you, which explains why my heart feels shredded right now and I can't—" She squeezed her eyes shut against the tears leaking out.

He waited a good ten seconds and then said, "I'm not in love with her. The only person I'm pining over is you."

She sobbed. "Yeah?"

His voice went molten. "Yeah. I love you, Judit."

"I love you too." She sobbed again, grinning. "I wish you were here right now."

"I can be up there tonight," he said, his voice close to a growl.

She shivered. "Then get up here."

He arrived on the next flight, carrying a backpack and wearing a mask. When she opened the door, they stared at each other for a moment before she threw herself at him. He caught her, wrapping her in his arms and they held each other for a long time before she reached up and gently removed his mask. "I'm sorry I didn't call sooner. Thank you for being patient with me."

He kissed her. Judit lost time in the way his lips moved against her, his fingers on her hips, his tongue—

Someone cleared their throat. Judit and Patrick came up for air, blinking at Helen.

"Look," Helen said. "There's one door out of this place and I'm trying to clear out to give you some privacy but—" She gestured at how they were blocking the doorway.

Awkwardly, Patrick and Judit clung together and shuffled to the side. It was probably the least effective way to hide his boner, but whatever.

"Have fun!" Helen saluted them as she slid by. "And close the damn door."

Judit closed the door behind them and they stood together in the sudden silence before breaking into laughter. "Could that be any more awkward?"

He grinned. "Probably but let's not tempt fate." He kissed her nose, then her cheek, her lips... "Bed?"

She took his hand and dragged him into the room she and Helen shared. After they'd gotten thoroughly reacquainted, they lay jammed together on her twin bed, cuddled together. "So," she said. "How would this work?"

He smoothed back the hair sticking to her face. "Well, I'm free of NoN so I have a lot of time on my hands right now. I'm open to ideas."

She sat up. "I want to get this out of the way: my income is limited. I can't travel frequently because I'm working like three jobs until I find something better and I have no idea what to do with my five-year plan and I'm a mess and my health insurance is up soon and..."

He waited until she ran out of words then said, "You know how much of a mess I am, why would I begrudge your messiness?"

She exhaled hard and shrugged.

He covered her hand with his. "We can work on our plans together. We love each other and we're willing to work to keep this going, right?" His tone was reassuring but she could see the spark of worry in his expression.

"Yes," she said. "Of course. I'm just—I'm scared."

"Me too," he replied. "But I'm more scared of losing you than I am of trying."

She smiled. "Damn, hard to argue with that."

"We have time." He smiled back. "Maybe one day you'll end up in LA, maybe I'll end up here. Maybe we'll be somewhere else. But for as long as we want to be, we'll be together."

"You make it sound simple."

He shook his head. "It's not. Staying together is hard, but I've been able to communicate with you better than any of my past partners. Being with you feels so possible, it gives me hope that we can do this."

She leaned into him and kissed his bare shoulder. "Me too. Is it too soon to say I want to include you in my five-year plan?"

He laughed and kissed her temple. "You better."

EPILOGUE

"Okay, you got this," Judit muttered to herself, checking her make-up in the flip-down visor of Patrick's car.

The man himself gave her knee a reassuring rub from the passenger seat. She glanced at him, catching his smile. She would never get over how lovely he was. Thank the universe he was here, she didn't want to do this alone.

"Ready?" He asked.

"I think so? Are you?"

He chuckled. "You made me watch so many movies. I've

been having reunion dreams for the last week. Though." He peered out the windshield. "I thought these things were supposed to be at the gym, canonically."

Judit shrugged. "COVID, I guess. Okay, let's do this."

He gave her knee one last pat and slid his sunglasses on. She stepped out, pushing hers up the bridge of her nose and smoothing the skirt of her dress. It was a lush purple with Major Arcana cards dancing along the hem and non-constricting lines. Designed by Helen, of course.

The large park spread before them, green, if slightly damp from the winter rains. A gentle slope put the park in a giant bowl and the reunion, according to her evite, was somewhere in the basin.

You're really interesting, she reminded herself. *Fuck anyone who implies otherwise.* Yeah, she now worked an office job doing admin work (full-time with benefits and mostly remote!).

With her fibromyalgia diagnosis (Patrick had been there to hold her hand through the whole appointment) she'd been able to get some Reasonable Accommodations to ensure the days she did come to the office weren't too debilitating.

She'd had to pull back on her freelance psychic work because working full-time was no joke, but she still made sure to keep her hand in. She wasn't giving up on her career yet. But still, it wasn't exactly interesting, was it?

Patrick came up beside her, his fingers finding hers. Holding his hand grounded her and she led the way to the picnic area.

They almost walked right by the reunion. A few picnic tables with balloons in the school colors (yellow and black, go bumblebees!), and fifteen or so people milling around snacks were easy to miss.

Judit checked the time. They were a good thirty minutes after the start time, exactly as she'd hoped. Patrick raised his eyebrows at her. She shrugged and they entered the (mild) fray.

She didn't recognize most of the people, except for the two organizers who she'd been friendly acquaintances with. Despite this, everyone wanted to hug. Patrick hung back while she was engulfed one by one by people she'd been everything from okay with to outright disliked ten years ago.

One girl told her unprompted about how social media accounts spontaneously become bots that will hack your account then squinted suspiciously at Judit like she was a real-life bot. A guy who'd famously had his stomach pumped in the ninth grade talked wistfully about his new wife and how they'd one day have kids like the ones playing nearby. A person who she'd barely talked to told her a solid ten minutes of gossip about people who hadn't attended and who Judit didn't really know anyhow. No one asked what she did, though one girl was definitely working up the nerve to ask if Patrick was really who she thought he was.

Finally, Judit escaped to the snacks where Patrick was inspecting the packaging of an almond butter cup.

"How's it going?" he asked, unwrapping it.

She thought about it. "Kind of banal. None of my friends are here."

"Maybe they'll show up soon?"

"Who are your friends?" asked one of the organizers, who'd been sitting at a nearby table. She wore all black like she had in high school (she looked like she hadn't changed much at all in the last ten years). Judit was pretty sure she'd moved out of Clementine the day after graduation. (What was her name?) Judit remembered her as being nice enough if blunt. "Sorry," she said to Patrick. "I'm Miri. You didn't go to Clemmy High, did you?"

"That obvious?" he asked.

She nodded. "You're too hot. Also, I have the guest list." She tilted her head at Judit. "Who are you waiting for? I'll tell you if they RSVP'd."

Judit rattled off the names of all the friends she'd lost touch with. Miri consulted her phone but she shook her head after each name. "Sorry hun, we're in the same boat."

"You organized this and *your* friends didn't show up?" Judit was shocked.

Miri shrugged. "Let me put it this way: the original organizing committee was ten people. Only me and Zach showed up. People are flakes."

"Be nice, Miri." The man Judit vaguely recognized as Zach sidled up to them. "People are busy, it's the holidays, and we're still in a pandemic."

Miri narrowed her eyes at him. "Stop being reasonable. It's rude."

Zach laughed. "Would it help if I reminded you that we have a date with the bar around the corner in two hours?"

"So much," Miri said. "Hold that thought. I'm going to slap that idiot for drinking in a public park." She stomped off towards Mr. Got His Stomach Pumped in the Ninth Grade and the paperbag-wrapped bottle he'd produced from nowhere.

"You're welcome to join us later," Zach told Judit and Patrick. Which is how they ended up in a bar with the organizers and their partners, day drunk and laughing at antics from high school. Zach eventually clocked Patrick and made him sign a napkin as well as his shirt sleeve. Patrick drew the line at signing Zach's arm.

Judit and Patrick stumbled out of the bar afterwards, in search of food to soak up the alcohol.

"Was that all you were hoping for?" Patrick asked.

Judit shook her head, stumbled, and turned them towards Badlands Diner. "It was weirder, which was maybe better?" She laughed. "I can't believe the guy with the vanlife cult didn't show up. I was hoping to find out what that actually entailed."

"They don't have a website?"

"It's very barebones," Judit said mournfully. "Did you have a good time?"

Patrick looked at her. "I did. It was nice to have a second-hand high school experience."

Judit snorted. "You sound like you just went on an anthropology expedition."

"Well, you made me study for it."

"Did not!"

"You were my favorite part of the expedition." He pulled her closer and kissed the top of her head. That made her melt, the way it always did. She couldn't believe they'd been doing this for months. It hadn't been easy exactly, especially when he opened his new studio. But they made it work, seeing each other at least once a month.

"Oh, hey," he said. "I got you something." He pulled out a card in a purple envelope. "It's nothing big but I figured this was a big deal for you. I know people don't usually give reunion presents but—" He shrugged and handed it to her.

She opened the envelope carefully, surprised and warmed by the gesture. He'd figured out pretty quickly that showing off the wealth gap between them made her uncomfortable but he still found a way to mark little occasions with thoughtful gestures. She tried to do the same.

Inside was a custom digital drawing of Sean Connery dressed like Zoey Deschanel, screaming "There can only be one!" It was just as she'd pictured it on their weird first not-date. She burst out laughing. "Ohmigod, Pat. I love this so much!"

He grinned. "Turn it over."

She flipped it. On the back, he'd written: "There can only be one for me and it's you. Yours always, Patrick."

"I almost went with 'Be your own manic pixie dream girl' but I thought you might like this better. Also, it's true."

She kissed him. "It's true for me too. I love you and your dorky thoughtfulness."

"I love you too. I was thinking..." He hesitated. "I was thinking about making you a key to the house if you wanted."

Judit bit her lip. "Actually, I wanted to show you something too." She pulled out her phone and opened her notes app.

Judit's Five Year Plan

Year 1: Full-time job, get health stuff under control, enjoy relationship with Patrick, build online following, upgrade website

Year 2: Take business classes, keep job, move in with Patrick?? LA?, make enough on readings to afford LA

Year 3: Work part-time job (figure out benefits), rent space to do readings (share with someone? Helen?), talk about marriage

Year 4: evaluate whether to keep part-time job, decide on marriage, teach tarot classes,

Year 5: quit job if possible, do something cool for 5 year anniversary, create own Tarot deck/book?

SHE FIDDLED with the hem of her dress. "It's got a lot of question marks but I finally finished."

He looked up, a soft smile on his face. "I'm in every year."

She smiled back. "Of course you are."

"You know, we don't have to wait two years if you want to move in sooner. No rush though."

She kissed his cheek. "I'll take that under consideration."

"Consider all you want," he said. "but I'll probably ask you to marry me not long after. Fair warning."

She laughed. "I'll probably say yes. Fair warning."

TEN MONTHS LATER...

Benji sat on the back steps of their Sacramento house, a ginger beer bottle dangling from their fingers, and stared at the disarray of their backyard. When they bought this somewhat rundown Victorian, they had a vague concept of how much work it would take to get it habitable. But after years of piece-meal work, it seemed like every time something got fixed another thing broke. Frustrating yes, but given they only lived here about half the year, it wasn't more than an inconvenience. Now, though, with NoN needing a venue for their songwriting retreat and Benji having a large, probably not haunted, house at their disposal... Well, now there was a timeline.

Benji sighed and stood, brushing off their ripped jeans and old long-sleeve shirt. They had about ten minutes before their mother came over with her band and some other Gen X punks to help remove the branches, construction trash, and two full-sized bathtubs that had been there since Benji bought the house. They were letting a few bands put on a show back here over the weekend. Mom's band, Razor Bitches, was trying to make a comeback and this would be their first show in years. So, of course, the band was headlining it.

It didn't give Benji heartburn at all. Rubbing their sternum, they grabbed their phone and checked social media. Not that they needed any more stress, but it was a habit, being in the know. Keeping tabs, not on anyone in particular. Mostly.

Angelica had just been so quiet over the last year or so. And they sometimes had a tickle in the back of their mind. A question. A what if. A bit of a fascination—which would fade.

It certainly didn't mean anything except they were not nearly as impervious to Angelica's persistence as they'd like to think. But that was fine. They doubted she'd push the issue further than her incompetent flirting and when—if she resurfaced, they would avoid her as much as possible in this incestuous industry.

As long as everything stayed that way, it'd all be fine. They didn't need any more stress.

In their app, a new alert popped up.

What's up, hell babies?? I'm baaaaack...
—@thatbitchangela

LOVED THIS BOOK? LEAVING A REVIEW HELPS OTHERS WHO MIGHT LOVE IT FIND IT (AND IT HELPS INDIE AUTHORS KEEP WRITING). THANK YOU!
<3
KATTA

READY FOR BOOK 3?

In the gospel according to Benji, there's no one worse than the self-proclaimed Bitch Queen Angie. In Angie's book, there's no safer crush than the one person who will *never* love her back. But what happens when their cat-and-mouse game brings them closer than they ever thought possible?
No Love in LA coming in 2025

ACKNOWLEDGMENTS

Hi, hello, it's me, the author. What a joy to be back here again! Writing the acknowledgments is kind of glorious in that it means I'm near the end of a lot of editing and also that I get to bask in how lucky I am to have wonderful people around me. If I left you out, I swear I still love you, my brain just wandered off into the fibro fog.

And yes, I gave Judit my pain and Patrick my anxiety. Sorry sweeties!

First off, I have to thank everyone who read and loved *Love in the Liner Notes*, especially those who told me and asked for Patrick's story. Y'all make my day. :] Extra thanks to my parents for buying copies, demanding I sign them, and reading my book.

Next, thank you so so much to my amazing beta readers including Karen A. Parker, Vee Thorn, ShanShan Guo, Belladonna Obscura, Shana, and C.A. Vargas. This book is a million times better thanks to your suggestions. Special thanks to those who pointed out things outside my experience.

I did a lot of research to make sure I did my best to portray the characters outside my experience of being a cis white woman but please note no one character is meant to represent the whole range of experiences for any one group. All mistakes are mine and mine alone. To learn more about people like my characters, please read and consume media by creators in those identity groups.

Thank you also to Liz at Magus Books and Herbs who gave me the foundation of my herbalism knowledge. Also to

Markus K. Ironwood aka Swamp Witch Stephanie, my favorite drag queen, for the name Steph Infection.

My writing discords helped me keep learning and growing my community while my writing group To Be Named was the best cheering squad and support team a girl could ask for. I got so damn lucky to have found you all.

Last but never least, to my favorite dork and chronic pain buddy who talks my books up to strangers, talks me out of my anxiety spirals, and supports me through my pain flares: love you, baby.

ABOUT THE AUTHOR

Katta Kis' first job was playing a vampire baby in a student film, sealing her fate as a goth child for life. After a variety pack of jobs and apartments, she is currently settled in Northern California. She cohabitates with her two adorable demon babies masquerading as cats and her high school romance which never ended. When not writing, she can usually be found reading or at a concert.

Keep up with her through her newsletter!

ALSO BY KATTA KIS

Love in the Liner Notes

Book 1 of the Pagans & Pop Stars series

Two ex-boy band heartthrobs.

A witchy sex educator.

The love triangle no one expected.

Cazzi has been in love with her childhood best friend Patrick since, well, forever. He's the only one who gets her paganism, her passion for sex education, and knows what happened on the worst night of her life. But when she kissed him, it ruined their friendship. Now Patrick is back in her life—until his old bandmate throws a wrench in their relationship.

Rohan is an ex-boy band heartthrob on his last bid for a comeback career. But this is jeopardized when Cazzi inspires him to leave his tempestuous girlfriend, causing a rift between Cazzi and Patrick in the process.

Between the emotional fallout and work drama, Cazzi is duct-taping her mental health together with ritual, marijuana, and the brownies Rohan bakes for her. As Cazzi and Rohan grow unexpectedly close can their relationship survive when the machinations of his ex threaten to expose her biggest secret?

Out now!

www.ingramcontent.com/pod-product-compliance
Lightning Source LLC
Chambersburg PA
CBHW011408310726
48972CB00011B/2890